Praise for the sensational first DOOMSDAY BRETHREN novel, TEMPT ME WITH DARKNESS

"Excellent story . . . wonderful characters . . . fast-paced . . . you won't want to put it down."

—*Romantic Times* (4½ stars)

"A hot, exciting romance filled with intriguing characters and a great storyline. I can't wait for more in this imaginative series!"

—*New York Times* bestselling author Lara Adrian

"Deliciously wicked and sexy hot. . . . Shayla Black keeps me turning the pages!"

—*New York Times* bestselling author Gena Showalter

"This orgasmic paranormal . . . will have Black's fans panting for the next installment."

—*Publishers Weekly*

"Fast-paced, emotional and thoroughly addicting . . ."

—*Romance Junkies*

More praise for national bestselling author
SHAYLA BLACK's novels

"Intense, erotic, and sizzling hot."

—*Fresh Fiction*

"Keeps the heat on high until the very last page."

—*Just Erotic Romance Reviews*

Look for a steamy FREE Doomsday Brethren novella, "Fated," available now on www.simonandschuster.com!

The Doomsday Brethren titles are also available as eBooks.

POSSESS ME
AT
Midnight

SHAYLA BLACK

POCKET BOOKS
New York   London   Toronto   Sydney

Pocket Books
A Division of Simon & Schuster, Inc.
1230 Avenue of the Americas
New York, NY 10020

This book is a work of fiction. Names, characters, places, and incidents either are products of the author's imagination or are used fictitiously. Any resemblance to actual events or locales or persons, living or dead, is entirely coincidental.

First Pocket Books paperback edition November 2009

POCKET and colophon are registered trademarks of Simon & Schuster, Inc.

For information about special discounts for bulk purchases, please contact Simon & Schuster Special Sales at 1-866-506-1949 or business@simonandschuster.com

The Simon & Schuster Speakers Bureau can bring authors to your live event. For more information or to book an event contact the Simon & Schuster Speakers Bureau at 1-866-248-3049 or visit our website at www.simonspeakers.com.

Illustration by Chris Cocozza.

Manufactured in the United States of America

10   9   8   7   6   5   4   3   2   1

ISBN 978-1-4165-7846-8
ISBN 978-1-4165-7863-5 (ebook)

To my family. For taking a huge leap of faith with me, for putting up with me when I'm on deadline . . . for still loving me. I'm so blessed to have you. I'll try to improve my bonbon-eating skills with each book. ☺

ACKNOWLEDGMENTS

To MY USUAL CAST of characters: Lee, Mel, Denise, Natalie, and Susan. I can't make it through a book without you! I'd be remiss if I didn't thank Laurie just for being so awesome, listening to me, and always being my cheerleader. To Annee, I've missed you in my life SO much, and I'm so thrilled you're back. Since you applied to be the president of the Doomsday Brethren fan club, you're hired!

To my agent, Kim Whalen, and my editor, Abby Zidle. Thank you both for your insightful comments, which made for a stronger book, and your shared enthusiasm for Ice and Sabelle. We make a great team!

CHAPTER ONE

SABELLE RION HEARD DEATH whisper, felt its breath on the back of her neck. *Bram*, it called. *Come with me.* She clutched her brother's hand, trying desperately to keep him anchored in this mortal plain.

Since becoming a fully transitioned witch at twenty-four, she'd had the ability to touch others and make them feel whatever she wished. In the last sixty years, she'd perfected the skill. Very few were immune to her gift. But she had no idea if Bram could feel the positive healing vibrations she now sent his way. If so, they weren't improving his condition.

Damn the black smoke surrounding her brother, slowly smothering his life and, she worried, his magic. And damn Mathias for attacking Bram with it! Fighting back angry tears, she clenched her fists, her fingernails cutting into her palms.

Just yesterday, they'd tangled with the evil wizard who had escaped after hundreds of years of exile. Last night, Conrad the healer and her aunt Millie had examined Bram. Neither knew what the deadly smoke was, exactly what damage it caused . . . or how to eradicate it.

They only knew it was draining the life of the person she loved most in this world.

"Can I come in?"

Sabelle looked over her shoulder as Lucan, her brother's best friend, entered the room. Following Mathias's abduction of his mate, Anka, and the breaking of their bond, Sabelle had cared for Lucan, providing him vital energy through sex while he'd been incoherent and suffering acute mate mourning. Bram had given him support, protection, and a roof over his head. It was no surprise that Lucan wanted to help care for Bram in return.

"Certainly."

"Any change?" He caressed her shoulder.

The gesture surprised Sabelle. Lucan had never touched her while bound to his former mate. But now that Anka was in the arms of another, and he knew Sabelle had recently provided the sexual energy needed to keep him alive, had that changed their friendship in his eyes?

Nibbling on her lip, she risked a glance in Lucan's direction. He was a beautiful man. Coffee-colored hair brushed wide shoulders. His shocking blue eyes lured a woman from between a thick fringe of black lashes. His mouth . . . He knew how to kiss; she'd learned that . . . eventually. Over time, he'd become less frenzied in his mate mourning and pressed his mouth to hers. The skill of it had stunned her. Someday, they would both need a mate. Becoming Lucan's would solve many problems . . .

She shook her head to clear the thought. His gesture meant nothing, was merely one of comfort. Lucan still had strong feelings for Anka. And it was impossible for Sabelle to think about her future when her beloved brother might soon pass to his nextlife.

"No change," Sabelle murmured.

Clutching her shoulders, Lucan urged her to her feet to face him. "Come eat. You're worrying yourself to exhaustion."

She pulled away. "I can't leave Bram. What if he wakes and needs me?"

"Spare yourself five minutes. Olivia and Sydney have been cooking—the human way. It's taken them hours to prepare enough food. They did it for you."

The tears that had been threatening all day speared the back of her eyes, closed up her throat. Though she'd only known the other women for a few weeks, she already considered them great friends. Yes, circumstance had thrown them together. Having Mathias on the loose required a magical army to defeat him. Bram had assembled the Doomsday Brethren, a group of warriors, mostly magical, willing to fight. Olivia and Sydney were mates to two of Bram's fighting force, and had not only stood by their men, but the group. They'd risked themselves to rid magickind of this cancer, though the fight wasn't theirs. Their efforts to help her touched Sabelle.

"Five minutes," she agreed reluctantly.

Lucan nodded and brought her close. "I'm worried about you. You can't carry all of Bram's responsibilities on your shoulders."

She cast him a desperate gaze. "I have to try. He's worked so hard to build this—"

"No one will allow it to crumble. Come see. Everyone is assembled downstairs, waiting for you."

Everyone? Surely not . . . "Shock?"

Lucan clenched his jaw. "No one wants the traitor here."

Especially not the traitor who was now shagging Lucan's former mate.

It touched her that the Doomsday Brethren had come to pay homage, but she feared only one person could help her brother. "Has anyone searched for Bram's mysterious mate? Emma's energy—"

"Might heal him. I know. But it's hard to find a woman when you know nothing more than her first name. Sydney has volunteered to call Aquarius, since she presumably knows Emma."

Sabelle shook her head. "Aquarius says she doesn't know Emma's whereabouts. Her flat is empty, her mobile phone disconnected. The shop she once worked in is closed tight. Bram already tried all those avenues. Clearly, the woman doesn't want to be found."

"In light of the situation, Sydney agreed to speak to Aquarius once more."

She prayed the woman would help them this time. If not . . . The looming possibility stabbed despair through her heart. Sabelle beat back a fresh batch of tears. She would not cry. Waste of time that solved nothing. She could fall apart later. Alone. Now, too much was at stake.

Lucan smoothed a thumb across her cheek. "You're one of the bravest women I know, Bella. Bram is my best friend. Let me help you. Lean on me."

The offer was tempting. Lucan was a strong wizard and warrior. But he'd lost his mate a mere month ago, and had only just learned that Anka sought refuge with an enemy. His whole life had been torn apart. He needed to get back on his own feet before worrying about her issues.

She plastered a smile on her face. "I'm fine, but thank you."

"Let me help. There wasn't time earlier for me to express . . ." He sighed. "Thank *you*. I know the sacrifice you made to save me, the risk you took in bedding someone feral to provide me proper energy to live and heal." Lucan threaded his hand thorough her pale hair. "I remember being with you. Your fear. Your determination. Your softness."

He remembered? Damn and blast. That would complicate everything. But it wasn't as if she'd forgotten the feel of Lucan either, his heat, his hardness, his single-minded intent. The unexpected desire. In their time together, Sabelle had come to know him as a lover . . . and she wasn't certain how she felt about it. Now was hardly the time to sort it out.

"Lucan, I—"

He brushed his lips over hers, cutting off her words. Soft but firm. Achingly gentle. He set his mouth on hers and merely felt her. Breathed her. Then he lifted his head.

"Anything you need, I will be here for you."

Why? Friendship? Gratitude? Passion?

Though she often tried to block others' thoughts, she peeked into Lucan's. Friendship, certainly, and gratitude by the bucketload, a bare hint of passion—and a welter of confusion. She related to that.

Slipping from his mind, she sent him a wan smile. "Lead the way."

Lucan took her hand and led her downstairs to the dining room. As he'd said, everyone was assembled. Marrok stood, tall and daunting as ever. Olivia, his mate, sat beside him as he rested a big hand on the crown of her dark head. Envy tore through Sabelle. She ached for the sort of love and affection they shared. Between her brother's protective streak and her obligation to marry well, she wondered if she'd ever find it.

"Are you all right?" Sydney asked gently.

The human redhead stood beside her wizard mate, Caden. Lucan and Caden exchanged a brotherly glance that she didn't have the energy to decipher.

"Fine," Sabelle reassured her. "Something smells good. Thank you for cooking."

"Come eat so you can get back to Bram." Sydney shoved a plate into her hands and gestured her toward the spread of food on the sideboard. Roasted hen, a flaky white fish, even a Beef Wellington, along with an array of vegetables and breads. The gesture touched her all over again, pricking her eyes with tears.

"Thank you so much." Sabelle sniffed and blinked, holding back the tears.

"Eat." Lucan pushed her toward the food, then accepted a plate from Sydney and stood protectively behind Sabelle.

She dished herself a few spoonfuls of food without looking at what she'd served herself. It was all just nutrients to help her tend Bram longer. Nothing else mattered.

Behind her, all the others plated up. Sabelle settled into her usual chair. Lucan sat directly to her left. Marrok and Olivia settled in at the far end of the table. Caden and Sydney plopped down beside Lucan. The Doomsday Brethren's newest member, Tynan O'Shea, sat glumly across from Marrok and began picking at his food. His vengeful thoughts blared past her mental barricades, along with his pain. His grief over his intended mate's murder by Mathias was affecting his appetite. Sabelle had no trouble understanding why.

Beside her, Bram's chair at the head of the table sat empty. The realization that he might never again sit there hit her like a blow to the belly. She lowered her fork and looked at her plate, now blurred through her tears.

"Sabelle." Simon Northam, the Duke of Hurstgrove, approached the table slowly.

Until the formation of the Doomsday Brethren, Bram and Duke hadn't known each other well, but despite his lofty human rank, he'd been a solid member of the group from day one.

She took a moment to swallow her tears, then raised her gaze. Being born a Rion, everyone expected her to lead by example, tamp down her fear, and move on. Bram, most of all, would demand it. For her brother, she'd stay strong.

"I'm fine."

Duke nodded, dark hair looking uncommonly shaggy, as he set his plate on the table and eased himself into Bram's chair. She swallowed an urge to jump up and rail at him. He could not take her brother's place!

"Would you rather sit here, or shall I?" he asked softly.

The angry wind left her sails. She took a deep breath, common sense prevailing. The group needed a leader, and Duke occupying Bram's chair signaled he was willing to take the job.

"You. I'm no warrior, and I'll have my hands full with Bram's Council business."

He cast her a sympathetic gaze, a silent promise of support, then looked down the table. This was for the best. Mathias was weakened, but in no way defeated. The Doomsday Brethren had to stay together and remain strong.

Duke opened his mouth to speak when the last of the warriors sat down—directly across from her.

Ice.

Sabelle felt that intense green gaze of his fasten on her. *Oh God.*

Though fearsome and reportedly insane, since becoming a member of the Doomsday Brethren Ice had been on his best behavior—around her, anyway. Hardworking. Polite. Even-tempered . . . mostly. But the constant staring and the naked want on his face tied her belly in knots. He was a puzzle she was utterly compelled to solve.

His fierce expression made her wonder exactly what he was thinking. Oddly, he was one of the few people whose mind she could not read. She'd tried. Nothing. Wondering what was in his head drove her mad. The one time Ice had put his arms around her to heal Sydney's injured friend, Aquarius, had been overwhelming. Combustive.

Forbidden.

Not only born to the Privileged class of magickind, she was among its elite, the closest thing to royalty in the magical world. Rions were descendants of Merlin, the greatest wizard of all time. While Ice . . . well, the Rykards were not only Deprived, but disliked and distrusted—Ice more than most. As if that didn't complicate their attraction enough, Bram hated him with a boundless passion.

Anything between her and Ice was impossible.

"Is something wrong?" Lucan asked, wrapping his warm fingers around her chilled ones.

Ice's fork clattered to his plate, his mouth tight. She didn't need to read his mind to feel his hostility. It raged across his face as he stared at her hand clasped in Lucan's. Her breath caught, and her first instinct was to pull away. She checked it. Nothing good could come of fostering an attraction between her and a man she could never have. Better to let him believe her attentions were otherwise engaged.

She gripped Lucan's hand in return, feeling his strength and fortitude.

"I'm fine." Sabelle realized with a start that the entire table was staring, and she flushed. "Truly. Everyone eat."

Silence reigned for long moments. No one spoke, and the dead air was painful. Often, Bram led the conversation—or dominated it, as was his wont. The quiet now only reminded her that her brother might not live long enough to control the conversation again.

Suddenly, Duke cleared his throat and addressed the group. "No one can replace Bram, but someone must oversee our leadership while he recovers. Does anyone else want the role?"

Marrok shook his head. "I know not magickind's people or how to help them in their time of need. I possess not Bram's diplomacy. Those who impede our cause would feel only the hack of my blade, if I had my way."

"Which is why you're a warrior, not a politician." Olivia, his American mate, smiled.

Their affection, as always, wrapped them in a world all their own.

"I will, if you wish it," Caden volunteered. "Though I think you have more experience to handle the difficult times ahead."

Though gratified by Caden's show of solidarity, Sabelle agreed.

"I formed the group with Bram," Lucan offered, then swallowed. "But my mourning has just ended. My temper is . . . uncertain."

Lucan spoke the truth. His emotions scraped closer to the surface than she'd ever seen. He revealed much with his gestures and expressions—too much to handle magical diplomacy now.

"I've been with this group less than a week," Tynan pointed out, his gray eyes the color of a foreboding rain cloud about to burst.

A fitting metaphor, Sabelle mused. Tynan himself was a ticking time bomb.

Everyone had spoken . . . except Ice.

Drawing in a shaky breath, Sabelle braced herself to look in his direction. He was still staring at her, hot, intent. Something in her belly tightened again. Was she actually shaking?

"Who is wont to listen to a madman?" Ice challenged with a raised brow.

Duke cleared his throat. "Then it's settled. We must resume fighting and weapons training again. Marrok?"

"Aye. Tomorrow at dawn. Everyone."

Caden rolled his eyes. "Oh-dark-hundred again. Great. I left the Marines, you know."

"Foolish on your part. They were nicer," Duke teased, then sobered again. "We'll need to add security to the house.

I've no notion how Bram's magical defenses are holding up in his weakened state."

"Not well," Sabelle admitted. She could feel it slipping by the hour . . . just as Bram was.

"After dinner, we'll develop a new network of magical security. This house is critical to our success. We need a place to meet, to regroup, to plan. Without it, I fear we'd be too disorganized to defeat Mathias. Does anyone disagree?"

Every man at the table shook his head.

Good. Another matter settled. Now if she only knew what to do about her brother's diminishing health . . .

". . . give us an update?" Duke asked.

It took her a moment to tune in to him, and she surmised that he asked about Bram. If he wanted new information, she had dealt with nothing else all day.

"Bram is resting, but weakening. Neither Conrad nor Millie know what ails him or how to heal him. I've no notion how to stop it unless we find Emma."

"I've got a call in to Aquarius," Sydney assured. "As soon as I hear from her, I'll let you know. We'll find Emma."

Even if they did, could they persuade her to come care for the mate she'd taken in a night of passion and abandoned before morning?

Silence overtook the group again, punctuated only by the clink of forks and heavy sighs. Sabelle blocked as many thoughts as she could and ate a few more bites of her dinner before admitting defeat. Even the smell of food was making her stomach roil.

She stood to leave, and Lucan stayed her with a hand at her elbow. Ice growled and glared at Lucan's touch. Ice wanted her, and an answering knot of desire grew again in her belly. He must suspect how she felt. If she ever found herself alone with him . . . nothing would be more dangerous.

"You cannot be finished," Lucan chided, scowling at her still-full plate.

"I am." She folded her napkin on the table. "I must get back to Bram. Thank you, ladies," she said to Sydney and Olivia.

Before she could extricate herself from Lucan's grip and depart, bells chimed through the house. A magical calling card. A request to enter the premises.

From Anka MacTavish, Lucan's former mate.

Beside her, Lucan tensed, his face a wrenching mixture of anger and yearning. Sabelle felt the intensity of his pain gripping her chest, sharp and panicky, like someone suffocating. No doubt, whatever Lucan felt for her paled in comparison to the consuming love he still harbored for Anka.

Marrok stomped out of the room and down the corridor. Sabelle heard him open the front door. "She is alone."

Assured that Shock or Mathias and his Anarki hadn't followed Anka, Sabelle released the last bit of security around the house so that Anka could enter the room.

The first thing Sabelle noticed was that the woman looked healthier than before . . . but not completely well. Was Anka not gathering enough energy in Shock's bed?

Lucan's gaze was still glued to his former mate. Despair tinged his thoughts, and Sabelle ached for him. She understood wanting someone beyond reach.

Anka glanced at Lucan, then at his hand upon Sabelle's. Hurt flared across her face before her amber stare skittered across the table and rested on Duke. "I'd like to see Bram."

Duke hesitated, cast a quick gaze at Lucan, who gave a small shake of his head.

"He's not here," Duke lied.

So, they'd surmised that because Anka was sleeping with a wizard they all presumed to be the enemy, she couldn't be trusted? The witch's thoughts revealed that, in throwing her lot in with Shock, she had run to the man most able to protect her and least likely to make demands after her ordeal at Mathias's hands.

Anka tossed fat, blond ringlets off her slender shoulders, her broken magical signature still matching Lucan's, indicating their severed mate bond.

"He doesn't seem to be anywhere," Anka said, clearly frustrated. "I've been calling for him since dusk."

"Council business. What do you need?" Duke snapped.

Anka pressed her lips together, sent Lucan another uncertain glance, then addressed Duke again. "Earlier this evening, Shock told me some alarming things. I—I couldn't keep this to myself. Not when there are so many people here I . . . care for."

Duke gestured her to the chair at the far end of the table. Anka sat, as did Sabelle and Lucan. He didn't relinquish his hold on Sabelle's arm, and she knew Lucan needed the support. He might turn to her because she was convenient and would expect nothing in return—but his heart belonged to Anka.

"According to Shock, the Anarki plans to attack you here tonight, sometime before midnight."

It was currently just after eight.

Sabelle opened up her mind a bit more to Anka. The woman wasn't lying, and she truly had been trying to tell Bram all evening. They'd been ignoring incoming messages and summons, uncertain how to handle them. *Bugger!*

Duke froze. "You're certain? Tonight?"

She nodded. "I warned you as soon as I could."

"Why should we believe you?" Ice asked impassively.

Her amber eyes burned. "I'm risking my life to be here."

Given Anka's fierce expression, Sabelle didn't doubt her

in the least—and she admired the other woman for her grit. But there was something Sabelle didn't understand.

"Why are you fucking the enemy if he works for the monster who raped you?" Lucan snarled. "Especially if you're stabbing him in the back?"

"Clearly, you haven't been alone, either," she shot back with a fiery glare. Hurt blasted from Anka's every thought before she folded her hands on the table in front of her and collected herself. "You don't understand what Mathias did to me."

"I know what he did." Regret tinged Lucan's tone. "I'm more sorry than you'll ever know that I wasn't there to protect you."

"What Mathias did changed me. I—I can't remember all of our mating, can't just resume life as the happy mate. I cannot pretend I'm not damaged—"

"The past doesn't matter. Nothing he did changes you in my eyes," Lucan vowed. "What you're doing with Shock—"

"You're expecting me to be the same woman I was before I was taken. I'm not. I can't undo that fact, even for you."

"You think I can't handle it? Or you no longer trust me to protect you?"

Anka bit her lip. "I can't discuss this now."

"Soon." Lucan stood so suddenly, his chair toppled over, clattered to the floor. Then he left, slamming the door in his wake.

Anka sprang up to chase him . . . then thought better of it. But the way Anka watched Lucan's retreating back, her thoughts riddled with both sadness and indecision, made Sabelle's heart wrench.

Duke cleared his throat. "I'm sorry. Go on."

Anka looked ready to cry. "I'm sorry to cause problems."

"Not at all. What else can you tell me about the attack? How many? Where around the estate? What do they seek to accomplish?"

"A large force. Shock didn't say how many. I don't know how they plan to get in. Maybe Shock knows a way . . ." She sobbed.

Clearly, seeing her former lover while turning on her new one wasn't easy.

Like Lucan, Sabelle had wondered why Anka remained with Shock. Now she understood that between his low station and low expectations, she found him "easy" to be with during this difficult time.

"They want the Doomsday Diary," Anka murmured.

Sabelle squeezed her eyes shut. Damn Morganna le Fay for creating a weapon that wizards had been willing to fight and die for since its rediscovery less than two months ago. Fifteen hundred years in hiding had swelled the book's legend so much that people would do anything to get their hands on it.

"Mathias can't use it," Sabelle pointed out. "And he knows it. He's not female."

Anka nodded. "They plan to take one of the females from this house."

"He will *not* take her."

Sabelle turned toward the booming declaration. Ice. His protective gaze was as tangible as a caress. She swallowed.

"Of course not," Duke assured. "Sabelle is too important to our cause."

Ice stormed around the table until he hovered beside her, mere inches away, his body heat pouring over her. "If there is a breath left in my body, he will not take her."

Duke turned to her with a silent question, but Sabelle ignored him. Ice's protective nature was similar to a mate's. Naturally, Duke would be curious about anything between her and Ice. A mating between them would be nothing short of shocking.

Ice was long rumored to be mad. Many whispered that he possessed a murderous temper. Sabelle didn't know why exactly, and she hadn't seen Ice behave erratically, but Bram had gone to great pains to keep distance between her and the warrior he saw as a necessary evil. Servants avoided him, refused to meet his challenging gaze that silently laughed at their fears. But when he looked at her, his stare held another sort of challenge altogether.

Sabelle stared anxiously at Duke's face, praying he and the others would ascribe Ice's possessive behavior to his alleged insanity. Whatever his motive, she couldn't accept anything Ice might offer . . . no matter how much everything inside her wanted to.

"I'll be all right," she whispered to Ice, daring to glance at him over her shoulder.

Still, he lingered beside her, so close she swore she could hear his heartbeat, smell his body, a musky blend of sage, cedar, and raw earth. That scent weakened her knees every time.

"Thank you, Anka," Sabelle said. "We'll take care to protect the house and the book."

"There's more," Anka said, then turned to Duke again. "Shock said that Mathias has decided the quickest way to ascend to power is to win a seat on the Council."

That made Sabelle's heart stop. "There are no open Council seats, haven't been for decades."

Anka's thoughts assailed her, and the devious truth made Sabelle gasp. She turned to look at Duke, who suddenly wore a grave expression.

"He's going to assassinate a Council member?" Sabelle's voice trembled.

"The plan is to start with one. But eventually . . ."

Mathias plotted to kill them all. How else would he gain complete control of the Council? That meant if he hadn't already targeted her brother, Bram was now on his hit list.

Her knees wobbled. Her stomach revolted. The stunning revelations came one after the other . . . and she melted toward the ground.

Before she came anywhere near the floor, she felt strong hands beneath her, assisting her to her feet, then lifting her into iron-band arms. Sabelle looked at her rescuer, but already knew she'd find a bare stubble of black hair and vivid green eyes penetrating her all the way to her soul.

Gently, he set her in her chair. "You're overdoing. Enough."

Clearly, her efforts weren't enough if Bram wasn't improving and Mathias was plotting to take down the Doomsday Brethren, steal the diary, and kill Council members. None of them had done enough.

"You're certain?" she asked Anka, her voice weak.

Biting her lip, Lucan's former mate nodded. "I ran to tell you. I know you have no reason to trust me. My association with Shock in no way transfers to Mathias. After what he did to me, I hope he burns in hell, and I'll do whatever I can to help, even pass information."

From her current lover to her previous one and his friends.

"We appreciate anything you can tell us," Sabelle assured.

The suspicion left Duke's expression. "Be careful."

With a sad smile and a lingering glance toward the stairs where Lucan had disappeared, Anka exited the house, then teleported away.

Sabelle closed the door, gathered her strength, then marched back to the table. "We need a plan. Immediately."

Duke nodded. "Everyone, pack your belongings. Caden,

you and Sydney find Lucan. Calm him down and tell him Anka has gone. Ice, can you and Tynan secure our weapons elsewhere? We can't let them fall into Mathias's hands."

His air of authority cleared the room quickly, though Ice lingered for a last look at Sabelle.

Once everyone had gone, Duke guided Sabelle to the nearby library and shut the door. "How quickly can we secure the house with our magic?"

"In a few hours' time, I don't think we can. Bram's magic is complicated. I can allow friends in, like Anka. I can undo the safeguards *I've* put around the house. But until he wakes, I have no idea how to unravel his protections, even if they are weakening."

"Can't we lay something over it?"

"Only with Bram's guidance and permission. We could manage in a few days, I think."

"We don't have a few days." Duke mentally cursed, his thoughts frustrated.

"Indeed." She paced.

"So we abandon the house."

Sabelle pressed trembling lips together. This was her home, and a million memories resided here. Bram loved this house. Its seclusion, its beauty. And she didn't know how to save it for him. Her life was spinning out of control.

"I know this is a lot of responsibility for you," Duke murmured, as if talking to a child.

"Don't placate me. I'll be fine." Resolution and fury stiffened her spine as she pointed out, "The book must be protected."

"You, Olivia, or Sydney must carry it. A female must possess the book to transport it; its magic ensures that it will dissolve instantly and return to its last female owner or the resting place in which she put it."

"I'll take it," she volunteered.

"Sabelle—"

"Olivia hasn't come into her power yet, and Marrok is both mortal and human. Were Mathias's minions to kill him, Olivia would be virtually without defense."

Duke sighed heavily. "Agreed. He's a legendary warrior, but a human without magic. Mathias would delight in tearing him apart. And Sydney is human as well."

"Indeed." Nor did the woman share Marrok's prowess on the battlefield. She'd become magickind's news correspondent, making Sydney a very tempting target. Coupled with the fact that her mate, Caden, was newly transitioned and still grappling with his magic, giving them the book to safeguard wasn't smart.

From the look on Duke's face, he had similar thoughts. "I can't send you alone."

"Duke . . ."

"If you plan to take the book, you need at least one warrior to protect you. I'll take your brother and make certain he's cared for."

"No!" The thought of being away from Bram, not knowing if he lived or died or needed her, filled her with panic. "He comes with me."

"Be reasonable."

"Be merciful. He's practically my last living relative." Her absent, selfish mother didn't count.

Duke rubbed his forehead with his hand. "You're making this difficult."

"Go with Caden and Sydney. Make certain the transcasts continue. Magickind needs the regular news she provides via their mirrors. Send Tynan with Marrok and Olivia. They'll need the extra protection."

"That leaves you with Lucan and Ice."

Sabelle sucked in a breath. Damn it, she'd painted herself

into a corner. Being alone with either man could be dangerous. She most trusted Ice to protect her, but not herself to
resist him. "I'll take Lucan."

"He admitted that his temper is uncertain. Given everything transpiring with Anka . . . he could quickly regress
into a dangerous state. You've been granting him energy. If
he turns feral, he may refuse sex from anyone else and force
the issue. We can't risk that. Take Ice, as well."

As much as she wanted to be self-sufficient, imagining
that she could, by herself, protect the book and care for her
brother, while dealing with a wizard who might slip back
into a mate mourning he couldn't control, and fight off pursuing Anarki seemed foolish.

"Bram wants Ice nowhere near me."

"He'd like you dying even less. Sabelle, the clock is ticking. We need to leave now."

Damn and blast! "I'll let them both accompany me. But
it will be your job to tell them to get along. I refuse to play
referee."

"Consider it done."

"I'll grab the book and a few items and be off. Tell Lucan
and Ice to bring Bram down and to meet me at the foot of the
stairs in thirty minutes."

Spitting mad and terrified at once, she charged toward
Bram's office and the Doomsday Diary's hiding place.
Bloody high-maintenance men. How the devil was she to
handle the odd tension between the three of them? Manage
Lucan's potential slips into illness and Ice's desire, while
maintaining Bram's expectations? Later. She couldn't worry
about it now.

Sabelle took a few moments to grab the book and scan her
brother's office, remembering all the times she'd seen him
here. Would he ever be back and thriving again?

Swallowing a lump of fear, she turned toward the study doors, feeling the clock tick down to danger.

Suddenly, the ground shook beneath her feet. A huge blast resounded in her ears. The walls shook. Smoke filled the air, choking her. She fell to her knees, clutching the book, then crawled into the hazy corridor.

Duke had managed to stagger to one of the front windows and looked out with dawning horror. "Get out, everyone! We're being attacked now!"

CHAPTER TWO

WHEN THE CEILING THUNDERED, and Ice heard a woman scream, his blood ran cold. *Sabelle!*

He and Tynan hadn't quite finished stashing the weapons when he heard the first rumblings. They were under attack. In a choice between preserving the hardware and saving Sabelle . . . no choice.

After collecting a few weapons for the warriors to carry, Ice quickly conjured thigh-deep water and doused the rest. That done, he whirled around and pumped his way up the stairs, to the first floor of the enormous house. Amid the smoky chaos and ceiling's crumbling plaster raining down, Ice scanned the corridor.

"Sabelle!" he shouted over and over as he stalked to Bram's office, the library, the dining room, broken glass crunching under his boots. All empty.

Duke stumbled toward him from the front door, bleeding from a gash in the forehead. "The Anarki will be inside the house in less than five minutes. Find Sabelle. Get her and the book out of here. And take Lucan."

With a curse under his breath, Ice nodded. The annoyance at taking Lucan was minimal compared to his fear. Sabelle, though he'd never hold her, was . . . everything. He'd never understood a wizard's urge to mate. After one look at her, he comprehended perfectly.

Though she might become Lucan's, no way would he lose her to Mathias.

"I've been screaming my throat raw to find her. Know where she is?"

"Sorry . . ." Duke said and ran toward the back of the house.

Ice cupped his hands around his mouth. "Sabelle!"

"Up here."

Ice barely heard her reply above another explosive boom, but the siren call of her voice was enough. He charged up the stairs and flung into one bedroom after another. In the middle of one that was golden and silken and sumptuous, he found her.

He resisted the urge to gather her in his arms. She would neither welcome nor allow it.

Sabelle had thrown on a pair of jeans, a creamy white sweater that was snug across her breasts. She shoved a few items into a black backpack. "I'm ready."

"The Doomsday Diary?"

She pointed to the backpack and darted past him, out of the room.

The closer he stayed to her, the safer she would be. He grabbed her arm to guide her down the stairs. Instead, she ripped from his grasp and sprinted down the hall.

Ice chased after her. "Where the hell . . . We must leave now!"

"Not without my brother," she called over her shoulder.

It was on the tip of Ice's tongue to suggest leaving the imperious bastard to rot, but Sabelle would waste valuable time arguing and trying to cart Bram down the stairs. The longer she stayed here, the greater the danger.

"Bloody hell," he muttered, on her heels.

Bram's room of heavy curtains, dark wood, and luxurious damasks was a study in wealth. Ice didn't spare the time to shake his head in annoyance. Right now, Sabelle was trying to use her magic to levitate her brother and evacuate him. A whole lot easier to sling the prat over his shoulder.

With a curse, he edged past Sabelle and grabbed Bram, hoisting his dead weight into a fireman's carry.

"Be careful! He's very ill."

As if he didn't know that. With his free hand, Ice grabbed Sabelle's hand and ran. "Let's go!"

Another boom resounded, shaking the whole house. Halfway down the stairs, the front door began to groan and heave intermittently under the magical equivalent of a battering ram. Collectively, the Anarki threw energy at the house as one, trying to shatter its magical protections. And Ice knew, soon, they would succeed.

Outside, a sea of voices chanted. Mathias's entire fucking army was here, and the Doomsday Brethren would be lucky if they managed to get out alive. Ice hardly cared if he did, but Sabelle . . . she mattered. Magickind needed her and the Doomsday Diary safe.

At the bottom of the stairs, he shoved her toward the back door. "Peek out the back windows. Have the Anarki surrounded the house?"

She stared at him, her gorgeous blue eyes rimmed in fear. But she bravely nodded and scampered off, dodging projectiles as another rattling boom shook the house. She was everything worthy in a female, and if he had more time, he'd tell her so.

But for now, he unloaded Bram's unconscious form on the floor, then took up a defensive position by the front door to face the pounding threat. Marrok, Olivia, and Tynan raced down the stairs. With a glance, Marrok saw Sabelle at the back of the house and sent Olivia in her direction. The once immortal warrior and Tynan lined up beside him to face the threat about to crash through their door.

Duke stumbled from Bram's office and joined them. "I've alerted the Council that we're under attack."

Old curmudgeons wouldn't do a damn thing, but Duke's belief in the nobility of the ruling class was understandable, given his title and background.

"Where are Lucan and Caden?" Duke barked.

He shrugged. Not his problem. His sole focus was to secure this door long enough for Sabelle to make it out alive with the book.

"I don't see Anarki in back," Sabelle shouted.

Hardly meant they weren't there. They could be concealed, but if he and the rest of the Doomsday Brethren waited much longer to take the women and leave, Anarki would be crawling everywhere. Escape would be impossible.

To his right, Caden and Sydney flew down the stairs, Lucan staggering behind, clutching a bleeding shoulder.

"What happened?" Duke asked.

"Flying glass. Someone can heal him once we're safe," Caden suggested.

At her mate's urging, Sydney darted for the other women. At the back door, Sabelle drew her wand, ready to fight, and Ice turned his body so he could see both doors with a subtle turn of his head. Sabelle wouldn't be the one battling for their survival.

Duke lifted the creamy silken drapes covering the windows on either side of the front door. Outside, the swell of black robes grew and grew. They began to fan around the house, scurrying like ants from one place to the next. More joined seconds later. Then more, until there weren't hundreds, but thousands.

Lucan and Caden exchanged a glance as they fell into the battle-ready group. The front door groaned and splintered.

It was going to break any minute, and Ice wanted Sabelle nowhere near the hell about to break loose.

"Take the Rions and the book. Lucan can help me defend the door. As soon as you're prepared, I'll send him with you," Duke insisted.

Ice wanted Lucan nowhere near him, but quarreling was a waste of time they didn't have. He bit his tongue to keep the argument inside. "Fine."

"Initially, we'll split up to confuse them, cut down their forces and make them chase us in all directions." Duke's face was grave with concern. "The book is most important. Keep it from Mathias no matter what."

"I'll contact you when it's safe. Where will you go?"

Duke winced when the door splintered again, and gray smoke crept in. The same sort of smoke that was slowly killing Bram.

The warriors shouted, cursed, began to back away as the insidious smoke clawed and crawled its way across the floor and walls. Mathias himself was likely here.

"Go now!" Duke shouted.

Ice didn't wait to be told twice. With Bram on his shoulder, he dashed to the back door, then pressed an urgent hand to the small of Sabelle's back. "Grab your backpack. Ease out the door. Stay in shadow. We've got two minutes, at most."

She sent him a shaky nod, but didn't panic. "Lucan?"

Who gives a shit? After losing his mate, the bastard thought to use Sabelle because she was beautiful, kind, and convenient? "Right behind us."

With a nod, she grabbed her belongings. "We're safe for the moment. Bram had more protection here, just in case we ever needed to escape."

Good to know. Still, as Ice opened the door, he checked to make certain no Anarki had made their way around the massive estate. He couldn't see any, but he could hear them, attacking Bram's weakened magical defenses, zapping and gnashing their way ever closer to the Doomsday Brethren's fallback position at the back door.

Ice urged Sabelle onto the terrace, in the shadow provided by the overhang, then slid out behind her, covering her body with his own. The December chill wrapped around him in welcome, and he thrived on the bite against his skin. Snow was beginning to fall. He hoped the Anarki bastards were having a miserable time. He'd be happy to speed the process along if they threatened his Sabelle.

Damn it, she isn't yours. Ice shushed the unwelcome voice in his head, then wrapped an arm around her to guide her into the terrace's corner while laying Bram at her feet in case he needed both hands to fight. With concrete at her back and sides, he could protect her. Holding his back to her, he pinned her against the wall and scanned for potential threats, watching as Marrok, Olivia, and Tynan poured out of the house. They took a few steps forward before the wizard grabbed the other two and teleported them away. Sydney and Caden followed.

Where the hell was Lucan? The prick had ten seconds before Ice left him to his own defenses.

Duke stumbled through the door, dragging an injured Lucan behind him, who was now bloody from head to toe.

Behind him, Sabelle gasped and tried to wriggle free. Ice whirled on her and mercilessly flattened her to the wall with his body, pressing her deep into the corner. "Can't you hear the Anarki? They're nearly upon us. You are not rushing through the danger to tend MacTavish."

"But he may need—"

"He is a full-fledged wizard with others around who can care for him. He'll escape."

"But I've been caring for him since Anka . . ."

Something on his face must have shown his fury and the soul-deep willpower he used to squeeze it down. He'd known that Sabelle had become MacTavish's willing carnal sacrifice as he healed, and it lit a fire of jealousy and hatred in his gut. Lucan loved Anka still, but he'd use Sabelle's body, her sweetness and softness, for his own ends. The bloody shit of it was that Sabelle encouraged him. Because she loved him? Ice knew Sabelle would never be his, but he'd be damned if he stood by and watched Lucan use her.

"Would you rather have Lucan die or the Doomsday Diary fall into Mathias's hands?"

She drew in a shuddering breath, and the feel of her breasts against his chest was damn near his undoing. But this wasn't the time or place. There never would be one.

"You're right. I—I wasn't thinking." Her breath misted the cold air, and he wanted to kiss her so desperately. He didn't dare.

"Ice!" Duke called through the dark chill.

Damn it! He pinned Lord High-and-Mighty with a stare and a raised brow.

"The Anarki is through the door and into the house. That gray smoke is everywhere. Take Sabelle and go. Lucan is too injured to be anything but a liability to you now. I'll bring him with me."

Best notion he'd heard all day. "Let's go, princess."

He grabbed her around the waist. She clutched his wrists and, panting, tried to pull him away. "Where?"

Ice knew of many remote places between here and his boyhood home. He could find a million places to hide—and stay hidden as long as necessary to ensure Sabelle stayed safe.

"Anyplace they're not."

Curling his arm more tightly around her waist, Ice tried not to think about how perfectly she fit against him, how soft her breasts felt cushioning his chest, how easy it would be to curl one hand under her backside and urge her legs around his waist as he rode her . . .

Not happening, he chided himself.

Focusing on Wye Valley in the Welsh Mountains, he willed himself, Sabelle, and Bram there. His knees left him as darkness and a keen sense of weightless disorientation swallowed him. But he was conscious of his arm around Sabelle, of her clinging to him as he hoisted Bram's limp form.

Moments later, the ground rushed up under them, and they landed in a heap within a cluster of trees, the river trickling nearby. Lights from the adjoining village glowed in the distance

Ice helped Sabelle to her feet and began leading her in the opposite direction. "Are you all right?"

In the silvery moonlight, she nodded, all those pale curls of hers shimmering around her face, cupping her breasts. "Where are we?"

Not a good idea to think about her breasts now—or ever. "Herefordshire. I know it well. Let's go."

Ice secured Bram over his shoulder, took her hand, and hauled her deeper into the copse of trees. If memory served him, there was an abandoned house built into the nearby hillside. It would be easy to defend and should shelter them for the night. After he reestablished communication with Duke and the others, they could decide on a rendezvous point.

They'd taken only a handful of steps under the shelter of the trees when he heard a *whoosh!* behind him.

"Where are they?" a deep voice boomed. "Find them. The spell Rhea cast on the book told us that it's been transported here. Spread out!"

Mathias. Motherfucking hell. The evil bastard himself had given chase. Not good.

Evidently Rhea, Mathias's witch, had put a spell on the diary. The Anarki would know the Doomsday Diary's exact location as soon as someone teleported with the book.

Question was, could the spell track them as easily on foot?

Sabelle gave the tiniest of gasps, and Ice gripped her hand more tightly and ran faster, hoping she could keep up. If she couldn't, he'd carry her—whatever was needed for her and the Doomsday Diary to stay safe. Despite the fact his legs were longer, Sabelle stayed with him, every step. His admiration for her went up another notch.

Quietly, they zigzagged around trees, gradually turning toward the abandoned house. They couldn't stay there now, of course. Likely the first place the Anarki would look. He and Sabelle would have to keep going.

Thanking God for the darkness that covered their tracks in the mud and for the fact it hadn't snowed in Herefordshire today, he and Sabelle trekked toward the hill on the west side of the valley. Behind him, Ice heard the pursuit of several wizards, the curses when one tripped over a branch.

"Are you certain they ran in this direction?" one asked.

"Not entirely. If she teleports anywhere, we'll find her," Mathias assured. "Whoever the bitch is, she cannot outrun us. When we find her, I will happily strip her bare and make certain she knows who her master is."

Over my dead body, Ice mentally growled.

But the conversation told him one thing: as long as he and Sabelle were on foot, unless the Anarki spotted them, they couldn't track the book. He thought briefly of hiding the book in a tree and teleporting away, but the risk was too great. If the Anarki found it . . . No, they must press on.

Sabelle stumbled in the dark, tumbling into him. Ice secured her with an arm around her waist. She must be getting tired, yet he didn't dare slow their pace.

"Can you go a bit farther?" he whispered.

"I will," she panted.

Ice wasn't certain she could manage, but he prayed she'd find the strength.

Without a word, he stripped the pack from her back and carted it over his shoulder. Bram's dead weight flopped over the other, but like the book, he didn't dare leave Bram behind for the enemy to find and use against them.

Sweat poured off Ice and his heart pounded a constant, violent tattoo. His lungs were about to burst, and his thighs burned. But he couldn't stop.

Finally, they approached the hill leading out of the valley. Ice was more than ready to be gone from here, find a car in the nearby town and drive to safety.

Just then the moon peeked out from the clouds, shining into the valley below. The trees leading up the side of the hills were few and far between. Now that Sabelle was no longer carrying the pack, he realized how her white sweater all but glowed in the dark. *Damn it!*

They were going to have to improvise—and quickly. If she was anyone else, he'd simply slop mud over her clothes. Her shiny blond hair, too. But Sabelle Rion? Did she even know what mud was? Regardless, they didn't have time for it. Behind him, Ice heard more Anarki, sounding closer than before.

Though he might be able to coax Sabelle into running north, parallel to the river, he feared running into searching Anarki. Same with running south. The cliff was east, the river west.

They were virtually trapped.

Think, he demanded of himself. *Think!* If they couldn't run safely in any direction, and they couldn't teleport away, how the bloody hell was he supposed to keep the book safe and Sabelle in one piece?

"Ice," she panted in his ear. "I know we shouldn't rest, but . . . perhaps we can take refuge in a tree? Maybe we would be able to spot an escape route if we were up high?"

He turned to her, his jaw dropping in surprise, his heart bursting with gratitude. "Perfect."

With a frantic gaze he looked around until he found a stout old tree with several low-hanging branches. He helped her up, then handed the pack to her. Ice heard Anarki trampling closer. Too close. Perhaps he could teleport into the tree and balance on a branch before Mathias's minions found him? Maybe . . . but he wasn't willing to take a chance while this close to the book. They needed a distraction, something to send the Anarki scrambling in another direction.

"Ice!" she hissed.

Their pursuers were coming closer still. He had to decide—now.

With a silent grunt, he heaved Bram off his shoulder and hoisted him into the next tree over. He wasn't well hidden, but between the dark and Bram's black clothing, this spot might suffice long enough to fool Mathias and his goons.

Still, he needed a distraction. . . .

"Careful," Sabelle whispered urgently. "He's so ill."

But not dead yet. He would be if Mathias found him.

A glance later made Ice pause. Sabelle's white sweater flared in the moonlight like a damn beacon, and as the Anarki crept ever closer, a tree stripped by winter of its foliage provided little camouflage.

"Give me your sweater." He whispered his demand standing at the base of the tree.

Sabelle recoiled. "What?"

So very near now, a muttered curse and footsteps shuffling through dried leaves. The Anarki were maybe a few hundred meters away. He and Sabelle had only seconds left before discovery.

"Your sweater. Now!"

Sabelle glanced down. Understanding dawned a moment later. Without pause, she crossed her arms around her waist and peeled the sweater off, then tossed it to him.

Ice tried not to think about what she might—or might not—be wearing now that she'd pulled off the thin cashmere. He glimpsed lots of bare, golden skin. Damn it all. Not only was she a temptation, but she wouldn't stay warm for long like that. Then again, time wasn't on their side.

"I'll be back. If the Anarki finds you, transport yourself and the book somewhere you'll have help."

"And leave you and Bram? No." She crossed her arms over her chest.

For a princess, she was terribly stubborn. "Promise me."

She shook her head.

"Now," he demanded in a low voice the wind swept away.

"Bloody cold!" an invading wizard shouted fifty meters to their left. "Hate winter."

Ice dodged around the trunk of the tree and sent Sabelle another demanding glare, mouthing, "Please."

Finally, she rolled her eyes. And nodded.

With her sweater wrapped around his hand, he tried not to think that his soiled hands had probably dirtied it. Or that he could smell her light peachy feminine musk rising to his nostrils.

"I'll come back for you," he mouthed.

Wishing he didn't have to leave her, Ice took a gamble, teleporting to the other side of the river bank, inside a cluster of smaller trees. Crouched in the mud, he smelled the recent rain. His heart pounded in a violent rhythm that matched the beat of his thoughts. *Must return to Sabelle. Must return to Sabelle.*

He could find no Anarki on this side of the river. They were all near her, and she'd been so brave when he left. His distraction must be enough to draw them away, to where he now stood.

Reaching above him, he grabbed the nearest branch with one hand and lifted himself, then slung his leg over. Shimmying down the branch toward the junction of several branches, he positioned Sabelle's white sweater in the shadowed wooden valley, then leapt to the ground and darted to the next tree.

Thankfully, no shouts from the other bank of the river, no signs of discovery—yet.

Clambering up the old tree, fighting a cold sweat of fear for Sabelle, he made his way into the giant tree, frantically glancing around for one of the younger limbs. Spotting one above, he climbed toward it.

"Over here!" he heard from a distance. "I think I see something!"

Time to draw them away now.

Ice edged out onto the limb and, with a roar, jumped high, then landed on the fragile wood, right in the middle. A sharp crack rent the air, echoing with his primal scream.

"I hear them!" Mathias called. "On the far bank. Capture them!"

Running through a few of the trees on the other side of the river and shaking branches, making as much noise as possible, he listened as a horde of Mathias's minions worked back toward him. He stomped hard on the earth, crunching leaves with his boots.

Finally, he heard the Anarki racing in his direction. By the time they figured out it was a ruse, he and Sabelle would be long gone. Hopefully.

In a flash, he teleported back across the river, to the base of the tree in which Sabelle huddled. She'd smartly pulled her long, golden curls behind her back so that only the crown of her hair glowed in the moonlight. For both warmth and concealment, she'd curled up into a ball, clutching her knees, clothed in dark denim, against her chest. And she shivered.

He grabbed one of the sturdy low-lying branches and reached for the next one above it, then hauled himself up until he neared Sabelle.

"We're not leaving yet?" she whispered. "They fell for your ruse."

He held up a finger to stay more questions, just in case some of the Anarki had remained behind to keep watch on this side of the river. He and Sabelle couldn't afford to give away their position or give the evil underlings chasing them any means of getting their hands on the Doomsday Diary. Since a woman could write her true wish in the book and have it granted, even the commencement of doomsday if she had the proper power and passion, they could not afford to allow Mathias anywhere near the book again.

Balancing his big feet on branches that flanked Sabelle, he reached down and lifted her into his arms. She drew in a sharp breath and tensed, but quickly forced herself to relax. He settled her in his lap, pulling her back against his chest into the warmth of his body. She snuggled against him, teeth chattering.

Ice tried not to notice how bloody soft she was, how the bottom curve of her breast brushed one of his thumbs when she exhaled, or her amazing scent. He willed his erection to stand down, but around her it was no use. Sabelle got him hard. Every time. It had been that way since he'd first laid eyes on her. Might as well get her used to that now. He wasn't certain how long they'd be alone together, how many hours or days it might be before they reconnected with Duke and the rest of the Doomsday Brethren. The fact they couldn't teleport without being detected threw a serious wrench into every plan he'd made.

But work with it he would. He had no choice.

Energy, however, he worried about. What would he do when his magic needed the charge he obtained from sex? His usual outlet was hundreds of kilometers away. And Sabelle sat in his lap.

Impossible. Somehow, he'd have to rile her up and have her send all her furious energy to him in lieu of the sexual kind. It wasn't optimal. He'd rather cut off his arm than hurt her. But better to anger her than insult her with his touch.

"Don't move," he murmured right into her ear. Dear God, even her hair smelled incredible. "I think they've fallen for my distraction, but I want to make certain that there are no Anarki on this side of the bank before we make a run to the village just north of here."

She nodded. "Thank you for acting when you did. They were creeping close."

Ice shuddered, imagining what scum like the Anarki might have done when they realized they held magickind's most prized female in their possession.

He tightened his arms around her and breathed her essence in deeply. No one, least of all Mathias, would ever touch a hair on her head.

But in order to keep that vow, he had to get them out of this valley alive.

CHAPTER THREE

THREE BLESSEDLY SILENT MINUTES passed, punctuated by the occasional sound of Anarki across the river, still beating the trees to find him and Sabelle. The fog rolled in. The temperature dropped. Ice feared rain soon. He could withstand it, but Sabelle . . . Bloody hell. He needed to get her to shelter quickly.

Clambering down from the tree quietly, he peeled off his brown sweater, ignoring the bite of the early December chill. It would be too big for her and smell like him. Hopefully, she wouldn't mind. He had nothing else to offer her . . . but wasn't that a metaphor for everything between them?

"Take this." He handed his sweater up to her. "Put it on."

She shook her head. "You'll freeze."

Ice stared. Who cared? She must know that no one would. "No time to argue. Put it on."

Reluctantly, she grabbed the warm sweater, and he watched with perverse pride as she donned it. Miles too big, it all but swallowed her whole, but the fact it touched her skin made him harder than an iron pike.

Bloody stupid bastard. She's surviving, not letting you put some stamp of ownership on her.

Scooping up handfuls of mud, he rubbed it all over his torso, camouflage in case they were spotted fleeing from the other side of the river. He winced against the cold sludge, but applied it as evenly as possible. Sabelle watched him, blinking and stunned.

Grimacing, he reached up for Bram, carefully lowering him out of the tree. As much as he hated the miserable bastard, Ice knew all this jostling wasn't good for him. But it couldn't be helped. Damn bad luck that none of them had realized that, when Mathias briefly possessed the Doomsday Diary before Sydney had stolen it back, he'd had a witch write in it as well.

Securing Bram in his grasp, he reached up to help Sabelle to her feet. He caught her around the waist, and she slid slowly down his body. Bloody hell, she smelled luscious. His growing appetite for peaches surged—the blonde was a succulent fruit so beautiful, she made his teeth ache . . . along with everything south of his waist.

Get your mind off the princess. Get to safety!

Knowing they had no time to waste, Ice took Sabelle by the hand, hating like hell that he had to dirty her. "Tuck your hair inside the sweater, princess. We're going to run for it."

Quickly, she did as asked, then he crouched and began to run. Sabelle mimicked him, staying low to the ground as they trekked north, away from the river. Away from Mathias.

They put one foot in front of the other for a minute, two, three, five . . . slowly wending their way out of the valley. Behind him, he could hear Sabelle begin to breathe heavily. They had at least another three kilometers to go, and he prayed she could endure. He could use his magic to carry both her and Bram, but since they'd traced the book via teleportation, he feared using any measure of magic around the Doomsday Diary—at least until he knew what Mathias's witch had written.

"You're doing well. Keep going. I've got you." He squeezed her hand.

She squeezed back. "I won't let you down."

Ice whipped his gaze back to her. She was running for her

life and cared about him? The woman amazed him. How was it possible that she and Bram were even of the same bloodline, much less shared a father? In his eyes, Sabelle was indeed a princess. But Bram was no prince charming.

They settled into a pace, slower than he might have liked, but she still jogged behind him. With each continued step, confidence infused him. He grinned when they reached the outskirts of town. They had escaped, without injury—and with the book!

Ice learned otherwise when, through the bushes covering the bend in the road, he saw three robed wizards fanned out across the route leading from the valley into town. *Bugger!* He clutched Sabelle about the waist to keep her close, safe.

Against him, she breathed hard. "How did they find us?"

"I don't think they did," he assured. "They don't appear to be looking, so I suspect they're guarding the road as a precaution."

And he wasn't certain how they would escape. Anarki at his front, back, and sides, no means of teleporting . . .

Sabelle took a deep breath. "Why don't you teleport across town, get a car, then—"

"Steal a car?"

"Unless you own one here, yes."

After being thought little better than a vagabond and thief most of his life, stealing didn't set well with him. In fact, he'd never done it in his life. But desperate times clearly called for desperate measures.

"I don't own a car."

"Steal one, drive to that church down the road and collect me. I should be able to sneak against the side of this cliff and escape detection."

Stealing aside, it was a solid plan, except . . . "I cannot drive. We'll stay together and—"

"And be caught trying to find a way out of this town. No. We'll reverse roles," she breathed against his cheek.

Ice gritted his teeth to stop himself from turning to her, kissing her . . . and likely blurting the words that would be the biggest mistake of his life. Already, she intrigued and compelled him beyond logic. Sabelle Rion mate to a Rykard? Sounded like one of those damnable human television comedies.

"You have the pack with the book. Give it to me." After he did so, she set it on the ground at his feet. Perfect. Now when she left, the diary would stay where she had placed it. He could get away, if need be, and hopefully it would remain hidden. "Stay here and stay quiet."

She stood, and he grabbed her wrist and pulled her back. "Where the bloody hell are you going?"

"To get a car and take it to the church. See the lights down the road, through the fog?" She pointed to some glimmering, distant point to his right.

"I do, but—"

"I'll take the car there, teleport back to you, then we'll sneak away with the book toward the church together."

Ice stared at her, conscious that he expended effort not to drop his jaw at her suggestion. *She* was going to steal a car? "Can you do that?"

"Drive? Certainly. Bram has fourteen cars. I often delight in sneaking one of his convertibles out and driving, just to feel the fresh air on my face and the wind in my hair."

He could picture that. Would, in fact, love to see her hair streaming out behind her as freedom beckoned her. Even more, he'd love to see her hair streaming across his pillow as he sank deep into her body . . .

Who the bloody hell was he kidding? Tonight was as close to Sabelle as he would ever be. When he'd first met her, Bram had refused to allow her to shake his hand. Half the time, she looked as if she couldn't decide if he was simply odd or truly frightening. And now she wanted to steal a car to help him get free? Yes, it was for her brother and the book, too. He understood. But she could have left him to his own devices after securing the car and driving away. Instead, she spoke as if they were a team . . . in this together.

Damn, even that made him hard. Well, harder.

Turning to her, their faces dangerously close, he nodded. "Go, then."

Ice wanted to kiss her cheek, but didn't dare. She wouldn't welcome the gesture, and he'd only be tantalizing himself with what he could never have.

"Wait here."

He nodded, hating to see her go alone, but it was the only way. "For thirty minutes. If you don't return, I will come for you."

"If I don't return, teleport to Duke's. Get him to bring Olivia or Sydney to collect the book. Don't waste your time chasing me." When he opened his mouth, she shook her head. "Don't argue."

Like hell. He cursed as fear started to gnaw at his gut. "Be careful."

Nearly midnight. Sabelle found herself in an unfamiliar Welsh village with a brother whose health had taken a downturn, judging by his intermittent coughing and moaning. Alone with Isdernus Rykard, the one man who scared her—even as he made her burn and ache.

The one man she could never have.

As the grandfather clock in the hall chimed the half-hour mark, Sabelle swallowed, hands wringing as she paced the bed-and-breakfast's wooden floors, and listened to the shower run, imagining the steamy water streaming down every muscle and vein of Ice's large male body.

Stop. Focus on Bram! Determined to give her brother her full attention, she crossed their rented cottage to check on him.

The evening had been a blur. Fleeing Mathias and the Anarki had been harrowing. All that climbing in trees and hunkering down inside bushes had been unnerving . . . but markedly less so with Ice's protective presence beside her. Thankfully, her plan had worked. His relief when she reappeared within the half hour had been foolishly intriguing. Did he actually care about her beyond his own survival? With that question swirling in her mind, they'd slipped away from the Anarki.

Covered in mud and uttering few syllables, Ice directed her southwest, just over the Welsh border to Monmouth. Not far out of town, they'd found this charming stone bed-and-breakfast. Very out of the way, and Sabelle had used some of her siren gifts to persuade the manager that they had reservations for the night and had paid in advance.

Once inside, they'd locked all the doors and windows, and she'd ringed the place with her magical securities. Ice had done the same. As far as they could tell, no Anarki had followed them, but better to play it safe.

Then, despite being covered in mud, Ice offered her the shower first.

Though labeled by magickind somewhere between crazy and dangerous, he had put both her safety and comfort above his own time after time. Odd, considering he hated Bram.

Then again, every time she got near Ice, his body told Sabelle that he wanted her.

Quickly, she'd showered and settled Bram into one of the cottage's two bedrooms. The smoke around her brother looked thicker, darker, than before. Cloying, choking. The labored sound of his breathing terrified her. His magical signature was fading . . . which meant his life would soon follow if they couldn't find a way to break Mathias's terrible spell.

Frustration eating at her like a disease, Sabelle slammed the door. She *hated* feeling helpless, but watching her brother die weighed her down with a sense of being powerless.

Taking Bram's hand in hers, she crouched at the side of his bed and bowed in prayer, her forehead touching his unresponsive hand. This was not her brother. Bram was vital and bossy and amazing—and the only parental figure she'd ever really had. Lord knew her selfish mother had never cared for her, beyond however much offspring with Merlin's blood in her veins was worth. Losing Bram . . . Devastating wouldn't begin to describe her loss. She'd envisioned him beside her as she took a mate, had younglings, grew older. They'd laughed and fought and helped each other. Their bond, always strong, had become stronger since Mathias's return. Eradicating magickind of the cancer the evil wizard spread through society was Bram's most passionate cause. Sabelle didn't know how she'd finish that work without him.

Hot tears stabbed at her eyes again. Exhaustion and fear overtook her defenses. Two minutes. She'd give in that long, then put on her brave face. Ice would want nothing to do with her tears. They had no time for foolishness.

Suddenly, the door to Bram's bedroom *whooshed* open and bounced off the wall beside him. There stood Ice.

Sabelle leapt to her feet with a startled gasp, aware of hot tears burning her cheeks—and her stare glued to his body. Wearing nothing but a towel, he scanned the room for danger with wild eyes. Rivulets of water caressed their way down his corded neck, over his bulging shoulders that ate up the door frame, across a chest no doubt capable of bench-pressing a bus, and along the ridges of his six-pack abs . . . before being lapped up by the towel riding dangerously low on his lean hips. *Dear God.*

Finding the room empty of Anarki, Ice turned his fierce green eyes on her. They flared with heat. Her body sizzled as if she kissed a live wire.

"What's wrong?" he barked.

"I—I . . ." She couldn't find her tongue.

"I heard a door slam. Has anyone come? Are you in danger?"

Trembling, she ripped her gaze away from his massive chest rising and falling with each rushed breath.

"No." She swallowed. "Sorry. Just me. I . . . was frustrated. Bram's getting worse."

Tears threatened again, and she didn't want to show Ice her weakness. His body might want her, but the way he called her princess, almost a sneer . . . No. She wouldn't reveal her vulnerabilities and give him a reason to mock her later.

Despite her resolution, a fat tear rolled down her cheek and dropped onto the inn's black silk robe she'd wrapped around her. She swiped at her wet cheek.

Ice charged across the room. He reached out to take her hand, then stopped before touching her, his tattooed biceps flexing with restraint. Quickly, he glanced at Bram. His mouth took a grim turn down.

"Have you any other ideas that might heal him?"

Another painful weight settled on her heart. "None. Were you able to reach Duke and the others while I showered?"

"I don't dare. If they're being followed as well, any magical summons before we're truly safe could be dangerous for all of us. And I didn't have my damn mobile with me when the Anarki attacked."

"Me, either. The phone in this cottage only rings the front desk; I checked. We'll find a phone tomorrow."

Ice nodded, then edged back. "I ordered food earlier. It should be here shortly."

A lovely gesture, but Bram's condition ruined her appetite. What if her brother never opened his eyes again?

Fear welled up inside her, and to her horror, fresh tears rushed. She couldn't contain the flood. Her breath caught, and her vision blurred. Scalding tears rolled out of the corners of her eyes. She swiped at them, but couldn't catch them fast enough.

Oh, God. She was again crying in front of Isdernus Rykard, for whom sympathy was likely as welcome as syphilis. His personality often matched his name, and magickind regarded him as both ruthless and crazed. A man like him doubtless had no patience for weepy women, particularly not when times called for strong ones.

Sabelle slapped a hand over her mouth and raced past Ice toward the bedroom door. His hot hand clamped around her upper arm and hauled her back, dangerously close to his large, warm body, still beaded with water.

With his free hand, he pulled hers from her mouth, staring at her with an expression somewhere between probing and puzzled. "Don't fret. We will see him well."

The gentle note in his voice shocked her, brought forth a fresh well of tears. "How? Th-that smoke is a mystery. No one has b-been able to figure—"

"Shh." He laid a soft finger across her lips.

Ice's touch on her sensitive mouth jolted her, as if her entire body was connected to her lips. "Don't think him into the grave."

She sent him a shaky nod. Positive thoughts would help her brother more than fear. "You're right." Drawing in a trembling breath, she felt the onslaught of more tears. Angrily, she wiped them away. "I'm sorry to be a weepy mess."

He drew in a deep breath, his chest expanding. She winced, waiting for him to scold or bellow at her. Instead, he pulled her against him, pressing her body to his with an arm around her waist. He buried his fingers in her hair. A million starbursts erupted, scattered over her scalp, her very skin. The sensation sank bone deep, fracturing her thoughts, her composure, her heartbeat. His heat seeped into her, cementing his impact on her, searing it inside her. He was hard. Again. Sabelle sucked in a breath.

"No apologies for tears. Bonds between siblings can be strong."

He had siblings? Apparently. His statement proved how little she knew of him, and for once, it was frustrating not to be able to read someone's mind.

"Tears won't help now. I know that," she offered. "I should be planning what else I can do to help Bram, how I can get him to safety, where I go from here, what—"

"We," Ice murmured in her ear as gently as his rough voice allowed. "My shoulders are strong. Let me take some of the weight of that responsibility. Now, we must rely on each other."

So solid against her, he didn't feel like her brother's enemy. He didn't sound insane, but capable and willing. She wondered exactly who Ice was.

Sabelle pulled back and stared as if she could reason him out like a puzzle. "You're awfully kind to me."

His face closed up. "Any reason I shouldn't be?"

"You and my brother . . ." *Hate each other? Try to kill one another at every possible turn?*

"The enmity between Bram and me has nothing to do with you."

His eyes glowed so green in the low light filtering in from the next room and moonlight beaming through the fog-shrouded window. He looked so intense in every way: determined thoughts, dominant stare, fierce desire.

It had been easy to write Ice off as a madman, especially given his mysterious and eternal hatred for Bram. But he'd given her the very sweater off his back, then soothed her grief about a man he loathed. Why?

Sabelle doubted he would answer if she asked. Besides, she had to focus now on Bram.

"I don't know what else to do for him." Her gaze flickered back to her brother. Fear raked its cold claws through her, and she tried to suppress the shiver.

"Right now? Nothing."

That reality brought a new cascade of tears. God, her eyes were gritty now. Fatigue beat at her, and crying didn't help. Why couldn't she stop?

"Damn it," Ice muttered.

Sabelle cringed. Of course he was annoyed. Tears accomplished nothing. He didn't need to be dancing attendance to her, but keeping them safe and getting the Doomsday Diary back into hiding. This foolishness needed to stop.

Before she could apologize again, Ice bent to her, lifting her in his arms against that inferno chest. She choked in surprise, and her stomach fluttered. Actually fluttered as if she'd swallowed butterflies, as it never had in her nearly eighty-five years.

Then he marched out of Bram's bedroom and back into the main room. He set her on the sofa, near the cheery fire he'd started as soon as the cottage had been secured. He sat beside her and reached for her hand. The contact charged her with an electric need. Yet with him, she felt safe. Cared for, even, though she had no doubt that Bram would forbid this or any kind of comfort from Ice.

She stared at his hand over hers, his hair-roughened knuckles swallowing her fingers. "Ice, I'm so sorry."

"Stop apologizing. You're worried about your brother. I understand."

How could he possibly? "Do you have a brother?"

"No." Something in his face warned her to stop asking questions. She took the silent advice. After his kindness, she shouldn't pry.

"It's just . . . Bram has practically raised me. I owe him everything."

Ice clenched his jaw, but nodded. "Of course."

Right, then. Time for a change of subject. He wasn't one for chatter, clearly. Tonight, she yearned to pour out her fears and feelings. Exhaustion and fear overwhelmed her. All her support . . . scattered to the winds. Olivia and Sydney were hopefully hiding safely with their mates. Bram was unconscious. Lucan had gone with his brother.

She was completely alone with a man she barely knew, one most regarded as mad.

Sabelle bit her lip. A glance told her that Ice still watched her, his stare unblinking. *What the devil was he thinking?*

He shifted closer, and the towel parted, leaving one powerful thigh—and the dark shadows in between—exposed. Sabelle tried not to stare. But the dusting of dark hair on his thighs grew more dense at the top of his leg, and she found herself insanely curious about what he had under that towel, if *all* of him was that large.

Heat crept up her face. Damn. She was probably turning ten shades of red.

"Do you . . . ah, need to finish your shower now?" She looked anywhere but at him.

The fire crackled. The air stilled. The silence deafened. Her mouth turned dry.

"No." He grabbed her chin and forced her to look at him. "Are you all right?"

Sabelle tore away from his grasp. Times were serious. Desperate. She had no business staring, no matter how much her eyes fancied the visual candy. "Fine."

"Don't lie."

My, he is *blunt*. Then again, everything about him was. Hair, manner, stare, words—all of it no-nonsense. She needed to adjust, remember he was no diplomat, nothing like the Council members she'd dealt with of late. Clearly, Ice was used to rolling up his sleeves and accomplishing whatever he set out to achieve.

"Don't push," she shot back. "It's not important now."

"The devil it's not. If you need something—"

"I will deal with it."

His green eyes flashed, then his expression turned flat, cold. He withdrew his hand from hers, that tattooed biceps flexing again, now in anger. "Naturally."

There was a wealth of meaning behind that one word. "What does that mean?"

He raised a slash of dark brow. The firelight illuminated his face, and she noticed for the first time a slashing diagonal scar through the middle of that brow. In fact, he bore the proof of a nasty gash on the top of his shoulder, and a mark around each wrist. Magickind healed faster and more efficiently than humans. It was fairly rare to retain scarring for more than a few months. But these wounds looked very old, indeed.

"Do my scars bother you, princess?"

Did he think that she would not want to be in his presence because he wasn't perfect? "I wonder what you must have suffered. I can only imagine the pain—"

"Don't." He shook his head and leaned against the back of the sofa, putting distance between them.

In other words, he refused to discuss it. His business, of course. But Sabelle couldn't deny that his refusal upset her. She wasn't hurt, exactly. But sensed a deep well of pain, and she had no idea where it stemmed from. And she hated being shut out . . . though she'd done the same to him.

"Do you need anything else?" His gravel voice raked over her.

"Do you?" Sabelle couldn't stop herself from reaching across the sofa and laying her fingers on his arm. After all he'd done for her and her brother today, the least she could do was ease his pain. But when she opened her senses to send him joyful and peaceful thoughts, he ripped his arm away and stood.

"I don't need your siren abilities to force happiness on me, princess. I'm just fine."

"I—I'm sorry. I simply thought . . . I brought up something painful, and—"

"I'll live. I didn't grow up with rainbows and sunshine. I don't need them now." He took a deep breath, then another, staring down at her.

Sabelle felt instantly contrite. "I'm sorry."

He sighed, and the anger seemed to drain from him. "So am I."

With that obscure apology, he pivoted away and headed again for the bathroom, closing the door behind him.

He didn't want to hear about Bram, and now that they weren't fighting for survival, every other conversation with Ice was strained and confusing. A few words. Less than five minutes, and she was mystified. And completely curious.

Where had the scars come from? What exactly had his life been like before the Doomsday Brethren, as a member of the Deprived? Why did he and Bram despise each other?

The wind outside howled, reminding her that the enemy awaited them just on the other side of that door. None of her questions mattered now. Nor did the answers, not until they were safe.

Ice walked back in wearing the other dressing gown supplied by the bed-and-breakfast. Black, sleek, it draped lovingly over his muscles, clinging to every physical feature that fascinated her.

He finished belting the garment around his waist, then looked up. The green of his eyes stood out, grabbed her by the throat. Sabelle's heart pounded.

"Food should be here soon."

And then what? Sabelle shook her head. Much better to focus on that question than gawk at Ice's body—again.

"What shall we do next?" she breathed.

As soon as the words slipped out, an image of his big body tangled with hers as he captured her mouth under his and aligned their bodies so he could press deep inside battered her better sense. She forced herself to ignore the ache that image created.

He froze. "Besides sleep?"

Ice wasn't exactly suggesting anything. But horrified that her thoughts showed on her face, she shook her head. "I—I meant tomorrow."

With a sigh, Ice sat beside her again. "We can't stay here. You're probably tired and want to rest for a few days—"

"We don't dare."

The measuring glance he sent her revealed surprise. "Exactly."

Damn it. Perhaps the fact she couldn't read Ice's thoughts was a good thing. He probably thought she was a stupid Privileged siren blonde, with nothing more to do each day than worry about her outfit and the state of her hair.

"We must warn the Council members their lives are in jeopardy."

Ice sneered. "Let's hope they believe it."

Indeed. "We have to get Bram some help as well."

"He's seen a healer, right?"

"Did no good, so I've been thinking . . . I have help." She nodded toward the Doomsday Diary sitting on the leather ottoman in front of the sofa.

Ice's gaze fell on the little red book. He frowned. "Do we know what it will do? Olivia never wrote in the book. Sydney wrote only her sexual fantasies. You're talking about reversing dark magic, nearly stopping death. What are the repercussions of tampering with something so magical?"

"What are the repercussions of doing nothing?" she shot back.

"If Mathias can track it when we teleport it, it may be possible for him to track the book when we use it."

Good point. "Perhaps. It may be worth the risk to find out." Though writing in the diary scared her, Sabelle didn't see many other options. "I fear he'll die if I don't."

"Understood. But if using the book makes it traceable, Mathias will find and kill us all if you do."

Ice could well be right. "I'll have to think on it. Perhaps there's a way to use it that he can't track?"

"If there is, I'll help you find it."

Surprise skittered through Sabelle. He wanted to help her help Bram? "Thank you."

Ice nodded, and Sabelle found herself hard-pressed not to stare. Everything about him shouted masculinity. He was solid, like a rock, both in strength and spirit. It would take a lot to make him crumble. That didn't surprise her, really. But she had to admit that she felt extraordinarily safe with him. And she was certain that her sudden, unruly attraction had everything—and yet nothing—to do with those characteristics. From the first, she'd thought he was unbearably sexy. That hadn't changed one whit.

A knock sounded at the door. Only a human could approach the door with the magic they'd placed around the cottage—this must be dinner.

"I'll get it." Ice rose and urged her back with a hand. "Stay here . . . just in case."

He opened the door to a smallish woman, young with very fair skin and nearly-black hair. She took one look at Ice in the black dressing gown and flushed beet red.

"I-I'll just put your meal over here." Her voice shook as she placed a tray on a nearby table, then snuck another glance at Ice. "R-ring the front house if you need anything else."

"Thank you." Ice walked toward the door, clearly ready to be rid of her.

The woman lingered, then smiled at Sabelle. "Honeymoon?"

Lacking a better response, she nodded. Then glanced at Ice for his reaction. Did he know what the human word meant?

"It's romantic here. We usually do a little wedding cake for all the newlyweds. We knew you were coming. I'm sure we did one for you. I'll check the kitchen for it."

Understanding dawned across Ice's face, and suddenly Sabelle wished a hole would open in the ground and swallow her up.

"That won't be necessary," Ice assured. "We simply want privacy tonight and are leaving early in the morning. You understand."

The little woman flushed red again. "Indeed. I'll just . . . go. Congratulations!"

Backing out the door with a last glance at Ice and a wave, the bed-and-breakfast clerk left. Sabelle watched Ice's face for reaction, but he gave away nothing.

"She thinks we're newly mated?"

Sabelle felt certain that she was turning many shades of red. Again, she wished she could read Ice's thoughts. Was he laughing? Annoyed? Aroused?

"Indeed. Not that we . . ."

Ice frowned, and she stopped babbling.

"That we . . . what?" he asked with a raised brow. "Would ever have sex?"

Even his words blasted her with unbearable heat. If he ever touched her, she'd combust. She pressed her lips together to stave off her need. Now wasn't the time. Ice wasn't the man . . . no matter how badly her body wished otherwise.

"Ever mate?" he added.

It was imperative that she divert this conversation now. They couldn't ever mate, and pointing out all the reasons why was pointless. He knew them every bit as well as she.

"I didn't correct her because I thought posing as newlyweds would be better cover if Mathias tracked us here." Time to drop this sensitive topic altogether. "Shall we eat before the food grows cold?"

He nodded and crossed the room. She followed and uncovered the plates. Beef tips in a rich burgundy sauce, potatoes, delicate asparagus stalks, French bread, a lemon tart, and a bottle of rich red wine to polish it off. Ice's choices surprised her. They seemed so . . . sophisticated.

"I ordered what I guessed you might like. If you don't care for anything—"

"It's lovely." She tried to smile.

The expression must have passed muster, since he opened

the wine, poured her a glass, then grabbed another plate and uncovered the dish. An enormous pot pie, steaming and fresh, and a huge glass of water. As he grabbed a napkin and fork, then sat and dug in, she frowned.

"You don't want beef tips and wine?"

"This is fine." He plucked up a forkful of pastry, chicken, and carrots.

She should let it go, she knew. Maybe he didn't like beef or particularly loved pot pie . . . but she didn't think that was the case.

"I would have eaten pot pie as well. You didn't have to order anything special for me."

"Of course I did, princess."

There it was again. The name, the slight sneer. She lost what little appetite she'd possessed and threw her fork down with a clatter.

"I don't think I deserve your name calling. I've hardly stood about like a damsel in distress, moaning over chipped fingernails and the like. It's December, and I gave you my jumper. I slogged through the mud beside you. I *stole* a car. Yet you persist in mocking me. Just because I'm female hardly means I'm incapable."

He raised his gaze, then considered her with a long stare. "It has nothing to do with you being female."

Right, then. It had everything to do with the fact she was Bram's sister.

Jumping from her chair, Sabelle stormed across the room to hover over him, hands on her hips. "This is war. I understand that. I'm willing to throw my lot in, sacrifice and fight as need be. Just because I grew up Privileged doesn't mean I expect to be pampered. So don't you dare deride me or treat me as if I'm helpless."

"You think I'm insulting you?"

Hadn't she just explained that in some detail? Yes, he'd done a great deal to comfort and protect her tonight. But his mocking pet name grated. Clearly, it wasn't meant to be polite. "How else could I possibly interpret the manner in which you call me 'princess'?"

Ice drained his huge water glass in four long swallows. She watched his throat work and gulped herself. *Oh dear God.* He was huge, and made her insides jump with a need she could barely fight.

Slamming his glass down on the table, he stared at her. "Good. Keep taking it that way."

Good? "What the devil does that mean? I'm not your enemy. We're supposed to work together. You said you'd help—"

"And I will. But if you're angry, we won't be speaking more than necessary."

What? Perhaps the wizard *was* mad. "And you think that's a good thing?"

"Indeed. I have only two choices: keep you angry or give in to my every urge to kiss you senseless. Which would you prefer?"

CHAPTER FOUR

ICE DIDN'T MOVE A MUSCLE. He sat, breath held, awaiting Sabelle's response.

She blinked, wide-eyed, shell-shocked. Silent.

Bloody hell. Clearly, he had not opened his mouth and inserted his foot, but his whole damn leg. He couldn't take it back.

Still, even if he could, he wouldn't.

From the moment he'd seen her roaming Bram's posh estate two months past, serving hungry warriors a steaming dinner with a genuine smile and that halo of golden hair curling nearly down to the breath-catching sway of her hips, he'd been captivated. His head told him he had zero chance of spending any personal time with the princess. Parts south continued to hope.

Suddenly, that possibility lay between them. How would she react if he kissed her?

For that matter, how would he?

Slowly, Ice stood. Her blue eyes followed him up, up. Vulnerable. Alluring. Intrigued. *Interesting* . . . She flushed, her rosy lips parted, her breaths quickened. He fisted his hands, scouring his resolve for the will not to devour her that instant. Right away, he feared it was a losing battle.

As he stepped closer, his heart chugged. In the air between them, he smelled peaches . . . and her arousal.

His hands clenched into fists at his sides. A sign. He just needed any sign from her. A bare hint of receptiveness and like a freight train with no brakes, he wouldn't be responsible for how quickly he rolled her beneath him. She'd barely draw in a breath before he'd be deep inside her.

"Which would you prefer, Sabelle?" he murmured.

She blinked, then dropped her stare, breaking the breathless connection. *Damn it!* His stomach dropped to his knees. Well, he likely had his answer.

He fucking didn't like it . . . but he'd expected it. Still, to have any hope of keeping his distance, he needed to hear her say that she didn't want him.

Though he had no business touching the princess without her permission, he couldn't stop himself from propping a finger under her chin and lifting her gaze to his. "Answer me."

Drawing in a rattled breath, she lifted her hand to his chest. It shook. Did she intend to touch him? Or to keep him at bay? Either way, when her fingertips settled on his skin, it seared him. Ice's mind raced nearly as fast as his blood rushed through his body and settled into his cock. Hell, was there any left for his brain? Gazing at her upturned face, shining blue eyes, red cheeks and mouth, honeyed skin—incredible beauty, inside and out—he didn't think so.

"I—I don't like being angry," she whispered.

Again, she hadn't exactly rebuffed him. This could be the biggest mistake of his life, but Sabelle's nearness compelled him to touch her. Somewhere. Anywhere. He brushed his way down her shoulder, then caressed the curve of her waist. She drew in another shuddering breath. Her whole body trembled now. The scent of her arousal thickened. He swallowed, his knees turning dangerously weak.

She didn't screech at him to stop, didn't break the contact.

His heart tripped into hyperspeed, and he could barely hear his breathing over the roar. He felt poised on the edge of the cliff, looking down at the freefall likely to kill him . . . and still he couldn't stop from making the perilous leap.

His hand on her waist tightened. "Do you like being kissed?"

"I shouldn't." Her voice shook.

True, she shouldn't, at least not by him. Neither should he want her so badly. But maybe this once, amid chaos and possible death, duty and class wouldn't stop her from allowing him one small taste . . .

"That isn't what I asked. Do you?"

Her lashes fluttered again. Her breasts rose as she took a deep breath. Her head fell back, eased forward. Then she repeated the process again, this time more quickly. Was she nodding?

"Yes."

Barely a whisper. Her blue eyes held hesitation . . . and desire. Sabelle Rion, the most Privileged, beautiful witch in centuries, wasn't repulsed by the idea of his kiss.

Desire fired through him like turbo-charged lightning, a torch scorching his veins. He cupped her face in his hands and dragged her against him. Bent his head to her. Crashed his mouth over hers. He meant to be gentle, but . . . bloody hell. Lips so pliant. Sweet. He didn't linger. Couldn't. Later. Hunger roared at him. *Deeper. Taste her. Now.*

As he sank into her mouth, Sabelle parted for him. He swept inside her, devouring as much of her as he could in a single sweep of his tongue. Her taste overwhelmed him in less than a second. Hot. Sweet.

Instincts followed, flaring to life, then roared. *His!*

He took off the brakes, discarded the last of his care and caution. Turned every shred of his ravenous hunger on her, taking the kiss so deep, he didn't know how he'd ever find a way out of her mouth. And he didn't care. He must make her understand exactly how seriously he not only desired her, but had to possess her. Always.

Slipping his arms around her waist, he pulled her closer still, until she was crushed against him. A new icy-hot wave slammed him, drowning him in sensation, in her flavor. A skin-tingling fever of need followed. Sabelle moaned, then curled her fingers around his neck, over the stubble of hair on his head, drawing him closer still. Her kiss tasted of hot surprise and desire. Cocking her head to meet his onslaught, her lips clung, electrifying him. Her surprising acceptance fried his brain.

Until she tore her mouth away suddenly, panting. "Ice . . ."

Her expression was a question. What now? Why were they doing this? How could they stop?

Familiar words chanted through his mind, demanding he speak them. He tried to bite his tongue. Now was hardly the time, and she'd likely laugh. Once spoken, the words would bind him to her for the rest of his life, even if she refused him, which was likely. And once she did, he could never touch another . . . not that he'd want to, since he hadn't almost from the moment he clapped eyes on her. Unless . . . what if she spoke the Binding?

Whatever she decided, the Mating Call was forever.

Despite that, he could not stop. "Become a part of me, as I become a part of you. And ever after—"

"Oh my God." She gasped. "Ice, I—"

"I promise myself to thee."

Sabelle might not want him to finish this Call, and saying it might doom him, but the taste of her still rolled around on his tongue like ambrosia. Instinct reeled, roared. No way would she stop him from trying to stake his claim and make her his.

"Ice," she implored. "My brother—"

"Is *not* involved here." He felt his eyes burning into her. "This is between you and me."

"But . . . I—I don't. . . . He won't approve."

Bram wouldn't. That went without question. And right now, he could give a shit. But he noticed that she hadn't said she didn't want him. "What do *you* want? Because I know I want you, princess. Any and every way you'll let me have you."

God, her lips were right beneath his, and he needed another taste of her so badly, every cell in his body craved it. Damning caution, he layered his mouth over hers again. She was like sinking into sugar, sweet, light, tempting . . . addictive. He nibbled at her lips, then prowled deeper, engaging her tongue. Then deeper still, consuming as much of her as he could with a single taste.

Again, the urge to claim, to mate, scraped down his instincts, clear, loud, strong. He lifted his mouth, panting over her lips. "Each day we share, I shall be honest, good, and true. If this you seek, heed my call. From—"

"Stop!" She grabbed him by the sleeves of his robe. "Ice, think. If you say the rest, it's done. Even if I refuse, as long as I live, you'll be bound to me."

"I want nothing else." He stared deep into her eyes, as a feeling of rightness, inevitability settled into his gut. "From this moment on, there is no other for me but you."

The moment the words were out, fire slammed across his senses. *Take her! Claim her!* The voice in his head raged at him, chanting. *Now, now, now!* He restrained it— barely—grimacing as he clutched her waist and tried to wait for her response. Would she Bind herself to him? Renounce him? Most likely the latter. Even so, hope torqued up his gut.

She reached up, stroked the side of his face. Tears shimmered. Like she was going to a funeral. No doubt his. *Damn it!*

"Why?" she murmured.

"Why Call to you? Instinct," he growled out the truth. "You know wizards sense their mates in a single taste."

And he wanted another taste right now, deeper, more intimate. Everything she could give him. The need to consume her clawed at him. He tried to ignore it. In the part of his brain still running the show, he *needed* to hear her response before this went further.

Her gaze skittered away. "I don't know what to say."

"You don't know the Binding words? Can't sense them?" *Was that even possible?*

"I know them, but the wisdom of saying them . . . Most witches aren't blessed with the instinct, you know. We must choose. You and I . . . we've barely spent an hour alone together when we haven't been buffered by Bram or running for our lives."

Something in his chest softened like melted butter. She wasn't saying no exactly; she was overwrought. Bram was her priority, and rightfully so. The day had been harrowing. Pushing her wasn't productive, and as much as he yearned for a reply now, maybe waiting would persuade her to Bind to him.

"Sabelle. My princess . . ." Pure reverence welled straight from his chest, resonated in his tone. He hoped she understood his sincerity. From tonight on, no one would ever be more important to him.

She sobbed at his words, staring at him in pained confusion that tore at his chest.

"Shh." He pressed a kiss to her forehead. "I've spoken the Call. You know I could never hurt you, will always put you above me. If you need time to know me—"

"I do, but . . ." Her blue eyes turned bleak. "Even if you

were my best friend and lover combined, my brother would never give his blessing."

"Do you need it?" He tucked a golden curl behind her ear and caressed her cheek. "You're a grown witch, able to make your own decisions. Bram may not be thrilled. I'm not keen on having the backstabbing bastard as a brother by mating, but—"

"Stop! Whatever bad blood is between you and Bram doesn't matter. He's made me promise not to take a mate without his blessing. I won't break that vow."

He stared at her in puzzled shock. "You're fully transitioned. An adult. Certainly you're not going to let your brother make your decisions for you. What do *you* want?"

"Not to alienate my brother. I'll only be eighty-five next month—"

So young? Ice winced. He was nearly two hundred fifty. Yet another obstacle . . . "That makes you young, but not stupid. Are you saying that, even if you fell in love with me, you would never speak the Binding and take me as your mate?"

"It's not that simple."

He forced himself to remove his hands from her waist and step back. "It's a yes or no question, princess."

"You don't understand. My family, everyone I know . . . matings aren't allowed until they're sanctioned by the family."

"Allowed?" he roared. "Once the Call and the Binding have been spoken, there's no taking them back. The mating is sealed. You know that, yes?"

"I do," she conceded. "But being Privileged . . . everything is different."

"And I can't understand because I'm not as good as you?"

She sucked in a breath. "That is not what I said."

"Prettier words, but basically, it was." He held up a hand, dread sliding through him in a thick sludge. He'd *known* when he'd spoken the Call that little could come of this but doom. Damn instinct. "Never mind. Speak the Renunciation and be done. I expected it anyway."

Frowning, she murmured, "Why?"

"I'm Deprived. Everyone thinks I'm mad. Hardly the sort who deserves a princess."

With a stomp of her feet and a shake of her head, she railed, "I am not a princess. And I haven't seen any evidence that you're truly mad."

He raised a brow. "But you said yourself, you hardly know me. C'mon, Sabelle. The Renunciation, if you please. Let's be done with this."

Biting her lip, she hesitated. "I should."

"I'm waiting."

And those words were going to hurt like hell, every syllable ripping out his insides and replacing them with acid. Ice braced himself, eyes closed, head down, shoulders taut. Why couldn't he have kept his fucking mouth shut? For that matter, why had he tasted her in the first place? He'd been fairly certain what would happen. Now, he'd have to spend an eternity knowing exactly what he was missing. That delectable flavor, the soft sensuality of her kiss, the little catches of breath just before she moaned. Sugary, spicy, so incredibly female.

All gone. Forever.

Suddenly, she touched his arm softly. "You will remain a part of me, though—"

Just as her first words eviscerated him, they ended on a sob. Ice opened his eyes as she wrapped her arms around her waist, looking as if she might burst into tears again.

Confusion and impatience detonated inside him. By God,

if she was going to put her brother above his devotion for her, the least she could do was end his suffering. "Now, princess. You know the words. 'I am no part of you. Ever after, I will not promise myself to thee—"

"Stop it!" She shook her head, golden curls brushing her waist. God, she looked so beautiful . . . and so confused. Pain contorted her expression, as if hearing the Renunciation agonized her. "No more."

Ice gritted his teeth, trying to understand. Either she was going to Bind herself to him or Renounce him. Until she did, the uncertainty was only causing her unnecessary pain. And witnessing that was killing him.

"Why won't you give me the words?" he whispered. "Say them and stop hurting yourself. I'll keep my distance."

She remained silent for long moments. Fresh tears welled in her eyes. Even in anguish she looked so damn exquisite he could hardly breathe.

"I can't."

Before he could ask why, Sabelle charged at him and flung herself into his arms. She pressed herself against him and sought his mouth with hers. Without pause, he opened to her. Was this a yes?

Hope slashed into his heart, hacking at his defenses and good intentions like an ax. God, the witch had become everything to him in the span of a few hours.

He embraced her, lifting her feet from the floor and completely against him. She moaned, and tilted her head to receive him completely. Her taste blindsided him. He knew it would . . . but her flavor was so unique, getting it on his tongue was like discovering her all over again. His instincts solidified. She was his mate. No error. No doubt. He prayed this kiss was her way of embracing him as her other half, Bram be damned.

Unwrapping one arm around her long enough to sweep their dishes off the table, Ice ignored them as they clattered to the floor, shattering into pieces. Instead, he lay Sabelle across the surface and followed her down, their mouths still fused. Quickly, he unbelted her silky dressing gown and thrust the edges apart.

God, beneath the robe, she was naked. And glorious. Lush breasts, an intriguing dip to her waist, enticing curve of her hips, supple thighs slightly parted, hinting at every tempting secret in between.

Bloody hell, her beauty blinded him, as she stared up at him aroused and uncertain. Trembling. So close to perfect, he didn't deserve her. He vowed to do everything possible every day to make her happy. Make her smile. Keep her satisfied.

And he wanted to show her that now.

"Ice . . ."

"Feel me, princess," he murmured as he kissed his way down her neck. "Know how much I desire your pleasure and happiness."

He fanned a hand over her breast, his thumb brushing the taut nipple, and she gasped. She moved restlessly under him. Ice settled his mouth on her nipple, sucking it inside, teasing her with his tongue. Gasping, Sabelle reached for the edges of the table and arched up in offering.

Ice sank into the flavor of her skin. Passion pounded him, tightening every muscle. He nipped at the hard tip of her breast with his teeth, and she cried out. He smiled. If she let him, he would keep her splayed across the table and make an all-night feast of her. And he would love her forever.

Images blasted through his head faster than a strobe light. In every one, Sabelle surrendered to him utterly—as his mate. He could visualize them together so clearly, perfectly, it tore the leash from his restraint.

Taking this slowly wasn't an option.

Ice slid down her body, his hands trailing. Get his mouth on her. He had to. Taste her essence and desire.

Face poised over her mound, he anchored his palms on the inside of her thighs and pushed them wide. And stared. Pretty. Pink. Wet.

Mine.

He inhaled, and her scent made him mad with need. Succulent and humid with spice. She looked ripe for his taking, and he wanted her every way possible.

Sabelle tensed. "Ice . . ."

Foreboding shivered down his spine. He came to his senses. Damn it, she hadn't spoken the Binding. She wasn't all his. And her tone warned him that she likely wouldn't be.

Pain gashed through his chest, and he closed his eyes. "Princess, don't. I need—"

"Which is why I can't do this to you," she said, scrambling out from under him and securing her dressing gown around her again. "I'm sorry. It was unfair of me to lean on you, to kiss you, when I can't answer your Call."

He shoved away from the table, not giving a damn that his hard cock so obviously tented his robe. "Can't?" *Fuck!* "Or won't?"

"I . . . I'm completely confused." She crossed her arms over her stomach, as if holding herself in. "Bram will never approve . . . and yet, I'd be lying if I said you didn't beguile me."

Beguiled or not, Sabelle Binding to him was unlikely. A blizzard in July was more likely. Still, that didn't stop him from wishing that she felt enough for him to do the impossible. He was nearly begging, damn it.

"We are meant to be," he vowed.

"I'm not certain we *can* be!" A tear made a silvery path down her face, and spit fire on Ice's guts.

Pushing her was both pointless and painful—for both of them. He needed to stop now. "Do what you know you will eventually. Renounce me."

Slowly, she shook her head. "Please don't make me. I'm . . . not ready to let you go. I know that sounds terribly selfish, but . . . not yet. I'd like to know you better, see how we get on together." She sighed. "I want to talk to my brother."

Which would end any prayer he had of making her his mate.

"You know Bram will never approve." He hissed a curse, and she jumped at the ugly word. "Sabelle, a wizard's mating instinct doesn't lie. I've never professed undying devotion for anyone. Until you. I've never even understood why wizards bothered to mate. Until you. I can accept the fact you don't know me well enough to trust my instinct yet. I can't accept that you're ignoring your own heart and would bow to Bram's will instead."

Sabelle grabbed his hand, and the connection jolted clear through his cock and wound its way to his heart. "He'll disown me if I do. Times are difficult with Mathias free. He's made it quite clear that he expects me to mate with the son of a Council member to further our political advantage."

Not an impoverished Deprived everyone believed mad.

"Who? He's got Sterling MacTavish in his pocket. And since Tynan O'Shea has joined the Doomsday Brethren, I've little doubt his grandfather Clifden will cooperate as well. No sense in you mating with any male in those lines. Thomas MacKinnett had no children, other than the daughter Mathias murdered. So who?"

She shrugged and looked away. "Sebastian Blackbourne or Rye Spencer, I suppose. We . . . never actually discussed names."

"So you're going to let your brother pawn you off on

another Privileged prick, even if he has no instinct to mate you, so Bram can secure his power on the Council? Regardless of whether you're happy? Are you willing to sacrifice the rest of your life for his ambition?"

Fresh tears spilled from the dark fringe of her blue eyes. "You make him sound so calculating."

Fury scalded his veins. Though it would not endear him to Sabelle, he couldn't hold in his snarl. "Isn't he?"

"You don't understand."

"Sacrificing your happiness is something I never will."

End of conversation, at least for now. If he continued to malign the brother she revered, Ice knew she would Renounce him on the spot. As matters stood, he had only the slimmest hope that she would even consider his Call.

"Ice—"

"We will leave early tomorrow, in case the Anarki is on our trail. I suggest you retire to your room, princess."

"Or?" She crossed her arms over her chest, golden hair clinging to her shoulders.

"You'll spend the entire night naked and under me. Your choice." It was an empty threat, and he knew it. He'd never force her.

Sabelle's rosy mouth parted, formed an O. Her cheeks flushed. He didn't have to sniff to scent her arousal. His good intentions teetered. She had three seconds to leave the room . . . or he feared the primal side of him desperate to take his mate would obliterate all good sense.

Standing utterly still, he began counting in his head. *One* . . . She put a hand to her chest and stared straight at him with a hot, torn gaze. *Two* . . . Ice clenched his hands into fists and stepped forward, beyond ready to rip the dressing gown from her body and carry her to bed. *Three* . . .

"Good night," she murmured as she stepped back,

grabbed the Doomsday Diary, then retreated into her bedroom, closing the door behind her.

Sabelle leaned against the door, struggling to catch her breath. Oh, dear God. Isdernus Rykard had spoken the Call to *her*. Even the thought of it left her breathless. Something desperate inside her had yearned to Bind to him.

Clutching the book to her chest, she shook her head. Foolish. Completely impossible. Bram would never agree . . . *You're fully transitioned. An adult. Certainly you're not going to let your brother make your decisions for you. What do you want?* Ice's words rang in her head. He wasn't wrong, but he didn't understand. She couldn't feel his mating instinct. Lust, yes. A thousand yeses. But anything more certain, no. In order to Bind to Ice, she had to trust him. And not imagine for a moment that he Called to her—then pushed her to say yes—as a means of revenge against Bram.

Unfortunately, once she'd recovered from the shock of his Call, that had been her first thought. But when he'd touched her, said "My princess" as if he'd never held anyone so dear to him, she'd wondered. What if he was sincere?

It *was* possible. Isdernus struck her as many things: hotheaded, impulsive, so very male. But a liar?

Sabelle sighed. That question couldn't be answered so easily. On the surface, he seemed incapable of deception. He was unflinchingly honest, even to his detriment. Of course she didn't know him well. How far would he go to infuriate Bram and gain the upper hand in their long-standing feud?

No clue. She wasn't even certain why Bram and Ice hated each other.

Another mystery for another day. Right now, exhaustion seeped into her bones, so deep, she wondered if she would ever recover. The clock on the little bedside table said the time neared three a.m.

Eight hours ago she'd been eating dinner in her house. As she collapsed onto the bed's cozy mattress, reality struck. She'd never see the house again. God knew where the other Doomsday Brethren were, if they'd made it out alive. She wondered, too, could they reach the Council members in time to warn them of Mathias's threat? Who would believe them? And she had no idea how much damage all this running and shuffling might have done to her brother . . .

Sabelle sat on the bed in that circle of light and opened the Doomsday Diary. It looked innocuous enough. Small. Red cover. Odd symbol on the front she now knew represented Morganna le Fay, the book's creator. It hardly looked like the sort of thing that could bring about the end of the world.

Looks were deceiving.

With a quiver, she stared at the empty, yellowed pages. She was so tempted to conjure a pen and write the perfect words to cure Bram. But if she couldn't teleport with the book, Mathias could possibly pinpoint her if she tried to use it. Best not to risk it until they were someplace safer, more defensible. That was the one thing she and Ice could agree on.

So you're going to let your brother pawn you off on another Privileged prick, even if he has no instinct to mate you, so Bram can secure his power on the Council? Regardless of whether you're happy?

Ice's words hammered her. Put like that, Bram sounded so cold. Sabelle shook her head and settled herself against the downy pillows, bedside lamp on. Ice couldn't possibly understand what they stood to lose if she didn't mate wisely.

She closed her eyes—but her thoughts wouldn't stop.

Bram himself hadn't mated wisely. Instead, he'd Called to a human who had disappeared mere hours after capturing the heart of the most sought-after bachelor in all magickind. He hadn't Called to a Council member's daughter.

Sabelle opened her eyes, nibbled on her bottom lip. She'd met Rye Spencer but once. Nice enough fellow, but he'd never incited the fury of desire in her that Ice did. And Sebastian Blackbourne, the arrogant devil, would be no man's pawn and no woman's docile mate. He would take and take and take, then demand more.

None of that mattered a whit now. Only Bram—his health first, then his political position . . . if he lived long enough to care. She was ashamed that she'd allowed herself to be distracted by Ice's Call and the ensuing argument instead of assessing her brother's condition once more. Time to remedy that.

Except Ice would be curled up on the sofa. Not asleep. Did he even have a blanket to cover him on this December night?

Slipping from the warmth of the bed, Sabelle prowled the room, looking for a spare quilt. Nothing, not in the sturdy walnut wardrobe, not in the chest at the foot of the bed. She couldn't leave the man with no blanket on a sofa that was two miles too short for his body. Earlier, she'd offered to let him have the bed. He'd dismissed her.

Gathering the quilt off her bed, she draped it over her arm, then opened the door between them. She crept into the main room. Firelight licked over Ice's prone form, sprawled on his back, as he spilled over the quaint little sofa. His neck propped up on the arm rest looked most uncomfortable. His calves and feet hung over the other end. Sabelle again regretted her reluctant acceptance of the room's last spare bed.

"What is it?" He watched her with intent green eyes.

Even in the shadows, she sensed the heat of his stare. The desire burning off his body. Couldn't miss the sizable bulge between his legs. Every nerve in her body answered with a ping, a zing, a demand. She swallowed it down.

"I thought you might be cold." She spread the blanket over him, doing her best to cover his feet, though it left most of his torso uncovered.

He stared at the blanket, then looked back to her. "This is from your bed. Take it."

"I have another blanket," she lied. "I'll be plenty cozy."

"Take it. I have the fire for warmth."

She shook her head. "I'm checking on my brother, then going to bed."

"Have you been thinking of writing in the Doomsday Diary?"

"Yes. I know that's risky, but . . ." She bit her lip in indecision. "Hopefully soon."

He crossed his arms over his massive chest. "Is that wise?"

"I cannot do nothing and watch my brother die when I have the power to save him. I'll have to hope it doesn't kill us both in the process," Sabelle answered with a shrug. "If we find that Mathias can't track the diary through usage, then I'll regret not trying it. Beyond that, I know the diary's rules. Whatever I write cannot be too big for my magic, and it must be my heart's deepest desire."

"You're powerful. The way you uphold your brother, he's clearly your heart's priority. You should have no problem."

Meaning Ice clearly wasn't her priority. The dig shouldn't bother her. It did.

"Family is important to me," she defended.

He raised a black brow at her. "Indeed."

"You cannot make me feel guilty for loving my brother."

"Of course not." He slanted a look of hot challenge. "I'm

just puzzled that you seem not to have room in your heart for another."

"I do," she protested hotly.

"Then your refusal to answer my Call is specific to me. How many Calls have you received, Sabelle? How many have you Renounced?"

Was he insinuating that she enjoyed toying with wizards? "None. I would never purposefully—" She shook her head. "First you cast me in the role of stupid blond siren. Now the heartless bitch. I can't imagine why you Called to me, if you think so little of me."

"Instinct aside, I'm not certain either. A mistake, regardless."

His words were well-aimed barbs. He was trying to make her hurt as she'd hurt him, most likely. But even knowing that didn't stop the gibes from finding their mark. Or the pain from spreading all through her, radiating a hot, debilitating agony.

"I tried to stop you."

"Renounce me."

This again? "In the morning. I'm tending to my brother, then I'm going to sleep. We have to be up in a few hours."

"Won't you sleep better with this off your chest?"

He was pushing her again, for some reason she couldn't understand. His words said to reject him, but his face . . . that burning laser gaze of his, so green and full of desire . . . Renouncing him was the last thing he wanted.

"Good night."

Before he could reply to that, she made her way into the second bedroom, where Bram lay still as death. The cloud of black smoke had thickened in the last hour. His magical signature flickered, faded. Sabelle bit her lip to hold in tears. She was too tired to spend more. Didn't have the emotional energy or luxury of crying. Tend to business. Get sleep. Start again tomorrow. Don't linger, don't think, don't feel.

If she elected to take a chance and write in the diary tomorrow, she clearly needed to wish for his physical health first. If she could bring back his robust nature, perhaps she could eventually conquer the magical black smoke.

If you do, what are its side effects?

She'd worry about that later.

Dragging his covers over him, Sabelle kissed Bram's forehead, then smoothed his hair from his forehead. He needed a shower. She needed a phone to resume searching for his mate. Energy would help him, and she had no way to give him enough to recover. Besides, Bram was now mated and would most efficiently grasp energy from his mate. Without this Emma she'd never met, he could die.

What a damn mess.

Fighting tears again—and angry because she hated them—she tiptoed back through the main room, purposely not looking at Ice. If she did, he'd only engage her. They'd talk. Fight. She didn't have any more fight in her right now.

Pushing open the door to her room again, the little bedside lamp bathed a corner of the room in golden light, including the bed. On top laid the quilt, neatly spread and tucked in. Something in her heart twisted. Even when she refused to answer his Call, he put her needs first.

Stomping across the floor, she yanked the door open, ready to challenge him. Before she could say a word, he beat her to it.

"Not a word, princess. And don't lie to me anymore. Shut the door and go to sleep."

"You're bossy."

"I'm restraining myself. Unless you'd rather I didn't . . ."

He was baiting her, and she knew it. Damn man. But it

worked. She slammed the door, then huffed to the bed, trying to maintain her anger.

All she really wanted was to open the door and call his bluff, invite him into the bed to share the blanket. She more than suspected where that would lead . . . and then neither of them would need the damn quilt.

CHAPTER FIVE

SABELLE GRIPPED THE STEERING wheel of their stolen ve-
hicle as the sun rose over the hills around Monmouth and
glared at Ice. He'd been grouchy since she emerged from her
bedroom to find him dressed and staring into the cold fireplace. His mood was not improving with their argument.

"We cannot simply make a mad dash to your home and
hide," she pointed out. "Swansea takes us a hundred kilometers west, away from Duke and the rest of the Doomsday
Brethren."

"No one will find you under my roof. *No one*," Ice vowed,
stone-faced. It sent a shiver through her. "If the Anarki can't
find you, they can't hurt you. They can't find the book or
your brother either. It's safer."

From the perspective of an overprotective mate, yes.
Newly mated wizards were often irrational. She hadn't
spoken the Binding to him, but by Calling to her, Ice had
declared himself hers—and now acted accordingly. Sabelle
found it both annoying and touching.

"It's isolated." She shook her head. "We have to find the
others and warn the Council members. Thomas MacKinnett
lives in Ludlow, not terribly far from here. It's closer to the
other warriors. We can warn MacKinnett and, through him,
the rest of the Council."

If anything, Ice's expression turned more remote. "I
worry far less about the Council than you, princess."

His surly words softened her, damn it. After a mostly

sleepless night contemplating his Call and all the ways it would destroy her life if she accepted, she ached, down to her very bones. She wasn't in the mood to deal with these conflicting emotions. "I've taken care of myself for eighty-four years. I don't suddenly need you to do it for me."

Ice froze over even more, then squinted out the windshield at the rising sun. "Have you decided that I am not your mate, then?"

She'd said it wrong; he'd taken it wrong. "I meant only that I'm not helpless."

Ice scanned the remote Welsh landscape that reflected his expression. Bloody hell, he'd continue to take her words as some sign of pending Renunciation until she said it. And she should. Now. Bram would be appalled that she was hesitating. Sabelle wasn't certain why she couldn't manage to say no.

Except that she knew once she said those words, she'd never see Ice again. The prospect disturbed her.

And she couldn't bear the thought that she would cause him pain.

"Ice." She laid her hand on his forearm, driving with her right. The muscles were so hard and male. Heat radiated through her palm.

He turned, pierced her with a fiery green gaze. "I don't recommend touching me now."

Or . . . he would jump on her and make passionate love to her? The burn generated by his touch spread through her body at the thought. For prudence's sake, she reluctantly lifted her palm away, then gripped the steering wheel again. Instantly, she felt cold without him.

"Sorry."

"You've aroused me too much. My instinct screams for me to take you in every way possible."

She frowned. "I did nothing to arouse you."

He clenched his jaw, his stare growing more aggressive. "You breathed."

Oh God. She had to end this road trip as soon as possible or this . . . thing between them would take a disastrous turn.

"Relax," he said softly. "I'm merely being honest, not preparing to bloody assault you."

Sabelle took a deep breath, then realized she was gripping the steering wheel so tightly, her fingers were white. She forced her shoulders to relax. "Sorry. The whole situation makes me a bit tense. I'd feel better if we headed for MacKinnett's. It's closer. They'll have plenty of ways to contact Duke and the others. There's more civilization for us to lose ourselves in until we're all reunited and have a strategy."

"Yes, and more civilization for the Anarki to blend into, as well. Go to Swansea. Stay there with the book. I will teleport to MacKinnett's, warn him, then find Duke."

"Do you know Thomas MacKinnett?"

"No, but I'd like to believe that if one of the Doomsday Brethren arrived to tell him that Mathias planned to kill him, he'd be smart enough to listen. Since the pisshead murdered his daughter, I'm guessing he's one of the few on the Council who believes Mathias has returned?"

"He's old, not stupid. He believes, and Auropha's murder made him paranoid," she said, referring to the young witch Mathias had killed during his first night out of exile. "He won't see anyone he doesn't know. Since his daughter's death, I've spent a great deal of time with the man, devising a way to convince the rest of the Council that Mathias is, indeed, back. But if you've never met him, you won't step toe on his land."

"I'm not putting the safety of this Council prick above yours."

Sabelle paused and counted to ten. Ice meant well, but she had to make him see reason. "Without the Council, chaos would ensue—prime conditions for Mathias to overtake magickind. Then there would be no safe place anywhere."

Beside her, Ice gnashed his teeth as if grinding up glass.

"They are a necessary evil, and you know it." Her soft murmur closed the lid on his argument; they both knew it.

"Fine. Stay close to me. Every moment. This is foolish and risky, and I won't have you in additional danger."

Even in the midst of all this danger, his words made her ridiculously giddy. Sabelle bit her lip to hold in her smile. "Of course. Right beside you."

Finally, Ice turned back to her, his gaze a burning green. "Where you belong."

Less than an hour later, Sabelle insisted they stop in Hereford to switch cars. Their current ride being stolen, she worried the human police would be looking for it and arrest them. Normally, that wasn't an issue, but without the ability to teleport, it was a potentially serious problem.

Ice clenched his fists as a shiver crawled up the back of his neck. This whole trip made him wary, from Sabelle's odd reluctance to Renounce him and end the drama, to the gut feeling they were headed straight into danger.

In town, they encountered a cattle market with farmers milling about cold, dusty lots, waiting to sell their animals. Sabelle exited the car and shrugged on her backpack. She glanced in the backseat at her unconscious brother, who looked like a napping traveler. With a sigh, she motioned Ice out of the car.

"Walk to the end of the block and wait there," she murmured, then turned away.

Ice grabbed her arm and spun her back around. She stumbled

and fell against him. A jolt of desire thundered through him, and he wrapped an arm around her waist to keep her close.

"Let me loose." She wriggled.

Not on your life. "Where are you going?"

"To get another car. I won't get out of your sight, Ice. But we can't spend time soothing your territorial feathers now. The Anarki could be on our tail; we don't know. Let me do this, then we'll be back on the road."

Blast it all, why was the woman so bloody logical? He was proud of her, yes. Dazzled by her cool head under pressure. Usually, that was his role. But the woman had so turned him upside down that Ice couldn't think past his need to keep her safe—or his desire to lay her across his bed and show her exactly how he wanted her.

"I don't like it."

"I hardly expected you to. Maybe you can find a bite we can take on the road and a phone to ring Duke?"

Her tone rankled. She talked to him as if she planned to do something he wouldn't like, and he was too thick to catch her. But he'd play along. For now. And watch her every move.

His instincts screaming, he skulked to a café at the end of the block. It was a bit late for breakfast, a bit early for lunch, and the establishment was largely empty, though he heard voices in the kitchen.

Near the cash register, some absent member of the wait-staff had left their mobile phone. Quickly, he grabbed it and punched in Duke's number, grateful that he remembered it. He stared out the window as Sabelle looked about. One ring, two, three . . . voicemail. *Bugger!* He left a quick message: He and Sabelle had no phone with them and would call back when possible. No hint of location . . . just in case Duke's mobile—or Duke himself—was under Mathias's control. When he looked up, Sabelle was nowhere to be seen.

Cursing, Ice conjured a bit of human money and left it, grabbing a few scones and muffins. He made for the French doors near the back, exiting onto the street once more and rounding the first corner.

There. His little witch was occupied. Ice stopped, watched as she stood near a human male, drawing him close to her. Young, strapping, he smiled, looking dazed by her beauty. In turn, she sent the man a welcoming smile, punctuated by a flip of that golden hair Ice ached to feel across his chest, over his cock. She reached out to touch the male's hand. The male gripped her hand in return.

Ice snapped. Sabelle might not belong to him, but by God if she was going to touch another as he watched.

Hell-bent, he stalked across the car park. "Sabelle."

She whipped her gaze in his direction and gave him a go-away glare. *Like hell*.

He barreled toward them, pausing mere inches from her. Unwisely, she still gripped the human's hand. To his credit, the man tried to pull his hand from the minx's grip, but she held firm.

"This is James," she said before he could warn the man to get the hell away from his woman. "He's very graciously offered to let us borrow his car for a few days."

When she held up the keys, Ice dragged in a deep breath. She'd done it for escape. To be fair, faithlessness wasn't a question, since she had not committed to him. Even so, he could barely stomach the sight of another man's hand on her. But in allowing a stranger she would never see again to hold her hand and be influenced by her siren abilities, she had secured a new car that would not trouble them with the authorities. That one touch allowed them to escape and continue their quest.

He should feel thankful, not homicidal.

"Nice to meet you." James's voice shook as he extended his free hand in Ice's direction.

Ice did his best to suppress his scowl and took the man's hand. Sweaty. Shaking. Rather liking the idea of James's fear, Ice smiled, not nicely.

"Ice is my very protective . . . cousin."

"Cousin?"

Just like that, his tolerance snapped. Cousin was one step from brother, and he hoped to hell Sabelle didn't see him in that light. Hard to imagine when she'd allowed him to strip her bare on a table and wrap his lips around those tight, berry red nipples. He would have no problem ensuring she saw him as a man once they were alone again.

James glanced nervously between Ice and Sabelle, as if he sensed something wasn't quite right, but the witch's grip on his hand muted his logic. Self-preservation kicked in.

"I'll see you when we bring the car back." Sabelle leaned close to the human male, lips pursed.

Ice scented the lust pouring from James and, gnashing his teeth, grabbed Sabelle's arm to jerk her away. Touching her was a mistake. For that moment, she shot him a wave of soothing peace that smothered his jealous rage. In that instant, she planted a soft kiss on James's cheek.

Wearing a dreamy smile, James nodded. "Take as long as you need, love."

"Thank you for your kindness. Isn't he lovely?" Sabelle turned to Ice. When he failed to respond on the spot, she elbowed him. "Isn't he?"

Only to prevent annoying James, who might leave with his auto, did Ice nod. "Indeed."

Sabelle elbowed him in the ribs again.

Moments later, James left them, looking euphoric and happily confused. Sabelle watched, palming his keys.

"Let's go. Did you reach Duke?"

"No answer."

Concern darkened Sabelle's face. "What do you think that means?"

"Could be anything." He shrugged, trying not to think the worst. "Like us, he may not have had his phone with him when Mathias attacked."

"He did, on his belt." She bit her lip. "Do you think they were captured? Killed?"

The possibility so terrified her. Ice wasn't about to mention that had crossed his mind at least a dozen times as well. "They are able to teleport, which is a huge advantage. We're still alive, so it's likely they are, as well."

"I hope you're right. I'm not certain we can fight Mathias alone."

You can't, he wanted to say. He'd tried, after all, taking down nearly a hundred Anarki by himself. Yes, that had been two hundred years ago, and he'd been much more rash and stupid. He'd been lucky to escape with his life, though that hadn't been his intention. And he'd learned a valuable lesson: Mathias's army was like an octopus. An evil that could reach in all directions to drag a wizard in and devour him whole if he hadn't the proper tools and allies.

Which is why you can't make a bloody big deal about this car, he reminded himself. Escape. Getting Mathias. Lopping off as many arms of the monster as possible should be uppermost in his mind. Claiming the woman? Foolish and ill-timed. She would never say yes, and he shouldn't expect her to in the midst of crisis.

Time to move on . . .

"Let's retrieve Bram and get on the road again," he commanded.

Sabelle nodded. "Did you get food?"

Indeed. But when he looked down at his fist, he realized that witnessing Sabelle touch James had made him angry enough to turn the scones and muffins into little more than crumbs for birds.

With a curse, he dropped them. "We'll find something in the next town."

Around midday, Sabelle and Ice arrived at the outskirts of Ludlow. Thomas MacKinnett lived in a renovated nineteenth-century estate about five kilometers from Stokesay Castle. The golden sun burned through the haze to shine in a perfect blue sky. Everything here was lovely in a stark, December sort of way, and she had no reason to shiver. But she did. The air felt disturbed. Even without seeing the house yet, she knew something was wrong.

"It's quiet out here." Ice frowned. The farther up the winding dirt road she drove, the more his frown deepened.

Too quiet. Ice may not have said it, but he likely thought it. "Indeed."

"MacKinnett had no children other than Auropha?"

"No. And his mate died over a decade ago. Other than servants, he lived alone."

"Perhaps that's why it's so quiet."

Sabelle wasn't convinced. She stepped on the accelerator and moved their borrowed car farther up the muddy lane. When the house came into view, she slammed on the brakes.

Sun filtered through the clouds, sending down patchy rays of light playing on the battered roof. Age stains and ivy crawled across the stone facade. MacKinnett had closed the shutters over every window.

The house seemed frozen, as if terrified to even take a breath. Utterly unmoving. Even the trees didn't dare sway with the breeze.

"Bloody eerie," Ice murmured.

"Indeed. Do you sense any magic protecting the house?"

Ice paused, and his frown turned to a scowl. "Nothing. Hardly the actions of a paranoid sort of bloke."

"Exactly. Bram wondered if the tottering old man had gone completely mad with grief. But he was never reckless. We were here a few weeks ago. He had magical protections all over the house, up the lane. Early warning sensors . . . Now, nothing."

It worried her.

Gripping the steering wheel, she directed the car to the front of the house. Columns lined the wide porch. Elegant plaster designs hinted at wealth. The well-manicured garden looked dormant . . . neglected. She shivered.

Parking the auto, she peered under the shadowed eaves and finally caught a glimpse of the front door. It stood wide open.

"I think we're too late," Ice muttered with a curse.

Silently, Sabelle feared he was right. "We'll have to enter with caution. Maybe . . . he's left? After all, Mathias knew he lived here. Perhaps someone warned him in advance, and he fled before he could be slaughtered."

Ice nodded slowly, then turned to her. She tried to stop trembling, but she didn't believe a word she said. Clearly, neither did he. Fear permeated her.

"You all right?" he asked, taking her hand in his. Warm. Protective. Engulfing.

Sabelle placed her other hand over his, so very grateful for his strength. "Fine. Let's have a look around."

He shook his head. "You stay here. Wait in the car. Keep the motor running. Guard Bram. I'll take a look inside. If it's safe, I'll come for you."

Not a chance. Sabelle stepped away from the car and toward the waiting tragedy she feared was just beyond that gaping door.

"I'm coming with you." When Ice opened his mouth to argue, she cut him off. "I feel safer with you than sitting in the car by myself."

While the appeal played to his protective nature, it wasn't altogether untrue. Ice had this air of invincibility about him. At the very least, she knew he would fight with all his considerable skill and power to ensure the book remained out of Mathias's hands. At the moment, she couldn't hope for more.

With a sharp nod, Ice exited the car, placed some protections around Bram and the car, then began the trek uphill to the waiting house. It wailed in silence, seeped an odd sense of suppressed violence and distress. What would they find inside?

At her side, Ice gripped her hand. "I've got you."

She sent him a distracted smile. "Thanks. Do you sense anyone else here?"

He shook his head. "No one. It's feels like a battleground after the fighting is over. Filled with ghosts. Stay close to me."

He'd get no arguments from her on that score.

Together, they stepped onto the porch, past the stately plaster columns, through the open door, into the foyer.

Chaos everywhere. Furniture overturned, walls smashed, glass shattered and littering the stone floor. Evil lingered in the air, bled from the walls. There was no doubt Mathias had been here.

"Oh God," she murmured, her heart pounding roughly as she pulled the straps of her backpack tighter to feel the book closer to her body.

"Shh. Hopefully MacKinnett escaped. It's possible he did."

Maybe. She hoped. Or . . . she didn't want to think about the *or*.

"The problem is, if Mathias wanted to eliminate a Council member so he could put himself in the wizard's seat, he would have to either eliminate the Councilman's entire family or murder one without issue. Thomas MacKinnett, having had his daughter and brother murdered earlier this year, had no remaining heirs."

In other words, a prime target.

"Fuck," Ice muttered.

Sabelle never said the word. But at this moment, she couldn't agree more.

She bent and retrieved a smashed picture of Thomas and his late daughter, Auropha. The frame was bent, the glass in pieces. The picture had clearly been taken during happier times. She held it to her chest and shoved back an inconvenient onslaught of tears. Now was hardly the time.

Ice took her aside and wrapped his arms around her. "This is hard for you."

He didn't ask; somehow, he knew better. She was grateful for his intuition.

"I've known him most of my life. Thomas and my father were good friends. I remember him visiting shortly after my transition. He brought me biscuits and candy and told me to regain my strength." Her voice cracked. "That magickind had just inducted one of the most important witches ever. Nonsense, but such kind words when I was feeling so weak and overwhelmed."

The tears welled again, and she tried to focus on where to search next: upstairs or cellar? The choice filled her with irrational fear.

"Was he one of Bram's allies?"

"Since Mathias's return? One of the few, yes."

She swallowed when she thought of those implications. Sabelle had known that Bram was on the evil wizard's hit list. But seeing MacKinnett's noble estate in shambles somehow made it more real.

"Only MacKinnett would believe that Mathias had returned," she murmured. "He could hardly deny it, since the bastard had taken his daughter from him and used her so callously she bled to—"

"I know," Ice cut in and tightened his grip around her. "But we cannot stand here like targets. We must check the rest of the house."

She knew that, but the prospect terrified her. "Maybe we shouldn't leave Bram alone in the car."

"He's protected, and it's a calculated risk. We can search the house more effectively without him. If we need to fight off the Anarki, we won't have to protect him or ourselves with our hands full, so to speak."

True. She just didn't like it.

"If you'd like to wait in the car, I'll check the house alone."

And leave Ice to face the fear and danger alone? No. She wasn't a coward or the sort of witch to let others do the difficult work on her behalf, like her mother. She wouldn't start that rubbish now.

She shook her head. "Let's go upstairs first."

With a squeeze of her hand, Ice led her upstairs. She was ridiculously grateful for his support. He was like a rock. As much as being here frightened her, Sabelle knew she would be ten times more afraid without him. And he shouldered her fear without comment or question. Ice would make some witch a wonderful mate someday, and she cursed the fact it couldn't be her.

At the top of the stairs, more destruction abounded. Furniture tumbled about and smashed into pieces like matchsticks. Charred walls and floor. And the smell . . . Something sickly sweet assaulted her nose.

They entered the hallway. Every door was closed, and Ice put his hand on the first door's latch. Sabelle's stomach clenched as she stood behind his broad back. He swept the door open.

"Oh God!" Ice bellowed before slamming the door.

He sounded like he might be sick. Still, he pushed her away from the door and tried to force her down the stairs. But she was faster. Shutting her out so that she didn't know just how ruthless an enemy they fought wasn't an option.

She ducked under Ice's tattooed arm and opened the door again. The odor assaulted her first. Terror and blood and death. In the middle of the room huddled a group of corpses, frozen in death. Men staked with knifes to the walls, bleeding at wrists, ankles, and neck. The women all naked, wrists bound, branded with Mathias's symbol on their red, bare mounds. Blood oozed between their thighs. Even more tragic were the children in a circle, dangling by their crooked necks from ropes knotted to the rafters above.

Sabelle slapped a hand over her mouth. There was the strapping manservant who had always helped Sabelle with her luggage and his wife, their two children. The maid, the cook, the butler and his son. Humans, all of them. Now dead for a cause they knew nothing about.

Ice grabbed her by the shoulders and shoved her into the hall, shutting the door behind him. "When I push you away, witch, it's for a reason."

Through tear-blurred eyes, she looked at him. Fear set in, so cold and absolute, like a hard knot in her belly, she shivered. "I had to know. I can't hide from reality. None of us can."

His shoulders tensed, and frustration flashed across his harsh features. "No one doubts your bravery."

"Then stop acting as if you do. This is terrible and wretched and the worst thing I've ever seen in my life, but we have to move forward. MacKinnett . . ."

She couldn't finish that sentence, and Ice didn't force the issue. "Let's find him."

Her teeth chattered, and she wrapped her arms around herself. Swearing, Ice grabbed her hand again, squeezing it, bringing her near. His heat warmed her almost instantly, and again she was incredibly grateful for his presence. For *him*. Bram would have immediately ordered her away from this horrific scene. Marrok, Duke, Lucan—all like overprotective brothers. Shock and Tynan . . . the first would look out for himself, and the latter she didn't know well enough to trust. But Ice, he let her participate, help, even if reluctantly. Again, it struck her that in the middle of madness, he was the one sane person she could rely on.

Leading her to the next door, Ice tensed as he approached. No sounds, no stirring of life. Just the sickening smell of death and fire.

Behind the second door, they found nothing but destruction. Furniture, pictures, pottery, draperies—all smashed, fractured, shredded. But thankfully, no more bodies.

Behind a third door and a fourth, the same. They'd reached the end of the hall.

Which left only the cellar.

"Is it possible he escaped?" Ice asked.

"MacKinnett had human connections through his late mate. He wasn't the sort of wizard to leave his wife's human companions to suffer their deaths alone. I want to think, for magickind's sake, that perhaps he got away. But . . ."

Ice drew her cold frame against him, clasping his fingers

in her hair, soothing her with his palm. Again, she felt oddly comforted merely with his presence.

"Let's check the cellar, then."

She didn't want to, God knew. It was likely to be a chamber of horrors. But she had to be strong. Magickind needed heroes. That had always been Bram's role. Without him, she and Ice would have to do.

Silently, they trekked down the stairs, back to the foyer, then to the kitchen. This room, too, lay in shambles. Pans littered the floor. Flour scattered over every surface of the counters and stove. An apron tossed over a lamp . . . and the rest of a cook's clothes scattered across the counters. The Anarki had rigged ropes at each corner of the nook's table. Blood darkened one side of the ropes, and Sabelle could almost hear the screams still echoing.

A little boy's toy truck lay under the table in a pool of blood.

She looked away, shuddering, fighting tears. Ice drew her closer, kissed her cheek. "Go back to the car, check Bram."

Bless him, Ice was trying to spare her the horror to come. Shaking her head, she dug down for strength, refusing to give in to fear. She would not leave magickind without hope. She would not stop fighting.

"Let's go to the cellar." When Ice opened his mouth to argue, Sabelle pleaded, "Please. I need to do this."

Clenching his jaw and no doubt holding in a curse, he nodded and opened the door that led down to a dark, windowless cavern.

And opened the door immediately to the scents of charred flesh, blood, and hell. A shiver shot through her again, and Sabelle took a deep breath to ward it off.

"Stay here," Ice barked.

"If you go, I follow. Do you see a light?"

With a grim shake of his head, he started down the dark steps into the utterly black room. Hands on the hard ridges of his shoulders, Sabelle followed, her legs so weak and shivery beneath her that she feared tumbling down the stairs. But she pushed on.

At the bottom, she groped the nearby wall for a switch. He did the same. A moment later, artificial light flooded the room, glaring and stark. And Sabelle screamed.

Inches from them Thomas MacKinnett had been stretched across a makeshift grate, his wand broken and his body set aflame—burned away to ashes. They'd stopped the fire halfway up his torso. His mouth gaped open in a horrific scream. His eyes bulged wide as he witnessed the last terrible moments of his life.

MacKinnett's death proved in the ugliest, most tangible manner that Anka hadn't been lying. Whatever her association with Shock, and his with Mathias, Lucan's former mate had been telling the truth. Mathias truly planned to put himself in a Council seat.

God help them.

CHAPTER SIX

A QUARTER HOUR LATER, Ice and Sabelle sat inside the manor's old coach house, which squatted on a parcel of winter-dried grass behind the manor and had been converted to guest quarters. These rooms were, thankfully, undisturbed. Ice pressed a cup of water into her cold hands, then sat across the table, his big body and larger presence taking up most of the narrow, quaint room.

Since she completed spells to keep Bram hydrated and his body functioning properly, shadows draped her brother as he lay on the sofa. Here, it felt peaceful, quiet except for the softly falling rain. The appearance of serenity was both temporary and a lie. Sabelle shivered as flashes of senseless murder and spilled blood tattooed her mind.

"We can't stay here," she said. "We need to warn the other Councilmen, then flee."

Braced on his elbows, Ice leaned on the table, shoulders bulging and wide. "No. We should stay."

Was he mad? "The Anarki can invade this place and do . . . terrible things," she choked. "As they already have. And they'd take the diary, besides. Why would we stay in harm's way?"

"Precisely because they have already been and think their mayhem here is done. They've no need to return."

After a pause, she realized he was right. As much as Sabelle wanted distance between herself and the house of horrors just outside, where a man she'd been fond of and his servants had all been slaughtered painfully and viciously, she knew better. Why would the Anarki return here when they'd been so recently and completed their terrible task so effectively?

"All right. But we stay here in the coach house. I won't sleep in the manor."

Ice paused, frowned, then reached across the table for her hand. His warmth embraced her chilled fingers and she was absurdly grateful for his support. Sabelle hadn't realized how badly she needed it. But somehow, he'd known.

"I wouldn't ask that of you," he assured. "We'll stay in the coach house. I'll keep watch."

"You need sleep as well."

He hesitated. "There is only one bed."

Sabelle's gaze flitted to it, a cozy cherry wood tester bed trimmed in gauzy curtains and piled with comfortable quilts. A bed designed and outfitted for romance. She imagined Ice's body next to hers, hard and dusted in hair where she was soft and smooth, putting off heat like a broiling oven. Her pulse jumped. Very bad thoughts, indeed.

Hiding a wince, she turned back to the warrior. She'd offer the sofa to Ice, but Bram was draped over it limply, his condition unchanged. "We'll manage."

Ice closed his eyes. Looked down. Swallowed. When his gaze bounced up to hers again, fire flared. Transfixed, she stared.

"Princess, if we share that bed, neither of us will get any sleep. All night."

She sucked in a breath as a hot ache balled in her stomach. Worse, the feeling was beginning to sink down and settle right between her thighs. She could only imagine the nuclear reactor sort of energy she and Ice would generate, the blistering pleasure. His intimated offer was so tempting. *He* was so tempting. An utter puzzle, hard one minute, tender the next, alternately kind, possessive, insistent, infuriating. He enthralled her.

God, she was a fool. If she spoke the Binding and became his mate, the Privileged would be devastated, her brother sick, her famous grandfather, Merlin, turning over in his grave . . .

Ice wanted her. Not for a tumble, but forever. His actions seemed to match, but always that voice in the back of Sabelle's head reminded her how much he and Bram hated each other. What would he be willing to do to cause her brother serious pain? How far would he go?

She had no answers.

"I don't think that's wise," she said finally.

He released her hand, eased back in his chair, eyes unreadable. "Of course not."

What did he mean by that? Sabelle frowned and wanted to ask, but it was pointless, really. These few days alone with him were some page out of time, never occurred before and never would again. Eventually, perhaps when she was less worried for Bram and they weren't running for their lives and focused on saving magickind, she would find the will to Renounce Ice. Until then, what point was there in building their relationship?

None.

"We should focus on reaching the other Councilmen, warning them."

"How?" he barked. "How do we do that without alerting the Anarki or their sympathizers that we're here? We can't teleport without leaving the diary behind. I've seen no phone . . ."

"When any Councilman ascends, they are given a special transcast mirror for communication. It connects only with other such mirrors. This is not something many know, and they are always hidden."

"I'd wondered why Mathias decimated the manor house, but if there's a communication device . . . You think he sought that when he tore apart the house?"

"Likely."

"We could search for MacKinnett's." Ice paused, then sighed. "How badly do we need it? Think about it, princess. Maybe we say nothing about MacKinnett's fate or warn the others yet. Would it truly serve Mathias's interest to kill other Council members just now?"

"They stand in his way. Why wouldn't he want them all dead so he could he take over?"

"That's likely his ultimate goal. But if the Council suddenly ceased to exist, Mathias could have an uprising on his hands, with the Doomsday Brethren still standing in his way. He's evil, not daft. The more cunning approach is to start smaller, work his way up to power, *then* take action and fill the Council with like-minded puppets until he rules magickind with his iron fist."

"Impossible. You know if a Council member passes to his nextlife and has no heir to claim his seat, the Council itself selects and elects its own members. I cannot imagine the current body voting Mathias to occupy MacKinnett's vacant seat."

"Unless Mathias has a Councilman in his back pocket."

"What do you mean?"

"Well, Mathias must have a plan. I don't think it likely that he would plot and murder to occupy a Council seat without a member willing to champion him and sway the rest to vote."

Sabelle frowned. "Who would possibly do that?"

"You know better than I. Let's talk about the Councilmen."

"Well, clearly not Bram. Sterling MacTavish is Lucan and

Caden's uncle, and I've known that man my whole life. He would never aid Mathias. He lost friends during Mathias's first terror. He's also elderly and knows he no longer possesses the strength to fight."

"So he continues to deny the bastard is back?" Ice asked, his tone razor sharp.

"Exactly. Clifden O'Shea, Tynan's grandfather, is of the same ilk. Helmsley Camden has no issue, having never mated. Given that he waged a fierce political campaign against Mathias in the past, I'm hard-pressed to believe Camden would assist Mathias now."

"The others?"

Sabelle bit her lip. Now matters got murky. "I scarcely know Kelmscott Spencer and Carlisle Blackbourne. It's likely Bram desired alliances with one of them, through my mating to either of their sons, to solidify his position and hold them in check. Both Rye Spencer and Sebastian Blackbourne will someday assume their fathers' seats. I'm sure Bram wanted to be assured of at least one of their votes."

"Blackbourne's family once supported Mathias," Ice pointed out.

"As did Spencer's. Though both have long since rescinded their positions."

"Yes, but for show?"

That, Sabelle couldn't say for certain.

What a terrible political tangle. Yes, she had been assisting Bram with Council matters, but she was hardly the expert. Her brother knew how to finesse or manipulate them. He'd learned which battles could be won and which were hopeless. Sabelle felt as if she'd dived off a cliff blindfolded and had nothing but intuition and new wings to guide her.

"Perhaps you're right," Sabelle conceded. "If Blackbourne

and Spencer are on his side, perhaps they seek to persuade someone like Camden that it's in his best interest to approve Mathias. And if he refuses . . ."

His head could well be on the chopping block next.

"Still," she went on, "Mathias would have only three votes. The other three would be against him."

"How do they settle a tie?"

"According to Bram, the Council's eldest member decides the issue with a challenge."

"And the eldest member is . . . ?"

"Blackbourne."

"There you go." Ice nodded.

A chill swept across Sabelle. Ice's thinking looked damned possible. And Ice had figured this out. A very intelligent theory from a supposed madman.

"Let's look at the other likely scenario. If Blackbourne and Spencer aren't colluding with evil, maybe Mathias intends to use terror tactics to muscle his way onto the Council by threatening Councilmen's families. We should warn them of that possibility."

Ice paused. "It's not that simple, princess. If we warn Councilmen who are, in fact, Mathias sympathizers, the Anarki will know we're at MacKinnett's manor. They will begin hunting us again. We're slower, traveling by human means. We're easy prey if they find us."

Sabelle didn't want to risk Councilmen's families being hurt or killed because of their silence, but Ice was right. Besides Bram, they had the Doomsday Diary to protect. If it fell into Mathias's hands, it could mean the destruction of magickind.

"We should at least warn Camden that Mathias may have painted a target on his back. If Mathias is going to kill more Council members now, Camden is the most likely, both because he's without an heir and has made no secret of the fact he despises the evil bastard."

Ice nodded. "I agree. Warn Camden alone, perhaps enlist his help. He may be best equipped during Bram's illness to help us understand the politics of the Council and who can be trusted."

"Indeed." Sabelle rose from her seat.

With a frown, Ice grabbed her wrist and stayed her. "It can wait until morning, when you've rested and feel more ready to face what's in that house again."

The idea was tempting, push it all aside until tomorrow. But Mathias and the Anarki were quick and remorseless. She didn't want Helmsley Camden's blood on her hands.

"No, it can't."

Night had fallen and the temperature had dropped when they entered the manor again. Ice viewed the melee with new eyes. The chaos and destruction? All the Anarki's attempt to find the Councilman's transcast mirror. It made sense that Mathias would want to intercept important, secret means of communication between magickind's remaining six leaders.

Behind him, Ice heard Sabelle's hesitant steps, sensed her fear. It took everything inside him not to turn around, comfort her, send her back to the coach house. He didn't want to let her out of his sight . . . just in case. And likely, she would have better luck finding and using the Council's magical mirror since she knew what sort of item she sought. He knew only that it was small and would be disguised, perhaps as a family symbol.

The rooms on the first floor netted nothing except stark reminders of violence that made his blood boil. He hated to think of what these human women had endured at Mathias's hands. It only made him picture his sister's suffering the same fate before her life, too, had ended brutally. And that filled him with an anger so overwhelming, he could scarcely control his violent urge for revenge. That side, the one that had earned him the reputation for being mad, he didn't want to show Sabelle.

Instead, he took a deep breath.

"Upstairs now, or to the cellar?" Sabelle interrupted his musings.

He wanted her nowhere near the bodies. They clearly disturbed her, and for all Sabelle's strength, conviction, and courage, she possessed a compassionate heart. Gorgeous, smart, generous . . . No wonder he'd wanted to mate with her after one taste. He'd been half in love with her since first setting eyes on her.

Ice turned to face her. "We divide and conquer. I'll check the first door upstairs on the left and the cellar. You search the other rooms upstairs."

Sabelle bit her lip, hesitating. "That's hardly fair to you."

"It is. You'll be searching twice the number of rooms."

"But you'll be forced to see all the bodies again."

He shrugged, and she looked so pale and torn. Ice couldn't help himself; he cupped her shoulder and brought her against him. Damn, she was cold and shaking. He wrapped his other arm around her, cursing when the pack containing the diary blocked his caresses up and down her spine.

"I've seen it all before, princess. It's all right."

Slowly, she nodded, then pulled back. "Thank you. I found some candles in the kitchen. I didn't think it wise to turn on lights, just in case Mathias or the Anarki decide to return and check on the house."

Smart woman, he thought with a faint smile. "Excellent."

He took a candle from her. With a flick of his wand, he lit

both. Her hand shook so hard that the flame flickered, the wax dripped.

"Careful, now." He steadied her hand, then urged her toward the stairs. "Up you go."

Sabelle glided silently up the staircase. Despite wearing yesterday's clothes and securing her golden hair in a braid that followed the line of her spine, Ice still thought her the most beautiful woman he'd ever seen.

Stupid sap. He had it so bad for her.

Once on the landing, he disappeared inside the first room, a parlor or sorts, with all the bodies of the human servants. The men he could look at. The abused women and butchered children . . . no. Every glance pained him like a serrated knife slicing his gut.

Turning his back on the corpses, he searched everywhere else. Floor, ceiling, furniture—or what was left of it. Nothing. Damn it. Mathias had already succeeded in killing one of the seven most powerful wizards in all magickind. He didn't want the prick obtaining any device that might bring him closer to the others.

Twenty minutes later, Ice gave up on the room and closed the door. Later tonight, after Sabelle slept, he would remove the bodies, give them a decent burial. It was the least he could do after all they'd suffered for a cause they would never understand. And it would give him something to do besides watch Sabelle as she slept and burn to seduce her. Possess her.

"I'm going down to the cellar," he said as he peeked into one of the upstairs bedrooms, which Sabelle currently searched, one hand on a lush hip, the other clutching her candle.

Was the bedroom MacKinnett's? It was certainly grand enough, all chocolate browns, golds, wine reds. Heavy draperies, rich coverlets. A fireplace on the wall across from the bed, and a long, flat screen above the mantel. Ice had never embraced the idea of human television. Their news was not his, their shows too trivial for his taste, but many in magickind enjoyed keeping up with their less magical cousins. He shrugged.

"I'll meet you in MacKinnett's office when I'm finished."

"Agreed. Shout for me, should you need anything."

She sent him a soft, grateful glance. "You spared me the worst, and I thank you. I'll be fine."

Before he read too much into her gratitude and convinced himself it was the desire and devotion he wanted so badly from her, Ice turned away and headed for the cellar.

Down the winding stairs he went. The acrid char of burned flesh completely smothered the normally damp, dank scent of this sort of room. The odor had grown stronger in the past few hours as the body decomposed. Ice swallowed against his gag reflex and set his candle aside. No windows in the cellar, so he could turn the lights on and be certain no one outside would see.

The room itself was vast with a cement floor that had a slightly damp tinge to it. Dusty wine bottles lined one wall, all neatly lined in racks. Hundreds of them, some no doubt very old and rare. He'd never understood such collections, but then his family had never had the money for luxuries and his father would have scorned them. Sabelle, however, would likely think such a wine collection not only desirable, but a necessity.

Frowning, he turned away. Nowhere to hide the mirror there.

The next wall to his right was both narrow and completely bare. To the right again, the wall behind MacKinnett's body was floor to ceiling shelves filled with family treasures. Jour-

nals, heirloom goblets, a crystal ball. He smirked. No one had
used one of those in easily five hundred years. A few skulls, a
cauldron—all the Dark Ages sort of stuff. But nothing that
looked like a family crest or a magical mirror.

At the far end of the room stood another narrow wall.
Furniture had been stacked against it. A sofa blocked the
whole wall, enormous and dusty. He suspected it had once
been white. A massive dining table rested in front of it, its
pedestal carved from a gnarled, massive tree trunk. The remnants of a few of its chairs were in small pieces around the
room. A table that size had likely seated twenty or more, and
Ice suspected the rest of the chairs had been destroyed and
used as the kindling to burn MacKinnett at the stake.

Damn Mathias!

But Ice did wonder . . . The sofa looked so dusty, it
couldn't have been disturbed like everything else in the
house. Was it possible the Anarki had already found the
mirror before burning the manor's master alive? Is that why
they'd stopped their search? Or had they merely been too
lazy to move such massive pieces of furniture? Or arrogant
enough to assume that one man could not possibly outsmart
them all?

Determined to leave no stone unturned, Ice moved the
table, lifting and grunting until he dragged it a few feet from
the wall. Yes, he could have used his wand, but he was running low on magical energy and needed to conserve. Bound
now to Sabelle only, unless she shared his bed—and soon—
he would have to find some other way to acquire a boost.
Something that didn't involve another woman. Not only
was it impossible to fuck another since speaking the Call
to Sabelle, he didn't want to. Ever. Besides, if Marrok had
taught him one thing since training the Doomsday Brethren in human combat, it was that he liked challenging his

body, forcing his muscles to perform more difficult feats of strength every day.

The sofa was a behemoth and it made him sweat when he lifted it. Dust flew, and he choked, but it took his mind off the dead Councilman in the middle of the room.

With a grunt, he hefted one corner of the massive sofa away from the wall, then shuffled to the other end and lifted it as well. Then he frowned. Behind the sofa, low on the wall, he saw the faint outline of something. A small door? A crawl space?

After moving the sofa farther from the wall, he knelt and ran his finger around the edge of the perfect square of raised stone. A cutout of some variety. Wedging his fingertips around the edges, he pulled. It barely gave, but he pulled again and again until he could grip the heavy stone block with his whole hand. Then, with one last mighty yank, the piece clattered to the floor. Ice grabbed his candle and peeked inside.

A crawl space, definitely. He sat at the edge and shoved his candle in deeper. *Big* crawl space. In fact, a hiding place big enough for an entire family. Ice looked back to MacKinnett and his half-charred form. Had the Councilman been trying to reach this space when the Anarki caught him?

Ice eased in farther. The space opened to winding stairs that led ever deeper underground. He crawled until he reached the stairs, stooping over to avoid battering his head on the low ceiling. As he descended, still clutching the candle, he smelled water and soil. Sure enough, at the bottom, he found a tunnel. He'd be willing to bet his life that the tunnel led to the nearby village.

Smart. Very smart. Next time Bram built a sprawling estate and had half the Doomsday Brethren living with him, he'd tell the prat to create a few of these escape routes. Too bad MacKinnett had been unable to reach his in time.

Turning away from the dark, dank tunnel, he took the winding stairs two at a time, the light of the cellar leading him back. When he crawled out of the space, he wiped his hands on his jeans and sighed. Only one place here left to look for the magical transcasting mirror: the Councilman's body. Dismally, he wondered if there was anything left to find in the burned rubble, then set the candle aside and walked toward the corpse.

Sabelle searched yet another sumptuous bedroom, this one in muted greens and golds, trimmed in silk ribbons and large tassels, all of which had been ripped off and tossed to the floor. It was stately despite its disarray, even more so than the previous bedrooms.

She opened a huge armoire filled with electronic gadgets that Bram would salivate over, were he conscious to appreciate the display. A large fireplace, blackened from frequent use, and bamboo flooring with colorful area rugs strewn about set the mood. A robe littered the floor, just beneath a convenient hook on the back of the door.

MacKinnett had used this room. His smell lingered. His thoughts, even. He'd always been a scholar, and despite the destruction, his essence permeated the walls. The well-loved tomes on magical theory and human science that she suspected had once rested on the nightstand had been slammed to the floor, their spines split by the force. The sight filled her with an anger she could barely understand or contain.

But she couldn't succumb to emotion now. They didn't have time. They had to warn Camden, then she had to convince Ice to leave here. If they hadn't found it, she had a terrible feeling the Anarki would return to search again for the mirror.

Shaking her head, she moved to his fireplace and searched

beneath the mantel, inside the pit, up the chimney walls. Nothing. Wiping away the soot, she crossed the room to the armoire and checked beneath the television, game console, iPod dock, and other assorted treasures. Nothing, either inside the armoire nor out.

This was the last room, and she was running out of options. If Mathias had found MacKinnett's secret transcasting mirror . . . Bram had hinted once or twice that an enemy finding such a device would be bad indeed. She thanked God again that she had seen fit to hide his mirror at Olivia's little art gallery, A Touch of Magic, after the black cloud had swallowed him. She'd feared the house's defenses would be weak, and she'd been right.

With a weary sigh, Sabelle bent and righted the night table, retrieved the books and put them back in place. Then she opened the drawers. Virtually nothing in them. Some reading glasses. A date book from several years past. A few pens.

She shoved them back inside the open drawer. As she did, the top of her hand brushed something odd. Protruding.

Excitement bubbled as she yanked the drawer from the night table and set it on the nearby rug. Then she flattened her palm and slid it across the panel above the open cavity. There! Something raised. Her fingers traced carvings. It was octagonal, like Bram's mirror. This had to be it.

Curling her fingers around the edges, she pulled once, twice . . . finally it came free.

Quickly, she extracted it. And smiled. The MacKinnett family crest seemingly carved in stone. It looked like a paperweight or something one might affix to a mantel for decoration. She knew better, for Bram's looked nearly identical, family crest excepting.

She rubbed her hand across the top three times clockwise, one counterclockwise. Suddenly, it popped open, much like a human female's compact. Sabelle jumped to her feet and opened her mouth to shout for Ice. She closed it. This was Council business. She was acting on her brother's behalf. Camden didn't know her well, but well enough to know she would never lie about MacKinnett's death. Ice . . . given his reputation as an anger-fueled madman, perhaps she'd be better served to talk to Camden alone.

The mirror was fogged, not uncommon when it wasn't in use. Around the edges appeared six other crests and one symbol at the top, which she assumed allowed one to reach all the other Councilmen simultaneously. She avoided that button, and struggled to recall the exact crest belonging to Camden's family. But the memory wouldn't come. What did she recall about the Council? Protocol. Yes, the Council loved that, and it saved her now.

The eldest member of the Council was Blackbourne. Accordingly, his family crest was the first etched into the glass near the top. Spencer's would be just beneath his. O'Shea's and MacTavish's she recognized beneath that. Which led to Camden's. Beneath that, MacKinnett's symbol had gone black. Sabelle hoped, prayed, it displayed thus on all the mirrors. It would certainly lend credence to her message.

The Rion family crest was last, and the symbol had gone a dark gray. He was ill, very ill. She'd shoved aside worries about him since she'd cried at the bed-and-breakfast in Monmouth, but they always lingered, plaguing her mind like a disease. The mirror proved she was right to worry.

Shoving the thought aside, she focused on what must be done.

Touching her finger to Camden's symbol, she waited. Within moments, he appeared, looking ready to shout. When he saw her face, he closed his mouth and sent a puzzled frown instead.

"Lady Sabelle. You have MacKinnett's mirror. His symbol is black. Is he truly dead? Are you all right, girl?"

Thank God, she didn't have to explain a great deal. "Yes, I have his mirror. Yes, he's dead. My brother is unwell." She swallowed. "I know you don't wish to hear this. None of the Council does, but Mathias and the Anarki attacked and killed Thomas. Burned him alive." Her voice cracked. "All his human servants dead—"

His expression closed up, his wiry gray brows knitting. "You're prattling nonsense, girl. Mathias is in exile."

"*Was* in exile. He killed Auropha and George MacKinnett and . . . and now he's finished off Thomas. The entire house is in shambles. The Anarki symbol has been branded into all the women's bodies."

Camden hesitated, the shook his head. "No. How would Mathias possibly have gotten free?"

"I don't know, and right now, I don't care. I hailed you and you alone because I think Mathias may be after you next."

"What? Outrageous! That is impossible."

She held in a grunt of frustration. "It's not only possible, it's likely. Look!"

Holding the glass away from her, she retrieved the candle. Using them together, she slowly scanned the annihilated bedroom, then made her way out the door, down the hall, to the bodies in the first room. She swallowed, hating to show disrespect by using them to prove her point, but she was running out of options.

Once she pointed the mirror toward one of the human female's naked forms, complete with dried blood and the angry brand on her naked, intimate skin, she heard Camden's indrawn breath.

"Dear God," he breathed.

She flipped the mirror around and faced the wizard again.

"He attacked my home as well. Destroyed it, I'm certain. Mathias struck Bram with a terrible spell that I cannot reverse. Please . . ."

"I—I . . . Mathias cannot be back. I am but an old man. How could *I* fight such a monster?"

"Just keep yourself safe. That's all I ask. We believe Mathias killed MacKinnett so that he could put himself on the Council. You are the only other member without an heir."

Camden cursed, but nodded.

Sabelle weighed her next words carefully. Secrecy had been vital to Bram's efforts thus far . . . but MacKinnett's murder and Mathias's plans had changed everything. She only hoped honesty would reassure Camden and underscore the urgency of the situation.

"Before his illness, Bram began quietly gathering a fighting force to destroy Mathias, the Doomsday Brethren. Let them do their work. Help us by hiding well."

He blew out a shaky breath. "Indeed. Can I do anything to help you?"

"Yes. Listen to me: if there are others on the Council whom you know without any shred of doubt would never support Mathias, would you wish to warn them?"

Camden paused for a long moment. "No. The elders above me will never believe this without proof. I would suffer what Bram has endured since he began talking about Mathias's return, I'm sure."

Sabelle feared he'd say that. "Right, then. Keep the information to yourself for now. We'll deal with the rest of the Council later. I have to get Bram healed—somehow—and protect MacKinnett's mirror." There was the matter of keeping the Doomsday Diary safe as well, but no need to stun Camden with more huge news, in case Bram had never told him about the diary's rediscovery.

"Yes. Yes, of course. Check in with me, girl. Keep yourself safe. You're doing a very brave thing. I'm only sorry that . . ."

He'd basically called her brother a liar for the past month? Water under the bridge now. "Thank you. I'm sure Bram will appreciate it once he's up and about again."

"Yes. Well . . . Take care of yourself, then."

Sabelle nodded. "Contact me periodically to let me know you're well."

"Of course."

They ended the contact, and Sabelle backed out of the room piled high with corpses and tragedy, then ran down the stairs. "Ice?" Silence. She jogged down to the cellar and called his name again.

This time, he growled a skin-crawling, blood-chilling scream of pain so rife with torture, it made Sabelle's heart stop.

"Ice!" she screamed as she flung open the cellar door.

CHAPTER SEVEN

HEART POUNDING, SABELLE DARTED to the bottom of the stairs, desperate to reach Ice. She thrust her candle aside. The cellar lights revealed a nightmare: Ice slumped against the concrete wall, straining, twitching—fighting some invisible battle. Sweat popped up across his face and head, despite the cellar's chilly air. He gripped his thighs and screamed.

"Ice!" She rushed over to him, skidding to a stop at his side. "What's happened?"

He opened his mouth, convulsed again and gritted his teeth as he wrapped his arms around his middle, then strained with effort again. A moment later, ice flowed from his fingertips. He dug under his sweater, trying to reach bare skin. Sabelle pushed and shoved at the garment until it raised well up his muscled torso. Her hands came away warm and sticky with his blood.

Gasping in a huge breath, he applied ice-coated hands to his abdomen. The muscles rippled and tensed as the first blast of cold hit his bare skin. He roared out in pain.

Sabelle tried to tamp down panic, but it breathed hard and heavy on her. "Ice?"

"Trap." He took shallow, uneven breaths. "Magical mine."

Oh, dear God. Then its energy was likely still fixed on Ice. She had to get him as far away as possible, to someplace she could help him. Now. Magical mines could be deadly in minutes, and she cursed the fact she hadn't foreseen that Mathias might lay such a trap. But she couldn't act rashly.

"What is the source of the mine?"

Jaw clenched, he fought off pain. Tendons stuck out in the thick column of his neck. Sweat beaded on his forehead, at his temples. "The. Body."

MacKinnett himself? Sabelle dug quickly into the pack and grabbed her wand. Then she hesitated. "I have to move you. It's going to hurt."

He sent her a shaky nod. "Do it."

Biting her lip, she flicked her wrist. Ice raised a few inches from the floor and cursed. Sabelle used her wand to direct him up the stairs, away from the corpse. The farther from the mine they traveled, the better for him.

As fast as she dared, she raised Ice out of the cellar, through the house. Setting him in one of the bedrooms was closer, but all the furniture had been destroyed, every bed in shambles. So she led him through the ruined foyer and the wreckage of the kitchen, then out toward the coach house behind the manor.

The December night bombarded them with cold from all directions. The air smelled of impending snow. Ice shuddered at the icy wind over his body, then slowly, he relaxed.

The magical mine had been all but cooking his insides. He'd needed the outdoor's chill to recover, though she found it unpleasant. Fighting the urge to rub her freezing hands together, she hesitated instead, lingering for Ice's benefit as much as she dared. Seconds ticked by, then minutes. Sabelle watched Ice's breath cloud the air about his face. Finally, he drew his icy fingers away from his belly and legs. He formed fists at his side.

"Inside," he rasped through chattering teeth.

Hers had long since begun to rattle from the cold.

After an absent nod, she used her wand to urge his levitated form closer to the coach house.

"Walk," he demanded with a cracking voice.

He wanted what? "No. You will do nothing until I discern how serious your injury is."

"Princess—"

"That growl may intimidate others. I'm not listening. You can shout later. Now, I'm taking you to safety."

He muttered something, then winced, grabbed his thighs as if warding off fresh pain. Foolish man wanted to walk . . . Stubborn pride. He had loads of it.

Sabelle welcomed anger and the sense of purpose. Right now, those feelings alone stood between her and complete screaming panic. Magical mines had been known to kill. Often.

He still isn't out of danger, a voice in her head whispered.

Fear threatened to overtake her. And a sense of dread. Not that she would be alone in taking the Doomsday Diary to safety. She was crafty and knew enough to blend in with humanity, should she need to, at least until she could reach Duke or one of the other Doomsday Brethren. But the idea of doing without Ice, of never seeing him again . . . Horror clutched at her and squeezed mercilessly.

Sabelle nearly stopped breathing, her chest stuttering. Do without Ice? Someday, she would have to, yes. *Please not today . . .*

Barreling inside the coach house's door, she maneuvered Ice toward the curtained bed, kicking the door shut behind her. Bram's waxen face, smothered by the ominous black cloud, brought her a new level of fear. And hate. Goddamn Mathias for tearing apart her family, her loved ones— Well, she didn't know Ice well enough to love him, of course. But she couldn't deny a certain attachment . . .

Later. She could worry later how to classify Ice's place in her heart. First, she had to make certain he would actually live.

Finally, she reached the bed and gently lowered him to it, shoving the covers out of his way. She tucked her wand back into her pack, then attacked Ice's boots, sweater, and jeans. And gasped.

He wore absolutely nothing under them.

His body was massive. She'd known it logically, but seeing him completely naked . . . She drew in a shaky breath. Hard shoulders and bulging arms were a road map of maleness with a dusting of dark hair and stark, raised veins. More dark hair lightly furred his solid pectorals and covered the ripples of his abdomen. The center of his stomach was bisected with a deep groove of muscle, and more hair grew there. Darker. An odd lure to touch him, follow the path straight down to his . . .

Stop there. Right there. Ice could be dying, and she gawking as if she'd never seen a man.

But she'd never seen a man like this. So overtly masculine, so overwhelming and massive—in every way.

She blinked, turning her gaze away. *Must stop now.*

With trembling fingers, she grabbed the sheet and the army of quilts and covered everything below his pectorals. Blood oozed from a wound to the front of his left shoulder. More from a gash on the right side of his rib cage. The magical mine's entry wounds. And they were open—wide. Whatever the spell, it had made a clean and complete entry. Even now, it could be decimating his insides.

"Can you tell me what's happening to you? So I know how to heal you."

He kicked off the blankets, all of them, exposing every inch of his body. Sabelle tried not to look. Truly tried. But not looking at the man who intrigued and lured her, made her sweat and want and wish for the impossible? She couldn't manage it.

"Hot. Inside. Outside."

"The magical mine still burns you, yes? That's why you were trying to use your freezing ability on yourself?" she asked, throwing her braid over her shoulder.

"Yeah." He choked, then grabbed her hand. "Felt my insides frying. Fought it off. Directed freeze inward. Took most of my energy. Being near you renews me."

She smoothed her free hand across the dark stubble over his scalp, over the top, to the back of his head—and came away with blood.

Gasping, she grabbed his shoulders and lifted him up enough to look at the long line of his spine wrapped in layer after layer of muscle. More blood rolled down his skin.

Dashing to the coach house's bathroom, she dragged down spare towels, turned the sink on full blast and threw two cloths into the basin. The rest she carted to the table beside the bed. Then she retrieved the soaking rags and turned off the water.

Carefully, she laid the first cold, wet cloth across his skin. "Hurt?"

He gritted his teeth. "No."

Liar. But what use was there in fighting about it?

Instead, she quickly wiped every inch of his torso and back with the wet rags, applying pressure and employing a dash of soap until she was satisfied the wounds were clean and no longer bleeding. She used her wand to put a little anti-infection spell on them and did her best to close them. Her magical medical skill had never been good, and now she cursed the fact that her talents lay elsewhere. How dearly she would have loved to call her aunt Millie. She, at least, could have discerned the extent of Ice's internal injuries. As it was,

Sabelle had no clue how to check for such things. She would have to rely on Ice to tell her.

With a final wave of her wand, she sent the towels back to the bathroom and made the sheets fresh once more.

"Better?" she asked.

Gingerly, he nodded. He looked white and exhausted and utterly depleted.

"Internal damage?"

"Healing." He squeezed her hand. "I stopped the burn in time."

A whole sentence. And now, he was breathing easier. His injuries were healing. "You're certain?"

Again, he nodded. More a jerk of his stubbled chin than anything, but enough. "The damage stopped when you dragged me from the cellar. If you hadn't come for me—"

"Of course I would." Did he just assume she would leave him there to die?

"You could have run straight into danger, Sabelle." He swallowed and fought for a breath, squeezed her hand again. "When I'm well, I'm putting you over my knee for that."

Despite the gravity of the situation, her face flamed. "You'll do no such thing."

He rolled his eyes. "Don't take away all my fun."

A joke? He'd nearly died ten minutes ago, and now he was telling a joke. He didn't wish her to know the extent of his injuries, clearly.

"Amusing, indeed."

"Infuriating," he corrected. "No more chances with your safety. On this point, Bram and I agree. You're into magickind's troubles too deeply."

"I'll tell you what I told Bram: I won't sit about like some helpless princess while the rest of magickind fights. It's my cause too."

"Your funeral as well, if you're not careful."

"It could be anyone's," she argued. "Everyone's. That's Mathias's doing. Not mine. Now, stop arguing and tell me how you feel. The internal damage has stopped?"

"Yes. I fought it off in the cellar, then you took me away. Between distance and your touch, I've improved."

"Anything else?"

He hesitated. "My head. When the mine hit me, the force of it thrust me back. My head hit the wall. I heard a loud thump."

Judiciously avoiding looking at the lower half of his very naked body, she gripped his large calloused hand in hers. Closing her eyes, she gathered up her power and summoned the siren in her. To Ice, she sent waves of healing, peace, sleep.

He growled. Suddenly, a wall shot up between them, blocking her well-meaning sentiments. Sabelle gasped. Where had that come from? Ice? Did he have the energy for that? Or was the mine still working its dark magic?

Then the barricade crumbled, and she felt Ice again. But this time, he sent her a blast of something else—desire that was thick, hot, screaming with lust and sex and need.

With a gasp, she pulled back.

A tired smile creased his face, and despite his exhaustion, his arrogance shone through. "Felt that, did you? I told you, I've no need for your happy sunshine and rainbows."

"I sent you peaceful healing," she argued. "You do need it."

"Rubbish. I let you feel what I truly need."

That overwhelming battering ram of desires and yearning? She placed a hand to her chest and forced herself to breathe evenly. Knowing he wanted her that badly staggered her. She blinked, looked at Ice, focusing on those green eyes of his that glowed with unquestionable want. Exhaustion still etched his face, and she knew that sending her any emotion had cost precious energy he didn't have. Why bother?

"No one has ever bombarded me with their emotions like that."

"You tell others what to feel and they abide?"

She frowned. "I try to be helpful and soothe the troubles or worries others have. I'm hardly forcing unwanted feelings upon them."

"I didn't want to sleep, princess."

Sabelle felt her face flush again. "So I gathered."

"Glad we're clear."

"Ice, you hardly have the energy to be wasting on such things. My touch has given you some, I suppose. But the sleep was to help you. I meant no insult. You must concede, your energy is dangerously low. Your magical signature is nearly transparent."

He pressed his lips together and said nothing.

"Is—is that why you sent me the sexual vibrations?" She bit her lip and felt her cheeks flame up again. What was it about Ice that made her feel so feminine? "You need . . . energy?"

He stared, heavy, glowing, jaw clenched. "Sabelle . . ."

"You do." She swallowed, studying his increasingly sheer magical signature. Normally a bold green laced with a fiery red. Black rimmed it, and she'd always worried that was a commentary on his sanity or his soul. But now, she could see straight through it all. And that frightened her. Without recharging, he would be unable to run, flee, help her evade Mathias. Yes, her touch, because he had Called to her, provided a bit of energy. But without a full dose of power, eventually he would die.

She eased off the bed and rose to her feet. With trembling hands, she pulled off her shirt. Instantly, she felt his gaze on the slope of her shoulder, the curve of her neck, the lacy cups of her bra. His icy-hot eyes made her shiver. She locked stares with him, unable to look away.

Sabelle reached for the button of her jeans. Instead, he reached up and clamped his hands around her wrists. "Don't."

"But you need energy."

"Yes, but—"

"You Called to me, so you can touch no other. And . . . I have no anger in me now to try to boost you that way. You want me and—"

"You know it. But I will be damned if I'll let you make me into your next Lucan: a patient, a duty, a burden. What passes between us will never be an act you endure merely to heal me." He squeezed on her wrists. "I would rather die."

"Your pride is misplaced. My opinion is neither here nor there. Your life—"

"Will mean little if I have to swallow the bitter pill of being nothing to you. I hardly expect you to Bind to me, but I won't have your pity."

His passionate speech had used up more energy he could ill afford. The stubborn man! Frustration built inside her, a crescendo that trumpeted into fury. Ice could *die*, and he wanted to debate the meaning of an act intended to save his life? He sought to force her admission that she trembled for his touch before he allowed her into his bed. The energy exchange would be clean, simple, if he would merely accept her help. Did he not understand that crowding it with words and confessions would only make matters more difficult?

She tore her wrists from his grip, stepped away, and stripped off her pants and knickers. Her bra quickly followed. Ice's eyes clamped onto her. His nostrils flared. His entire body tensed, and though she swore she would not look down, her gaze drifted across the harsh rise and fall of his chest, the undulation of his abdomen . . . and fixed on the hard stalk of his cock rising between his well-muscled thighs. A sudden gush of dampness slicked her intimately, where she now ached. She swallowed against the riot of sensations, a need unlike anything she'd ever felt.

If she admitted that to Ice, he would use this desire against her mercilessly.

Sabelle wanted to believe, more than anything, that Ice was motivated strictly by his desire to possess the witch he perceived as his mate. But niggling doubt made her wonder if revenge fueled him more.

"You have my help." Her voice trembled as she sat on the edge of the bed next to him. "You need no more than that."

Ice raised a dark brow. "You have no idea what I need."

Before she could argue, he grabbed her around the waist and threw her under him, until her back hugged the sheets steeped in his warmth and earthy scent. He loomed over her, his shoulders blocking out most of the room's light. She felt surrounded, enveloped. Overwhelmed.

"Did you come for him?"

His big, hot hands gripped her hips, and slid up her torso until his palms cradled her breasts. And his touch burned her. She bit her lip to hold in a gasp, but the aftershocks of their contact reverberated, crashing wave after wave of desire through her body. She softened. Her nipples peaked. She grew wetter.

He stopped. Sniffed. Smiled. "You want me."

"My body is ready." She dared not admit more.

His smile slipped, and he grunted. "Bloody answer me."

Damn it all, she'd forgotten the question. "I've no idea what you're talking about."

"Lucan," he growled. "Did you want him? Did he give you pleasure? Bring you to peak?"

Very direct questions. That shouldn't surprise her. But she couldn't answer him. No answer would satisfy him. In either event, he'd turn this into some sort of chest-beating competition. And the truth would only cause . . . issues.

"It's hardly relevant. You need me, and I am offering. Nothing more or less."

He flicked his thumbs across her nipples. Slowly. Back and forth. Until she gasped.

"I plan to make certain it is much, much more."

With a wave of his hands, Ice closed the drape around the bed, shutting her off from the rest of the world. Then he flattened her to the bed, covering her body with his own. The hardness and heat of him overloaded her senses. His hair-roughened body abraded against her, and her skin became a living, breathing, aching entity. It craved more of his touch and possession. Tingles . . . God, everywhere.

Her will couldn't overcome her need to clasp her arms around him and draw him closer. His lips glided up her neck. His tongue flirted with her lobe until her attention focused solely on his mouth. Then he moved in for the kill, nipping at the sensitive skin with his teeth.

A shiver scraped its way down her spine. No way of hiding that reaction from him. No way to mitigate how he made her feel.

"That's it, princess. Show me the woman you hide."

He knew that? How had he grasped that she hid so much of herself and her desires from everyone?

"Ice, stop." Her breathy voice trembled, and Sabelle knew that her tone told him that the last thing she wanted was for him to stop.

He heard it too.

"Have I hurt you?" he murmured against her lips. His gaze dug right into hers, making her insides jump, pulse.

"N-no."

"Given you reason to believe I'll hurt you?"

"No."

"Have I scared you?" he challenged.

Yes, but not in the way he meant. She knew, deep in her bones, that he would never hurt her. He'd gone out of his way time and again to see to her safety, her comfort. Even if he had Called to her to spite Bram more than claim her, the magical words themselves afforded her his undying protection and loyalty. Sabelle had no doubt that Ice would cut off his own arm before harming her. She only feared how much of herself he would demand in surrender. Would he wrest away a part of herself that she'd never reclaim? And if she admitted that fear, she'd be completely compromised. He'd have her then, in any way, every way, he wanted.

"O-of course not."

He smiled as if he knew she lied. "Good."

Sabelle couldn't find a reason or the words to stay him before Ice curled his hands around her thighs and pulled them apart. His hips sank between them, and his enormous erection pressed against her mound, rubbing right over the one spot guaranteed to send her reeling.

Her fingernails dug into his shoulders, and he threw back his head with a hiss. "Yes."

Mad. Ice was mad, just as his reputation claimed. What else could this insanity be?

"I want more of you," he murmured.

Then he blindsided her, not with a kiss, but a complete possession of her mouth. The force of his lips sank her head deeper into the pillow as he thrust deep. Then deeper still. He entered as if he planned to stay. Forever. And God help her, she opened to him in return. She flirted, her tongue touching his, then retreating, teasing him to chase her. And he did. Repeatedly. Until she lost her breath, her mind, her will to resist.

When he finally lifted his mouth, she drew in a huge gulp of air.

"I want you." He shook his head, his gaze riveted to hers until she felt locked to him. "Need you. Princess . . ."

He dragged his fingers through her hair and cupped the back of her head, then devoured her mouth again, filling her with the tangy taste of him that, no matter how Sabelle had tried, she hadn't quite forgotten. He dragged that flavor against her tongue again and again until she felt addicted to him. Blood pulsed, raced. Her heartbeat roared in her ears. Her female flesh more than damp and achy, but drenched and cramping with demand.

When he lifted his mouth from hers, she whimpered and tried to follow.

"Did you come for Lucan?"

The question shocked her out of her bliss, and she recoiled. "It hardly matters. Forget him."

"I won't," he vowed, gripping her face in his hands, his green gaze scoring its way into her soul. "Until I'm certain you have."

Sabelle dragged in a breath, trying to ready arguments in her scrambling brain. But nothing could have prepared her for the slide of his body down hers, the hot suction of his mouth on her breast.

Lightning shot to the bead of her nipple as he flicked his tongue over it, nipped at it with his teeth, caressed it with his lips. Thunder boomed through her body when he repeated the process with her other breast. She arched to him, an offering, a plea. Growling, Ice wrapped his arm around her waist and brought her closer to his voracious mouth. He consumed the soft skin with firm lips, rasping his stubble gently across the tender sides until she shivered.

"Tell me," he whispered against her belly. "Did he give you pleasure?"

Sabelle frowned, her body aching so badly, she didn't want to think about the past, about reality—about anything more than Ice pushing deep inside her and demanding she take pleasure.

"Stop. Focus on this. Right now." She panted. "The fact we're together. What you make me feel."

Ice slid farther down her body, then anchored his palms on the inside of her thighs and pushed them wide. "That's not enough, princess. I want everything. All of you. I won't rest until I've erased his memory—and every other man's—from your mind."

Had anyone else said that, she would have laughed. In the last sixty years, she'd had her share of lovers and taken few seriously. Yes, she turned down more than she accepted. Far more. But she never wanted for men and had never been shy about embracing her needs.

Ice changed everything.

He'd yet to make love to her, and already she could scarcely remember another man's touch. She trembled as she never had. Shy yes . . . yet she was so bloody eager to join with him. But if she told him any of that, he would overtake her completely. Of that, Sabelle had no doubt. Once he had any chunk of her soul, he would take more the next time he touched her. And more the time after that. Worse, she feared that she'd lack the will to stop him.

She would then gladly Bind to him—and lose her brother.

Hot breath heated her wet flesh, and Sabelle knew Ice hovered above her, watching. She shivered, panting. Everything inside her strained up to him, and not just for the pleasure she knew he would give her. Pleasure, while nice, was fleeting. No, she felt certain that whatever they were about to share would change her life forever. It scared her . . . but she wouldn't—couldn't—stop him.

Somewhere in the room, the clock began to strike. The twelve gongs penetrated her fuzzy brain. Midnight. Deep in the darkness, yet the beginning of a new day.

Then Ice dropped his mouth to her, right on her clit. He dragged his tongue through her wet slit, greedily lapping at her once, twice . . . until she began to lose her mind.

Pleasure tilted her, careening out of control. It gathered, built, grew, stretched, crowded her sanity, then hovered her over the edge of an abyss she'd never experienced before. Her body beat like a drum, pounding with need, and the feel of him tasting her in the most intimate way, staking his claim, annihilating her restraint.

"Ice!"

She clawed at him, but the stubble of hair was too short for her to grasp. Blindly, she groped for his shoulders. Something inside her settled when her fingers dug deep into the hard, bunching flesh there as he took another sweet taste of her flesh and moaned.

Sabelle trembled and burned. Everywhere. The impact he had on her was like a tidal wave, rolling over her, drowning good sense, flooding her landscape until he claimed her completely.

"Sweet princess," he murmured against her flesh, then licked her again, moaning.

Digging her fingers deeper into his shoulders, Sabelle tightened. Close. So bloody close, and now his mouth lingered over her, not quite touching. And she needed. How badly she needed him. Right now.

"Please, Ice. Please . . ." She knew she begged, but couldn't seem to stop.

He sucked her clit into his mouth, flicked it with his tongue. Her breath hitched. Sabelle hadn't thought it possible, but she inched even closer to an explosion so huge, she feared it would blow her soul wide open. But she didn't fight it. Right now, she couldn't. She welcomed the shattering pleasure he dangled right in front of her. "Please."

"Did you come for Lucan?"

God, that question again. Had she answered it earlier, would he have demanded this utter submission to his will, to her pleasure? She didn't know, and it didn't matter. The truth? Concealing it was no longer possible. This moment was too raw to hide behind lies or redirections. From the first, Ice had revealed his emotions to her with such candor, believing he'd be rebuffed. Anything less than truth from her now, while easy and uncomplicated, would be cowardly and wrong. If she couldn't have Ice forever, she could take comfort in the fact she hadn't evaded when he needed the answer she could give. Just as she needed him to know that, in this moment, she cared too much to lie.

Now, she only hoped he didn't hate her for the truth.

"O-once."

His face froze over, and determination fueled an implacable determination in his eyes that made her shiver. "Just once? You'll find I can do better."

CHAPTER EIGHT

ONCE. WHAT THE BLOODY HELL was he to make of that? If Sabelle had never found pleasure with MacTavish, Ice would know she had no lasting feelings for the other wizard. He could use tonight to show her that he would always put her and her pleasure first.

If MacTavish had always brought her pleasure, Ice could surmise that she had deep feelings for Lucan and would have nothing to do with himself. He could have ended tonight with precious memories of her, then tried to repair his heart tomorrow.

But once? *Something* lay between them. But what? Ice doubted that Sabelle would respond to a man in an animal state like Lucan's if she didn't care for him at least a bit. Since the bloke hadn't been in his right mind, he couldn't have focused on her pleasure. In fact, Lucan had done nothing more than use her body, and Sabelle had borne it without complaint. Yet she had come for him. Once. Out of friendship? Or more?

Ice had hardly expected Sabelle to be an inexperienced woman. Having transitioned some sixty years ago, she'd had lovers. Ice didn't like that fact, but he understood. Sex was a necessity to magickind. Life depended on energy. But Sabelle taking Lucan to her bed—and potentially having feelings for the wizard—distressed him. No. It made him want to tear apart the Privileged bastard with his bare hands until MacTavish's blood ran in the streets.

But there were other impediments to Sabelle accepting his Call: class, family, prestige . . . he and the princess would likely never overcome those issues. Still, he wanted more than merely her body. He yearned for something he would never have: her heart.

Unfortunately, Sabelle's answer hadn't told him if Lucan had already captured it. If MacTavish had, it was up to Ice to replace him in Sabelle's affections, show her exactly how precious she was to him. But if she responded to him, came for him, if she utterly surrendered . . . he would at least have hope that she cared.

"Ice?" Sabelle breathed, her golden hair floating around her shoulders and waist. An angel ready for sin. He hadn't believed it possible, but his cock got harder.

He met her gaze. Surrounded by her heart-shaped face and rosy cheeks, her eyes flashed neon blue, like a sign, drawing him nearer. She lay spread out before him on the bed, a naked, writhing, fantasy come to life. The smell of her arousal was driving him mad.

"Please don't st— Oh my God!"

He cut her off by setting his mouth back over her clit and sucking it in. She cried out, keening, her back bowed, legs taut. She clutched the quilt and groaned. So beautiful and sweet.

A thousand things he wanted to do to her. A million ways he wanted to possess her body and touch her heart. But he hesitated. She was like magickind's princess, and other than Lucan with his animal fury, she had probably taken polite lovers. That wasn't Ice. He gave and took hard, demanded everything of a woman without apology. But he could hardly do the same with Sabelle. How would ravishing her from head to toe in an urgent, dominant sweep convince her of his love? He was accustomed to women who wanted anything from a friendly romp to a vigorous fuck. Sabelle was, no doubt, used to being worshipped.

He felt her hard little bud swell and begin to pulse on his tongue . . . and he pulled back. He had to know if she could respond to him while he was buried deep inside her and they lay, gazes locked, heart to heart. That would tell him if he had any chance at all to win her love. It would have to be enough—for now.

"Ice! No. Please." Her body shook. "Don't stop . . ."

He raised up on all fours and kissed her belly. "Shh. I won't. Ever. Until you tell me to."

Then he lowered himself over her, cradling himself between her thighs, grabbing her hips, making his intent clear.

Trailing kisses over the swells of her breasts and her neck, he reached down to toy with the button of her clit again until she drew in a sweet, shuddering breath. *Slow, steady,* he told himself. *Gentle.*

Carefully, he took his cock in hand and aligned their bodies, then paused. "I ask only one thing in return: never hold anything back from me."

She wriggled her hips, driving him completely mad with the feel of her wet flesh caressing his sensitive tip. "I won't. Please . . ."

"Give me everything."

"Yes," she panted as he pushed forward, thrusting deep. *"YES!"*

Bloody hell. With a word, she nearly undid him, to say nothing of the feel of her tight and slick around him. Sabelle Rion, here under him, crying out for him. A fantasy in the flesh, feeling so good that it hurt. His blood boiled in an instant. Need ramped up, made him sweat, made him dizzy. He craved more of her. Now. Sooner than now. Had to feel her screaming and pulsing and accepting him.

Ice drew back, then thrust forward again. To the hilt. "I'll take every part of you."

Body and soul.

He swore that now she had allowed him into her bed, he was never leaving. Ever. Wrapping his arms around her and sinking even deeper only reaffirmed what he knew: she was his.

He pulled back, tried to ease off, but her body clung to him, tightening around him. She looped her arms around his neck and peppered frantic kisses across his shoulder. She was close, and Ice swallowed. Now he'd find out exactly how invested she was in him because he had no doubt that her body was tied to her heart. And his heart was irrevocably tied to hers.

Ice tangled his fingers into her hair, this thumb braced against Sabelle's jaw. Her face and chest were rosy by candlelight, and her eyes were closed in impending bliss. Unacceptable.

"Look at me," He had to make certain she *knew* who was deep inside her, that she could not imagine Lucan or anyone else in his place. Best that she get used to him being right here. Often.

Slowly, her eyes fluttered open, revealing dilated pupils, and she gazed at his face.

His heart jumped. His libido kicked up another notch, and he slammed home in one powerful stroke, nudging the end of her channel. The hitch in her breath spiked triumph through him as much as the increased tightening of her slick walls around him. He wasn't giving up. If he had to sweat and strain all night, he would earn her pleasure and a place in her heart.

"Don't look away," he warned.

Sabelle shook her head, her gaze never wavering. Her acceptance and the exquisite feel of her was killing the remaining bits of his self-control. He had to grab hold of his need and keep it tightly under wraps, couldn't unleash the full extent of his lust on her. Pushing or frightening her would get him nowhere.

The warning chanting in his brain did no good.

Lowering his hands to her hips, he tilted her toward him and drove into her with a strong, rapid rhythm. The impact changed her face immediately. Her mouth fell open, eyes widening. She tensed and gasped again, clutching him tighter.

"You're going to come for me." It wasn't a question because he wasn't giving her an option.

"Y-yes."

Impossible to miss the catch in her voice. It drove him to thrust deeper, clutch her hips and hold her in place so she felt the friction. As he did, he drowned in a sea of darkening blue eyes and thick brown lashes. He didn't dare blink for fear of missing a moment between them.

Suddenly, her legs tightened around him. She began to whimper. It grew loud, then louder. He held the pace steady, sweat beading all over. Seconds later she clamped down on him with a scream that rattled the windows. Fluttering around him, then squeezing, she released.

Satisfaction doused his veins as she pulsed around him, keening out her pleasure. He continued his pace, dragging against the sensitive spot he'd discovered, prolonging her ecstasy.

She no more than caught her breath before he began to pound that same spot again, still holding her gaze. He knew he should ease away, back off until she recovered. But when she experienced ecstasy, he swore he could see so deep into her soul, and she was beautiful to him all over again. Even more than before. Her kindness had always impressed him, for she'd never treated him as anything but a warrior wizard. Her intelligence amazed him. She was a clever girl able to manipulate Council politics as easily as she helped deal with the centuries-old Doomsday Diary. Her sensuality . . . That he had always suspected she kept beneath her surface, but basking in it now, he nearly drowned. She was . . . everything, and he wanted nothing more than to hear her cry out in pleasure for him again.

Closer. Somehow he had to get closer, deeper, take even more of her. Now. He raised her legs over his hips, and they curled around his waist. It still wasn't enough. He put more force behind each stroke, sank deeper still. The bed shook with every thrust. And still it wasn't enough. He pressed his face closer to hers, losing himself even more in the blue heaven of her stare. Still not enough. Would it ever be?

"I could do this to you all night," he murmured. "I want to."

Her eyes flared again, and she didn't speak, but she moaned, lower than the last time she neared orgasm. Longer. Joy raced like fire through his veins as she tightened on him again. A little more, then . . .

"Ice!" Sabelle screamed, her nails digging frantically into his shoulders.

The pain spurred him on, and he pistoned into her like a madman. His pleasure spiraled nearly beyond his control, but he held on to it for the sheer thrill of watching the frantic need on her face transform into the most beautiful bliss. And trust. She *trusted* him to care for her. Nothing was more beautiful.

As her second orgasm ended, gratification and need hit him at once, almost conflicting. Yes, he'd managed to hurtle her into pleasure more than once, and he could only pray that meant he held a deeper place in her heart than Lucan. But twice didn't satisfy him. Not even close.

Don't push her anymore, he told himself. *Slow. Gentle. Pull back. She's not ready for more.*

He told the voice in his head to fuck off.

Rolling over, he laid on his back, then lifted her off his erection, which ached for more of the soft suction of her body. Then he wrapped his arms around her, tattoo bulging with his biceps, and lifted her up his body, settling her wet, swollen sex over his mouth.

Without hesitation, he began to feast, his gut tightening. The taste of her very essence screamed at him, his instincts flaring anew. *My mate. Mine!*

"Ice," she panted. "Wait. I—I can't. Let me catch a breath."

He closed his eyes, trying to get a grip. As he trembled and felt a haze of need shut down his brain, he realized that grasping for self-control was a waste of time . . .

"Need more now," he growled, then devoured her again, sucking the little swollen bud into his mouth and teasing it with his tongue.

She came again, against his lips, with a shout that tapered off into a crackling, hoarse cry. And still he wanted more. Way more.

Maneuvering her down his body with one hand, he lifted his cock with the other and raised up into the tight clench of her body. She closed around him in welcome.

"Yes. Ice. Oh God . . . Yes!"

His favorite word from her.

Sabelle caught his mood and gyrated down onto his aching shaft, her chest against his. Her gaze locked with his once more.

Almost immediately, she cried out again in a raspy roar,

her fingers digging into his arms. Her body held him so tightly, Ice wondered if she'd kill all the blood to his erection, but the strong contractions allowed plenty of time for the rest of the blood in his body to plummet to his cock and make him even harder.

The need to let go and find his own pleasure was strong, but he ground his teeth and tamped it down. As long as Sabelle had any remaining desire, he wanted it directed it at him. Whatever happened tomorrow, he wanted this to be a night she would never forget. God knew he never would.

Swallowing a curse, he lifted her off him, kissing away her protest with a harsh press of his mouth over hers. He swallowed her cry and urged her back to the bed. Without a bit of prompting on his part, she parted those sweet, golden thighs, and the invitation was nearly too strong. But he wanted—needed—to have her in the most submissive way. If she responded with equal passion and trust when he had her beneath him and open, maybe he'd be satisfied.

Even as he called himself twenty kinds of fool, he rolled her to her stomach and lowered himself over her, spreading her legs again with his feet. Then he gripped her hips.

"Ice? What—"

"Feel me," he demanded, then pressed deep, relishing this position where she could feel everything and control nothing.

He latched his mouth on the back of her neck, and she cried out. Satisfaction broiled deep inside him when she arched up, giving him a better angle to sink deep inside her. He took ruthless advantage of it.

One unrelenting stroke after another. Ice reached beneath her, and his fingers found her distended button of nerves and swiped his cream-coated fingers across it.

"Ice. Ice!" She could barely find her breath now. "I can't—"

"You can. I need it."

In the next moment, she clamped down on him again, her explosion of pleasure mere moments away. And still something drove him.

"You feel me?" he growled.

"Yes!" She looped one of her arms over his, linking their fingers together.

Sabelle wanted to be closer to him, and that fact renewed his frenzy. Squeezing her fingers, Ice blocked out his need to release with her. Instead, he read the cues of her body. Just once more. Then surely he would be satisfied with her response.

His fingers swept across her wet flesh, and he hammered her with rapid strokes, thrilling to the feel of her tensing beneath him, her gasps and moans.

"Who is deep inside you?" he demanded.

"*Ice!*"

She bucked and screamed beneath him, and he swore he was even deeper inside her than before.

Bloody hell, it wasn't enough. But his control was fraying, his blood screaming for release. The ache building in his groin was eroding everything but the need to mark her in the most basic way, with his seed.

Withdrawing again, this time to the sounds of her weak protest, Ice rolled her to her back once more and slid between her relaxed thighs. Pushing back inside her swollen sex required patience he didn't have and nearly shoved him over the edge. She wasn't done yet, not without him. One more climb to the pinnacle of pleasure . . .

Again, he linked their gazes and hands. The connection was electric and shuddered down his spine. His steady strokes turned urgent, and Sabelle, his sweet princess, rose up to meet him. Her stare locked with his, and he read the growing pleasure, the rising need, then the dawning of surprise. He clenched his jaw. Yes, the explosion was big. Huge. Monumental.

Sweat broke out across his back, his forehead, as he pushed his way inside her ever-tightening body and acceptance glided across her face, as welcome as a cool breeze on a broiling summer day. Perfect. Then she was chanting his name and falling over the edge. And clinging to him with her hands, her lips, her gaze. Ice fell down into her as the need crashed past the last of his resistance, and he soared into a pleasure so intense, so sublime, it shook him to the core. *She* shook him.

He'd sworn that tonight would change Sabelle and her feelings for him. Instead, being with her had changed him forever. He'd believed he loved her before. Now he knew it was an abiding, enduring devotion. As he'd said when he spoke the Call, there was no other for him but her.

"Princess?"

Sabelle's drowsy, half-open eyes and her tilted smile focused him. "Hmm?"

She sounded drowsy, dreamy, and Ice couldn't hold back a smile as joy whipped inside him.

"You should do that more," she whispered.

"Make love to you? Oh, I plan to."

Biting her lip, she closed her eyes, suddenly shy. Had he ever seen a more beautiful woman? Gorgeous in pleasure, she was stunning in satisfaction. That he had put the look on her face awed him.

"Smile, I meant," she corrected.

He hadn't had much to smile about in two hundred years, since Gailene's death. But now . . . he widened his smile. For her. Yes, happiness was fleeting, and Sabelle would likely never be his mate. But no one could take this moment from him, and he planned to savor it for the rest of his life.

* * *

Early the next morning, Sabelle stretched, eyes closed, feeling peaceful. And energetic. Brimming, actually. She felt well rested for the first time in days. Despite the wind howling outside, and the still darkness before sunrise, a sense of warmth and protection from the December chill settled over her.

She rolled over, encountered a hard body radiating furnace-like temperatures. Her eyes flew open.

Ice.

Oh God. Everything they had done together last night rushed back to her in stunningly clear memories. She'd never forget looking into his eyes as he penetrated deep inside her, sending her hurtling into pleasure. The memory of the tenderness etched onto the hard lines of his face melted her. And the pleasure he had driven her to, over and over.

He'd been relentless, unyielding, demanding. Competing with a wizard who wasn't even in the room. After last night, Ice had more than proven that whatever she'd felt for Lucan whilst she'd cared for the wizard during his mate mourning was less than a pale imitation of the vibrant, white-hot need Ice roused, the attentive way he sought to fulfill her every desire. He'd treated her like a woman, not a china doll. And she'd never experienced such ecstatic bliss.

Slowly, she opened her eyes to the harsh lines of his cheekbones, the black wings of his brows over closed eyes, his strong jaw. Her heart skipped. Actually skipped. Something had changed between them last night. She'd always been interested in Ice. Curious. This . . . was more. Somehow in these past few days, he'd gained a foothold in her heart.

Sex for her had always been easy, fun . . . and fairly meaningless. She'd rarely found more than fleeting pleasure. But she had stored energy, which was all she'd needed in the past.

After Ice, Sabelle didn't think she could ever settle for less than fierce, stunning desire again. He'd given her so much, shown her so many possibilities, looked at her with such adoration.

You could have that forever, a voice whispered to her. Speak the Binding. Become his mate.

And what would Bram say? The Council? The rest of the Privileged? Could she endure the possibility of being shunned? What about the mating of political necessity Bram needed?

She sighed. Bram had mated where he wished. But wondering where the fairness was in that did her no good. As Merlin's granddaughter, celebrated from the time she'd entered magickind, she was heaped with expectations from the moment she'd cast her first spell. No, life wasn't fair. It never would be, and resenting her brother for following his urges and heart only made her feel petty.

Rolling away, Sabelle sat up, glanced over her shoulder at Ice again. He occupied three quarters of the bed, and she recalled his arm twisted about her in slumber, his leg draped over her, hard breathing on her neck. She'd felt cherished. And protected.

Gathering up the courage to Renounce him today would hurt. But she had to do it. Continuing to give Ice hope when she could not be free of her station in life was nothing but unfair to him.

Tears stabbed her eyes, and she shoved the gauzy drape aside and stumbled from the bed, covering her face with her hands and holding in her sobs. She wanted Ice. Wanted him now. Again. God help her, she feared she wanted him for always and no one else would do. A reckless part of her wanted to crawl back into bed with him and Bind to him so it could never be undone.

Duty. Desire. Family. Her heart. All were important, and she didn't know which way to turn.

Sabelle reached for her clothes and thrust them on, so utterly confused, her mind adrift . . .

Until a sudden shrill clanging in her head warned her.

She rushed to the bed to shake Ice awake, but he was already jumping up and shoving on his jeans.

"The Anarki are here," he muttered, grim-faced.

Swallowing, she nodded. "They haven't penetrated our magic yet."

He paused. "Won't be long. I sense great numbers."

As soon as he said the words, a bombardment of mental activity penetrated her. Thoughts. Puzzlement. Anger. Triumph.

"Whoever is out there knows we're inside and potentially cornered. We must escape now."

Ice hesitated. "*You* must escape now. I'll help you. Hide you and Bram. Take the Doomsday Diary—"

Sabelle gripped his hand. "You're coming with me."

He caressed her cheek. "No, princess. They believe they have someone cornered. If they break through our magic and find the premises empty, they will only know we've fled and continue chasing us. If they find me here, they may believe they've won and leave you to escape with Bram and the book."

Horror crossed her face, blanched her veins. "Ice, no . . . You can't. If they find you, they'll torture—"

He placed a soft kiss over her mouth, ending her sentence. "We've no time to argue. Let me get you hidden. I know a place. I found it in the cellar. If I can, I'll teleport away and meet you in the village in an hour."

"Do you promise?"

Something resolute drifted across his face, and it scared

her to death. "If I'm not there in an hour, take a car and go without me. No objection, princess. Magickind is counting on you."

His assurance that he'd teleport away . . . a lie. He was going to let the Anarki take him to better her chances of escaping. And if they caught him . . .

A sob caught in her throat. Ice was sacrificing his life for hers.

"Please don't do this . . ." Tears welled in her eyes. "Please."

"Princess, we must go. If you're to escape, we can't waste time." He brushed past her, and she watched his wide back retreat, then bend as he lifted Bram, still shrouded in the black cloud, over his shoulder. "Grab your pack. Let's go."

This couldn't happen. She couldn't let this deep, passionate wizard give himself over to evil and unspeakable torture to save her.

With all her strength, she latched on to his elbow and swung him around to face her. "As I become a part of you, you become a part of me. I will be honest, good, and—"

Ice covered her mouth with his hand, his body tense, his eyes rife with pain. It killed him to stop her. So why had he?

"You don't mean that—any of it. Speaking sacred words to keep me with you . . . No. For me to allow that would be dishonorable. And I won't have you suffer should something happen to me."

How had she ever believed that he could Call to her with revenge in his heart and mind? She felt like such a fool. She could not give him up now, especially to the Anarki.

"But—"

"We did our best, princess. We tried to escape and we failed. I love you. Know that. If you wish to make my dying thoughts happy, escape for me. Be safe."

He turned away again, let himself out of the coach house, heading through the early dawn mist toward the manor house. He loved her? Fresh tears stung her eyes as she strapped her pack on her back and hurried after him, her stomach in knots. She was numb to the danger and the fear. But doing without him? God, the thought of it even crushed her. How had he come to mean so much to her in a few short days?

As she chased after him, her mind raced. There must be some way, any way, to convince him to escape with her. Or try. Maybe the Anarki didn't know he was here.

But in the next moment, as she ran after him across the iced grass and it crunched beneath her feet in the ghostly fog, she sensed the Anarki's thoughts. *Zain*'s thoughts and voice, calling out for Ice. Somehow, Zain had identified Ice's magic.

She scanned the protections they had placed around the house.

A new horror rolled over her as she jogged to Ice's side. "You covered my magic with yours? They cannot sense any magic except your spell. Why? You put yourself in danger."

Ice cut her a sidelong glance. "I did what was necessary to protect you and ensure Mathias never hurts another woman."

And then he was off again, striding into the manor house. She followed, her thoughts flying . . . but she was out of options.

She raced to him again. This time, she wrapped her arms around his neck and pulled his face inches from hers. Tears spilled down her cheeks. "Please . . . Don't go. I th-think I love you too."

"That thought will be the reason for my last smile. Thank you." With a caress of her cheek, he wiped away her tears with his broad thumb. "Now down to the cellar. They're getting closer."

They were. Sabelle could feel them—a collective evil quickly unraveling the magic they had laced around the estate in their hurry and exhaustion.

"Ice, you can't sacrifice yourself like this."

He plunged into the cellar and flipped on the light, wincing as the magical mine's dark magic zeroed in on him again. "I would do anything to keep you safe, and I pledged long ago to kill Mathias. With any luck, the Anarki will capture me and take me to him. They fear me, and Mathias will want me brought to him alive. That's all the chance I need to fulfill my mission and allow you to escape."

"Why?"

He pushed a huge dusty sofa away from the stone wall, revealing a square stone opening. Kneeling, he drew Bram off his shoulder and eased her brother inside the hole. "Get in."

"Ice . . ."

A crash, a slam, a mass of footsteps on the floor above them. The Anarki flooded into the manor and quickly spread out.

"Now, Sabelle. Time is running out."

"Come with me!" she cried.

With a shake of his stubbled head and a tight jaw, he shoved her inside the hole, then conjured water. Instantly, it flooded the cellar knee-deep.

"What are you doing?"

He shook his head and picked up the stone block to lock her and Bram in. "Use your magic to lift Bram and travel the tunnel to the village. Take a car. Be safe. Do *not* come after me, Sabelle. Promise."

He staggered back. The mine's destructive energy would weaken him quickly. If he had any hope of escaping the

Anarki, he would need all his strength. She had to let the stubborn wizard go.

But it was so damn painful.

"Why are you willing to give your life for the chance to kill Mathias?" She latched on to his wrist, holding back her tears.

"Ask Bram. He'll explain."

Then Ice pressed a hard kiss to her mouth. Before Sabelle could pull him into the space with her, he shoved the stone back into the wall, shutting out her view of his beloved face and most of the light. She heard the scraping of the sofa across the floor and the tug of something else dragging across the stone. A rush of cold water and a blast of cold air later, she understood. He hadn't simply blocked her exit; he'd frozen it.

Finally, lone footsteps faded away. The slam of a door resounded with finality.

Ice had left the cellar and gone to meet his death.

CHAPTER NINE

SHE HATED THIS PLAN. The Doomsday Diary and her brother had to be protected; that went without saying. But Sabelle knew she could fight. She refused to simply let the Anarki take Ice from her.

Taking the wand from her pack, she moved Bram and the diary beneath the tunnel's narrow stairs. It provided little cover, but hopefully enough for the moment. It was a big risk, she understood. But magickind could not afford to do without a warrior any more than it could be without more Councilmen. And she wasn't at all certain her heart could tolerate life without Ice.

Somehow, some way . . . she feared she truly had fallen in love with him.

Digging through the pack, she extracted MacKinnett's transcast mirror. The dead Councilman's blacked out symbol on the glass reminded her of the gravity of the situation. She couldn't hesitate or falter.

Quickly, she pressed the symbol to reach Sterling Mac-Tavish. Another calculated risk. He had never believed Bram's assertions that Mathias had returned from exile and had again gathered the Anarki, but she prayed that one of his nephews had shaken some sense into the elder and he was now willing to send Lucan and Caden her way. It was the only hope she had.

Stomping footsteps overhead reminded her that time was short. Scuffling, running. A shout like a battle cry. Ice!

As Sabelle's ears rang and her heartbeat roared, Sterling's aging face came into view. Gray hair and beard. Same piercing blue eyes his nephews had inherited. Silvery brows lowered when he saw her in MacKinnett's mirror.

"Sabelle Rion?"

"I haven't much time," she whispered. "The Anarki attacked Thomas MacKinnett. He was burned to death in his cellar. All his human servants murdered, the women raped."

Sterling sighed. "Not you, too. First your brother . . . Where is he?"

"With me at Thomas's house. We're hiding, and Bram is unconscious, felled by some spell of Mathias's a few days past. Sterling, you must listen to me. The Anarki *have* returned. Right now, Isdernus Rykard is fighting them alone—"

"Won't be the first time. When Mathias was alive, the nutter attacked their quarters by himself and killed nearly a hundred."

She'd heard rumors about Ice, but nothing concrete. Were they true? Only a madman would raid Mathias's compound alone. *They fear me, and Mathias will want me brought to him alive.* Ice's words haunted her. Yes, they'd bring him in alive . . . so they could kill him slowly, with maximum pain.

Above her, she heard the slamming of doors, more shuffling. She heard grunts of pain, shrieks of terror. Sabelle held in a gasp.

Ice's battle roar rose above the din. He wasn't going down without a fight. But what was one man against so many? If Sterling's story was true, he'd had the element of surprise in his favor before. Now, he had no one but her.

She had to get out of here.

"Sterling, if you don't want to believe Mathias is back, believe that someone has killed Thomas MacKinnett. Look at your mirror."

The old wizard peered at it, then frowned. "His symbol. It's black."

"I've seen his body with my own eyes. All of the bodies. You can add Bram, Ice, and me to the list of the dead unless you send help here now."

"H-help? I'm hardly in fighting shape. Magickind hasn't needed anyone to enforce the rules really since—"

"Mathias, right?"

The old wizard sighed. "Are you certain this isn't much ado about nothing?"

Sabelle gritted her teeth. "Locate Lucan and Caden. Ask them to come here. Right now. You are our only hope. Please . . ."

"You younger ones are so easily excitable and so certain you've seen a ghost." Another sigh. "All right, then. I will find my nephews."

"Thank you."

Closing the lid on the mirror, she tucked it into her pack and sat it beside Bram. With wand in hand, she crept up the stairs and listened. Stomping, shuffling, shouts, some of pain—all abovestairs. The odds were against her, and she might be captured. But she had surprise on her side and she was *not* going to leave Ice to his doom.

Bracing her palms on the stone block in the wall, she pushed with all her might. It didn't budge. Damn and blast! She muttered a curse, then pointed her wand at it, envisioning it wiggling free of the ice and falling to the floor below. The stone trembled in the wall, shuddered, then fell still.

The only reason her spell would fail: Ice had sealed it off, put his magic into that frozen water to make opening the little tunnel again impossible. He'd made certain she couldn't leave the relative safety of her hiding place to help him.

Tears choked her. That big, stupid, noble, idiotic, incredible man. So willing to protect her at the cost of his own life. Didn't he understand that she would and could have fought by his side? Yes. And despite hating her brother, he cared enough for her to ensure her safety, even at the expense of his own.

Somehow, she had to rescue him. She had to escape this tunnel and save him.

Above her, shouts erupted. Something—someone?—banged the walls. Repeatedly. More stampeding across the floor. A door slammed.

"NO!"

Sabelle's blood froze. *Ice!* She'd know his voice anywhere; it was imprinted on her heart.

Whispering a prayer that her brother and the diary would be safe and remain undetected here until either she returned or Lucan and Caden arrived, Sabelle teleported to the back of the house and crept toward the kitchen door.

"Bloody fucking wankers." Ice again. Thank God he was alive.

She peered through the glass in the door, barely peeking above the edge. What she saw jumped her heart into her throat. Blood ran in vivid crimson rivulets down his face. One ribbon dripped right between his eyes, soaking the thirsty sweater across his torso. He held his wand high and backed out of the room.

"Kill me, then. I won't tell you where the diary is."

The half-dozen wizards with their backs to Sabelle laughed.

One sauntered forward, his swagger infuriating her. "I'm certain Mathias will change your mind."

Ice raised his chin, full of challenge and sneer. "He can try."

The wizards nearest the door charged toward Ice. Sabelle's heart jumped in her throat. He was terribly outnumbered. And agitating the other wizards to act. Was he utterly mad?

With a slash of his wand, three of the pursuing wizards stopped. Ceased completely and simply fell down. Sabelle had never been one for bloodshed, but she sincerely hoped they were dead.

Nor would she allow the remaining three to reach him, she vowed as she eased the door open behind them, determined to keep surprise on her side.

Ice's eyes flashed when he spotted her. The swagger slipped, and terror overtook his face. "No!"

From the side door between the kitchen and the formal dining room, Zain popped out and raised his wand with malicious glee. "Thought you could kill another hundred of us again, did you? You only got eighty."

"Because the other twenty ran like cowards."

Zain roared, "Your bloodshed stops now!"

Sabelle cast a spell at the three heading for Ice, hoping he would take out Zain, and they would be free. Instead, he pointed his wand at her with fear and apology in his eyes. And love.

Then she felt her entire body being propelled out the open door again as if someone had grabbed her by the waist and pulled back, tossing her as if she weighed nothing. She landed moments later on the icy lawn, flat on her bum.

Hot anger and fortitude juiced her as she shot to her feet and teleported into the kitchen. The stillness of the room—of the house—assaulted her. She was too late. Instead of using his magic to kill the last few Anarki and free himself, he had spent the time getting her out of the way. Those few moments of distraction had allowed Zain to capture him.

In a tearing panic, she searched the house, every crevice, hoping against the odds. In addition to the servants and MacKinnett's body, she found dead Anarki everywhere. Ice had wreaked havoc. But she couldn't count, didn't cheer. She prowled from room to room, trying to ignore the carnage, praying they'd simply moved the fighting elsewhere.

Five minutes of howling silence and eerie stillness later, she knew the Anarki had taken Ice. To almost certain death.

God, the urge to fall to her knees and cry out her grief nearly overcame her. She took a deep breath. *Be strong.* Magickind needed her. Bram, the Doomsday Diary, Ice . . . none of them could be healed, hidden, or rescued without her now.

So she sniffed back her tears and made her way to the cellar. She had to collect her pack, her brother and the diary, get into the car, find Duke and the others. She'd hoped that Lucan and Caden might arrive in time to help . . . But they hadn't.

Damn, Sterling had likely not contacted them yet. He had no idea the urgency of her request. She shook her head, holding in the towering urge to rail and scream and cry. It would do no good. She was going to have to save Ice alone.

As she brought her brother and the pack upstairs, she heard the front door crash open. The back door followed, and she was suddenly surrounded by Lucan, Caden, Duke, and Tynan.

"Where—" Duke looked around the room. His eyes widened and his mouth snapped shut. "Ice did this?"

Hooded and robed Anarki bodies lay strewn all over the foyer. At least fifty of them, some pinned permanently into the wall, with the collection of swords that used to decorate the room. The undead dripped black blood in oily rivers down their warped faces. Another stack of Anarki had been piled shoulder-high when Ice ripped off the handrail from the wrought iron staircase, then shoved them on the up-thrust rails. The black blood of the undead mixed with the red wizard blood, creating a murky pool that slowly spread across the floor as the bodies continued to drain. The rest of the undead had met untimely ends at the business end of an ax. The wizards looked stricken where they fell.

How on earth had he killed this many this quickly all by himself? It was terrible and horrific, but Sabelle was struck by the amazing skill such a feat must have taken. Marrok would be proud.

"Zain said Ice killed eighty of them."

"I'll be damned," Caden murmured. "The Marines would love him."

Lucan shot his younger brother a cross look, then turned to Sabelle. "And they have him now?"

"Yes. We have to get him back." Her voice trembled, and it took all her strength to hold in her emotions and tears.

Now wasn't the time for the rest of the Doomsday Brethren to ask questions about her attachment to Ice. The clock was ticking, and every second could be the difference between his life and death. She needed to persuade Lucan and Caden that they couldn't do without this fierce warrior. Because the cause needed him. So, she feared, did she.

"We will." Lucan wrapped a gentle arm around her shoulder, and it was all Sabelle could do not to push him and his unwelcome touch away. "They won't kill him, at least not right away. They need the information he has too badly."

Which meant they would torture the big, brave wizard. Her heart wept for Ice.

"I see Bram's condition is unchanged," Duke commented. "The Doomsday Diary?"

"In my pack. What will we do about Ice? We can't leave him at Mathias's mercy!"

Duke and Lucan exchanged a glance. Already, they were wondering what emotions lay between her and Ice, and clearly they disapproved. She didn't care. They should be worried about saving one of their own.

But they likely didn't see Ice as one of their own, being Deprived, and therefore expendable. Sabelle wanted to scream.

"We need a plan." Duke approached her, the self-appointed voice of reason. "Come with us back to my uncle's and—"

"I can't." She explained that one of Mathias's witches had placed a spell on the book that allowed it to be tracked whenever its owner teleported. "I must travel by human means. Car, train, plane . . ."

Astonishment transformed all four warriors' faces.

"That makes our trip vastly more difficult," Duke mused.

Tynan snorted. "You mean fucked up."

"It's a miracle Ice by himself managed to keep you from being captured." Lucan squeezed her shoulder.

Sabelle stormed away, unable to stand his touch. "We need a plan *now*! I've got an auto outside. I'm going to drive—"

"I'm going with you," Lucan said immediately. "You need protection. My uncle has a veritable fortress near Birmingham. We can travel there and devise a plan."

A glance told her that he was low on energy, as well. Sabelle thrust the thought aside. Wondering if he needed her body was more than she could bear now.

"Lucan, you teleport to your uncle's and ready him to have the rest of us invade his home. I hate to impose, but—"

"No. Everything now is difficult. There's safety in numbers." Lucan turned to his brother. "Caden?"

The youngest wizard sent Sabelle a curious stare, then nodded. "I'll go with you."

Tynan raised a hand to lift Bram from the ground. "The car out front?"

"Yes." Sabelle raced for the door, then stopped. One more thing, in case Sterling MacTavish was still reluctant to believe Mathias and the Anarki were back. She extracted MacKinnett's mirror from her pack, flipped it open and chose Sterling's crest again.

"You again?" he grumbled. "I sent my nephews. They've

just returned and told me they found you. I've agreed to open up my home, though this is nonsense, I'm sure and—"

Sabelle turned the mirror to display the carnage Ice left in his wake—all the bloody Anarki robes skewered and hacked up everywhere. The last sounds she heard from Sterling were a gasp and something that sounded suspiciously like retching.

"If you think this is still nonsense, someone should bury you deep in Bedlam." She snapped the mirror shut, then turned to Duke. "Let's go."

Hard, measured footsteps against the chilled concrete alerted Ice that he was no longer alone. With his wand snapped in two at his feet and his hands clamped behind his back, secured with something that prevented him from moving at all, he'd lost all ability to perform the sort of magic that would allow him to escape—or at least turn to face the new threat.

Not that Mathias would let him leave this dungeon alive. The pain of being hoisted off the ground and hung by his bound wrists, his shoulders dislocating from their sockets, was a bitch. But not the worst of what they could or would do. Since Zain had failed at extracting the diary's location, he figured it was only a matter of time before someone more brutal put in an appearance.

Right on schedule, he thought as the footsteps drew closer.

"Mr. Rykard."

Mathias himself. Ice supposed the evil wizard's patience must be running thin, to appear so quickly. The thought made him smile.

"Mr. D'Arc," he shot back.

"I understand you killed eighty-one of my best. Impressive. But it quite puts me out . . . after your friend Caden MacTavish destroyed my means to quickly convert strong humans to Anarki, you understand why I'm so reluctant to lose new recruits."

"A thousand pardons. They tried to capture me, you see, so I defended myself. I felt certain allowing them to take me would lead to my death. Am I wrong?"

"Not at all," Mathias said lightly. "Unless . . . you reconsider your loyalties. It's a disgrace to Deprived everywhere that the head of one of their most established families is openly supporting a Privileged cause. And why? Are you still hoping to curry favor with Bram so he'll give you a modicum of power?"

"No. Mostly hoping to kill murderous, scum-sucking shitholes like you."

"Still angry about Gailene?" Mathias taunted.

Ice ground his teeth so hard he swore they might turn to dust. But he refused to give Mathias the knowledge that his words were a stab in the heart. He remained silent.

"I sense you are. As you said so sincerely, 'a thousand apologies.' My actual purpose for this visit, I'm sure you know, is not ancient history, but the Doomsday Diary. Where is it? Which female has it?"

Ice stared straight ahead at the concrete wall and said nothing.

"You want me to guess? A game. How quaint. Let's see . . . Olivia has experience with the book, and of course, a familial connection, being Morganna's descendant. Her magic, once she transitions, will be very strong. The younger MacTavish's tasty new treat is another possibility. Despite being human, she's both sassy and strong. She's clever enough to hide it. And then there is Bram Rion's very elegant sister, Sabelle. She is quite one of the most beautiful females ever. I would very much enjoy having her bound to my bed."

Biting the inside of his lip so hard he drew blood, Ice forced himself to remain silent. Anything he said in defense of Sabelle now, anything that made Mathias believe that Sabelle had his heart, would only paint a target on her back.

"You've nothing to say?" Mathias prodded.

Ice closed his eyes, resolved that whatever the evil wizard said or did, he would not talk. He would not put his princess in further danger.

"Hmm." Mathias sounded put out. "I understand from Zain that withholding oxygen made you pass out briefly, but did little to loosen your tongue. He advises me that he spent an hour nearly crushing your stones to get you to talk."

Grimacing at the memory, Ice still kept quiet. His bloody stones still throbbed. Ice knew he would never get to repay the favor, but hoped another of the Doomsday Brethren would.

"You have remained very loyal in the face of immense pain. Pity you won't reconsider your future." Mathias paused, as if he hoped Ice would now plead for mercy. Then he sighed. "Unluckily for you, I can be quite good at extracting details from someone's mind, and it isn't very pleasant. My methods are especially effective once the subject has been weakened by pain. I advise that you tell me where the book is and which female is its guardian and spare yourself the difficulty."

"Fuck off."

"Determined to be defiant, I see. Must run in the family. It took a great deal of effort to hold Gailene down so I and the others could take my pleasure until her death."

Ice tried to stop the mental image, but it came at him like a jet barreling down a runway. Gailene . . . so young, so innocent, her tiny form spread wide open for Mathias and his minions' brutal pleasure and her utter pain. The regrets and recriminations Ice had lashed himself for the past two hundred years haunted him anew. Why hadn't he seen, guessed, what would happen?

Still, he said nothing, refusing to give Mathias a new way to torture him.

Mathias crept closer. Ice knew from the brush of air at his back and the stench of evil. He tensed, bracing himself, certain the wizard had more torture in store.

Instead, Mathias whispered in his ear, "You *will* tell me how to get my hands on the Doomsday Diary. I have more ways to ply you with pain than you have stamina to resist. And I have patience. If you insist on being difficult, you should know I'll very much enjoy breaking you."

Ice didn't doubt that Mathias could find limitless ways to cause him pain. But no matter what, Ice would never put Sabelle in this madman's path. His own life was all but over. Sabelle . . . Magickind needed her, and Ice needed to know she lived on well and happily.

"Fuck off."

"Let's see how brave you are in, say, a half hour. I've found the most interesting human, with the most deliciously twisted mind. I tested this one on MacKinnett before I burned him. Such gratifying screaming. I'm hoping you'll prove equally entertaining."

With a snap of his fingers, the heavy metal door swung open on creaky hinges. More footsteps. Heavy ones. Whoever had just entered was bulky. And he dragged something light but solid on the ground. He'd find out what it was soon enough, but had no doubt it would prove excruciating. Humans relied on torture since they had no magical means to coerce cooperation.

"This one?" A rough male voice asked.

"Indeed. Spare no mercy," the evil wizard went on. "He's particularly troublesome."

The newcomer said nothing, but simply laughed, the sound like gravel rattling in a metal cage.

In the next moment, Ice heard a *whoosh*, followed by the snap of a whip. Then a line of fire broke out across his back. Agony. In seconds, blood seeped from the wound and dripped down his back. He barely had time to assimilate the impact of the first blow before the second came, then the third. Sweat broke out all over his body, despite the freezing room. He bit the inside of his cheek to hold a scream in. But, oh God, he could feel the whip ripping through skin, tearing into muscle, seeking bone.

One breath at a time. Ice focused on drawing air in, out. He turned his thoughts to Sabelle, desperate to focus on anything but the next lash, which wrapped around his waist, its coil snapping just below his navel and drawing fresh blood. Or the blow after, which opened up the sensitive flesh at the back of his neck.

Beauty. Kindness. Bravery. Intelligence. Goodness. Sabelle. He'd held her a short time, but the knowledge that he wouldn't be suffering this torture if Mathias knew who had the book gratified him. In his mind, Ice sidled up to her, wrapped an arm around her, buried his face in her neck . . .

Then he felt Mathias's hands on his shoulder and the bastard working inside his head, probing his thoughts. In the blink of an eye, Ice erased them completely.

"What were you thinking of, warrior?" Mathias demanded. "Who?"

Fuck off. Ice sent the thought to Mathias, a pained grin spreading his dry lips.

With a mental roar, Mathias shoved his way inside Ice's head, just as the lash of the whip landed on his shoulder and around his biceps, tearing his flesh open. He dripped blood over every inch of his back, which soaked into the waistband of his trousers. Without Sabelle to focus on, fresh pain rushed in, and the flaying from the whip rushed to the front of his consciousness. He missed the mental escape that thoughts of her brought, but refused to risk her.

His knees collapsed under him, but he forced himself to stagger to his feet. The whip bit him again, this time across his hip, tearing his pants, his skin. Still, he refused to cry out or give in.

Mathias squeezed his shoulder and pushed deeper into his thoughts, and Ice focused inward again, almost grateful for something to tend to. He shoved at the evil wizard, barring him from every memory he could, judiciously protecting the events of the last few days. That joy was his, and his alone.

Undeterred, Mathias attacked his mind like a demon, serrating his defenses with claws and teeth and determination. Diverting his energy to his mental defense, Ice let his legs crumble, let himself cry out. Pride meant nothing if it kept Sabelle safe. Instead, he locked down his thoughts, trembling with the effort to bar Mathias, using the powerful energy his night of passion had generated.

The snap of the whip landed again at the small of his back, slicing through skin and tendon, straight toward bone. He cried out, rolled to avoid the pain.

He lifted his head. Blood. Lots of blood oozed out of his pores, ran down his face—the cost of his effort to resist Mathias's mental invasion. But at least with Mathias's touch absent, the fucker couldn't get back into his head.

Ice stumbled to his feet, lurched to the side. Dizziness assailed him. His energy flagged. Still, he put everything he had into protecting his thoughts as he crumbled to the ground and found blessed peace. Here was a good place to die. Now was a good time to do it.

Then the whip snapped across his skin again, over his biceps and ribs, ending right between his shoulders. Blood warmed the concrete around him. He regretted he had not avenged Gailene. He could only hope she forgave him if he saw her in his nextlife. But he could not be sad that, even with his dying breath, he'd protected the angel he held dear now.

It was his final thought before he slipped into a black chasm of peace.

Sabelle, Duke, and Tynan arrived at Sterling MacTavish's estate via auto just over an hour after leaving Ludlow. From the moment they walked in the door, bedlam ensued.

"Is this possible?" Lucan demanded of his uncle Sterling. Caden sat by his side, Sydney in his lap, looking both rapt and confused.

Sterling MacTavish, nine hundred if he was a day, was a lean post of a man with gray hair and whiskers, well-groomed and well-dressed. Sabelle was used to seeing the haughty, learned man in a position of power. Now he simply looked scared.

"It's not *im*possible," Sterling frowned. "And what are we to do? With Thomas dead, Bram unconscious, Helmsley Camden deep in hiding . . . I don't trust Blackbourne. I've never been more than acquaintances with O'Shea or Spencer."

"You must call upon someone," Lucan insisted. "We know how serious this threat is."

"What threat?" Duke asked from the door, beating Sabelle to the question on the tip of her tongue.

Sterling looked across the room and rose, trembling, to his full height. "Mathias sent a missive, declaring that he will run for MacKinnett's empty Council seat. Blackbourne has backed him."

Foreboding rushed like a flood through her system.

"Thomas had no heirs," Sterling went on, "and Mathias's

grounds are that he's kin, albeit distantly, to the Chillingham line, who sat on the Council six centuries ago."

"Unless he's willing to admit that he and the Anarki murdered Thomas MacKinnett, how does he supposedly know about the man's death?" Sabelle challenged. "I told Caden so he could protect himself, but I doubt he told anyone. So how will Mathias explain that to the Council and magickind?"

Sydney winced. "I transcasted the news nearly an hour past to all of magickind, as soon as you contacted Uncle Sterling. We thought it wise to inform the public quickly of the murder of one of their leaders."

Of course. Mathias wasn't stupid. At least it sounded like Sterling was finally a believer.

"And," the former reporter continued, "I contacted my old boss Holly at *Out of This Realm*. She's unhappy, but willing to sit on the story. Only magickind knows the truth."

Sabelle reassured Sydney, "You did the right thing."

"Mathias declared he'd been nominated for the Council a quarter hour later." Sterling sighed, looking defeated. "Blackbourne then sent a message, championing Mathias."

"According to Mathias, his intent is to bring 'balance' to the Council," Caden spat.

"That's important, I grant you." Sabelle sighed, frustration rising like lava inside her. "But in order to fight Mathias, we must have Ice back. We need a plan now."

"Agreed." Duke nodded, looking grave.

Tynan hissed a harsh curse. "You must nominate someone to run against him. Lucan is a good choice."

"You know the Council frowns upon having two members of the same family sit on the Council. Supposed to prevent a family from taking over magickind *and* ruining a family's line of succession."

"In extreme situations, it has been done," Tynan countered. "The bigger impediment now would be that Lucan has no heir and no mate upon whom to get one. The Council won't like that, especially now."

Lucan closed his eyes. Sabelle avoided his thoughts, so she wasn't certain what he hid, but pain and humiliation likely ranked at the top of the list.

"Perhaps you can nominate Duke," Sydney suggested.

"Unlikely," Duke drawled. "I'm too human for most of magickind. I may be wealthy and well-connected by human standards, but my magic comes from my grandmother, whose family was neither well-known nor well connected. I don't know if I'd pass the Council's scrutiny."

Sabelle sighed in frustration. They had more pressing matters to attend first. "First, we must rescue Ice!"

"You're right," Duke said. "We should—"

"Isdernus is merely a Rykard. Not important. The Council, however, is. We must think of magickind's stability, not a Deprived who's more than half out of his mind. Use your common sense, girl," Sterling rebuked Sabelle.

Sabelle wasn't naive. She knew that most of magickind held that view of Ice. But she refused to stand still. "Where is your compassion? Ice saved my life at the risk of his own."

"Then he finally did some good." Sterling dismissed her. "Now, if no one in Duke's grandmother's family ever sat on the Council, he won't pass scrutiny. Mathias still has his sympathizers out there, and people like Blackbourne wield a great deal of clout. He will try to convince some to vote Mathias's way."

"And coupled with Mathias's likely threats to kill loved ones and wipe out entire families if he does not win his way, I would not be surprised if some of the Council approves him," Tynan pointed out. He knew Council politics well, because his grandfather sat elbow to elbow with Bram.

"We need a strong claim to the seat." Sterling rested his chin on his fist in thought.

"Later, Sterling. We bloody need to rescue Ice now. Mathias captured him. He'll torture and kill him, and the man sacrificed himself to keep me safe. I won't leave him to die. Mathias's bid for the Council can wait a few hours."

Silence descended on the room for an instant, then Duke nodded. "Right, then. Ice first. The vote can't be conducted until we locate the others and see if any come forward with a candidate. If only Bram were well, he could nominate—"

"Focus on Ice!" she demanded.

"Of course." Duke wiped at tired eyes, then slanted a glance at Lucan again.

Sabelle knew they suspected she had deeper feelings for Ice than she should for a mere Doomsday Brethren warrior and she didn't care.

"Someone best fetch Marrok," Caden suggested.

"Where is he?" Tynan searched the cozy, fire-lit room with a frown.

"Putting the new volunteers through their paces, find out if they're manly enough for the cause and all that," Olivia put in. "I'll bring him in."

"New volunteers?"

Sydney shrugged. "Tynan brought Raiden and Ronan here."

The Wolvesey twins? As unruly as they'd always been, they were the least of her worries. Sabelle winced.

"I see that look," Lucan said. "They're hardly the same boys who pulled on your hair when you were in nappies."

Olivia opened the door, and Marrok, along with the two green-eyed wizards, entered behind him. Everyone was here.

"Doomsday Brethren," Duke called. "Gather round. We need a plan."

CHAPTER TEN

ANOTHER FIFTEEN MINUTES SLID by, and still the warriors had no strategy. Sterling insisted that Ice, being Deprived, was expendable and constantly changed the subject from plotting the warrior's rescue to thwarting Mathias's scheme to sit on the Council. Caden finally redirected his uncle to locate an obscure bit of Council law, for which Sabelle could have kissed him.

But among the Doomsday Brethren, tempers ran short. The warriors argued about how to rescue Ice. No one knew where he was being held. The only possible source of information was Shock—and no one trusted him.

Hearing the *tick-tock* of the clock, Sabelle dashed upstairs with an excuse that she needed to check her brother and store the Doomsday Diary in a safer place. She sent Olivia and Sydney meaningful glances, then disappeared into the first available bedroom in Sterling's sprawling estate.

Moments later, the other two ladies entered behind her.

"I'm going to get him back," she said as they entered.

Olivia and Sydney exchanged a glance. Yes, they both suspected that she and Ice had formed more than a friendship while on the run. Wisely, neither said a word.

Sabelle unzipped her pack and opened the book, then shot Olivia and Sydney direct stares. "How do I use this?"

"The Doomsday Diary?" Olivia asked. "Are you sure that's a good idea?"

"Do you have a better one? We'd be mad to assume that

those warriors downstairs could infiltrate Mathias's compound, wherever it might be, guarded by all those Anarki, and have no injuries or casualties. Why risk them if the Doomsday Diary can help? I didn't know for certain how to use it and had no time when Ice was first taken. But now they've left me no choice. Help me."

They hesitated, then Sydney nodded. Olivia did the same.

"I always started with a 'Dear Magical Diary,' as that's what I believed the book to be. Of course, I believed it merely granted sexual fantasies. Anyway . . ." She flushed, her pale skin turning rosy. "All you must do is write down your wish."

Olivia searched the room for a pen, then handed it to Sabelle. "We now know that for your wish to come true, you must have a powerful desire to have it granted. The bigger the wish, the more you must want it. Saving Ice must be your heart's deepest desire."

Not at problem, at all. Fear gnawed at Sabelle's belly, and she ached without him. Every moment that slid by when she didn't know if he lived was pure torture. She wanted him beside her where she could wrap her arms around him, so they might have a chance to untangle the future together.

"Perfect." Sabelle touched the pen to the page, preparing her thoughts.

"It takes time," Sydney warned. "The diary, I mean. It doesn't work like the snap of a finger."

Quickly, Sabelle wrote out a few sentences in which she begged for Ice's safe return. Then she snapped the book shut. If the magic was traceable, they'd deal with it.

"I won't leave Ice's fate to the whims of a book. I'm going to visit Shock."

Olivia gasped.

"Are you out of your bloody mind?" Sydney rounded on her. "He's most likely sided with Mathias, and may view your presence as an opportunity to abduct you to make his master happy."

Possible. They knew little about the wizard except that he claimed to be working for the Doomsday Brethren, appeared when it suited him, then disappeared again just as quickly. Secretive in the extreme, Shock was ever a mystery. And at this point, she saw few options.

"The Doomsday Diary originated from Morganna le Fay's capricious magic. None of us know a great deal about the book's workings. I can't rely on it alone. So I'm going to seek out Shock. I'm aware he's neither safe nor predictable, but he didn't hurt you when he could have," she pointed out to Sydney. "Besides, it's possible he'll be away and Anka will know something useful."

Then again, Shock could be there and abduct her on sight. But she couldn't wait around for the men downstairs to come to a decision that would risk their lives. She'd rather go alone and if she was hurt or killed . . . Well, she wasn't as vital to the cause as Ice.

"Let us go with you," Sydney urged.

"No! Mathias would love to stop the anti-Anarki voice of the transcasts, and Olivia has an enormous target on her head, being Morganna le Fay's great-granddaughter. Besides, I need her to take the diary under her wing." Sabelle handed the book to Olivia. "I don't have to tell you to guard it with your life. And Sydney, I need you to talk fast so the wizards downstairs aren't aware of my absence."

"Certainly. But if you're not back in two hours, we're coming after you," Sydney warned.

In two hours, she'd either be successful or dead.

* * *

Sabelle teleported to Shock's house. On a seedy London street close to Canary Wharf, it was one of many nondescript brick buildings that had withstood wind, water, and war for centuries. Renovations in the form of a new coat of paint or a window washing had done little to disguise the place's less-than-distinguished feel.

Briefly closing her eyes, Sabelle sent out her personal ring, asking Shock for admittance. She hoped, in fact, that he was elsewhere and she could talk to Anka alone.

Luck wasn't on her side. A moment later, Shock pulled the door open wearing sunglasses, a glower, leather trousers— and nothing else. The power of his half-bare body roared out at her through the portal. Towering height, bulging shoulders, cabled biceps, ridged abdomen, well-muscled thighs. Imposing, definitely. But he intentionally projected that message.

"To what do I owe this displeasure? Has your brother sent you in his place with some inane message? Does he imagine that I won't hurt the messenger if she's pretty?"

If necessary, Sabelle figured she could play games, mince words and not reveal her purpose right off. Shock alone likely knew where Ice was being held. If she played this right and if he chose to help her, she could save Ice soon.

Big if, especially since Shock kept her on his doorstep, shivering in the December chill. Snow had fallen in London, and the damp wind cut through her clothes.

"No. When we freed Sydney from Mathias a few days past, he hit my brother with a spell none of us has ever seen or knows how to counter. It's slowly been killing him. I've merely been able to make him comfortable and hope his absent mate appears. But that's not—"

"What sort of spell?" he demanded.

"I hardly know. Something that's wrapped him in a dark

cloud and nearly smothered him. But as trying as that may be, I'm here to discuss Ice."

Shock stood stock-still. Something crossed his face, and Sabelle knew that he was aware of Ice's captivity.

"What about him?"

"You and I know he will not make it through the night if you don't help me reach him. Can I come in?"

Again, Shock hesitated, then glanced above her head, to the left and right, as if searching for spies.

"Three minutes," he finally barked, then stepped aside.

Sabelle entered the surprisingly warm little place. Shock's decor or lack thereof didn't interest her, but every wall was white, every stick of furniture black. Scratched hardwood floors with threadbare rugs ran in a mismatched scattering all over the place.

"You want to discuss Ice or compare living spaces?"

With a guilty grimace, she shook her head. "Sorry. Have you seen him?"

He shrugged, indicating that he really didn't care whether she'd stared or apologized. "I suspected Bram or Duke would come to plead Rykard's case to me. I never expected you."

"Bram cannot, and Duke is busy with Mathias's nomination to the Council after MacKinnett's murder."

"Are you surprised that Mathias has no use for the Councilmen and seeks to replace them? Look, little girl. Mathias has no use for any of the Council, your brother especially. And if he tried to kill Bram with that black cloud and your brother is still alive, that's a testament to Bram's strength of will. Something is keeping him alive. What is it?"

Sabelle shrugged. Revenge, his mate, pure stubbornness?

"Do the rest of the Doomsday Brethren know you're here?"

She hesitated. The truth might make her vulnerable, but

Sabelle suspected that Shock would quickly ferret out a lie . . . and he wouldn't take it well. "No."

"Duke should have come. Perhaps Marrok. You have no business dabbling in what you scarcely understand."

She was far beyond the point of dabbling, damn him. "I understand perfectly that this is very dangerous. None of them could come. They don't trust you."

"And you do?"

"Not entirely, no. My only consolation is that I don't believe you have any reason to personally dislike me or want Mathias to dispense his personal brand of rape on me."

Shock paced the floor. When he retreated, Sabelle saw a tattoo sprawled across his back, an abstract Celtic knot/lightning bolt design that swept from shoulder to shoulder. Nothing but black ink, bronze skin, and the incredible pain he must have endured.

Then the wizard turned again. "I saw Ice. Mopped up the blood after his first . . . conversation with Mathias. I took him a bit of food. His signature has changed since I saw him last."

Sabelle closed her eyes, knowing where this line of questioning was headed, but she played along. "Yes, he Called to me."

"You didn't Bind to him." It wasn't a question; Shock could see that in her magical signature.

"I want to speak to my brother first."

Shock raised a black brow. "You certain either of them will live for that conversation?"

"No." Her hands trembled as she clasped them in front of her.

"You have any interest in Binding to Rykard?"

This might stun Shock down to his big, hairy toes, but . . . "Yes."

Suddenly, he started laughing. "Won't that fuck with your brother's mood?"

Yes, and she was losing patience with his odd mind games. Shock was always unpredictable, but tonight had her tied up in knots. Not for anything would she tell him so. "Will you help me or not?"

"What do you expect me to do? And why do you think I would do it when none of the Doomsday Brethren trust me?"

"You answered my brother's summons when he first formed the group. You threw your lot in with them and have assisted the cause . . . in your way. I like to think you give the appearance of helping both sides so you can eventually deal Mathias his death blow."

Shock shrugged, the inky gloss of his straight black hair brushing his shoulders. "Do you now? Anyone ever called you idealistic?"

"Probably, but it's better than being a dodgy prick."

Shock laughed again. "Part of my charm."

Personally, she was certain the man had none, but since he had the ability to read minds, as she did, she buried that thought very deep.

"If you don't wish to assist me openly, tell me the location of Mathias's compound. I'll go there myself and find some way to free Ice."

The tight smile disappeared beneath an ominous scowl in seconds. "Don't be stupid. You know the fate you'll suffer. And if you're not convinced it's a terrible one, I'll wake Anka so she can talk to you about the joys of *Terriforz*."

Sabelle shuddered at the reminder of Mathias's mentally controlled rape. Anka wasn't the same witch she'd been before Mathias's abduction and abuse. The strong, sparkling female who adored her mate had been replaced by an angry, skittish witch who had left Lucan in favor of the wizard before her. Anka hadn't finished dealing with her experience, and Sabelle could only hope that her friend's cohabitation with a wizard of Shock's low caliber was somehow helpful and temporary.

"Low caliber? Tsk-tsk," Shock mocked.

Damn it, she had to remember to bury her thoughts.

"That would help," he added. "But the truth is, I'm not certain I can help you. I refuse to send you to Mathias. Alone, he would kill you like a pesky fly—quickly and mercilessly. And in case you're securing the information of Mathias's whereabouts for the rest of the warriors . . . well, I don't think he would appreciate me giving away the location of his new lair."

"Help me. Please." She wasn't above begging, and if it would help Ice, she would plead all night long.

"A Rion begging *me*. There's a sight no one would believe."

"What do you want from me?" she asked, wishing she could stare into his eyes and read his thoughts. But as always, those blasted sunglasses ensured she saw nothing. "Tell me what you wish for, and I will find some way to grant it if you will help Ice."

"You have nothing I want. Not now . . ." He cocked his head. "The time may come, however. Or maybe not. Your three minutes are up. Go."

Oh God. Shock was going to throw her out, and she was no closer to securing his agreement to help. "Will you help me?"

Shock shrugged. "I see no reason for you to go near Mathias's compound. Or for you to return here. So don't."

With a mental shove, Shock forced her out the door and back into the nearly frozen December air. On the surface, it seemed that Shock would not lift a finger to help her . . . but with Shock, one never knew. Would he assist Ice—or was she on her own?

Sabelle returned to Sterling's estate, dejected. She really had believed that Shock was doing his part to assist the Doomsday Brethren, even if he didn't come when called or like to admit that he was one of the good guys. He'd even explained his frequent absences to Bram a few weeks earlier as keeping up appearances for Mathias's sake. But it seemed that, as soon as the warriors had shown Shock open doubt about his loyalties, his attitude had become less clandestine double agent and more "fuck off."

Trying to block out the fact that Ice would likely die soon, she pushed open the door to the room she'd tucked Bram into shortly after arriving, the one beside hers. Olivia sat next to him, perched on the edge of the bed. Sydney sat in a nearby wing chair, a phone pressed to her ear.

"Thank God you're back. What happened?" Olivia asked, her dark hair hugging her shoulders, violet eyes bright with concern.

Nothing she wanted to discuss. She simply shook her head and mumbled, "Dead end. How is my brother?"

Sabelle could see for herself that Bram was unchanged, and the truth pierced her heart. Bram was slowly dying. If anything, his skin looked more gray today than yesterday, and she wondered what, if anything, would cure him. She performed a few quick spells to keep his body hydrated and functioning. But there was nothing more she could do.

With a glance at Sydney on the phone, Sabelle turned back to Olivia. "Has she been able to locate the mysterious Emma yet?"

As soon as she finished speaking, Sydney rang off and put the phone down with a clatter of finality. "I spoke with Aquarius. Emma is, apparently, an old school chum of Aquarius's. You'll recall she received the Doomsday Diary from Emma just before giving it to me. After uni, Emma moved to Manchester. They lost touch. Emma turned up one night very nervous. Afraid. She shoved what she called a magical diary into Aquarius's hands and said she should hide it. She seemed to think it had something to do with the series of articles I'd been writing for *Out of This Realm*. But Emma refused to say more."

"Lovely history lesson," Sabelle grated. "How do I find the woman now? Bram might recover if we could locate Emma."

"Aquarius has been looking since the first time I called. But it's as if Emma has disappeared. She used to work for a human who dealt in rare antiquities. But her attempts to reach him have been unsuccessful. She peeked into the store's windows and saw only clutter and chaos. I wonder if Mathias found him whilst looking for the book?"

Yes, that was possible. Even probable, since Mathias had been following the little magical book closely. Could Emma be inside the shop? Possible, but if she was dead, Bram's signature would reflect his loss, and so far, hints of Emma's personality shone in earthy greens and browns inside the bold slashes of Bram's magical signature.

The woman was alive somewhere, and Sabelle had to find her.

"I'm assuming Aquarius has tried to call Emma directly?"

"Oh, a hundred times. Number's been disconnected."

Of course.

Reality hit Sabelle square in the chest like a battering ram, and she caved into the pressure for a few precious moments. Bram's unstoppable journey to an untimely death, Ice's imminent peril, magickind's danger—all because of

Mathias. She hated that wizard for what he'd done to her family, her friends, her society. If, by some miracle, she managed to save everyone who mattered to her, she would hunt him down with every bit of her determination and do her best to slaughter the bastard.

"It's all right." Olivia hooked an arm around her shoulder, and Sabelle realized only then that she'd begun crying.

She brushed her tears away with impatient fingers. "No time for this now. I have to keep searching, hoping, trying . . ."

"You need sleep. It's nearly midnight."

There was no possible way she would sleep, knowing that Ice was enduring hell—if he was still alive.

"I'm fine. I need coffee and to talk to Duke. Are they still belowstairs?"

Olivia looked like she wanted to argue, but nodded. "I'll stay here with your brother. He was a good friend to me when I first moved to London. I miss his smart-ass remarks."

Though Sabelle had often cursed them, she did as well. "Find me if there's any change."

"I'll keep trying to reach Emma. Someone, somewhere, knows where this woman is."

Yes. She just hoped that someone wasn't Mathias.

As soon as Sabelle loped down the stairs, she found a group of angry warriors waiting for her. Damn, apparently Sydney hadn't talked fast enough to keep her out of trouble.

Duke and Marrok had the look of concerned fathers. Caden and Tynan both looked at her as if she'd lost her mind. And perhaps she had. Raiden and Ronan Wolvesey, whom she had not seen in seventy-five years, smirked, clearly not at all surprised to see that she was in trouble. And Lucan . . . she winced. Pure rage, and not that of a parent, brother, or friend. He was taking a more personal interest in this evening's event.

"We overheard Olivia and Sydney talking. You visited Shock?" Lucan exploded. "Without telling any of us and letting us accompany you?"

"Without allowing us the opportunity to talk some sense into you?" Duke raised a dark brow that suggested a bit of common sense would be in order.

"This is precisely why. I'm neither a child, nor stupid, and being female does not make me helpless. I had a gut instinct that Shock would not hurt me, and I was correct. Unfortunately, he was also no help, so—"

"Shock may not have been, but I am."

Sabelle whirled to the sound of the witch's voice. There Anka stood beside a dark-colored figure. Sabelle cast a guarded glance at Lucan, who remained on the far side of the room, arms over his chest, gaze firmly on the wall behind Sabelle's head.

Giving her former mate a wide berth, Anka approached Sabelle. "Shock told me of your visit, of Bram's condition. I insisted he find someone to help Bram."

Could anyone actually help her brother? "If Shock knew anything about the spell that's felled Bram, he didn't say so."

Anka lifted a dainty shoulder, her blond curls sliding across her back. "That's Shock's way. He doesn't say even half of what he knows. Sometimes, I can get him to talk."

Sabelle bet she knew exactly how the lovely witch enticed Shock. A glance across the room at Lucan showed that her former mate had reached the same conclusion and was angry enough to spit glass.

"He told me about a healer. A dark one. She may be the only one who can help Bram." Anka gestured to the figure beside her.

A dark healer? Sabelle hesitated. She wanted her

brother well, absolutely. But someone who dabbled in the dark arts . . . dangerous indeed.

On the other hand, what awaited Bram if she failed to act except certain death?

"Bring her up to see him."

"Sabelle!" Lucan snapped.

She flipped her gaze in Lucan's direction. "He's *my* brother, and whatever has passed between us gives you no right to gainsay me when it comes to my own flesh and blood."

Lucan rushed across the room and grabbed her by the arm. She stumbled down a stair, right into his chest. "I should take you over my knee."

"Try it and lose a hand."

Refusing to hear more on the subject, she wrenched away from him and marched upstairs. Anka motioned to a little black-hooded woman who followed moments later. Sabelle cast a glance over her shoulder to see Lucan and Anka exchange a pained glance.

At the top of the stairs, she showed the women into the spacious blue-hued bedroom Bram occupied. Anka hovered in the doorway. The black-hooded witch darted immediately to the bed. Sabelle wished she could see something of the woman under the hood, but the lighting and her disguise ensured she saw nothing of the witch's face. There was something so familiar about the witch's magical signature, but she was too exhausted to place it.

The woman's dash across the room gave Sabelle the impression of youth and urgency. But then she sat slowly on the bed at Bram's side, which made her seem very old indeed. Long moments passed before the witch took Bram's hand in her own.

Sabelle would be lying if she said she wasn't both curious and skeptical. She knew many of magickind's dark healers—or knew of them. She had no idea which of these dabblers in the dark arts had come and was currently latched on to her brother.

"What is your name?" she asked. "I'd like the honor of knowing the kind soul who is helping my brother."

The witch stiffened, and Sabelle had the distinct impression that she fought the urge to face her. Instead, she murmured, "My name is not important."

As answers went, that wasn't helpful. "Have you ever seen a spell such as this?"

She shook her head. "But I know what must be done. Leave us."

Leave her defenseless brother alone with a dark healer sent by Shock, whose loyalties were questionable at best? "Impossible."

"Shock said this witch will know exactly how to heal Bram, but we must let her do her job without protest or interference."

I'm certain he did. "And how do we know Shock has Bram's best interests at heart?"

"I vowed to him that if something ill happened to Bram, I would take it out of his hide."

Sabelle wanted to take Anka aside and ask if her friend was well and happy living under Shock's roof, in Shock's bed. The difference between being Lucan's mate and Shock's lover must be extreme. Lucan had always treasured Anka, put her first, provided well for her, encouraged her. Shock . . . Well, Sabelle didn't see him being the warm, fuzzy type.

Anka read the question in her eyes and turned away. Sabelle sighed. Just as well. Tonight was about Bram. Pray God this worked.

"If I do nothing, Bram will die, so I've no other choice but to leave him here with you." She teared up, hating to show her weakness to another. "Please help him. He's . . ." Her father, her brother, her best friend all rolled into one. "He's important."

The small hooded figure nodded. "Return at dawn. I'll do all I can by then."

Then Anka left the room. Nerves flaying her insides, Sabelle followed suit to wait.

Dawn neared, Sabelle sensed. It was, perhaps, an hour or two away. She couldn't sleep. She strained to hear any sounds in the bedroom beside hers where the mysterious witch had locked herself in with Bram. She'd heard a cry, the woman chanting Bram's name, her brother moaning. Nothing more in the last hour.

And still she couldn't sleep.

Ice weighed heavily on her mind. She'd written in the book nearly twenty-four hours ago—and nothing had happened yet. Certainly saving Ice was her heart's desire. Granted, Sydney said that the fulfillment of her wish would take time . . . but she sensed it was time Ice didn't have.

Sabelle bit her lip to hold in her cry. Yes, an entire night without sleep after a day fraught with danger was not helping her keep her composure or her emotions in check, but the thought of losing Ice had the power to destroy her. How could she possibly do without him when she had just realized how very dear he was to her?

Punching her limp pillow, she rolled to her side—and encountered something massive and hard. No, someone. A person very cold and still.

With a gasp, she sat up and whirled around, pressing a hand to her chest. And she stared through the dark, hardly able to see more than the outline of a man. A man in her bed. A large man, unmoving except his ragged breathing. And she smelled blood.

Heart drumming as she searched the shadows, Sabelle quickly flicked her wrist. Soft golden lights flooded the room, and she shrieked as her gaze returned to the man beside her.

Ice!

CHAPTER ELEVEN

"YOU'RE HERE! YOU'RE SAFE!" Sabelle flung herself at Ice, and he groaned.

At the pained sound, Sabelle pulled back and studied him. The joy tripping through her heart quickly gave way to horror. Both his eyes were swollen shut, his cheekbones and jaw bruised blue-black. He lay shirtless on his stomach, and the sight of his back had her recoiling. Someone had whipped him viciously. Repeatedly. The flesh was in shreds, still oozing blood and swelling angrily. Fresh blood wreathed his head, as dried rivulets looked frozen on his face.

Sabelle had no doubt that, had Ice remained with Mathias even another few hours, he would have died.

She backed away and took his hand. "Can you hear me?"

He struggled to draw in a rasping breath. His chest rattled with the effort. "Princess."

Tears stung her eyes. "You're safe now. I'll care for you."

Vaulting off the bed, she ran to the en suite bathroom and grabbed washcloths and towels. She wet one, then carried the lot back to the bed. The limp set of his shoulders and slightly slack mouth told her he had fallen asleep. Likely better for what she had to do.

Swallowing hard, fearing she would hurt him, she first mopped the blood from his head, face, and neck. He barely moved until she encountered an open gash at his nape. She rinsed the washcloth in the sink, then returned to tend the shreds of his back.

Gently, she patted the wet cloth over his destroyed flesh. God, the pain he must have endured. To protect her. How cruel Mathias must have been, and yet she knew Ice would never tell Mathias who had the diary or where to find her.

How had she ever thought this man less than worthy? How had anyone ever thought him mad? Her brother had shown him nothing but contempt and disdain, and yet Ice had opened his heart and used his body to protect her.

He humbled her.

Once she'd cleaned Ice as best she could, she removed his pants. They were filthy and torn—and she saw fresh lashes under the ragged garment. He oozed blood from his hip, his thigh, and Sabelle tended him here, as well, wishing she could curl up against him and somehow heal him, make his pain end.

Instead, she withdrew her wand from her pack. She wasn't magickind's best healer, but she'd healed Bram through more than a few scrapes. Ice's road to wellness might take a bit longer and a bit more energy, but she vowed with everything in her soul that he would be well.

With a wave of her wand, she focused on stopping the blood, mending the skin, closing the wounds. She would provide vitality and energy as soon as he awoke.

After discarding the soiled towels, she rested beside him, cuddling as close as she dared. She grabbed his hand and closed her eyes, thanking God that he was here beside her and would live. Had it been a miracle? The Doomsday Diary's magic? She didn't know, and at the moment, she didn't care.

He was with her.

"Where am I?" he muttered sleepily.

"Sterling MacTavish's estate. We've stopped here temporarily."

"The others?"

When he'd come so near death, he worried about the other warriors and their mates? Ice humbled her all over again. "Fine. Everyone is unscathed."

"You escaped MacKinnett's." He smiled. "Good girl."

She would have never done it without him. "Don't ever sacrifice yourself for me like that again."

He pried open swollen lids that were already recovering, thanks to her touch and her magic. "I would do it a thousand times over to keep you safe."

Sabelle's heart bumped and rattled in her chest. Ice had already proven his worth, yet he kept ensnaring her heart with his protection and caring. Binding to him and becoming his mate would be the greatest privilege.

But would following that impulse lose her the only family she'd ever known? That question was for another moment.

She pressed a soft kiss to his forehead. "I missed you."

Ice lifted that oh-so-green gaze of his and caressed her face. "Are you well?"

"Better now that you're here." She smiled, then faced reality again. "How did you escape?"

"I don't recall. One minute I was on the ground hearing Mathias's footsteps walk away, certain I was about to pass into my nextlife. The next, I opened my eyes to Shock's boots beside me."

Sabelle gasped. Had the wizard actually helped? "And?"

Ice frowned, clearly trying to piece it together. "He came with food and unshackled me. I spit it at him."

With a grimace, Sabelle felt certain that, even if Shock had come to help Ice, after that stunt, Shock would have been only too happy to show Ice to his doom.

"We traded insults. Oddly enough, he didn't hit me, just yelled. I did all I could to prolong the argument. His fury was giving me energy, and I'd used it all up fighting off Mathias's mental invasion."

"He was determined to know where the diary was and which female carried it?" Sabelle asked, but she already knew the answer.

Ice nodded. "Shock stomped out in a huff, either blind or stupid. He left me uncuffed and the door unlocked. I remember wandering into the hall, searching for the stairs, since I was dizzy and bleeding, believing myself too weak to teleport. Yet here I am."

Yes, and whether Shock had aided his escape or the Doomsday Diary had snatched him from evil and delivered him to safety, she didn't care. Ice was back with her, safe now.

"Nothing pleases me more." She took his hand in hers.

He squeezed her hand. "Sabelle, I know I have no right to ask this of you, but I need . . ."

Need what? She scanned him from head to toe. The black eyes and beaten jaw were faintly marred with yellowish bruises now. The wounds on his back were closing up, scabbing over, the blood and the pus and the ragged flesh no more. The wound on his hip and thigh was all but healed.

Then Ice rolled to his side and revealed his need in the turgid length of his erection.

She jerked her stare back up to his face and melted. He needed to touch her, know in the most tangible way possible that she was safe, to reconnect with life. He needed to share himself with her, bond with her as much as she would allow. He needed to know, at least in this shadowed, predawn moment, she was his.

Sabelle needed that too.

Caressing his cheek, she fought back emotion as she pressed her mouth to his. He waited, his body trembling with the effort to hold back. But for her, he did, remaining nearly still while she swept into his mouth with a slow kiss of worship that left her panting when she lifted her head.

"I worried about you. So much," she whispered.

With a gentle nudge, he rolled her to her back, then half covered her body with his own, his massive shoulders blocking out the rest of the room. He was hot now, an inferno blast that flowed inside her, bringing golden light to the places inside her that had grown dark in his absence.

He covered her lips with his own, soft but urgent, lingering but demanding. With his kiss alone, he reached deep inside her and found her heart, her need, and he embraced them. She sighed against him, desire and more rising. She could no more keep her hands from roaming his face, neck, and shoulders than she could resist taking her next breath.

"That's it, princess. Touch me," he invited.

She didn't need to be told twice. With reverent fingers, she skimmed his back gently, gratified to feel his wounds nearly healed. Her palm glided down his arms, her thumb brushed over his mouth. He repaid her with a kiss that started like gossamer and ended like a hammer. Soft, then, deeper, harder, burning, until she couldn't breathe, couldn't think—and didn't want to.

Ice, as he did most things, dominated the kiss. The rhythm, cadence, and fury of it. The pleasure drowned Sabelle, setting her adrift. Thoughts? Gone. The outside world? Not important. Only now. This man, this moment, this promise of devotion. She opened to him and gave all.

With greedy strokes of his mouth, he took again and again, as if he couldn't get enough. And that suited her; she couldn't either.

When they'd first made love at MacKinnett's, Ice's touch had been a blend of possession, insistence, and mastery. He'd pushed her far and hard, well beyond any former lover. She'd gloried in his ability to please her without a word, and Sabelle yearned to please him as much in return.

Now, reverence, joy, fascination tinged his embrace, as though the beautiful man had cheated death and wanted to share his soul with her.

Slowly, he lifted his lips from hers, his gaze fastened on her face. "You're beautiful, princess. Not because you're part siren. Because you care."

"You're beautiful as well."

"If it's because I care, too, then I must be bloody gorgeous." He smiled, then it faded to something solemn. "I haven't cared about anything, anyone, in nearly two hundred years."

The grief that crossed his face was an endless dark chasm, and Sabelle ached for him. "Why?"

He shook his head. "Now isn't the time. At the moment, I need to love you."

Sabelle hesitated, then nodded. Unless she spoke the Binding to him, she had no right to demand the truth. His expression told her that he meant to make this moment special, not cloud it with the past.

"I'm here for you, Isdernus."

Without a word, he removed her nightgown and laid her out over the white sheets, spreading kisses all over her body. He laved the side of her breast, palmed her hip, nipped at her navel, stroked her thighs.

Mere touches, and her body burned. Ice had that effect on her. From the moment they first met, when Bram refused to allow them to shake hands, Ice called to her in a way no wizard had.

But for the first time, she was nervous. She didn't want to lie on her back and wait passively for him to touch her.

Their first time together, he'd given her no opportunity to explore his muscled, heavily veined body. No time to learn textures, experiment with his taste, discover ways to please him. She yearned to . . . but would he welcome a more intimate touch?

"How is your back?" she whispered.

He lifted his mouth from the flat plane of her stomach. "Better. Every moment I'm with you heals me more."

Perfect. She anchored her hands on his shoulders and gave him a gentle shove. A question loomed on his face, but he followed her lead and rolled to his back. She raised herself over him and whispered, "Let me."

Ice stilled for a moment, then spread his arms wide, his body still. A mischievous smile lifted the corners of his mouth. "Anything you want, princess."

Just what she wanted to hear. Catching his gaze, snared by the desire burning in his eyes, she placed a kiss below his collarbones, on the swell of his pectorals. She brushed his small male nipple with her thumb, and he hissed. The little bud turned hard. Gently, she scraped her fingernail over the other. It, too, stood erect.

At the smallest touch, he responded. The reality was so heady she tested her reaction to him again, this time smoothing her fingers down the ridges of his abdominal muscles. They bunched, tightened, rippled. She sighed. Amazing. Every part of him so gorgeous, his body so attuned to her—she'd never known her smallest touch to make such an impact.

Her gaze drifted down to the hard stalk of flesh rising in an angry jut from between heavy thighs. Ice followed her stare.

"Sabelle . . ." His voice was a warning: don't toy with him unless she meant it. He wouldn't be responsible for the consequences.

It was a warning she couldn't heed, not when she needed to touch him, take him in her hand, feel the power, stoke his desire.

She lowered her palm just above his knee. His body jolted. When she caressed her way up his thigh, he closed his eyes and groaned. "Yes. God, yes."

Closer she crept to his erection and the heavy sacs beneath. Would he feel smooth and hot and strong? Sabelle ran her fingertips up his hip, swirled around his navel, and slowly began to follow the line of hair back down, working up the courage to answer her question.

"Please, princess . . ."

Big, bad, not-quite-sane Isdernus begging her? She smiled and granted his wish.

When her hand closed around him, they both gasped. His shoulders came off the bed, and his eyes flared like an inferno—hot and unstoppable. Incredible. Tingles skipped down her arm. Gripping him was like holding power in her hand. Her hand didn't quite wrap around all his girth, so she wrapped her other around him as well.

An earthy curse slipped from his lips. "I dreamed of this. God, so often. The minute I met you, I could only think of having you with me, naked, touching me, letting me touch you . . ."

She rubbed her thumb over the damp head of his cock. He sucked in a breath. Reducing Ice to nothing but gasps and moans filled her with both power and peace. She was where she belonged. No other wizard had ever felt so right. But still, she wanted more.

Throwing her hair over one shoulder, she bent to him. Ice tensed, and when her tongue laved his erection then took him deeper in her mouth, he dissolved into sheet-fisting groans. He tasted harsh and hot and so exquisitely salty and male.

She savored him, the slow learning of his body and pleasures. In the past, sex had been anything from a mere energy exchange to a fun, flirty way to pass time. But being with Ice . . . a treasure, a moment of worship, a quickly burgeoning addiction.

"Yes," he murmured, then raised a hand to her hair. Fingers filtering through the strands, anchoring against her scalp, he arched his hips, sinking his stiff flesh deeper into her mouth.

Amazingly, he grew harder, longer, his motions more insistent and urgent. Sabelle reveled in the fact that she could bring such a fierce warrior and wizard so much bliss.

Moments passed that lapsed into long minutes. His fever rose, and he grasped her hair in both hands, guiding her to deeper, faster strokes. Then suddenly he stilled and gritted his teeth.

"No more." Gently, he lifted her head away from him, then raised her face to his. "Thank you for the incredible pleasure, princess, but I want to share the sensations with you, feel you all around me. I need that now."

Before she could reply, he rolled her beneath him, lodged himself in the cradle of her thighs, and plunged deep. She was wet, of course. Simply being in the same room with Ice excited her, and her body was all too eager to receive every hard inch. But he surged into her fast and deep, and she gasped as his cock scraped every one of her nerve endings as he buried himself to the hilt.

"You drive me to madness." He gripped her hips, then gasped when he sank in deeper. "Give me your pleasure."

It was impossible to merge his body with hers and not feel as if she was drowning in ecstasy. He unleashed a firestorm of furious need, thrusting in slow, deep strokes that quickly had her gasping and tightening around him. Ice's lips brushed across hers, then he melded their mouths together.

The double assault on her defenses overwhelmed her in moments. Ice surrounded her, and she didn't just feel his kiss or his passion, but his very soul as he poured it into her with measured, relentless strokes that quickly pushed her over the edge, into a realm where sensation ruled and he was king. With a cry, her heart followed.

Still, Ice wasn't satisfied. The release of her power into him invigorated and energized him. He picked up the pace, shuttling into her with increasing demand. By rights, after a release as powerful as the one she'd just experienced, she should be somewhere between sated and numb, but Ice would not be denied.

He palmed her breast, his thumb brushing the sensitive peak as he continued to delve her mouth and body with a determination that stunned her. Shockingly, the heat and pressure between her legs built again, this time darker and more demanding than before. Up, up, up her need clawed. Sabelle feared Ice must still carry the wounds of his mistreatment at Mathias's hands, but she couldn't stop herself from digging her fingers into his shoulders, wrapping her legs around his waist and meeting him stroke for stroke until she dissolved into a million pieces.

Moments later, Ice remade her as he ground out a harsh male cry and emptied every bit of himself—breath, heart, seed—deep into her.

In the moment, she wondered if life as his mate would be like this. If so, she wanted it badly.

The Binding words hovered on the tip of her tongue as they each recovered their breathing. She wanted to speak them—so much. But Bram . . .

Ice raised up on his elbows and peered down into her face with eyes so green and tender, her heart melted all over again. "Princess, something ails your mind already?"

She forced a smile. How simple it would be to tell him that she intended to become his mate. But Sabelle didn't deceive herself. Getting her brother's blessing would take more than a few moments and require her best logic. And she wanted Bram's approval. Giving up her family and all she'd known for a wizard she'd never spoken to until a few days past, a man clearly haunted by secrets . . . it hardly made sense. She wished she had a wizard's mating instinct. They had the luxury of taking a single taste and knowing the right female for them. Witches had nothing but their hearts. Still, something tugged at her, telling her that, without Ice, she'd live a half-life.

"I don't know what to do," she confessed. "About this. About us."

Ice sucked in a deep breath. "Sabelle, you know what I want. My wishes have not changed. But if you will not Bind to me, please say so."

"I can't make myself Renounce you. I've tried, for my brother's sake." Tears broke her voice and regret welled deep inside her, a burn in her chest she wished she could ignore. "But my heart . . ."

"Wants more than a loveless political marriage." He cupped her face. "You deserve more, princess. Become my mate. Everything else, we will work out together."

Sabelle hesitated. Ice made the matter sound so simple when she knew it was anything but. "I cannot do that to my brother. I owe him my well-being and happiness, my respect and allegiance. He removed me from the clutches of a selfish mother. When I was but six, she was already seeking to sell my future to the highest bidder, promising the most powerful wizard that I would mate with them or their sons upon my transition."

He blanched, turned white. His face closed up. "You were a child! Bram rescued you?"

"Yes. Before he came for me, I had never met or heard of him. I knew what my mother plotted, and it terrified me. Wizards who were five hundred or more, many of whom had acquired their power by nefarious means, all openly vying for the chance to mate with Merlin's granddaughter. They knew nothing of me, the real me inside. Just my bloodline."

Ice swallowed, looked away. "You owe him a great debt, yes, but the rest of your life?"

"Today, my brother may be well." Sabelle glanced out the window to see pale edges of gray creeping into the lace-draped window. A fist-tight tension gripped her stomach. Soon, she'd know if the dark healer had healed Bram. "Then I'm hoping to speak to him."

With a sigh, Ice rolled away. "It will do no good."

Sabelle frowned, reminded again that she knew nothing about the enmity between her brother and Ice. "Why? Why do you hate each other so much?"

Rising from the bed, Ice padded to the bathroom. She heard water splashing, something that sounded suspiciously like a fist pounding the wall, before Ice reappeared, a white towel wrapped around his waist.

Suddenly, Sabelle felt naked, exposed. She grabbed the bedsheet and covered herself.

"He will never let you mate with a Deprived, especially me. I've been foolish to hope, but—"

"How do you know? If I tell him that you make me happy, certainly he'll listen. I've never seen my brother treat anyone differently because of their birth."

"Then you have not seen the true Bram."

Her brother, prejudiced against the Deprived?

With that ugly accusation, Ice returned to the bathroom, this time closing the door. She scowled and bounded from the bed, dashed across the room, determined to unravel this issue. But when she lifted the latch to the door, she found it locked. Yes, she could have entered with a bit of magic, but Ice had silently spoken. She would not invade his privacy for her own satisfaction. Besides, dawn was upon them, and she needed to tend to her brother—and hope the night and Shock's mysterious dark healer had revived Bram for good.

By the time Sabelle dressed and brought some semblance of order to her hair, Ice stepped from the bathroom, freshly showered. He prowled around the room and grabbed his shredded camo trousers from the floor with a curse.

Wizards were notoriously poor with domestic magic; cooking, mending, and cleaning spells were often beyond them. Looked like Ice was no exception, given the regretful way he eyed the garment. Despite the tension between them, she hated the frustration on his face.

Quickly retrieving her wand, Sabelle waved it in the direction of his trousers. In moments, they looked completely new, tears mended, bloodstains gone.

His gaze bounced up to her, gratitude shining there. "Thank you. You're quite good at that."

She shrugged and shoved her feet into trainers. "Loads of practice. I need to see if Bram is awake. Ice . . . No matter what happens, whether you escaped after Shock's visit to your cell or because of the Doomsday Diary's magic, I'm glad you're here and safe."

Before she said anything more, she turned away. Ice put a soft hand on her shoulder, the touch a question, a request. It was nearly her undoing. After this morning, she'd hoped . . . But she wondered if fate, culture, and family would always stand between them.

"You wrote in the Doomsday Diary for my safe return?"

She nodded, knowing the next question he would ask and

that she could only give him the truth. "It was my heart's deepest desire. I wanted you here with me. I still do."

Ice closed his eyes, shook his head. "So fucking futile."

"Why? Why are you so certain my brother will refuse?"

Ice sighed. "There's no point in dredging up the past when it will not change the future. I'd rather say nothing. I don't want you to think ill of the brother who clearly did so much for you. The fact he extended me no such courtesy is of no concern to you."

With that, Ice shouldered his way past her, shirtless, his back nearly healed. He looked back and reached out for her hand. Sabelle tucked her palm inside his, and he squeezed. "Go see your brother. I'll be beside you, in case you need me."

Releasing her hand, he left the room. Sabelle followed, dread and uncertainty brewing in her gut. Her brother's health, her relationship with Ice, the threat to magickind—all of it so consuming and hammering her at once. Still, she must bear it. Endure. A Rion could do no less. She had the spine; time to use it.

She hurried down the hall, turning toward the closed door to Bram's quarters, then pushed the door open. Ice followed.

Inside, Bram lay still, eyes closed. The black cloud was gone.

Duke sat in the wing chair in the corner. Lucan perched on the edge of the bed near Bram. Both looked up when she and Ice entered.

Lucan peered at her, then at Ice. His blue eyes narrowed, and Sabelle knew that one glance at Ice's magical signature, coupled with the fact they both must be glowing with energy, all but shouted the truth.

"You fucking bastard, you *dare* to touch her?" Lucan leapt to his feet.

Ice met him in the middle of the room. "At least I wasn't a dangerous madman, mourning another witch while I did. *I* would never hurt or use her."

Sabelle tried to wedge between them, certain that if she didn't they would start trading blows or hexes.

"Is this how you plan to get revenge against Bram, crush him by taking his only sister?" Lucan accused. "Tit for tat?"

She gasped. Ice had a sister, and Bram had somehow taken her?

"I think that is a very good question."

"Bram!"

Relief lifted a thousand pounds off her psyche when she found her brother sitting up in bed, his glare squarely on Ice. She ran to Bram, throwing her arms around the sibling who had always represented safety and comfort. He held her by the shoulders and stared over her shoulder at Ice with a malevolence that stunned her. He looked ready to kill.

"Answer Lucan," Bram demanded of Ice. "This, I want to hear."

Ice cast her a pained glance, then turned back to Lucan with a growl. "I Called to Sabelle because my instinct told me she is mine, not because I sought any sort of revenge. *I* treasure her, while you merely saw her as a source of energy. Take your righteous anger and shove it up your arse."

"I would rather shove something down your throat, like my fist." Veins popped out in Lucan's neck, and he looked ready to attack at any moment.

"You're welcome to try." Ice raised a black brow, not backing down an inch.

"Stop it! All of you! This is not the time to worry about my romantic life. We have more pressing concerns."

Her brother wouldn't let it go. "I told you never to shake her hand. To know that you fu—"

"Bram, stop! I'm a grown witch, and magickind needs your guidance far more than I."

"That remains to be seen." Her brother arched a brow. "Where the bloody hell am I?"

"Sterling MacTavish's estate. Mathias and the Anarki attacked our home. The defenses were down with you unconscious. We had no opportunity to build them back up before . . ." She swallowed. "I'm certain it's destroyed."

He closed his eyes, growled, then opened them, revealing a frosty glare. She stepped back. He was Bram . . . and yet something about his eyes looked foreign, as if he wasn't quite himself.

Sabelle shook at the thought. "The healer, what did she do?"

For a long moment, he turned his stare to Ice, who did nothing but stand tall, his pose deceptively casual. Finally, Bram dismissed Ice and gave Sabelle his attention.

"You sent a witch into heal me?" At her nod, he frowned. "So there *was* a female here. I don't know what she did to heal me. It felt much like a dream. It must have been."

Bram glowed, a beacon of vitality and energy, the likes of which she had not seen since the morning after he first mated . . .

Sabelle gasped. Emma? "Was the female familiar?"

"I don't remember much. Did she give her name?"

"No. Did you see her, speak to her?"

"Not exactly."

Exasperation made her sigh. "What happened?"

"A hooded woman told me to break through the darkness inside me and held my hand while I . . ." He gripped his head as if warding off pain. "I fought, but it choked me with anger. And a clawing need to . . . rule magickind, run it correctly. The feelings . . . overwhelmed me. Nearly crushed me. I couldn't breathe." He sighed. "I don't understand."

Sabelle gasped and gripped her brother tighter. She didn't know what that meant, either, but didn't think for a moment that Bram's anger or ambition were good. Had Mathias's spell infested him with something evil, or just brought out his worst tendencies? Or maybe this was all part of the dark cure? None of them knew, and now only time would tell. Sabelle would watch Bram . . . just as she knew the others would as well.

"Then she was there . . . naked under her robes. She made love to me." Bran swept a tired hand across his face. "Everything was like a dream. It must have been."

Because if it hadn't been, that meant his "dark witch" was his missing mate.

"Was Emma in your 'dream?'" Sabelle asked.

"Impossible," Bram snarled. "She's gone and isn't coming back."

Or she'd come and gone again with no intent to return. But who knew for certain? Maybe the dark witch had seeded a dream of his missing mate in her brother's mind. Sabelle dropped her gaze to the floor, a pang of despair filling her. Would the darkness inside Bram slowly rot him without a mate's love to save his soul?

"Dream or not, we have other problems," Duke said, rising to his feet. "Big problems. Welcome back from the relative dead, by the way."

Bram sat Sabelle beside him, glared again at Ice, then asked, "What problems?"

Duke quickly filled him in on MacKinnett's murder and Blackbourne's nomination of Mathias for the Council seat.

"Has anyone else on the Council suggested a nominee?" Bram barked the question.

Duke shook his head. "Despite Sydney's transcasts, most didn't believe in Mathias's return until yesterday, when he contacted them all and declared his intent. Blackbourne's nomination corroborated it."

"And still the rest of the prats have done nothing?" Angry incredulity exploded in his tone. "Spineless cowards, the lot of them."

Lucan cleared his throat. "You're under my uncle's roof, and he is quite shaken. I'm certain Tynan would not appreciate your description of his grandfather."

"The truth can be painful," Bram spat.

Sabelle inched away. Bram was back with her . . . yet this was not exactly him. Now, he seemed angrier, less patient, more confrontational. He'd always been a diplomat. A thinker. She prayed this was a mood, simply a side effect of the dark healing. That her brother wasn't fueled by some remnant of Mathias's magical rage.

"Name calling will hardly solve the problem," she pointed out. "A plan would be better."

"You know the cause of my anger, little sister." Bram's gaze slid again to Ice. The promise there on his face to kill the wizard filled her with dread.

Before she could protest, Bram interrupted. "But your point is a good one, and I think I know how to solve two problems at once. Lucan, your uncle has heirs independent of your father and his line."

"Indeed." The wizard nodded, his dark hair looking glossy and shaggy as dawn filtered through the windows. "He had three sons of his own, the eldest of whom now has his own son."

"Excellent." Bram smiled. "If I nominate you, no one can claim that I would be disturbing the line of succession to the traditional MacTavish seat."

"That was Tynan's suggestion as well," Lucan conceded.

"But will the Council protest two members from the same family?"

"In desperate times? When they've all shown such an appalling lack of leadership? I hope not. You've shown yourself to be a man of reason. I know they respect you."

"Perhaps, but my claim is not as strong as someone like Alfred Hexham, who was a mere boy when his father passed to his nextlife. Alfred Senior had no other heirs to keep the seat in the family, and the Council voted to bestow the seat on MacKinnett precisely because he was old and had no heirs. My uncle told me all assumed that by the time MacKinnett passed, Hexham would be ready."

"Alfred Hexham is an idiot who should not be allowed to make decisions about his own life, much less anyone else's. His presence on the Council should not be tolerated."

"He is not the wizard his father was," Lucan conceded, "But—"

"No buts. Your point is well taken, and we will simply give you a stronger claim, especially since you have no heirs currently. In order to keep Mathias off the Council, I will require solid allies who will vote in solidarity with me. If I can count on you, your uncle, and Clifden O'Shea, we'll have enough to keep Mathias out."

"True," Sabelle said. "But how will you give Lucan a stronger claim than Hexham?"

"By making an advantageous mating to a very Privileged witch with an impeccable bloodline." Bram smiled, slid Ice another nasty glare before turning back to her. "In short, dear sister, by mating him to you."

Chapter Twelve

"ARE YOU OUT OF YOUR bloody mind?" Sabelle shouted.

Bram raised a blond brow at her over an ominous stare. "Lucan is of good family. You know he makes a faithful, considerate mate. He cares for you. The mating will earn you both respect within magickind. His claim to MacKinnett's seat will be stronger because of your union, so Mathias will have less opportunity to wage his war from the Council and destroy innocent lives to satisfy his hunger for power. Why would you object?"

Every word Bram said was true and yet . . . Sabelle's heart railed against it. "Because my heart is engaged elsewhere."

No one spoke for a long moment, and she felt the vibrations of tension bouncing off the walls. When Bram's gaze slid over to Ice with a lethal bent, Sabelle knew she must explain—and fast. But not with an audience.

She glanced out the window at the foggy gray dawn, ignoring both Ice and Lucan staring at her over her shoulders. "Could everyone leave us for a moment please? I'd like to speak to my brother."

Duke all but ran out of the room, clearly eager to avoid more conflict. Lucan was slower to depart. He tried to catch her eye, reached out for her. Resolutely, she kept her profile averted and tensed against the touch she knew was coming. Instead, Lucan sighed, dropped his hand, and left with a curse. Now, just she, Bram, and Ice remained.

"Bram." Ice addressed her brother in a clear, forceful voice. He *would* be heard.

"Pleading your case to mate with my sister?" her brother challenged.

Sabelle's heart threatened to pop out of her chest. Would Ice truly press his suit with Bram now? Doing so was ill-conceived at best, a pending disaster at worst.

"Wait, Ice. I—"

"I intend to have my say with your brother before he continues with this farce."

"Farce, is it?" Bram crossed his arms over his chest. "Odd. I look at it as protecting my sister and magickind all at once."

Ice clenched his fists, refusing to back down. "I would care for Sabelle always, putting her needs and wishes above my own."

Bram scoffed. "Pretty words are easy. And I would expect no less of any wizard with whom she mates."

"Lucan does not love her. I do."

Sabelle's heart melted at his open declaration. Ice hid nothing, held back nothing from her brother. But Bram wasn't in the proper frame of mind to appreciate it.

"You presume to know what's in Lucan's heart?"

Ice leaned in and challenged, "Next time Lucan is in the same room with Anka, watch him, see the manner in which he watches her. Pines for her. Burns for her. Note the abiding love on his face. Unless you've turned blind in the name of your ambition to rule the Council, you'll see it. If Lucan loves Sabelle, it's as a friend. He is grateful for her care during his mate mourning, as he should be. But a mating between them would be wrong."

"No, mating her with *you* would be wrong. A mating with Lucan would be advantageous for all concerned, especially the innocents likely to be slaughtered should Mathias obtain the necessary votes to fill MacKinnett's seat. If Lucan does not yet love her, he will grow to in time."

"Bram," Sabelle cut in. "I'm a grown witch, capable of making my own choices. You saved me from my mother's terrible plans. But—"

"Because of that, I know what is best for you."

"How is your scheme better than hers?"

Her brother's jaw dropped in affront. "Lucan is your *friend*. You've known him most of your life. I know you're familiar with his touch. Yet you dare tell me you think I'm whoring your freedom to a stranger?"

Sabelle took a deep breath and told herself to tread carefully. This Bram, who had been shocked by Mathias's evil spell, wasn't the same Bram she knew and loved. His ambition to control the Council had always existed, but he'd checked it. Now . . . She'd never seen him so ruthless or obvious about it.

"Surely, there is another witch with whom Lucan could mate and gain credibility."

"Who? It must be someone closely related to a Council member. Mathias murdered MacKinnett's daughter, Auropha. O'Shea has no female descendants. Camden has no heirs at all. Blackbourne has apparently already chosen the other side. Spencer's only daughter has scarcely transitioned, and the lot of them are dodgy, besides. That leaves you."

It was all true. Frustration and temper boiled inside Sabelle. "You are sacrificing my happiness for your own."

Bram stared, blinked, then stood. Hurt ripped across his face as he crossed the room. "Sacrificing? You've long done everything possible to help the cause, even when I ordered you to cease. You understand, no one will know a shred of happiness if Mathias finds his way onto the Council. Casualties will be high, particularly among existing Councilmen and their families. You know he will seek to replace me and most of the others with his puppets. To do that, he must kill anyone on the Council and their relations, every last man, woman, and youngling."

Sabelle swallowed as dread spread through her body, swallowing up the futile anger. Despite Bram's reasons for pushing her to mate with Lucan, his logic could not be faulted. If Mathias earned MacKinnett's Council seat, he would quickly enslave or kill everyone he imagined to be his enemy. The women . . . She shuddered, remembering Anka's ordeal and its aftermath, the bodies of MacKinnett's female servants. If Mathias had his way, there would be thousands of those pitiful souls.

"Besides," Bram continued softly. "You may think that Rykard makes you happy now, but he has not the means to keep you as well as you prefer."

"Material things aren't important," she shot back. "The man is."

"The man . . . yes. Do you think he has no ulterior motive for wanting you to Bind to him?"

Sabelle wasn't quite certain how to answer that question. *No. Well, perhaps . . .* The real question, however: Were those potential reasons stronger than his feelings for her?

Ice stepped forward. "Bram—"

"Shut up," he snapped. "Does she know the truth?"

Foreboding slithered up Sabelle's spine.

Ice hesitated, resignation stealing across his face. "What purpose would telling her serve?"

"Telling me what? Stop talking about me as if I'm not standing before you both!"

Neither wizard spoke for a long moment. They merely glared at each other with equal measures of resentment and resolution. Finally, Ice sighed.

"Mathias killed my sister, Gailene, when she was but seventeen. He kept her for days, under the haze of *Terriforz*, before he tired of her and gave her to the Anarki. They delivered her shaved and branded body back to my doorstep."

Sabelle gasped, horror freezing her face. How had she not known this? How was it possible that no one had told her? Her heart went out to him, and his grief was visible.

"I was a new Councilman at the time," Bram provided. "Ice and I had been friends prior to Gailene's death."

Friends? Willingly spending time in each other's company?

"Impossible! Where did you meet?"

"I had been studying the Council," Ice said quietly. "I was still in school. Bram was my assigned mentor."

"And you were friends?" How, then, had they become such bitter enemies?

"Yes." Ice regarded her, his green eyes solemn. "After Gailene's murder, I came to Bram for help, hoping he could find me justice."

"No," Bram corrected. "You wanted me to use my influence on the Council to nominate you for the seat MacKinnett eventually occupied, so you could avenge your sister."

The idea was both idealistic and absurd. A Deprived on the Council? That hadn't happened in nearly half a millennium. Today, Bram might have the influence to make that happen. But when he had been a new Councilmember? No.

And Sabelle could guess what had happened next.

She turned to Ice. "Bram refused you."

"Yes."

"You felt betrayed?"

He gritted his teeth, then nodded, so taut she wondered if his jaw would shatter. "Yes."

"After trying to use my influence for his personal advantage and being refused, he grew bitter." Bram sent Ice a damning glare. "He said he hoped that someday he could show me the wretched feeling of losing a sister."

So he'd Called to her and tried to convince to Bind to him before she could talk to Bram, tried to separate her from her brother? Oh God. Sabelle felt her limbs collapse, her stomach curdle. As she eased onto the edge of the bed to steady her shaky knees, her mind turned over and over. *Please don't let it be true.*

"Is it true?" Her voice shook, and she knew her expression pleaded with Ice to refute the claim.

"Yes."

Sabelle's stomach plummeted to her knees. Ice admitted his vendetta, without hesitation, without blinking, while inside, her heart was crumbling.

"But that was two hundred years ago, princess. This is now, and I love you."

He'd said so before. But did he . . . truly?

"I can't hear this tripe," Bram moaned. "Do you expect her to believe you? When she knows how much you hate me and why?"

Sabelle still wanted to believe Ice. His stare locked on hers was steady, devoted, almost pleading. She bit her lip, turned her back on them both, her mind racing.

"Little sister, don't give him another moment of your time. Pretty words hardly make up for ugly deeds."

True. Ice hoping that Bram someday understood what it was like to lose his sister stuck with her. But maybe . . . he didn't have *all* the facts.

"Ice saved me from the Anarki," she explained. "The day after we found MacKinnett's body, the Anarki attacked us. He hid me—you, too, while you were unconscious—and he faced a small army alone. He marched to almost certain death after refusing my help. Had he wanted you to lose a sister, he could have turned me over to Mathias's minions then and there."

"Indeed?" Bram hardly sounded impressed. "Then what happened?"

"He killed most of the Anarki. I left my hiding place to help. Ice was captured trying to protect me. He nearly died for me."

Her brother shot Ice a contemptuous stare. "A pity he didn't."

"Bram!" she shrieked, appalled.

Never had she seen him so cruel. Was this the kind brother she'd grown up with, seen as her savior like a white knight of old? Suddenly, the blinders were off, and what she saw . . . He was like a stranger.

"Don't applaud him for giving himself to the Anarki. Did you think he did so just to save you?" Bram raised a brow.

"He did save me," she argued.

"Yes, and he also made himself look the hero while he got exactly what he wanted: the Anarki would take him to their master so he might have the opportunity to kill Mathias himself. Don't delude yourself, Sabelle. He didn't do it for you. This man who professes his love so sweetly would do anything for the opportunity to take Mathias apart, limb by limb, in the most painful way possible, even sacrifice you, me and anyone else. He'd say anything to have his revenge against me." Bram stared over her shoulder at the other wizard. "Ice isn't the sort to condone the death of innocent women, but there's more than one way for him to take my sister from me."

Ice said nothing, his stare just drilling back at her brother. Sabelle's mind raced as she tried to unravel his words. "What are you saying?"

"Dig deeper for his motives, Sabelle."

"If she does, she'll find nothing more than devotion and love," Ice insisted.

"Right." Bram shook this head, then faced her. "Decide whether you want to stake your entire future on his words, little sister. Because if you refuse to mate with Lucan and choose Ice, you will no longer be my kin. You'll leave me no choice but to disclaim you. Because I won't stand by and watch you put yourself forever in the grip of a madman with a vendetta, determined to hunt a homicidal tyrant whatever the cost. You will end up impoverished and mateless. Think on that before you decide."

After her brother's startling words, Sabelle fled him and Ice, running down the hall, the stairs, flinging Sterling's back door open to the frozen December garden. She wore no shoes against the cold stone, no coat to protect her from the chill. She barely felt it.

Her own brother would disclaim her if she mated with Ice.

Disclaiming was nearly unheard of these days . . . except among the most Privileged. She'd long known her brother expected her mating to bring some advantage to the family. With times as difficult as they were, she knew he could use the advantage of a good match, but she had truly believed that he had enough affection for her to allow her to mate happily. To discover that she was as much a pawn to him as she had been to her mother was a bitter pill to swallow.

Yet neither could she wholly trust Ice, knowing his vow of revenge against her brother.

Again, she wished she possessed the wizards' mating instinct. If she only knew for certain that Ice was the one for her . . . Her heart said so, but she had no experience in such matters. What if all his care had been but a ruse? What if his sacrifice to the Anarki had merely been a convenient way to dupe her while getting closer to the man he meant to kill at all costs? What if all the ways Ice made her body sing meant no more to him than a chest-beating comparison to all her other Privileged lovers? Or a slap in Bram's face?

Any of that could be possible. The truth was, she'd known Ice but a handful of days.

Sabelle swiped her hands across her face. A cold drizzle dampened her hair, and she began to shiver as she looked across the expanse of the wintery garden. Snow had fallen last night, and the remnants dusted the banks of the half-frozen pond. A stone lantern sat on the far banks. Bushes around it groaned with the precipitation's weight. The landscape seemed desolate, ravaged by the elements—much like her heart.

She didn't know what to believe. Yes, Bram had a reason to discredit Ice—a million of them, really. There was but one way Ice could be telling the truth: if he genuinely loved her.

How was she to know that for certain?

"You're freezing."

Lucan. His concerned voice slipped into her ear, even as his body warmth blanketed her back. He didn't touch her, merely draped a jacket around her shaking shoulders.

"I—I'm fine."

"You're going to catch your death, Sabelle. Come inside. I'll make you some hot cocoa. We'll discuss this."

For once, she didn't want to talk. She wanted to wail that she loved a man she could not mate with, who might not love her back. And the most terrible, awful pain was rending her insides to shreds, tearing her still-beating heart from her chest and leaving it to bleed at her feet.

But she could hardly say that to Lucan, her other suitor, without hurting him.

"I'll be in soon," she demurred.

"Sabelle . . ." He cupped her shoulders and sighed. "Sweetheart, we must discuss this. Time is running short. If we're going to cut Mathias off at the knees and prevent the rest of the Council from bumbling our defense, we've mere hours to do it. Tomorrow at the latest."

Hours. I must decide the rest of my life in a few ticks of the clock. The path had seemed so simple a few hours ago, wrapped deep in Ice's embrace. Now . . .

She squeezed her eyes shut and nodded. "I know."

"I would give you more time, but Mathias . . . And we don't know what the other Councilmen might do."

A spike of anger had her whirling on him, but she tamped it down. It has hardly Lucan's fault that he was right. She desperately wanted more time to sort through the tangle of these accusations and her own emotions. But if they waited, it would be too late to intercede. Mathias would be on the Council and disaster would already be unleashed.

"Do you truly want to be mated to me, Lucan?" She stared deep into his blue eyes, needing to see his expression for herself.

Lucan stood tall, familiar, and striking, the wind shipping his shaggy dark hair around his ears. He'd dug his hands deep into the pockets of his jeans, shoulders hunched in a T-shirt to ward off the cold. Stylish and pleasant where Ice was hard-edged and compelling. They represented two different worlds. Night and day. Neither was good nor bad . . . just different.

"We can help magickind, Sabelle. We can ward off the biggest threat to peace and security in two hundred years."

"What of your heart?" She looked at him with pleading eyes, begging to understand, for honesty.

He took one of his hands from his pockets and smoothed away a wet curl that blew across her face, held the skeins in his fingers, rubbing them together for a pregnant moment. An awareness she'd never seen from him passed through his gaze that had her sucking in a breath.

"When I told you last night at Bram's house that I remembered a bit about being with you, I wasn't completely honest. I remember *much* more."

That fact shone in his eyes, stunning her.

She drew in a trembling breath. "I remember, too. I know how many times you cried out for Anka. You don't love me."

"How many times did I call out for Anka the very last time?"

Sabelle thought back, and the answer stunned her.

"Not once," he supplied. "I think I knew it was you, deep down."

That had been the one time she had orgasmed with him.

He took her trembling hands in his. "We've always been friends, got on well together. I won't lie and tell you I don't desire you. Since I emerged from my mate mourning, you've . . . been on my mind."

Oh my . . . She covered her mouth with freezing fingers to stifle a gasp. Her brother's best friend, in lust with her?

"But you still love Anka."

Bitterness crossed his face in a pained frown, the hard clench of a jaw. "She isn't coming back. She's moved on, and I must do the same. To mate with someone I consider most dear for such a necessary cause, to have such a sparkling, intelligent female with whom I share a great many interests would be no hardship."

He was serious. Although this grand plan had been

Bram's, Lucan was perfectly willing to play along. And it wasn't because he coveted a Council seat; Sabelle knew that. While Ice, if she mated with him . . . didn't he win in every way? She would both destroy her relationship with her brother, thus losing him a sister, *and* Ice would improve his own connections potentially for a Council position.

A union between her and Lucan sounded perfectly logical and reasonable. She would mate someone she had long considered a friend, and Ice would not benefit from being less than honest with her. *If* he had been.

Nothing felt right. Her brain scrambled, her insides trembled with helpless fury. And her heart continued to want the untamed, unsuitable wizard who had stolen it. She yearned to throw politics aside. But how many people would die because she wanted to follow her heart?

"You're hesitating," Lucan pointed out.

Wasn't it obvious why? "You have no instinct to mate with me."

He shook his head. "That doesn't make the words any less binding, Sabelle. Certainly, you've long known Bram would make a political mating for you. But Ice . . . If you believe nothing I've said, believe that he likely has many reasons to make you his mate, none of which has a thing to do with love or instinct."

Sabelle bit her lip. Though ugly, it was quite possible Ice had kept the truth from her.

"With a long friendship to build on, we could do worse, Sabelle." He cupped her cheek. "But this isn't about us; it's about all the lives we will be saving."

That was the one truth she could not argue. Bram needed to nominate someone for the Council quickly to compete against Mathias. Of all Bram's allies, Lucan had one of the better claims to a seat through his uncle.

Even if Ice genuinely loved her, and God knew she loved him, nothing could change the fact magickind needed her to mate with the next wizard who occupied MacKinnett's seat. It had been a fairy tale to think that she would not be united for political advantage.

The reality filled her with a helpless rage.

"Sabelle." Lucan cupped her face in his warm hands, and the sting of his warmth against her cheeks brought her gaze up to his blue, blue eyes. "I will be good to you. Always."

Lucan leaned closer, erasing half the space between them, his lids half-closed. He wanted to kiss her. Was waiting for a sign from her.

She swallowed. Could she mate with Lucan? Could she share intimacies with him when she wasn't focused on providing energy and healing?

Clutching his forearms, she gulped and raised her chin a fraction, tilting her face toward his. Could she be with him? Could she honestly give herself to Lucan as a mate? Sabelle had to know.

She leaned closer. Exhaled. Then Lucan's mouth brushed hers, soft, lingering . . . compelling. She'd never experienced this side of Lucan while providing him energy. Then, he'd always been demanding, taking her greedily. Now, everything about his kiss cajoled and persuaded. The urgency was all in the finesse, and she'd be lying if she said she was oblivious to his touch. In fact, he roused a gentle desire as he dipped deeper into her mouth so she tasted the flavor of coffee and nascent longing on his tongue.

But he didn't scorch her, didn't make her ache and claw and beg for him.

It doesn't matter, she told herself. This wasn't awful or torturous. She and Lucan were going to save lives. She would give Bram no reason to disclaim her. And in case Ice was lying, she would prevent him from breaking her heart.

Sabelle eased out of the kiss, eyes closed, and turned her head away. "Speak the words, and I will Bind to you."

And break my own heart. For as pleasant as the kiss had been, she knew she would never love Lucan.

"Tomorrow?" Lucan asked.

So bloody soon . . . And yet she knew there was no time to spare. Mathias would realize his nefarious plan if Bram did not reach the others of the Council quickly.

"No!" A male's voice shouted, sharp with outrage and pain.

She opened her eyes to find Ice barreling toward her, his stomp and furious eyes both shouting possession.

"Back off," Lucan warned, reaching for her.

Ice grabbed her wrist first and dragged her closer. "Fuck off."

His touch exploded a thousand conflicting emotions inside her: need, duty, love, anger, desire, determination. They flashed through her like a strobe light, fast and blinding.

Suddenly, the chilly drizzle of Sterling's garden was gone, replaced by a bedroom housed in, of all things, a cave. A sprawling bed with mussed black sheets, sparse furniture, no windows. Utilitarian. Bleak. Cold. *Oh God.*

Ice had just teleported her to his bedroom.

Fury pounded through Ice as he stared at Sabelle, Lucan's kiss fresh on her lips. Every breath came in a harsh rush and exhalation, his chest working furiously.

Speak the words, and I will Bind to you. Ice heard Sabelle say that to Lucan over and over in his head, stabbing him in the heart with every echoed syllable.

"Were you going to Renounce me before you accepted

Lucan's claim? Do I not warrant at least a refusal now that your brother has painted me a villain? Certainly, you want to put me in my place."

Sabelle hesitated, looking at him with beseeching blue eyes that nearly imploded his chest. She silently begged for understanding. But the sight of her with Lucan, knowing she would accept a wizard who did not love her, bubbled him over his boiling point.

"Ice, the fact I must Renounce you has nothing to do with your station and everything to do with my role in stopping Mathias. Without me as Lucan's mate, Bram may not be able to sway the Council to vote against him. They're so fearful of their own shadows . . . we don't dare leave magickind's fate to chance. Besides, you were not completely honest with me. You vowed to show Bram what it was like to lose a sister and—"

"Meaningless words spoken in anger, long before your birth."

"Even so, you two hadn't spoken since, had you? When the opportunity to join the Doomsday Brethren arose, you must have seen the chance to join your two favorite causes: defeating Mathias and making Bram pay for not helping you with Gailene. Your suit was sudden, and left me no time to think. You Called to me nearly as soon as we were alone."

Did she really believe he could fake such passion and abiding love?

"Instinct, princess. I knew from the first kiss you were made for me. If I tasted you now, the same ripple of pleasurable certainty would slide down my spine and dig into my bones. The fact that you're brave, strong, giving, caring, and bright simply tells me I would have loved you, regardless of instinct."

Uncertainty tinged with disbelief tightened her face,

and Ice felt the crash of rage inside him again, like powerful waves pounding the craggy rocks on the shore outside his dwelling.

"And still, you don't believe me." He cursed.

Sabelle said nothing for long moments, as if she waged some inner battle. Finally, she exploded. "You said nothing to me of your sister or avenging her death! Not a word of being Bram's friend, seeking a Council seat. Stupidly, I believed that you and Bram disliked each other for no more reason than your resentment of his position, and his disdain for your behavior. You had a million chances to tell me all—any—of this. You remained silent. The only reason I can conceive is to hide your perfidy."

Bloody hell, that she thought so little of him was like an ax to his soul. He'd sought to protect her from the ugly truth and the worst skeletons in his family closet. They shamed him. He hadn't wished to taint Sabelle with the nasty history between him and Bram, or the other details.

Now, to have any chance of preventing her mating with Lucan MacTavish, the wanker, Ice must reveal all.

God. How badly would that hurt?

Ice loosed a rattling breath, then tightened his grip on Sabelle's wrist and dragged her closer. Surprise widened her eyes, and she stared at him before her gaze cut to the unmade bed with panic.

"No, I don't seek to work my way between your pretty thighs." *At least not yet.*

God willing, he hoped Sabelle would be his forever, and he would spend a great deal of time there absorbing her pleasure and listening to her cries of completion. First, he had to get through the next half hour.

"I want to show you something. I will tell you every fucking detail of the terrible reality I tried to keep to myself."

She dug in her heels but was no match for his strength and anger. He pulled her out of his room, down the cavernous hallway cut from the cave's grayish, windowless rock. His conscience twinged him, but he ruthlessly squashed it. Sabelle wanted the truth? She was about to get every last hideous grain of it.

Nor had he wanted to bring her here before their vows were exchanged. She was used to far finer. But it was done. Perhaps it was for the best. She'd known he was Deprived, yes, but did she really know what it meant?

"Ice, stop," she protested. "Where are you taking me?"

He said nothing. Almost there . . .

"Damn it, Ice. I—"

"If you want the truth, even the truth Bram didn't know, then shut up. You want me to tear off the scars so you can see inside my soul? To determine if I'm a liar and you should Renounce me? Then come along and listen."

A hopeless fury had come over him, the sort that hadn't gripped him in two centuries. After Sabelle heard about the train wreck of the past, instead of convincing her of his sincerity, she'd likely Renounce him on the spot. And the fact he was powerless to stop his beloved from leaving him for another crushed him just as profoundly as Gailene's murder.

At the end of the cold hall, he threw open a small door and pushed Sabelle inside. He knew exactly what she would see: a wardrobe, nearly empty, a palette of two ragtag blankets and a dirty, worn pillow, a faded red ribbon tied to a spur of the cave's stone wall.

He swallowed, throat tight, as he prepared to hammer the nails into his own coffin. "My father believed all females, unless used for pleasure or to breed sons, were useless. My mother gave birth to me, and much celebration ensued in the Rykard clan. Three years later, my mother gave birth to Gailene."

Sabelle paled. "Three years?"

Yes, she would be shocked by that, when the difference between magical siblings was often decades or centuries. A witch's fertile time did not come often unless . . .

"Which should tell you something about the frequency with which my father bedded her."

"C-constantly?"

Seeing Sabelle react exactly as he'd known she would was both gratifying and frustrating. From this, he knew precisely how she would feel about the rest of his story.

"So I'm told, yes. When Gailene was born, my father had no use for a girl child. In his eyes, she was but another mouth to feed. She would never add to our wealth or defend our dwelling. She would never advance our family in magical politics or marry well enough to distinguish us in any particular way. So the day she was born, he tried to kill her."

Sabelle gasped, and Ice could see the horror streaking across her face. But he wasn't done.

"My mother convinced him otherwise, and because he had high hopes of getting another son on her, and quickly, it behooved him to keep her happy. He allowed her to keep the girl child, with the understanding that their every spare moment would be consumed in the conception of another son. But the girl was to be given no comforts. Food was only hers if there were leftovers."

Hell, she looked at him now with a mixture of pity and horror, and it was all Ice could do to keep his fist from finding the nearest wall or breaking down the damned concrete wall he'd encased his tears in long ago.

"This . . . was Gailene's room?"

Ice nodded. "I gave her my blankets. She had none. I often

gave her my food. I tried to protect her from my father's rants and punishments. Though I told him I did those things in order to become a tougher wizard, he knew I lied. He mocked me and said that no warrior of merit had such a soft heart. He said it would be my downfall and resolved to cure me of it."

"Dear God, she was a child. You were protecting her. How could he be so cruel to his own flesh and blood?"

Ice shrugged. "My father was not a good man. He and my mother tried for many years to have another son, but after delivering two children so close together, my mother did not become fertile again as quickly as he liked. Finally, she conceived again when I was twenty, Gailene seventeen. My mother and infant brother died shortly thereafter. My father's only reason for allowing Gailene to stay in the house was dead."

"What did he do?" Her face said that she wasn't certain she wanted to know, and Ice hardly blamed her.

"My father, who had encouraged my friendship with Bram and others associated with the Council, ordered me away from our house." Ice remembered clearly the foreboding, the finality in his father's words. He'd tried every excuse imaginable to stay with Gailene.

"My father had promised me that he would allow Gailene to remain as long as I continued to cultivate the friendships that could return us to the glory the Rykards had known before the Social Order stripped us of our titles, wealth, and lands. For her, I made friends of many related to the Council, but I genuinely liked your brother. I saw that his ambition to rule the Council someday was motivated by a very clear vision of leadership for magickind. For that I was jealous, but I supported him. Believed in him.

"But that day, I came home. Gailene was gone."

"Your father let Mathias kill her?"

"He *sold* Gailene to Mathias and told the bastard that he cared not what became of her."

"And she was seventeen?" Sabelle's face had turned an even chalkier shade of white, and perverse satisfaction filled Ice.

"Yes. Mathias told me her screams as he took her virginity were delectable, but she became regrettably weepy, which forced him to give her to the Anarki, who quickly used her up. Finally, Mathias had one of his minions dump her body on the beach just outside. I found her."

Still he recalled the utter misery of finding the one person he loved so horribly abused and callously murdered. The fury, the desolation, the sense of failure . . .

"And so you attacked Mathias's compound and tried to kill as many Anarki as possible in revenge?"

"Yes."

"Which made everyone believe you'd gone mad. Then you tried to use your connection to Bram to secure an open Council seat so you could somehow punish Mathias?"

"Yes."

"And when he refused, you felt that he'd betrayed your friendship because he knew how important Gailene had been to you?"

Ice clenched his fists. "Yes."

"Oh, Ice."

She looked as if her heart broke for him. He didn't want her pity, just her understanding for the blow he knew would come next. And maybe, though he feared it would be too much to hope for, her understanding that he would never lie to her or use her.

"What did you say to your father?" she whispered.

"Nothing. I simply killed him."

CHAPTER THIRTEEN

SUDDENLY, SABELLE UNDERSTOOD with perfect clarity in that moment why everyone believed Ice insane: demanding a Council seat from Bram at the expense of their friendship, attacking Mathias in his own lair and slaughtering a hundred Anarki all alone, killing his father—all by age twenty. Put together with the fact he'd since isolated himself, came from a family many thought beneath them, and lived in a cave, Ice made the perfect picture of a social outcast.

His grief for Gailene was genuine. Sabelle might not know everything about Ice, but she didn't doubt the pain on his face. His utter stillness and the challenging set of his clenched jaw said he awaited her condemnation. Sabelle didn't want to hurt Ice more than he'd already been.

But one could not discount two facts: Ice had vowed revenge against her brother, and magickind would benefit if she mated elsewhere.

"Say something."

His choked demand made her heart clench for him. "I'm sorry for you, Ice. The terrible, awful way you lost Gailene. No brother with as much love as you clearly held for her should ever endure such torture."

"Did you hear me? I killed my father."

"I applaud you for it. I hope it was prolonged and painful. It was the least he deserved."

He exhaled, clearly relieved. "I could have killed him a

thousand times and it would never have been enough penance for Gailene's horrific death."

"You got your revenge against your father, nearly succeeded against Mathias. But what about my brother? Is that unfinished business?"

"Sabelle . . ." Ice shook his head. "When I first discovered Gailene's body, I was beyond rage and consolation. I wanted to hurt everyone who'd had a hand in her death. After killing my father, I demanded that your brother help me. But I quickly realized that he did not put my pain above his ambition and would not help me avenge my sister. I made stupid threats. He believed I'd gone mad. We ceased speaking." Ice shook his head. "Until he summoned me with the promise of a group designed to end Mathias, I had not spoken to him, so I'm certain that he only recalls my threats. But time has helped me to see that I asked too much of Bram." Ice grabbed her hands, honestly burning from his hard, square face. "I vow to you, I would never use you to hurt your brother. Ever."

Sabelle drew in a deep breath. Perhaps Ice was telling the truth. His earnest expression made her want to believe, so badly. Her breath caught, her heart bled. But her brother had warned her a hundred times while teaching her the ways of the Council not to be swayed by her emotions. Ice was playing every one she possessed, and it was so bloody hard not to be moved.

But now, she must face facts: Bram had behaved like a wanking bastard after emerging from the black cloud spell, but he had been telling the truth about the past. Ice *had* once hoped Bram would know the pain of losing a sister. Only his determination to have revenge had dimmed.

That wasn't her impression when she saw Ice and her brother argue, when she'd witnessed the Anarki carnage at MacKinnett's. Ice had killed Mathias's minions with abandon and relished it. He had killed his own father. Bram was unfinished business. Was it possible he'd been biding his time?

Despite his pretty speech, that possibility cast a shadow on all of his actions: his "possessive nature," his sacrifice of safety when the Anarki arrived at the MacKinnetts, his Call itself. Sabelle believed that Ice would never kill an innocent or condone that behavior, so it seemed logical that his seduction and Call could be his means of separating her from Bram.

Logical . . . though her gut told her that wasn't Ice's way.

Yet how was she to truly know? Her head and heart were at war.

"Thank you for that," she said finally, gently pulling her hands free.

Ice swallowed, then grabbed her hands in his own again. "Please . . . believe me. Don't mate with Lucan. When I said there was no other for me but you, I meant that with my whole—"

"It doesn't matter." She didn't mean to snap, sound cold, but her insides were breaking. "Whatever your motives for Calling to me, the fact is, Bram will nominate Lucan for MacKinnett's seat, but his appointment is by no means a certainty. Having me as his mate will secure his claim."

"Bloody hell, princess, you don't love him," he snarled.

She didn't, and whatever Ice may or may not be guilty of, she'd fallen hard and fast for the Deprived wizard who protected her, touched her with tender, wild passion, put her safety above his own. If he'd been genuine in all that, then she regretted deeply hurting him. But only time would tell the truth about Ice's motives.

Time was something they did not have.

"I don't love him," she confirmed. "But I love magickind. I won't see them crushed by Mathias."

Ice cursed, a long, loud string of crass words that had Sabelle flinching. "Would you say differently if you believed me? Your brother's words are ringing in your ears, and you still think I've used you for some elaborate revenge. But you're wrong. I love—"

"It doesn't matter!" Something inside her snapped.

If he convinced her of his love, doing what she must would nearly kill her. Already, it was difficult, knowing that her future would be with a wizard she regarded as a friend, not a lover. "None of it! Not what you feel, what I feel, what we might want, whether our love is real. Magickind *needs* me. Am I to turn my back on them? Watch Mathias make a thousand Gailenes? You, of all people, should want to see Mathias stopped at any cost."

"Not when it means your sacrifice, princess. You deserve happiness."

She frowned. "Everyone deserves happiness. I'm not any more special or deserving than any other witch or wizard."

"I think you are." Ice stared with solemn, burning green eyes. "You consistently put others' needs above your own. You're brave and resourceful, beautiful and kind—"

"Stop." She couldn't hear him heap praise on her, not and remain strong. "You were a strong, steadfast brother who didn't deserve to have his sister ripped away so young, yet that is reality. Not everyone achieves happiness. I've known my whole life that I would likely mate for political purposes. I will take solace in the fact that my sacrifice will help our people."

And she would cherish the memories of the few days she'd shared with Ice when following her heart had been a beautiful dream and she'd allowed herself to fall in love.

"You should take solace in that fact, too," she murmured.

"Until you speak vows with him, you are *mine*. I won't let you go easily. I love you. I believe you love me. You know our feelings are real."

No, she didn't know, but how badly she wanted to believe. Frustration wound up into a tangle of anger and tears. She tamped it down deep inside. "Ice, my course is set. By tomorrow, I will be Lucan's."

"Don't settle for a wizard who loves another when I would kill for you, die for you. You can't let him continue to use you for his ends. Stay with me. Bind to me." He grabbed her hands and brought her against the solid heat of his body. "Let me spend our lives proving that my love is real."

Ice had said once that their love was futile, and at the moment, Sabelle completely agreed. "We don't have a lifetime."

"What will it take to make you believe me?" he demanded.

"What I think does not signify."

"You're wrong. I cannot stand you thinking the worst of me when it's your love and respect I want most."

Though she sent him a sharp nod, her expression collected, his words shattered her into a million cold, black pieces. God, how badly she wanted to simply believe that he loved her, throw duty and caution to the wind, and Bind to him.

As I become a part of you, you become a part of me. I will be honest, good, and true . . .

She didn't dare. If she followed her heart, Bram would feel the pain of losing a sister. She would lose the only steady family she'd ever known. If she Bound to Ice, she would likely lose her mate to his vendetta against Mathias someday. If she chose her heart over duty, magickind might lose its freedom, see the slaughter of innocents.

Ice himself had given her the tools with which to end this discussion. Now it was up to her to be strong enough to use them.

"If my opinion matters so much, then let me do what must be done. Let me go to Lucan. If you do, I will know your true feelings." Sabelle tried to hold herself together, but the possibility that she was losing her chance with the wizard she loved crashed down on her. Tears scalded her eyes. "A-and I swear that, no matter how long I am mated to L-Lucan, I will love you."

Sabelle's words and tears stabbed Ice's heart until it tore, bled, damn near stopped beating. Let her go? Never hold or touch her again? Watch his princess mate with a wizard who neither loved nor appreciated her? That would be the hardest thing he'd ever done.

He pressed his lips together. Her sense of fairness and purpose were some of what he loved most about her, but this self-sacrifice for the greater good? He hated it, even as he admired her more.

"Princess . . ."

"Don't make this harder. Please." More tears ran down her cheeks. He was humbled that she would spend tears on him. Before he could brush them away, she swiped an angry hand across her face.

Damn Bram for putting Sabelle in this position and making her doubt him.

"Will you do that for me?" she whispered.

Honestly, he wasn't certain he could. Having her believe the worst of him shredded his guts, yet the thought of never holding her again—and knowing that MacTavish did—was every bit as painful.

Either way, he lost her. Unless he continued to fight like

hell . . . which would only serve to make him look more bent on revenge or so self centered she would lose all respect. *Bugger!*

An ominous gonging interrupted him.

Shit. Bram. That was all he needed.

"My brother? How did he find us so quickly?"

So Bram hadn't forgotten where he lived. Ice couldn't deny the wizard was smart, but demonic possession was also a possibility. Personally, Ice was hoping for the demonic possession. That would give him a reason other than anger to separate Bram's body from his head and end some of Sabelle's torment.

Then again, if he harmed her brother, Sabelle would hate him forever.

With a thick curse and dread multiplying, he opened his barriers. Bram barreled inside moments later, fury around him like a force field. His signature was muddled with the remnants of Mathias's spell. Something was not at all right with his former friend . . .

Rion stampeded in, rampage on his face. "If you ever steal my sister away again, I swear to God—"

"Bram, I am not ten and I hardly need you to conduct my personal affairs for me." Sabelle sighed. "We needed privacy to discuss our future."

"You definitely need me if you think you have any sort of future with this manipulative piece of rubbish."

"Asking a supposed friend for a favor," Ice growled. "Huge manipulation, all right. I'd rather be accused of crossing the line than stabbing someone in the back. Stupid of me to think you'd care that my innocent sister had been tortured and murdered by a madman."

"I *did* care. I grieved with you. I helped you bury her, then held you when you sobbed. I started the inquisition into her death. But I didn't have the power to grant you a Council seat."

"I asked you for a nomination," Ice growled. "Period. I would have explained my rationale, my qualifications—"

Bram grunted in frustration. "Everyone knew you were too young. Twenty and untransitioned, who would have taken you seriously? We both would have been mocked, and I would have lost all credibility—"

"Your precious reputation was worth more to you than my friendship. You made that quite clear."

"What good is a Councilman no one will listen to? I'd been on barely a decade. I was the most junior member. Even with my qualification, I had a difficult time getting the others to treat me as an equal. For you to insist on a nomination when you were not only young, but Deprived . . . You asked for the impossible."

"They'd been contemplating a change to the Social Order and balancing the Council with a Deprived. We'd talked before about the fact I'd be a good candidate, since my grandfather sat on the Council before the laws were changed."

Bram let loose a bitter laugh. "You really believed that would come to pass? The Council, the purveyors of change? Honestly, Ice . . ."

"Now I know otherwise, but at the time—"

"Which only shows how naive and ill-equipped to sit on the Council you were."

Ice gnashed his teeth. Point to Bram. "Why did you not say this? Why did you just say no and turn your back on me? You were my last fucking friend. My only—" He choked.

God, they hadn't discussed this in two centuries, and the first thing he did? Open his mouth and pour out the contents of his soul, showing Bram the actual pain his loss had wrought. During the dark days after Bram's departure, Ice often felt alone, wondered what the fuck he had to live for. And now, what must Sabelle think?

"You issued me an ultimatum, Ice. Nominate you or stop being my friend. What was I to do? I couldn't give you what you sought. You would have tried to direct all Council business into vendettas against Mathias. He needed to be dealt with, yes. But magickind had other problems you didn't care about. Nominating you would have been impossible and irresponsible."

Perhaps Bram was right. Likely, even. But Bram had never asked to see if the rest of the Council would accept the nomination. He'd simply said no.

"It's done. None of this matters. Leave my dwelling. I'll return your sister as soon as we've finished talking. Joining the Doomsday Brethren was a mistake. Consider my involvement at an end."

"Ice, damn it, no." Bram looked ready to hit him.

"The Doomsday Brethren needs you," Sabelle added.

He snorted, resentment searing his veins. "Yeah, you need your slave labor, just as you did during your early Council days. I'll bet you never told anyone I did most of your research or wrote a great many of your speeches."

Bram paused, looked away. Ice caught the surprise on Sabelle's face. *Score.*

"I'm good enough to break my back for you, but not good enough to be beside you in politics or family. Nice."

Bram cursed, then looked him in the eye. "No, it's not nice. But it's reality. The Council would have laughed at your nomination two hundred years ago, and today, magickind will benefit from Sabelle mating to Lucan. We cannot allow Mathias on the Council. But I need you at my side. We need good warriors, Ice. I freely admit you are the most fearless. The best."

"Please . . ." Sabelle wrapped her hand around his arm and squeezed. "Don't abandon the cause."

By God, they asked too much of him. Stay where he was not wanted but needed? Remain for the good of the bloody cause, where he would be forced to watch the witch he loved mate with another?

"What would Gailene have wanted?" Bram murmured.

It was a rotten question, but the answer was easy: for him to do the right thing. Gailene, bless her, had always had an unbending moral compass. She'd always done right, regardless of the pain or personal sacrifice. Her sense of rightness, fairness, always amazed him, especially since their father had shown her no such example.

Thoughts still raced through Ice's head when several more gongs sounded. MacTavish, Lucan, and Caden. A Wolvesey ring followed. What the hell, was he being invaded? Clearly, they'd all followed Bram. Difficult enough to bring Sabelle here and show her the painful plainness of his home. But to have every other Privileged warrior here as well? Give them a reason to forever mock him?

"Go the fuck away, all of you!" He turned and stormed from the room, down the hall, to the back of the cave, seeking the secret exit that led to the vast expanse of lake and forest and blessed privacy.

Instead, Caden's voice stopped him. "Ice, let us in! Tynan is injured, and Sydney is freezing."

Hell. He didn't want to see a decent wizard die unnecessarily, and because Ice hated Lucan MacTavish for stealing Sabelle didn't mean he wanted the wizard's sister-by-mating to suffer. But . . .

"Why the devil are all of you *here*?" he roared, marching to the front of the dwelling. "Certainly you didn't use all the rooms in Sterling's rambling estate."

The last thing Ice wanted was everyone invading his personal space and secretly mocking how he lived.

"My uncle's home is no longer safe," Lucan shouted through the door.

Frowning, Ice dropped his defenses long enough to let them all close, then flung the door open. First, he admitted the pretty redhead, who huddled in a jacket he recognized as Caden's. Her mate followed, carrying a limp, bleeding Tynan. Lucan and the Wolvesey twins sidled in out of the cold, Ronan curling a pretty blonde at his side. Their magical signatures declared them mated.

Sterling MacTavish emerged from the back of the pack and pushed his way in front of his nephews, just past Ice's front door. "Clifden O'Shea is dead. Attacked and slaughtered. Signs point to Anarki."

Oh dear God. Ice nearly stopped breathing. Mathias was moving bloody fast.

"Tynan went to visit him and was injured. He managed to get himself out," Duke added. "It's clear Mathias intended to finish off Clifden's heir, too. Damn near succeeded."

Ice cursed. Tynan, he'd somewhat liked. For a Privileged, he wasn't all bad.

"Can we come in?" Caden's blue eyes bore into his as he held the injured Tynan, who looked dirty, bloody, and completely unconscious. "If Tynan dies, Mathias will have another open Council seat to vie for."

Bloody hell.

"I must go," Lucan announced. "I merely came to check . . . the situation."

In other words, make certain Ice hadn't raped or harmed Sabelle. As if he could.

Ice snarled. "Everyone is alive and in one piece. No mad rages or mass slaughters. Yet."

Lucan cleared his throat, then made eye contact with Sabelle. She nodded once, and MacTavish visibly relaxed.

Ice swore inside. He'd known for two hundred years that everyone thought the worst of him. It had never bothered him until now. Until Sabelle.

"I'll be going, then." Lucan backed out. "I promised to help Duke, Marrok, and Olivia transport the Doomsday Diary here. Olivia and Duke can both drive a car, and I can lend protection."

Then, with a snap, Lucan was gone.

"Here?" Ice barked at no one in particular. "Why the hell would all of you come here?"

Ice glanced at Raiden Wolvesey, the unmated twin—he could only tell them apart because Raiden's hair was as pale as Ronan's was dark. Other than that, they had the same green eyes and wicked smiles.

"Bram's house is destroyed. When asked an hour ago, Sterling refused to back Mathias's bid for the Council, so we're fairly certain he's next on the Anarki's hit list. Marrok's cottage was destroyed by the Anarki months ago. Lucan's dwelling was breached when Anka was abducted," Caden recounted. "Duke's place is overrun with humans. And Ronan and Raiden have a . . . busy house."

And then some. Magickind's den of iniquity. The Wolvesey wizards were renowned for their sexual appetites. Ronan's mating was a surprise. Usually, the Wolvesey males just bedded one female after another until they got younglings on them. Considering the difficulty of conceiving a youngling between an unmated pair, that amount of effort said something about the single-minded pursuit of pleasure. Ice wondered vaguely why Ronan had broken tradition.

"So . . ." Caden winced, shifting Tynan's dead weight in his arms. "That leaves you."

Bram approached from behind, Sabelle on his heels. Ice sensed them, smelled his beloved's sweet fragrance.

"Your place is a veritable fortress, Ice," Bram commended. "Easy to defend. Damn near impossible to breach."

"And I must transcast the news of O'Shea's murder to all of magickind immediately. I'll be safe and uninterrupted here."

Ice bit back a curse. They asked too much, damn it. They asked him to give up Sabelle, to fight and perhaps give his life when none here liked or wanted him. They asked to invade his personal space, house and shelter them, when, if they saw him at one of magickind's functions, they'd likely ignore him at best or spit on him at worst. Certainly, none would accept, much less applaud, a union between him and Sabelle.

Yet what would become of the Doomsday Brethren if he didn't acquiesce? Clearly, they had nowhere safe to go, and if they all died, so too would magickind's best hope at vanquishing Mathias. Worse, Sabelle would never forgive him for turning his back, particularly if he might have prevented the slaughter by taking them in.

Hell. It wasn't as if he had no room. His father, mad prick that he'd been, had expanded the cave feverishly, hoping to fill it with a dozen sons. What it lacked in luxury, it more than made up for in space.

Plus, having them all here meant Sabelle stayed. Every day she was under his roof was one more day he might be able to persuade her to follow her heart and Bind to him.

"Fine." He snapped, then stepped back to let them all in. "My bedroom is the one at the very back. No one comes near it." He sent Sabelle a glance. "Unless you're invited. I like quiet and privacy. The locked door just down from mine is off limits. Transcast mirror is in the front room. This isn't a five-star hotel. Not every room has furniture, but I've plenty of pillows and blankets. I don't keep servants. You'll have to do your own cooking. Mine is dreadful. No bitching about the accommodations."

"Thank you," Caden said simply.

Then he nodded at Sydney, and carrying Tynan, led his mate and uncle down the hallway to the left. Plenty of bedrooms there—far from Ice. Excellent.

"Should I send for a healer?" Ice called after them. Blood oozing from the whole left side of O'Shea's body made Tynan look uncomfortably close to his nextlife.

Sabelle stepped up. "We don't dare yet. Let me look at him first. Maybe . . . it's not as serious as it looks."

Whatever ailed Tynan was serious enough for the wizard to lose consciousness and look as if he was at death's door. But he couldn't fault Sabelle's logic about being cautious in sending for a healer. No telling what means Mathias might use to track them all down.

"Let me know if you change your mind."

Sabelle merely nodded. "Thank you."

"You're not bad after all." Raiden shook his hand and smiled as they sauntered in. Ronan repeated the gesture. Along with his mate, they followed the MacTavish clan to the far side of the cave.

Ice made a mental note to put Tynan, Marrok and Olivia, and Bram on his side of the rambling stone dwelling. Excepting Bram, he found the rest tolerable. Sabelle, he'd keep in the room beside his and continue to hope for a miracle.

Sabelle sighed. It had to be late, though she couldn't be certain without windows. The heaviness of exhausted limbs and grittiness of tired eyes told her that her mating tomorrow morning was but hours away.

Resignation weighed on her. This morning she had awakened in Ice's arms. After she'd healed and loved him, she'd been prepared to fight her brother for the right to become his mate. Tomorrow, she would lie in the arms of another as his mate—the first of many times.

Yet she knew she'd always think of Ice.

As she looked around the surprisingly well-furnished chamber, the next task was one to which she both looked forward and dreaded.

Ice.

Sabelle pressed a trembling hand to her stomach and held back tears. She'd shed too many, and they'd done no good. Now was the time to buck up, do her duty, be proud of her contribution to magickind's safety. Lamenting her own heartbreak served no purpose.

Except the pain wouldn't stop.

Drawing in a deep breath, she stared at the room's two doors. One led to the hallway. The other . . . Sabelle had a sneaking suspicion that Ice had put her in a chamber that connected to his. She wanted—needed—to have these few private minutes alone with the man she loved.

And break the news to him.

On leaden feet, she approached the door and raised her hand to knock, dropped it, lifted it again. Closed her eyes. Then she forced herself to knock. No sense in prolonging what she could not change.

In seconds, Ice whipped the door open. His expression was a question, not harsh, but guarded. Hope haunted his beautiful green eyes, and she wished to God that she was seeking him out for any other reason. After what she'd already asked of him, it hardly seemed fair.

But nothing about this situation was.

"Do you want to come in?" he murmured.

She nodded and took a big step into his domain. Quietly, she shut the door behind her, then stepped closer.

"I'm glad you knocked. I—I have something to say and . . . If you require me to step aside, if you need that to believe that I love you . . ." He pressed his lips together, paused. "I await your Renunciation."

His words nearly yanked her heart from her chest. In a few short words, he'd erased most of her doubts. Yes, she supposed it could be another ploy . . . but Ice didn't seem the type. Straight and to the point, without subterfuge. One of the things she loved about him.

"Thank you," she choked. "I'm sorry it's . . . ended like this. Your cooperation for the cause—"

"I'm not relinquishing you to that wanking MacTavish for the cause. It's for *you*. I don't want you at odds with your brother. I feel every day without Gailene, and I won't have you suffering his loss. Your sense of duty to magickind would eventually bring you to regret becoming my mate if following your heart cost lives. I don't want you bearing that burden, either. I won't go in happiness, but I will go in peace, knowing that your family and conscience will be mollified and magickind served."

Was it enough for him? The sad answer was all over his face. Sabelle's heart crumbled all over again.

"I truly am sorry."

"You are many things, princess." He took her hand, clasped her fingers in his warm, strong ones. "Among them, too kind to hurt me on purpose."

Yet she was hurting him all the same. The air between them, the knowledge that this would be the last moment she was ever alone with him, ever allowed to touch him, was like a funeral dirge for her heart.

"Kiss me?"

Ice tensed, every muscle frozen. "I don't have the will-power to stop at kissing you."

Another chance to be in Ice's arms sounded heavenly. Tomorrow, she would give her future to another. The few precious hours that remained of tonight was theirs.

"I don't have the willpower to resist." Her voice shook.

He said nothing more, just looked into her eyes like she was the sun, his forever. A bittersweet smile stretched across his face.

Then he stepped back. "If you go to him tomorrow morning after spending the night with me, he will scent it. He will know."

A valid point, and one she should have considered. Lucan's decision to mate with her required sacrifice on his part as well, giving up all hope of ever reconciling with Anka. Still, she couldn't bring herself to care that Lucan would know she'd lain in Ice's arms. They both needed this last night to treasure what might have been before they faced a cold dawn.

"He'll know my feelings for you no matter what I do tonight. The mate bond and its sacred words will prevent us from ever having this moment again. Please . . . don't say no."

CHAPTER FOURTEEN

SAY NO? IMPOSSIBLE. WHEN it came to pleasing Sabelle, Ice could refuse her nothing.

He locked gazes with her, staring into the blue oceans of need and sorrow, straight into the shining light of her soul. Never had he known someone like her, so good and true. Kind. Real. Never would he forget a moment with her.

Tonight, he would have to make memories to last the rest of his life. Her torn expression said she would be doing the same.

Drawing in a shaky breath, he caressed his way down her arm, a slow brush of fingers, then laced his fingers in hers, giving her hand a squeeze.

She squeezed back. "Thank you. I know I've asked a great deal of you."

"There is nothing I have that I wouldn't gladly share with you."

Her face softened, and she cupped his cheek, clearly fighting tears. She barely won the battle. Her valiant effort touched him, though she needn't have fought at all. He would love her regardless.

With slow steps, he led her to his bed, glad they were making this last memory here, where he could lie at night and remember every soft sigh and treasured touch.

When they reached the edge of the bed, Ice lifted her pale sweater, palming his way up her torso, brushing her breasts, raising the garment over her head. She emerged a moment later, all tousled golden hair and trembling mouth. Again, he marveled that she could love him. And he cursed the fate destined to tear them apart.

Sabelle caressed his chest, hand trailing down his abdomen, until she reached the hem of his shirt and drew it up and away.

The need to touch her everywhere, all at once, jolted him. He pulled her against him, chest to chest, hampered only by the delicate lace of her bra. The warm press of skin made him sizzle, even as he drew in a shaking breath.

"Princess . . ." Ice began, but he had no words. What was there to say?

"I know." She sniffed. "But I won't cry tonight. I simply want to be with you."

Somehow, it would have to be enough.

Ice nodded, pushing aside the futility and rage beating at his heart, and gave himself to her. Everything good and hopeful and loving he'd been storing in his heart since Gailene's death he swore he'd give her tonight.

Below him, her lush pink lips beckoned, and he fused their mouths together, a brush, a breath, a sigh. With every kiss, he tasted the rightness of her on his tongue. Certainty shivered down his spine, rocking him to his core. No matter what words she spoke with Lucan in a few short hours, she was his.

And he would forevermore be hers.

Filtering his fingers through her soft curls, he cupped her head, brought her closer, dipped his head for another kiss, let her sumptuous taste slide across his senses again. She moaned, then peppered his face with slow, reverent presses of her lips. Ice felt the devotion pouring off her, and she humbled him all over again.

His fingers trembled as he unclasped her bra, slid her

jeans down her slender hips, brushed away her knickers, baring her. He'd never seen a more beautiful woman, true. But now he saw not just the golden-haired siren who had inherited the ability to ensnare any man with her wiles, but the angel inside who called to him with every move and breath.

Sabelle helped him out of his camouflage pants as he toed off his boots. Finally, they stood together, naked, heart to heart. He yearned to gobble her up quickly, but forced himself to savor her. Rarely was he given to indecision, but tonight . . . how could he reassure her he would always be here for her, yet send her to do her duty without leaving her to suffer guilt and regret for what could not be?

In the end, Sabelle guided him, lying back against the silken black sheets, arms raised to him. The easiest—and hardest—act in the world was to slide into those waiting arms and possess her parted lips again.

She opened like a flower to sunlight, her arms closing around him, her legs parting beneath him. He flowed over her, spreading heat and joy, as he caressed the soft mound of her breast, the graceful swell of her hip, then took her thigh in hand and lifted it to his side. She opened willingly.

An urge to take in every part of Sabelle rolled over him. Ice whispered butterfly kisses down her jaw, her neck, to the curves of her breasts. Hard nipples awaited, a treat he didn't resist. A stroke of his tongue, a pull of his mouth, and she moaned for him, arching to him, both seeking and offering succor.

Down her body he moved, dragging his tongue over the long, flat expanse of her abdomen. The creamy flavor of her skin, the sunshine scent, all mingled with the tart-sweet hint of her desire. The combined perfumes rushed to his head, and he delved deeper, where he feasted on her, lapping the concentrated essence of her desire for him. With patience and reverent kisses, he drew her higher, higher, joying to the feel of her tense hips in his hands and her pleas to fill her, to love her.

For a few bittersweet moments he resisted her siren call, content to shower her with pleasure, gratified when she reached the peak once, then again. Still, he didn't want to leave her, but he could not deny her breathy cries to become one with her.

Slowly he kissed his way up her body, cupping her bottom as he flowed into her, Sabelle's tight sheath closing around him in a caress of hot silk, a ripple of pleasure. Ice shuddered as Sabelle surrounded him everywhere, as if he felt her inside him, soothing his pained heart, glorying in these last few hours together. He frowned, wondering if she was using her siren abilities to make him feel whatever she wished, then realized no. It was simply her.

"Ice . . ." She touched his face, looked straight up into his eyes.

The jolt reached all the way to his heart as he slid deep into her body once more.

They remained like that, connected gazes, bodies, and hearts until she cried out beneath him, rosy cheeks flushed, pleasure transforming her face into the most beautiful sight ever. Then he joined her in a shimmering world of passion, the crash of it washing through his body as he poured his devotion and seed into her, lighting up his heart, where he knew she would stay forever.

Sabelle drew in a shuddering breath, and her eyes fluttered shut as a look of sublime peace settled over her. And he felt it too. The perfect moment. For this brief second in time, they could simply share a heart and a soul, and be one.

She drifted off to sleep cocooned in his arms, and he watched her, unmoving, as the hours slipped away. Having grown up in these caves, he'd developed a keen sense of time despite the lack of windows. He held her tighter as dawn approached, the sun rising to the day that would change everything between them forever.

Ice shifted to her side, pillowing her head on his chest, gripping her tighter. The gesture was futile. The black chasm of today and all his future days roared in, and Ice clenched his eyes shut against the reality. What the hell was he going to do with the rest of his life now besides fight and secretly hope that someday, somehow, she found her way back to his side?

Sabelle woke in Ice's arms. She knew it even before she opened her eyes. The strong arms, the pine and musk scent, the way he latched on to her as if he'd never let go. The feeling of joy and security like no other.

Reluctantly, she opened her eyes, faced the world, and found Ice studying her. Grief shadowed his eyes, the hollows of his cheeks, the pinch of his mouth.

She swallowed. "It's time, isn't it?"

He nodded and brushed his thumb over her cheek. "Sabelle, I—"

Pressing her lips to his, she stopped his words. "If you speak, I will only cry. And there is nothing we can say . . ."

Ice set his jaw, then nodded once. "When are you supposed to go to MacTavish?"

"As soon as I wake."

How she wished she had another few centuries to spend with Ice. But they didn't have even a few hours. Magickind might well depend on Lucan filling MacKinnett's vacant Council seat before Mathias somehow talked his way into it.

"If you'd like a shower, there's one through that door." He pointed across the room.

She didn't, actually. She'd rather let the scent of Ice cling to her as long as possible, revel in it for as long as she could. But it would be disrespectful to Lucan and do nothing but cause more strife between her brother and the man she loved.

"Thank you."

With wooden movements, she climbed into the sleek, black tiled box. Reluctantly, she lifted the soap to wash away the traces of Ice from her body. But she couldn't. Forehead against the cold tile, warm water beating down on her back, she clutched the slick, foaming bar and sobbed. In that moment, she hated her brother, hated the bloodline she'd been born to that forced duty and responsibility upon her. She hated being needed.

Still, it changed nothing, and that fact tore her heart in a hundred irreparable pieces with each tear.

Suddenly, she felt cool air, then a warm presence at her back blocking the spray of water. She felt more than saw Ice as he wrapped his arms around her and gently pried the soap from her hands.

He bathed her in slow strokes, carefully washing every inch of her, then grabbing the shampoo, lathered and rinsed her hair.

When he'd finished, he turned her to face him. "Say the word, and I will fight for you. Your brother, Lucan . . ."

The world assumed the big warrior was mad, but she saw the facade. He hid behind it, shutting off his caring and warmth. Because no one would believe it? Because he feared being hurt once more? Either way, she loved the man she'd uncovered. Her heart praised him with every beat.

"We've been over it," she said finally. "I should have known there were too many obstacles, too few possibilities before I fell for you. I will treasure every moment——"

Ice stopped her words with a kiss. "I will as well."

Clenching his jaw, he tossed his head back, eyes closed. Sabelle melted as Ice fought tears of his own.

"Come." He drew her from the shower and toweled her off, then pressed a soft kiss to her forehead. "No matter what, I am here for you."

She nodded and dressed as he did the same, then combed her hair. Exhaustion washed through her, along with the drag of despair. Today, she would be mated—an occasion she should await with great joy. Now, she could muster nothing but the urge to cling to Ice and cry again.

He approached her from behind, and she watched him clasp her shoulders in the mirror. "Turn and hold my hands. Renounce me, and let's be done."

Sabelle bit her lip as she faced him and grabbed his hands, fresh anger pouring through her. This is what she'd come to tell Ice last night and became tangled in his arms, lost in his kiss. And now she resented her brother all over again for forcing this cruelty on them both. "Bram insists on being present when I do. He wants Lucan to witness as well."

So there could be no question, no dispute. Not that there should be. Ice's magical signature would reflect the fact he'd been Renounced by her.

Ice cursed. "Determined to make this as difficult as possible, is he?"

Sabelle wished she could deny it. But the Bram who had emerged from Mathias's evil black cloud spared no thought for her anguish or Ice's. Likely, he would privately revel in Ice's humiliation. She'd argued until she could find no more words, and still Bram had not budged.

"So it seems." Her throat closed up, and she had no idea how she was going to force the next words out of her mouth. "He . . . also wants you to witness Lucan's Call."

"Bloody fucking bastard," he muttered, his grip tightening around her fingers. "No. I can't guarantee that I won't kill him if I have to watch you Bind to him."

"I understand." If their roles were reversed, Sabelle wasn't at all certain she could watch him pledge his life to another.

Ice sighed. "But to keep peace between you and your brother, I will try."

Her heart swelled with love again for this big selfless wizard. "I will never know a man as good as you, Isdernus."

"You have my heart always." Ice closed his eyes, frowned, the pressed his forehead to hers. They shared a breath, another hidden moment in time, then he eased away. "Let's go."

Ice led Sabelle from his bedroom, and she followed him down a winding hall filled with closed doors. At the intersection of two paths, he stopped at the entrance to an open room, an office of sorts with a cluttered desk, a worn brown sofa, threadbare rugs. A neglected layer of dust and air of hopelessness lingered.

Inside, Bram paced like a whirling dervish, his mad steps taking him across the room in a few short movements. Lucan perched on the edge of the sofa, watching with a pensive stare. Both gazes whipped to the front of the room when they appeared.

"It's well past dawn. You're late," Bram said tightly.

Ice clenched his fists at his sides. "Your sister is doing a great deal to save everyone's skin, and she doesn't need your harassment."

Bram's eyes narrowed. "Shut the door."

With a furious kick, Ice sent it slamming into the portal. "I've given you the roof over my head, the hope out of my soul, and the heart out of my chest. Don't ever ask me for anything again."

God, this was killing Ice as much as it was destroying her. Sabelle wished for the millionth time for a way to stop this parting, her mating to Lucan. But nothing had changed.

Bram sniffed at her. "You spent the night in his bed."

He hurled it like an accusation, and Sabelle felt her temper fry. "I spent it where I wished to, and it's none of your business how or with whom. I don't know what's happened to you since you awakened from Mathias's spell, but you're acting like a bullying prat. Be happy I'm here at all, and stop doing your utmost to make this unpleasant and humiliating."

Her brother rolled tense shoulders and raised a golden brow. "I seem in short supply of patience to curb my tongue or temper these days. For your sake, I will say no more. Speak the Renunciation to Rykard. Now."

Already? Bram's words crashed through her like a tornado, twisting away happiness and hope. She would be doing good for magickind, and that must be enough.

Hands shaking, she turned to Ice. She couldn't not look at him, couldn't dodge that green gaze that burned with love and regret and ultimate pain.

"You will remain a part of me, though I am . . ." *No part of you.* The words echoed in her head, but she could not open her mouth to speak them, to lie. Her lips parted. *No part of you.* The only thing that emerged was a sob. She curled her arms around herself and clutched her middle, trying to keep the pain, so much like acid, from spilling into every corner of her aching heart.

Impossible.

Ice stepped closer, brushed her hair from her face. "Deep breath, princess. You can do it."

"I can't!" Anger and futility raced through her. "I don't know how to break my own heart. I can't stand the thought that I'm breaking yours. That you'll never look at me again the way you're looking at me right now, as if I'm your whole world. I can't bear thinking that I'd have no right to simply take your hand in mine."

"Sabelle!" Bram barked. "Renounce him. Every moment you waste is a moment Mathias could be worming deeper into the Council and finding new ways to murder or enslave innocents."

"Don't you think I *know* that?" she shouted. "When have I ever failed to do my duty? I won't fail you now, either. But I won't ever forget your threat to disclaim me. I won't ever forgive the glee on your face as you tear me from the man I love."

"That's enough!" Bram wedged between her and Ice, shoving the other wizard away from her. "Have you forgotten that your future mate sits here? The last thing he wants to hear is you profess love for another, Sabelle."

Lucan sucked in a breath and rose from the sofa. "Stop, Bram. Just . . . stop. I'd wondered before how deep your sister's attachment for Rykard is, but now . . ." He shook his head. "One of the worst things I've ever endured was pouring out my devotion to Anka, trying to persuade her to be with me, when her heart now seems to be with . . . another." He gave a bitter laugh. "How big a fool would I be to make the same mistake with Sabelle?"

She gasped. What was he saying?

Bram whirled on him. "Nonsense! Do you think I should just give her to him? Give away one of your best political advantages?"

"No, friend. I am saying that I will not Call to her while there's another in her heart. No matter how much I like and respect her, even desire her beauty, she and I both know that I will never love her as Ice does. And the bond of the Call aside, I will never replace him in her heart."

Cursing, Bram raced across the floor. "This is war! Sacrifices must be made —"

"Don't speak to me of sacrifices!" Lucan snarled. "I lost the mate of my heart fighting for this cause, and live each day with the fact that she was tortured mercilessly as a means to weaken me, us. What have you given up? From here, it looks like you've merely used the war to grow your power."

Sabelle blinked, her mouth gaping open. Lucan was brutally honest with Bram, his best chum. And he'd said he would not have her. Though a surprise, his declaration made sense. Anka was, even now, sleeping in Shock's bed. Lucan knew vast pain.

"Bloody hell! Mathias could be consolidating his power, talking to Blackbourne and Spencer or any of the others and swaying the vote. We need to name a candidate today."

"I will agree to the nomination to fill MacKinnett's empty seat. I only say that, perhaps, we try to sway the Council without Sabelle as my mate."

Bram paused, tapping his toe impatiently. "Your nomination is far more likely to be rejected."

Lucan shrugged. "Then we will find another to nominate. But I will not Call to your sister."

Hope welling from Sabelle's every crevice and corner. She sent Lucan a watery stare. "Thank you."

A half smile lifted the corner of his mouth. "You could not speak the words to Renounce Ice. You certainly weren't going to be able to Bind to me. You *should* thank me. I saved you a great deal of stuttering, I suspect."

Relief and joy washed over her with all the explosive power of an emotional bomb. A hot wash of tears flooded her eyes. "I've no doubt."

She flung herself against Lucan, hugged him like the friend and big brother he was to her. Absently, he rubbed her back, then set her away, watching Ice with a cautious stare.

"Think about what you're doing," Bram demanded, mouth agape. "If they reject your nomination, we'll have lost precious time we don't have. I can't—"

"Ask them unofficially," Sabelle suggested. "Besides, you have your vote. Tynan will assume the O'Shea seat now that his grandfather has passed to his nextlife, like his father. Surely, you can get Sterling to vote with you. At worst, you'll have a tie. But if you're able to find out now how, say, Spencer or Helmsley will react to a well-placed suggestion of Lucan as a candidate . . ."

"It isn't done. Candidates are nominated, presented, then voted upon. A tie would bring about consequences . . . No."

"A tie is still better than a defeat," she pointed out.

Bram started tapping his toe again, biting his lip. Nervous energy rolled off him, and vaguely Sabelle wondered where he'd acquired such vigor, given the fact his mate was still missing.

"Do you still have MacKinnett's mirror?"

"Duke, Marrok, and Olivia will have it with the Doomsday Diary, I expect."

"They arrived a bit past midnight." With a short nod, he hustled from the room.

Sabelle stood alone with Lucan and Ice, one in front of her looking on with resignation, the other behind her, his body pinging with confusion and hope. She wished she knew what to say, the right words. Lucan might have refused to Call to her, but that hardly meant Bram would welcome Ice into the family. If she Bound to him now, she would still lose her brother. And Sabelle didn't delude herself; whatever had overcome Bram since awakening from Mathias's ugly spell would goad him into disclaiming her, as he'd threatened. She almost didn't care. Almost. But he was her brother, and cutting ties with the last of her family unless she had to . . . No. Maybe time, patience, a bit of soothing of the ways between Ice and Bram would allow her brother to accept her beloved. Someday.

"I should thank you, as well," Ice said quietly to Lucan. "You spared me what Shock did not spare you, when it would have been so simple to use your anger and show me how truly heartbreaking losing your mate must feel."

And Lucan's was many times worse than anything Ice would have experienced, given that he'd spent over a century with Anka.

Lucan closed his eyes for a moment, pain awashing his features. "No man should feel that kind of black anguish. I certainly had no wish to feel it twice. Sabelle would be easy to fall in love with . . . and hard to forget."

Ice had no reply. He just stuck out his hand to Lucan. "I am indebted."

Lucan shook it, and Sabelle's heart caught. Maybe . . . the first step in Bram accepting Ice in her life was encouraging a friendship between him and her brother's best friend. At least it was another avenue to help pave the way.

Just then, Bram stormed into the office again, clutching both his mirror and MacKinnett's. "Duke had the foresight to retrieve my mirror from Olivia's gallery."

Plopping down on the worn brown sofa, he lifted the lid and touched his finger to one of the crests. A moment later, a cultured voice greeted him. Kelmscott Spencer. He oozed political correctness, was always in favor of the path of least resistance. Sabelle could tolerate him—in small doses. But she never made the mistake of trusting him. The whole line was a bit shifty, in her opinion.

"You're in one piece, chap? Heard whispers that you were under the weather."

"Indeed. The Anarki nearly killed me. And now Black-bourne has nominated their master to the Council. What the devil is he thinking?"

Spencer cleared his throat—a subtle cue that Bram's badgering was both heavy-handed and unwelcome. "I think, as he does, that it's perhaps time to entertain a different point of view."

"What? Murder and mayhem? Slaughtering of innocents? Raping and enslaving? Murdering Thomas MacKinnett and Clifden O'Shea?"

"We have only circumstantial proof that he's involved in any of the atrocities. He's assured us they are rogue factions of the Anarki, and he's working to bring them under his control again and direct their efforts to matters more productive for magickind."

"You believe him?"

Bram's incredulity made Sabelle wince. Where was the brother who'd been able to use finesse and cajoling to win his way? This bull-in-the-china-shop approach would get him nothing but ignored and discredited.

Sabelle raced across the room and wrested the mirror from his hands, sending him a warning glance. "I've no idea what's wrong with you, but if you want to make friends, you might try a kind word, dear brother."

He lunged at her, groping for the mirror. To her surprise, Ice and Lucan each grabbed a shoulder and pushed him back to the sofa.

"Let her try," Lucan muttered. "She can't be any worse than you."

Bram cursed, fought, then finally sighed and slammed back into the sofa, arms crossed over his chest. "Fine, then."

He wore petulant sorely, but Sabelle couldn't spare another moment to think about that.

"Hello, Kelmscott." She smiled at the older man's thin-faced image, framed in gray hair and thick sideburns.

"Sabelle, dear. Lovely as always. What's gotten into your brother?"

"Bad mood. I've threatened to throw him to a pack of wild dogs if he fails to improve."

Spencer laughed. "Always a bright girl."

"Thank you. I think he was trying, somewhat indelicately, to ask if you had received any assurances from Mathias that he was not behind the violence or had heard any plans from him on how to progress and repair magickind. Bram has been somewhat out of pocket, you see."

"Of course, of course." The he shook his head. "Not exactly. But Mathias has advised us of potential unrest among the Deprived. They are at their wit's end with the Social Order. He warns of potential civil war if they are not . . . accommodated."

In other words, Mathias issued a veiled threat that he would bring the brunt of the Deprived anger down on the Council if they did not nominate and elect him. They had chosen the coward's way out and thought that placating Mathias now would spare difficulty later. Fools.

Sabelle pasted on a smile. "That is a grave warning. But can Mathias honestly state that he can quell any Deprived unrest if the Social Order is changed or repealed? I simply wonder—"

"He is their champion, my dear," Kelmscott reminded.

To her side, Ice snorted and shook his head.

"Well, he claims to be, yes. But he is not one of them, so how can he know who the Deprived will truly follow or what they want?"

"I don't think we can afford, at this point, to simply ignore the potential danger that refusing him would bring. If he is deceiving us all and is behind the recent attacks, perhaps keeping him close and controlled would put a stop to all this nonsense."

A bold, if not stupid, statement that had Sabelle gritting her teeth. Spencer and Blackbourne, two peas in a pod, had both determined that giving Mathias an inch would please him. Neither saw that he would, in fact, take a mile.

"Would another candidate, perhaps, sway you? I wonder if, in trying times, it might be best to consolidate our power and deal with Deprived unrest in a rational, well-planned manner. Is giving in to the fear of violence that Mathias suggests truly going to end it?"

Spencer frowned. "Who are you recommending, girl?"

"Lucan MacTavish would sit well in that seat—"

"No," Spencer barked back immediately. "Blackbourne and I discussed this, knew Bram would push it. Sterling and his nephew . . . The family ties are too close."

"Sterling has his own heirs. The seat should never pass down through Lucan."

"Perhaps not. But two MacTavish wizards on the same Council creates a potential impediment to fair voting on future issues."

Translation: the loss of power likely to result if the Mac-Tavish men created a voting bloc with Bram was something they would avoid at all costs. Shortsighted idiots.

"I see on your face that you're disappointed, Sabelle," Spencer said. "But I am quite set and speak for Blackbourne as well. The Council needs a change, and Lucan MacTavish would bring only more of the same."

Was it change they wanted, then? A smile curled the corners of her mouth, and she looked across the room to the three wizards watching, Bram with a watchful eyes, Lucan with more resignation, and Ice with a burgeoning grasp of the situation.

"A change. Excellent notion. If we're fearful of a Deprived uprising, which I completely understand, perhaps the way to show progress isn't to elect a Privileged who claims to represent one of them. Perhaps it would be better to actually nominate one of their own."

Spencer recoiled, his bushy gray brows forming a V over his prominent nose. "A Deprived, on the Council?"

"Indeed. Nothing would say change and progress to the Deprived more than that, and Mathias would have to champion that candidate if he truly favors their emancipation."

"Eh . . . Perhaps. We could discuss it. I'll talk to Blackbourne. We may be able to find someone . . ."

She glanced across the room at the three men again. Bram lunged up from the sofa. Lucan and Ice held him back once more while he grumbled and growled. After they subdued him, Ice looked at her once more and shook his head.

But she could see the hope on his face.

"I actually have someone in mind," she murmured. "Someone whose grandfather sat on the Council before the Social Order stripped him of his rank. Someone whose line is long, whose wishes to preserve magickind and peace are pure. Someone not terribly close to my brother."

"I see . . ." He looked genuinely intrigued, and hope curled inside Sabelle again. "I would be very interested."

"How would you feel about Isdernus Rykard?"

CHAPTER FIFTEEN

THE MOMENT SABELLE ENDED the connection with Spencer, Bram shook free and bolted to his feet, tearing across the room toward her. "Are you out of your fucking mind?"

As Ice grabbed Bram's arm again, holding him away from his sister, he wondered the same thing. Where had Sabelle gotten the mad idea to have Bram nominate him for the Council? He'd be damned before he asked Bram for help again, and Ice had no doubt the other wizard would cut off his right arm before lifting a finger to help him.

Sabelle turned on her brother with flashing blue eyes and pocketed Bram's transcast mirror. "Think with something besides the fury running your brain now. Blackbourne and Spencer are afraid. Mathias is more than they can take on, and they know it. They hope that, by appearing to be an ally, he will not turn his violence on them."

"Idiots."

"Obviously. But in this situation, the best I could do was use their arguments against them. They're afraid of a Deprived uprising because the group has no Council representation?"

"It's rubbish, Sabelle. They're afraid only of losing their own power. They've fought me since the day I stepped into the seat. They know change is coming, and that I will bring it."

"Of course. But see the beauty of this plan: If you nominate Ice, who should pacify the very people they claim to want to soothe, and Blackbourne and Spencer still vote for Mathias, you've boxed them into a corner. They have to appear to support evil. In time, that will lessen their influence. And we both know that Mathias will kill them once their usefulness is at an end. Either way, through their cowardice, they've signed their own death warrants."

The fight left Bram then, and Ice released him. Not that he could keep hold of the other wizard when Sabelle had shocked him all over again. He'd always known she was clever, but her mastery of politics astounded him. She understood the Councilmen well, what motivated them, what they wanted and feared. She'd found a way to use their lies against them. Pride burst from his chest . . . even as he knew he would have to decline her suggestion.

"Sabelle." He crossed the room and took her hand in his. "Bram was right to refuse to nominate me after Gailene's death. I'm . . . not Council material. They all think I'm mad. I don't hold my temper well. My birth alone will ensure they never listen—"

"That's crap," she interrupted. "You're strong and resilient. Smart. Once they get to know you, they'll learn you're not mad. Maybe they need a temper or two to shake them up."

She believed that? Despite being born Deprived, Ice had never felt less than equal until Bram's refusal and rejection all those years ago. He remembered that moment of shame, the bile sliding down his throat. The sting of humiliation. He'd never forgiven his former friend for that.

Could he get into political bed with someone he'd long regarded as an enemy? Did he have a choice?

"The Council elders have grown far too comfortable running the show," Sabelle pointed out. "They will listen to you *if* you and Bram learn to work together, vote together. Along with Sterling and Tynan, you four will control the Council. You will set the tone and standard. The policies."

Ice drank in her words, and they swam in his head. A Deprived who'd been born without a future suddenly becoming one of magickind's seven most powerful wizards? He'd never craved power, only wanted it to stop Mathias from spreading evil. Now . . . even if he and Bram could tolerate each other, what could he contribute to the Council? Bram had accused him of fixation on everything anti-Mathias. What had changed? What did he really know about governing magickind?

Sabelle turned to her brother. "With my suggestion of Ice, I've given you everything you wanted in the way of Council power: majority control. All you have to do is bury the hatchet with Ice."

Bram said nothing for long moments, merely stared at his sister with a mix of awe, anger, and exasperation. Ice related to the other wizard's feelings.

"The Social Order doesn't allow Ice to occupy a Council seat."

"It's crap and should be amended. You know it."

Bram shrugged noncommittally. Ice wondered what the devil was running through the other wizard's head.

"There is Helmsley Camden's vote to consider." Bram changed tactics. "He may agree to having Lucan on the Council and give us the necessary fourth vote."

Sabelle rolled her eyes. "Doubtful, dear brother. Clifden O'Shea refused to compromise his vote, and Mathias killed him for it. Why do you think Camden is still alive?"

Because he'd sold out. Sabelle was completely right. Again, clever, clever girl. Ice had always respected her, but today, his esteem for her raised by leaps and bounds.

"Think, Bram," she went on. "Blackbourne will vote for

Mathias. He nominated the bastard, and not voting for him would be bad form. But we have a chance swaying Spencer, perhaps, by convincing him that there's no love lost between you and Ice."

Not a hard sell, really.

Bram scrubbed a hand across his face. "Perhaps. I think you should let me talk to Camden, just in case. We can offer him protection in exchange for a vote for Lucan."

In the corner, Lucan cleared his throat. "Nominate Ice. It's a better move. Sabelle is right."

Whirling on his friend, Bram's glare shouted that Lucan's surprise statement was something he expected out of a Judas. "You're giving up, just like that?"

"No, deferring to the better plan. Think past your anger and that damned pride of yours. You and Ice don't see eye to eye. You both felt betrayed by each other. It was two centuries ago. If we're to prevent bloodshed going forward, we must use our heads."

Easy for Lucan to say; he hadn't been stabbed in the back. Given his scowl, Bram clearly didn't like Lucan's assertion any more than Ice. But damn it, the bloke was right. While Ice hardly believed he would make a stellar Councilman, for the sake of magickind and Gailene's memory, he would try.

"Thank you, Lucan." Sabelle nodded in the other man's direction, then turned back to her brother. "To confirm my suspicions, I'll contact Camden and see where his loyalties lie. I'm sure it's in self-preservation, but—"

"I'll contact him," Bram argued.

Sabelle raised a golden brow at him. "So you can conduct the same sort of delicate conversation you tried with Spencer? I think, dear brother, that until you learn to control your temper again, you should limit your conversations with others."

Raking his hand through his hair, Bram turned away with stiff shoulders. But he nodded.

"Good," she said. "I'm famished. Breakfast anyone?"

Lucan was quick to respond. "If you're cooking, yes."

Everything inside Ice demanded he follow Sabelle, keep Lucan far from her, be the only wizard to share her morning, her table . . . He pushed it down. *Logic*. Lucan wasn't going to Call to her. And as long as the others on the Council believed he was not Bram's ally, Sabelle could not be his.

Reeling under a stab of pain, he sent a long stare to his beloved. Something in her face, the pleading in her eyes, told him that she wanted him to extend an olive branch to Bram and let the healing begin.

His stomach balled up, a knot too big to have swallowed. Be the first to apologize to the "friend" who had slammed the door on his last beacon of hope to avenge his sister? Who had put him in his proper place with a few well-placed words centuries ago, then again when he'd Called to his sister? The wizard standing between him and happiness even now?

Sabelle asked much of him.

She and Lucan disappeared, closing the door behind them. The finality of the *click* resounded in the cavernous space between him and Bram. Ice stared at his nemesis. What the hell could he say? Virtually anything would be construed as a way of making his way onto the Council or into Sabelle's life. Both attempts would be spurned.

Bloody hell, he hadn't tried to use his diplomatic skills in nearly two hundred years. Once, he'd been promising in politics, pontificating, speech making. He'd let rage and hopelessness bury the promise. Now, as then, one man stood between him and salvation.

Shit.

"This is bloody awkward," Ice muttered.

Bram's gaze zipped in his direction. "Indeed. I don't like it."

"Me, either. Your sister is very clever."

He laughed. "Truer words are rarely spoken."

Silence ensued again, and Ice's thoughts raced. Once conversation between them had been easy, friendly, full of joking gibes and pranks. For years, his grief for Gailene had overshadowed nearly all feeling. But once he'd joined the Doomsday Brethren, that spirit of brotherhood he'd been missing had slammed him again with a different sort of sorrow. He believed in their cause, of course, but imagined that, as long as Bram led the charge, Ice would always be the outsider.

Sabelle, bless her, had given him a path to change it, perhaps. He couldn't stop to consider now what that meant for them. He had to focus on finding some way not to fuck it up.

"I . . . never thanked you for saving my sister," Bram said suddenly.

Those were the last words Ice ever expected to hear and they nearly knocked him over. "It was my privilege and pleasure. Whatever you think of my feelings for your sister, they are genuine. She is my heart, and I would give my life for hers."

Bram shrugged. "The issue now is MacKinnett's open Council post."

Which told Ice that Bram would not entertain notions of Sabelle Binding to his Call. Politics and necessity could blur lines of anger and enmity, but not love.

God, would he finally have everything he'd ever sought two hundred years ago, yet watch love slip through his grasp?

Fists clenched at his sides, Ice restrained the urge to grab Bram, shake some sense into him. Experience told him the harder he railed against Bram, the more the wizard would dig in his heels, and with this spell altering his temper and mood, Bram was more unpredictable than usual.

Someday, Sabelle. Someday . . . I will find a way to you.

He'd waited two hundred years to allow Gailene to rest peacefully for good. If he must, he'd wait another two hundred to have Sabelle in his arms again.

"It is," he agreed. "I want to be clear: I did not put this notion in Sabelle's head."

"No." Bram shook his head. "This was all Sabelle. I know the little minx." He rubbed the back of his neck. "I should probably thank her. It's a brilliant plan."

Bram's tone said that admission was a damn hard one to make, and Ice repressed a smile. "I find she's quite full of those."

"Always has been. From the time I met her, she was full of mischief. Had a way about her. Her siren beauty, I suppose."

Personally, Ice thought it was her inner light and goodness. "I'm certain that didn't hurt."

With methodical steps, Bram crossed the floor and sat on the sofa. "If I agree to nominate you, we must have an understanding in place."

Of course. Bram's terms and conditions. Ice swallowed a fresh ball of anger. He shouldn't have expected the last few moments to erase two centuries of distrust. "Spit it out."

"I need your voting loyalty. Not on every issue. I'm not seeking a puppet, but on matters of Mathias and magickind's safety—"

"Yes." That agreement was easy, since they shared the same views. "Provided the votes are not used to continually suppress the Deprived. Change must come about."

Bram hesitated, then nodded. "By changing laws, we'll not only do what's right, but take away Mathias's 'cause' and leave him without a base of power. The Deprived will have a new leader in you, one who doesn't feed off violence and death."

Crowning him a new leader seemed far-fetched to Ice, but if Bram needed to believe that, fine. Or maybe Bram saw something he couldn't? Either way . . . "Then we're agreed."

"Yes." Then the other wizard's blue stare zipped up to him.

Ice swallowed. Now the hard part of the conversation. *Please, don't ask me give up Sabelle.*

"My sister . . . The issue of your Call must be addressed."

"That's between your sister and me."

"I'm still her guardian," Bram snarled.

"She is a grown woman, a very bright one, as we've both established. Allow her to know her own mind and heart."

Bram shook his head. "If she mates with you, I must still disclaim her. Sabelle can be mated elsewhere for better political advantage, a stronger voting bloc on the Council. I will continue negotiations with Kelmscott Spencer. His son, Rye, would make a good candidate—"

"You son of a bitch! You're negotiating your sister's happiness for your political advantage, and your rejection will crush her. When you pulled her from her mother as a child because she was all but trying to sell Sabelle, you didn't do it out of the goodness of your heart or concern for what would become of the child, did you? You bought her from her mother so that you could use the fact Merlin's blood runs in your veins to greater political advantage. You've waited and bided your time for this day. Her happiness means nothing to you."

"I do this because I am convinced you are the last man in the world who could make her happy."

Ice knew he should shut up, stop arguing. But he couldn't let it be. He wanted Sabelle far more than a seat on the Council. Gailene, bless her, would have understood. "Why? Because I was born to a lower class in your mind? Because I haven't your connections?"

"Of course. What can you give her but misery?"

Ice clenched his jaw so tightly he thought it would snap. "I would *always* put her needs above my own, something you've clearly never done."

"That's my offer. Take it or leave it."

"Rescind your threat to disclaim Sabelle for mating with me. *Then* I will accept your nomination."

Bram's eyes narrowed. "You're in no position to negotiate."

Oh, but he was. Ice saw that now. "Then find another Deprived you know will vote with you in the next few hours and nominate him. I'll be with Sabelle, trying to convince her that I'll make her sublimely happy, regardless of your desertion."

Bram lunged off the sofa at him. "You bastard!"

Ice waved a hand between them and built a solid, frozen sheet between them. "Rescind it."

A calculating light entered those sharp blue eyes. "If you are elected, I will. That's my best offer."

Closing his eyes, Ice felt as if he'd negotiated with the devil. Bram would nominate Ice, and if elected, perhaps he and Sabelle could find a clear path to a happy future. Though nothing was assured, it was more than he'd dared to hope for.

"Deal. I give you fair warning: If I am elected, I will pursue your sister relentlessly until she Binds to me."

"Even if I don't disclaim her, she is loyal to her only brother, her only family. Don't be surprised if she remains so."

* * *

A few hours later, everyone under Ice's roof assembled in the dining hall. Ice sat at the head of his table, Sabelle to his right. He couldn't touch her, but he could feel her near, and it would be enough. For now.

Bram sat on his left, the transcast mirror he used to communicate with the Council on the big mahogany table in front of him, closed. Sterling and Tynan sat just down from Bram. They could not appear too chummy to the others, but recent events and the horrors of two Councilmen's murders created a bond between them that could not be ignored. Tynan's fresh grief for his grandfather settled into the hollows of his face, already deep with sorrow for his love, Auropha, murdered by Mathias several months past.

Across from the Councilmen, Raiden Wolvesey sat with a mischievous smile after inquiring to Ice about local witches who might be up for a bit of company. Ice wondered what sort of warrior he could possibly make when he never took anything seriously.

Bram clearly had the same notion. "Marrok, why don't you take Raiden and Ronan out for a bit of training? They're woefully behind."

Ronan smiled ruefully at his new mate, Kari, then kissed the pretty, petite blonde. Raiden just sighed. Marrok looked more than pleased to have new subjects to torment.

"I'll help," Caden volunteered, squeezing Sydney's hand on the way out.

The younger MacTavish seemed thrilled to have newer members of the group to rib. And the Wolvesey twins made such big, easy targets.

Lucan and Duke exchanged a glance and followed the group outside. Ice almost envied them. He'd rather have his arse kicked by one of Marrok's training exercises or practice his magical fighting skills with Duke than swallow down worry and wonder if his nomination would be rejected today and all would be lost.

Quietly, Sydney and Olivia cleared away the last of their evening meal and headed to the kitchen. Ice sat alone with Sabelle and the three Councilmen. They could afford to put off the nomination no longer. With every minute that ticked by, Blackbourne and possibly Spencer had more time to devise a counterstrategy that would play into Mathias's hands.

"Ready?" Bram asked with a glance around the table.

Ice resisted the stress-induced urge to vomit. Normally, he'd ignore what a bunch of Privileged pricks thought of him, but now . . . Too much was at stake. So for Gailene, for Sabelle and the future, he swallowed and held it in.

Sterling and Tynan both nodded, then Bram's stare fell on him. Ice felt Sabelle at his side, her reassuring presence. He didn't even have to look at her to know that she would catch him if he fell.

"Ready." Ice heard the growl in his voice and sighed.

Relax. How the hell would he possibly pass the nomination process if he already sounded as if he might take someone's head off?

With a nod, Bram opened his mirror, touched a few crests, then waved his hand. It expanded to something the size of a wall mirror. Ice reared back, surprised, though he supposed he shouldn't have been. They were, after all, magical. But not many saw the inner workings of the Council. Even during the time he'd studied with Bram as his mentor, he'd never attended any Council meeting.

A moment later, each Councilman's face appeared on the reflective surface of the mirror beside their crest. Blackbourne with his jet hair and jowls, pale skin, and beady, greedy eyes. Ice had disliked him at once, and held no illusions that the man would ever vote for or with him.

Spencer's familiar gray face popped up. The elder looked tired, almost defeated. And that was a damn sight better than Helmsley Camden, who looked positively petrified. A moment later, Ice saw why, as Mathias's golden, almost feline face appeared beside the muttonchopped elder. Camden, never long on courage by all accounts, had the most notorious wizard of the millennium sitting beside him. Ice knew immediately how his vote would fall.

Damn it!

Blackbourne convened the meeting, and began by addressing Tynan.

"Your grandfather's loss is a blow to us all," the elder intoned. "His service to magickind was respected, and he will be missed. May he rest in peace."

"Thank you." Tynan O'Shea said the words politely, but Ice saw the desire to spit at the disingenuous bastard.

A few short words later, Tynan bowed his head and accepted his role on the Council.

Some wizards prayed their whole lives to be noticed by the Council, much less considered for a position. To be in Tynan's place—hell, his own, Ice knew—should engender some reaction. Tynan simply laced his fingers and rested his hands on the table, looking impassive.

"And now to the business of filling MacKinnett's empty seat," Blackbourne went on. "I nominate Mathias d'Arc. He originates from a once-prominent family. No one can dispute that he is a wizard of great talents with the ability to inspire loyalty in others. That he's returned and is determined to do good and bring change for magickind's cause will benefit us, particularly since he may be the only one capable of quelling any pending Deprived uprising. Anyone opposed?"

Bram gritted his teeth, but nothing else gave away his disgust. Sterling and Tynan also remained silent. Denouncing Mathias now would do no good. He met the formal qualifications. His mettle would only be tested in the event of a tie as a result of the official vote. His character . . . only time would prove Blackbourne woefully wrong—after it was too late.

"Splendid," Blackbourne continued into the silence. "Let Mathias d'Arc's name be registered in the scrolls. If there are no more nominees, then—"

"I nominate Isdernus Rykard."

Bram's voice rang loud, clear. It sent a shiver across Ice's skin. He felt everything from surprise to outrage pouring from the others. Or maybe that was his own nervousness.

Blackbourne reared back. "Rykard, the mad one?"

"If it makes one mad to fight against Anarki who killed his sister, then yes."

"He's not Privileged," Camden argued. "He does not meet the qualifications."

"I propose a change to the Social Order, then. How can we effectively govern all when only one class is represented among us? If Mr. d'Arc is correct, and the Deprived are planning an uprising, might we not quell their anger by nominating one of their own?"

"This is quite abrupt," Spencer argued.

"So is replacing a Councilman who's been brutally murdered in his own home." Bram sent him a tight smile.

"Eh . . . indeed." Spencer's shoulders sagged.

"Honestly, I see no reason to refuse. It would be bad press during these difficult times if word reached the Deprived that we refused to consider a change in the Social Order to possibly include one of their own. Imagine the fever to rise up then."

"I assure you," Mathias spoke suddenly. "I can quiet them."

"The way you have the 'rogue' elements of the Anarki, sir?"

Bram's question was perfectly pointed. And with it, he took his life in his hands. Neatly, Bram had boxed Blackbourne and Spencer into a corner.

"Clearly not," Tynan added. "Or my grandfather would be with us."

With that, Bram called for a vote. Given that they had no logical argument, as they were suddenly espousing change, though they'd eschewed it for centuries, the Council elders all agreed, some clearly more reluctant than others, to change the Social Order to allow Deprived Council representation.

"Any other objections to Rykard's nomination?" Bram challenged.

Dead silence.

Ice swallowed a lump of nerves. A blast of amazement *whooshed* over him. The nomination to the Council seat that should have been his two hundred years ago was now in his grasp. It should have been sweet victory that the very man responsible for his defeat years ago was now his unwilling champion, but he couldn't spare a thought for petty irony now. Revenge wasn't sweet—or even his motive. Gailene's memory and Sabelle's love . . . nothing else mattered. Putting the past to rest. Getting his future on track.

One step closer . . .

"Shall we schedule the official vote for, say, three days hence at my estate?" Blackbourne queried. "That will give each of us time to carefully consider our votes."

And give Mathias a time and location where he could devise a plan to kill every Council member and instantly rule all of magickind? Give everyone a glimpse of his magical signature that would display to all the fact he had issued a Call to Sabelle?

Ice gaped across the table from Bram, ready to stand and protest. The other three wizards at the table beat him to it.

"I think times may be too critical to wait," Bram argued. "Everyone is present, and I see little reason for the delay."

Heart stuttering, Ice listened as the others grumbled their agreement. That suddenly, it was time to vote.

"I vote Mathias d'Arc," Blackbourne, the eldest, said, not surprisingly.

"As do I," Spencer chimed in.

Bloody hell. Ice had held out some hope, no matter how little, that Spencer had been swayed to vote with them. But clearly not.

"I vote Rykard," Sterling MacTavish told the others.

"Become Rion's lapdog, have you?" Spencer taunted.

"It's better than being Blackbourne's bitch."

Despite the tension in the room, Ice laughed. He'd never known the MacTavish clan well, any of them, always avoiding them because of their associations with the Rions. But now, he somewhat liked the outspoken wizards.

"I vote Mathias." Camden's voice shook as he entered his vote, and no wonder, with the evil man himself sitting there.

Again, Ice wished he could pour himself through the little mirror and attack Mathias, make him twist with pain and writhe in agony as he deserved. Instead, he clenched his fists and glanced at Sabelle for support. She smiled and nodded.

"One more vote for Mathias d'Arc decides it," Blackbourne reminded.

As if anyone needed to hear that.

"He won't have my vote," Bram vowed. "Rykard will represent the Deprived well. He knows them, will listen, and can carry our message to them, smooth relations, as it were."

Blackbourne snorted. "Your opinion. This is not the time for commentary. O'Shea? Keep in mind that a vote for Rykard sends us to a dreadful tie that should be avoided at all costs. No Council has ever had to enforce a challenge to dispute a tie."

Tynan cleared his throat. "Well, I'm sorry to say, then, that my first official vote as a Council member will bring about something dreadful, but my vote is for Rykard."

"Bloody stupid—" Blackbourne cursed, then huffed, as if getting himself under control. "Well, then. Tomorrow, an hour past dawn, both candidates will present themselves at the gate of my estate for the challenge. God help you both."

With that, Blackbourne severed the connection. The others followed suit. Ice paused, unease skittering through him. "Challenge?"

"Indeed." He exhaled, looked at Sabelle with regret, then shook his head. "I never imagined Blackbourne would actually enforce this. I thought for certain he would devise something else. It's his right as Council elder to do so."

"But he chose not to, so what happens next?" Sabelle demanded.

Bram swallowed. "Tomorrow morning, you will appear at Blackbourne's estate as instructed. You will battle with Mathias there for the right to the Council seat."

"What sort of battle?" Her eyes narrowed. "What do you mean?"

Bram sucked in a sharp breath, then looked at Ice with apology. "A battle that ends when one of you surrenders or dies."

CHAPTER SIXTEEN

"YOU'RE NOT GOING, SABELLE." Bram reiterated as if that was the end of the conversation, then sipped coffee.

Predawn gray gathered outside, and Sabelle felt the internal *tick-tock* of time passing down to the hour when the challenge for the disputed Council seat would take Ice away from her—possibly forever. Her gut cramped into a thousand knots, and she yearned for three minutes alone with Ice. To touch him, reassure herself. She wanted to Bind to him so badly. All night, she'd considered doing just that. But almost as if he'd known what was in her mind, her brother had monopolized Ice since the Council vote, discussing the challenge, developing a strategy, analyzing Mathias's potential weaknesses. Now, time slipped through her fingers, and the panic that she might never see Ice alive again froze her.

"You're not," Ice agreed with Bram, approaching from behind, coffee in hand.

She turned to Ice, close enough to smell the musky-pine scent of him . . . yet so far away. "It's taking all I've got not to plead with you to call off this challenge and withdraw your nomination. If I had known when I suggested your name what this fight would come to . . ."

Ice's face closed up. "I can't withdraw. Mathias can't be allowed to help govern magickind. I will not fail Gailene by taking the coward's way out."

Even at the expense of your life? But yes, she understood that he valued his sister's memory more. That, after two centu-

ries of grief, he needed this closure, this revenge. "I know, so
I've said nothing. But I beg you, do not leave me here to bite
my nails and wonder. Let me come with you and help."

"Only Councilmen and candidates attend the challenges."
Bram shrugged as if that settled the matter.

"Along with their mate or source of energy," she pointed
out. At their shocked expressions, she smiled. "Yes, I had a
little chat with Sterling last night. Most helpful."

Bram cursed. "Too clever by half."

Ice sat in the chair beside her at the long table and shook
his head. "I won't put you anywhere near Mathias. I know
the atrocities he's capable of. The energy I have will be suf-
ficient."

"To fight off one of the most powerful dark wizards ever?
Look at the spell he felled Bram with. It nearly killed him."

"Because I was unprepared," her brother protested. "He
caught me off guard. I had no time to put up a defense. Ice
will shield himself."

Sabelle banged her fist on the table. "Stop mollycoddling
me and use your brains! If Ice has to fight a prolonged battle,
no one can help him but me."

"I'll siphon and use the anger of others."

An ineffective energy source, and they all knew it. The
power he gleaned from another's anger would waver quickly
once he and Mathias were locked in mortal combat. But
pointing out the obvious wasn't working. Both men were too
protective, thinking of her, not the greater good. She had to
change tactics.

Facing Bram, she leaned across the table. "What happens
if Ice falters and loses this challenge because he had insuf-
ficient energy?"

"He won't." Bram ground his jaw.

"But if he did, what would happen?"

Sabelle knew the answer already, but wanted to hear Bram admit it. "Mathias would win the Council seat."

"He would." She nodded. "And then . . . ?"

Bram stared into his coffee cup, lifted a shoulder. "No one knows for certain."

"But we can guess, can't we? At best, he'll ramrod policies through using Blackbourne, Spencer, and Camden, who are all either corrupt or afraid of their bloody shadows. None of that will benefit magickind. At worst, he'll start destroying his opposition, likely beginning with you."

"He won't succeed." Fire burned in Bram's blue eyes.

"You don't know that."

"Well, I—"

"You don't!" she insisted. "And what happens if Mathias loses this battle for the Council? What will he do then?"

Her brother paused, frowned, looked across the table at Ice. "No one knows."

"But one thing we *do* know is that he would have to abandon hope of controlling the Council, at least for now. If Ice wins, you'll have a four-vote majority. If he loses, you'll have chaos and likely bloodshed. Given the stakes, it seems foolish to merely hope that Ice has enough energy for this fight. You and I know I am the only one who can serve him."

Bram frowned, gritted his teeth.

"I will prevail," Ice vowed.

She reached out to him and grabbed his hand. "You'll want to, but consider that Mathias can't *do* anything to harm me, not with so many Councilmen looking on."

"Don't be certain of that," rumbled a new voice from the doorway.

Sabelle looked up to find Shock standing with arms crossed over his chest, decked out in his usual leather, sunglasses, and bad attitude.

"Who the devil let you in here?" Ice exploded from his seat.

Sabelle stayed him with a light touch to his arm. "I did. I rang him earlier—"

"Are you trying to help Mathias?" Bram's voice boomed off the cavern walls. "Tell him where we're hiding now that he's destroyed my house?"

"Piss off!" she shouted. "I'm looking for help where I can."

"I don't have much for you," Shock said. "You can count on Mathias having a plan and discounting the rules, if need be."

"Exactly. Which is why I think we need to be smart and prepared."

"Who's to say that he won't take every word you say back to Mathias?" Bram stood. "How do you know Shock isn't a traitor?"

Shock shrugged. "You don't. But I can hear in your thoughts that you and Ice have discussed the challenge and battle tactics all night. You think you're prepared. Don't be surprised if he does something . . . unpredictable."

"Which is why I think we should be prepared to do the same," Sabelle added.

"I don't trust you." Bram growled at Shock.

"I don't care." Shock turned from him, then looked at Ice. "If you want to emerge from this alive, don't come prepared to fight. Come prepared to fight dirty."

Shock turned and headed for the door when Bram lunged at the mysterious warrior's back. "Whose bloody side are you on? Why come here at all, unless it's to spy on us for Mathias?"

"Do you really have time to worry about my motives?" Shock shot back, then headed for the door without another word.

Silence fell, then Ice and Bram both faced her, wearing almost identical questioning expressions. *What the hell were you thinking?* they asked. About the future. About Ice living to see the next sunrise.

"Why call Shock?" Bram barked. "Of all people, the one we can least trust—"

"You don't know that. I think he may have aided Ice's escape from Mathias's dungeons."

Bram paused, then turned a glare to Ice, who shrugged.

"It's possible. I don't recall much, except that he left my chains loose and my door open. Whether by oversight or design . . . I don't know."

"Right now, Shock's loyalty isn't my concern," Sabelle reiterated. "Ice is. I must be there in case he needs me. Bram, we can't afford to let him lose energy and thus the challenge."

Her brother sighed, worked his jaw. "I don't like it."

"No," Ice protested. "There is no force on earth that will induce me to put you in that bastard's path."

His protective nature had often been both tender and sigh-worthy. Now, she just found it exasperating. "There is no force on earth that will induce me to stay away. Come prepared to fight dirty, Shock said."

"I will fight and be watchful for Mathias's treachery, but I cannot break the rules. The Councilmen in favor of Mathias will be looking for any way to discredit me. I will not cheat."

Sabelle swallowed. Yes, Ice had a noble streak an ocean wide. He would not want to win any way but fairly. Unfortunately, Mathias wouldn't be quite so picky.

She wished that solving the matter was as simple as wrapping her arms around Ice and using her love and siren abilities to dissuade him from fighting, but Ice was relatively resistant to her gift of emotional suggestion.

*S*he was going with Ice. Already, she was devising a scheme. And she would be prepared to fight dirty.

Fog rose in eerie drifts, curling around the huge wrought iron gates of Blackbourne's estate. The Council elder and his family thought everyone else beneath them and shut themselves off from the world. Ice wondered briefly if a Deprived had ever crossed these gates as anything more than a servant.

His insides knotted as he, Bram, Tynan, Sterling, and Sabelle all sent their magical calls requesting admission. Moments later, the gates slowly parted. Blackbourne himself walked across the brown grass, through the ghostly white mists.

"You've arrived." He looked over the group with a sharp eye. "I wondered, Rion, why you brought your sister, but I see from Rykard's signature that he Called to her. You claimed he was no ally of yours."

Bram stiffened. "I can hardly stop him from babbling pointless words. You'll notice that my sister has not Bound to him. Nor will she."

"But—"

"Carlisle," Sabelle stepped forward and wrapped her hand around his arm.

Ice wanted to snap something in half at the sight, but swallowed the urge to do violence and forced himself to watch, listen.

"Do you imagine that my brother is eager to see me mated to Rykard?"

Ice's pride stung. Yes, he understood that it was in everyone's best interest for Blackbourne to believe there was no chance that he and Sabelle would unite. But the careless ploy still made him eager to prove to everyone else that Sabelle was, and would always be, his.

"Eh . . . no."

"Bram is still my guardian, so . . . Is your son Sebastian still unmated?"

"Indeed." Blackbourne relaxed, smiled at her.

Sabelle returned the gesture and Icc gritted his teeth. He wanted to kiss her in front of them all, put his arms around her, and demand she Bind to him instead of intimating that she'd welcome attention from Sebastian Blackbourne.

"The others are on the lawns behind the house," the elder directed. "Come with me."

Had Spencer, Camden, and Mathias all appeared together? Battle lines had been drawn, he supposed. Purposely, he hadn't spent a great deal of time thinking about exactly what magic he'd use to defeat Mathias. He'd prayed last night, asked himself what would most set Gailene's memory to rest, hoped that he could find an honorable way to win this seat, and someday, Sabelle.

Fear jangled inside him. Not fear of Mathias, actually. Fear of failure, of letting Gailene down again, of leaving this battle unfinished. Of never holding Sabelle again. Fates too terrible to contemplate.

All too soon, Blackbourne led them to the back of the massive stone estate. The bloody rambling place looked centuries old and had so many chimneys that Icc lost count. Windows everywhere. The smell of old power and corruption clung to every brick.

At the back of the large manor, Camden and Spencer sat sipping tea and eating scones, as if they hadn't a care in the world. And at the moment, they didn't. Who would believe Mathias could lose a battle to a common wizard?

Shoving the thought aside, Ice rounded the corner, which brought the rest of the back lawn into view. He braced himself for the jolt of anger, the urge to kill. But nothing could stop the visceral need that pumped through his body when he laid eyes on the wizard leaning indolently against a wooden pillar with a deceptively youthful appearance, golden hair whipping in the wind, looking somewhere between absent and bored.

Mathias d'Arc.

Ice fisted his hands so tightly his arms trembled. The corners of Mathias's mouth lifted in amusement. Smug. The son of a bitch had gleefully taken Gailene's innocence and life, then acted as if Ice's anger entertained him. How dearly he looked forward to the opportunity to kill the bastard. He might fail—and miserably—but Mathias would feel pain before he went down.

"My esteemed opponent. We meet again." Mathias eased away from the pillar, mischievous blue eyes clapped on him as he approached, hand outstretched. "Your last visit ended very abruptly, indeed. Let's see if we can settle in for a nice long . . . chat, shall we?"

No fucking way he would talk to Mathias more than necessary or shake his hand.

Bram intervened, ignoring Mathias and leading Ice to the far side of the lawn where a big concrete slab sat, surrounded by something that looked like a plastic bubble.

"A force field," Bram supplied. "The elders, Tynan, and I erected it a moment ago. Whatever spell either of you throw, it should not penetrate those walls and unwittingly hit someone else."

Slowly, Ice nodded. Right. Hitting someone with a blinding spell or unleashing a corporeal form of their inner demon would be bad, indeed. Best to keep the slaughter contained.

"And you must be Miss Rion," Mathias drawled from behind him. "Pity we've never met. A very lovely girl, indeed. After today's challenge, your brother and I should be working together more. It would be my pleasure to know you better."

Ice whirled on Mathias. To hell with waiting for the challenge; he wanted to fight now. Bram clapped a hand on his shoulder. Tynan darted over and grabbed the other.

"Steady. He's taunting you."

Bram was right, Ice knew. But he should have tied Sabelle to a chair—whatever necessary—to keep her away from the challenge ring. The thought of Mathias putting even a finger on Sabelle made his stomach curdle and rage pound.

"It seems I've made your would be mate a bit jealous," Mathias said in mock dismay. "Oh dear."

"We have nothing to say to each other, Mr. d'Arc," Sabelle told him.

Sensing Mathias on the move again, Ice tugged and pulled at Bram's and Tynan's grasp until he could see Sabelle. She held her own, chin lifted, an expression of well-practiced hauteur on her face. Even in jeans, trainers, and a fuzzy sweater, she managed to look like a princess.

Mathias sent her a false pout. "Has Rykard told you terrible lies about me?"

"I don't believe so, no. Since I saw the aftermath of your attack on Thomas MacKinnett's household, I'm inclined to think that what I've heard is fairly accurate."

With an affronted expression, Mathias sauntered closer to Sabelle. "Dear lady, you wound me. Rogue factions within the Anarki, I assure you."

"It took you no time at all after the discovery of Thomas's death to finagle a nomination for this Council seat."

"Indeed. I feel quite bad about the old chap's fate. How better to control these unauthorized elements of my former society than to make new governing policies and enforce rules?"

"By telling them to stop killing in the first place." Sabelle smiled sweetly. "Then there's the fact I saw the nasty business you performed on Ice's back with a whip."

Something in Mathias's eyes shifted, and Ice's heart dropped to his knees.

"Be careful what you accuse me of, Miss Rion. I do know more than one very intriguing way to stop a pretty mouth like yours from talking."

That was it, all he could take. Ice shook free of Bram and Tynan and charged at Mathias. Sabelle's hand curled around his biceps as he stormed past, but she couldn't hold him back with her grip. Her voice, however, stopped Ice where he stood.

"Please. It serves no purpose but his to allow yourself to be provoked. You'll look bad to the Council and likely violate some rule about this challenge, besides. Don't forfeit before you've even begun."

It also served to tell Mathias exactly where he was weak, Ice knew: Sabelle. Mathias had the advantage of superior age, experience, and evil. In Ice's favor, he was bigger and more determined. If he could be the smarter of the two, that might tip the battle.

Ice took one deep breath, then another, swallowing his anger, internalizing it. The force of it wended through his body, down his arms and legs, into his fingers and toes.

"I'm fine," he told Sabelle.

She watched him, checking his expression. With a nod, she dropped her hand, stepped away, having sensed his deadly calm.

"Are we ready, gentlemen?" Blackbourne called.

As if this were a bloody croquet match. Ice resisted the urge to curse and nodded.

"Indeed," Mathias drawled. "Quite."

Blackbourne directed them to the challenge ring and its force field. With a wave of his hand, an arch appeared. The elder motioned them through it, inside. With a jaunty step, Mathias breezed by, turning to examine the clear structure from all directions. When he caught Sabelle's gaze, he waved. She looked away, and Mathias laughed.

"Pretty thing," Mathias said to Ice, still staring at Sabelle. "After you're dead, I wonder how she'll feel underneath me. I do hope she's a screamer."

Ice tamped down fresh fury. Mathias was still goading him. He could see Ice's magical signature, knew he had Called to Sabelle. Even he, monster that he was, understood how protective a wizard was of any female he sought to mate, whether she answered in kind or not. Ice forced himself not to rise to Mathias's bait.

Camden waved an arm, and around the clear structure, plush chairs appeared. Three on the east side, which he, Blackbourne, and Spencer each occupied, and four on the west, which Bram, Tynan, Sterling, and Sabelle took.

"Before we start, there are a few rules," Blackbourne said. "The first, if anyone should wish to forfeit or withdraw their name from consideration, the challenge ends immediately. Any other spells cast by either nominee will be considered an act of aggression and treated accordingly. Also, should you believe that you have killed your opponent, you must signal me and pause the fight. I will establish the veracity of your claim. While I'm doing so, any spells cast will be treated as an act of aggression, as well. If you are still fighting in four hours, you will be granted a rest period, during which you may reacquire power by any means at your disposal. I see Mr. Rykard has brought Miss Rion. Mr. d'Arc?"

"The fight won't last that long, Carlisle," Mathias drawled. "If it does, Rhea awaits me upstairs."

Blackbourne nodded. "The rest period is fifteen minutes."

"Duly noted." Mathias nodded with the utmost civility.

Blackbourne resumed his announcements. "Should the fight extend another four hours, we will take a mandatory rest period for food and sleep. There is no limit to the sort or amount of spells you may cast, except that the release of any corporeal form you create must be contained within your challenge zone. It cannot move outside or above these walls. No one can leave these grounds until the fight is over for any reason. I've locked them down; teleporting is impossible. We will assume that any combatant who attempts such intends to cheat and will forfeit the challenge by default. And last, we will declare a winner once someone forfeits, withdraws their name, or dies. Any questions?"

No one moved or spoke. Ice heard only the revving of his heart as he studied Sabelle, who represented all he had to live for. Then he dragged his gaze over Mathias, who stood for all the evil he could squash.

"Ready?" the Council elder asked.

Ice simply nodded. It was time.

Blackbourne signaled, and the combatants on either side of the challenge ring dropped into a ready stance. Both had stripped down to the waist, oblivious to the December chill. Ice rolled his shoulders, every muscle rippling with repressed action as he clutched his new wand. It was clear he wanted this fight.

Sabelle wanted to vomit.

Lean as a whip, Mathias waited, looking as if he hadn't a care in the world.

God, if she had known when she suggested Ice for this Council post that it would place him in grave danger, she would never have mentioned his name.

"Stop blaming yourself," Bram whispered beside her.

"Who else am I to blame, then?"

"He could have declined. Ice wanted this . . . and perhaps I drove him to it as well. He wanted revenge against Mathias so badly after Gailene's murder. I stopped him. He was too young to fight Mathias. In my attempt to protect him, I only made him more desperate."

The truth of Bram's words washed an icy chill over her. Fear gripped her stomach. "I cannot simply sit and watch him die."

"Then don't. Send him your thoughts and good wishes. And don't underestimate him. When we were friends centuries ago, I saw huge promise in him, but knew it would never be achieved until he curbed his temper. He's come a long way since then. Let's hope it's enough."

Ice and Mathias began a slow circle, each sizing up the other. A glib smile played across Mathias's mouth, as if he mimicked Ice merely to toy with him. Ice ignored the silent jibe.

Dread slid through Sabelle. Her heart roared with disquiet, and she feared nothing good would come of this challenge. Ice was everything she wanted in a friend and mate. Sitting next to Bram and the others, watching Ice fight for his life, was eating at her composure.

Suddenly, Mathias raised his wand. She gripped her brother's hand, terror clutching her throat, as Mathias pooled water at the bottom of the ring, quickly making it into something of a fish bowl. Around and around, he swirled the water at his feet, then sent a tidal wave of water Ice's way.

With a mere hand, Ice froze the wave before it crashed over his head and swallowed him whole.

Mathias laughed. "So you can fight. Maybe today won't be deadly dull. How about this?"

With a flick of his wrist, Mathias blasted a wall of fire at the frozen wave. With a flash, it crashed into the icy barrier and began melting it. The resulting water rose to the ankle, then waist, again to the neck . . . and kept rising.

Treading water, Ice *whooshed* his wand in a circle. The water began to dissipate, mist floating at the top of the challenge ring's ceiling. It formed small clusters, then grew into big clouds in an angry gray.

Then snow began to fall, a light, harmless dusting of powdery brilliance.

Again, Mathias smiled "Interesting. Now that we've discussed the weather, are you going to try to kill me or not?"

Ice said nothing, just stared, his concentration unwavering.

Mathis sighed, then hurled a ball of fire Ice's way. Ice drew in a mighty breath and, waving his wand, blew snow directly into the ball's path with a howling wind. The fireball popped, sparked . . . fizzled.

"More childish games?" Mathias goaded.

Sloshing around in the snow, Ice continued to stare, circle him. "Fuck off."

"We've had this conversation before. I'd hoped you learned to be more eloquent since I introduced you to my friend with interesting toys. But alas . . ."

Sabelle shuddered into Ice's silence, thinking of the whip Mathias had flayed Ice with so viciously. But Ice said nothing, and minutes slid by. Mathias put out a hand, thumb and fingers curled toward Ice, who clutched his throat a moment later.

With his other hand, Ice sent a spell zinging to Mathias that was full of spark and electricity. Mathias tried to dodge it, but he'd been too preoccupied cutting off Ice's windpipe to oppose it. Instead, Mathias feinted to the right. The spell caught him in the arm, just above his elbow. He roared, his shoulder jerking with the effort to pull and tug at the muscle. It didn't move.

"Bloody bastard. You think to paralyze me temporarily? Is that a fair fight?"

"Choking me is?" Ice countered.

Mathias reared back, then lashed back at Ice, free arm raised, fingers bared like claws. A twisting fireball made its way toward Ice. Quickly, he threw up a sheet of frozen water between them, but before the spell reached it, the ball dissolved. But Sabelle sensed the spell wasn't broken.

A moment later, Ice clutched his eyes with a roar. "What the—"

"Burns, doesn't it?" Mathias sneered, trying to work his arm free of Ice's temporary paralysis. "Also keeps you from hexing me when I can't move."

Sabelle gasped and leapt to her feet to run to Ice's side. Bram and Tynan pulled her back down. "We're impartial observers only."

Her brother's words punched her in the stomach. "You would simply let him die?"

Bram ground his jaw. "We've no choice. These were the risks, and Ice knew it when he stepped into the ring."

"He wants revenge so badly . . ." She bit her lip, trying to hold still her trembling chin.

"And you," Bram admitted, then sighed. "He made me promise . . . *if* he managed to win the Council seat, that I would not disclaim you if you wished to mate with him."

Horror spread across Sabelle's face. In that moment, she both loved and hated her brother. He was making Ice prove his worth, earn a prominent place in magickind before allowing her to mate with him. That was a guardian's task, true, but did he care so little for her heart? For his former friend?

Yes, Ice wanted revenge. But he was willing to fight the

worst evil in a millennium, in part, for a chance to be with her. How stupid had she been not to Bind to him already? She had put Bram's blessing over Ice's heart, and now . . . This couldn't end soon enough. She had to talk to Ice.

"Bloody git!" Ice growled at Mathias.

Right now, Sabelle could say the same about her brother.

"I underestimated his love for you. Nor was I certain that you felt the same," Bram said. "It's my duty to be certain he's the best mate for you—"

"Excuses!" she hissed at him. "And you know it. Ever since you awakened from that black cloud of Mathias's you've been calculating and scheming. Unfeeling. You cared only that my mating allied you with someone advantageous. After you rescued me from my selfish mother . . . you became just like her."

"Sabelle—"

"I don't care whether you disclaim me or not, Ice will be my mate. You can go to hell."

She leapt up from her chair, relief and anxiety both pouring out of her. It was done; she was free of her brother's expectations. Whether Ice won or lost, she would mate with the man she loved.

If he survived this battle.

Ice growled. Inside the ring, something pinged. A flash of light bounced off one wall of the force field, then another.

"Missed me." Mathias laughed, finally shaking his hand free of the paralysis spell.

Clawing at his eyes, Ice dropped to one knee. Sabelle wrung her hands, willing him to concede this challenge. Somehow, they'd oust Mathias from the Council, expose him for what he was, but this challenge wasn't worth Ice's life. Their future together. Not to her.

"It's not over, prick." Ice grabbed a handful of the snow

remaining on the floor and wiped it over his face, grinding it into his eyes. He came up gasping, blinking, his eyes wide open. "Not by half."

Ice flicked his wand at Mathias. A whirling wind funnel appeared at his feet. He flung it toward the evil wizard with an angry roar. Then he scooped up more snow, crushed it in one big fist and tossed it at the tornado. The snow entered, then emerged on the other side as little projectiles of ice, headed directly for Mathias.

"Clever," he praised.

Mathias leapt above them, then levitated until all of the pellets ricocheted off the clear force field surrounding the ring and fell to the floor, harmless.

"But not clever enough. You'll have to try a bit harder."

Just then, Mathias raised his arms wide, bringing them down in a scooping motion near his hips. They were filled with something . . . little bodies that squirmed and wriggled. The evil wizard tossed them in Ice's direction. They seemed to multiply in midair, a few dozen becoming hundreds in the blink of an eye.

"My friends are hungry. Feed them."

Sabelle jerked her gaze from Mathias's dark glower to the little pale crawling creatures. They hit Ice like a wall, and he screamed, twisting and writhing, trying to fling them away.

Every one he dislodged left behind a bleeding little wound. Another quickly tried to take its place.

"Flesh-eating maggots?" Tynan reared back in disgust beside her.

They were. Oh, God . . . Dark magic, indeed. She'd read once they could eat a man alive in minutes.

Ice!

As if Ice heard her plea, he focused his energy, eyes closed. She ran closer to the force field, until scarcely more than a few meters and a clear wall separated them. Around Ice, more snow melted, slowly filling up the ring. Ice ducked, removing the last of the creatures from his shoulders and neck, and they floated away from him, unable to swim back for their meal.

When he came up for air, he froze the water with the flick of his wrist. It immobilized them instantly.

But the effort cost him. He looked pale and drained now, his green eyes dim beacons in a white face. No doubt, Ice needed her at that break—if he made it that long. Then she would go to him, assure him this challenge wasn't necessary, at least as far as her love was concerned.

Mathias nodded and crossed his arms over his chest. "I grow tired of toying with you. Your friend Rion enjoyed this one."

An evil smile settled over Mathias's features as he banged his wand in Ice's direction. A moment later, Sabelle's worst nightmare emerged.

The black cloud!

CHAPTER SEVENTEEN

SABELLE CLASPED HER HAND over her mouth to contain her clawing fear. Bram appeared at her side, and took her shoulders in hand, comforting her as she watched that deadly black cloud wisp its way toward Ice.

Behind her, Bram tensed, his breathing harsh. She wanted to turn to her brother, plead for help, but couldn't look away.

"What can we do?"

"Nothing. I don't know what the damnable thing is, but it will find him. Whatever his worst instincts, they will rise up and overwhelm him. Choke him."

In Bram's case, his ambition. She bit her lip. "It's painful?"

"Like your soul is being split in half."

Sagging against Bram, she looked for strength, refusing to let hopelessness defeat her.

Oh God. Ice would be a different man, *if* he came back to her. If he lived.

"How much longer until the break?" Maybe she could reach him quickly, somehow heal him before it did too much damage.

"Less than five minutes."

Please, Ice, hold out that long.

The black cloud drew closer. Ice watched it, taut shoulders rising up and down with harsh breaths. He was so bloody tired.

Levitating to avoid the mass nearly took more effort than he had. Though Ice lowered himself to the ground again, the cloud followed him, closing in on him. Next, he conjured a bottle. Perhaps he could contain the black cloud . . . somehow. Still, he would likely have to touch it, be affected by whatever disaster it promised.

His hand trembled as he held the bottle, its wide mouth open and directed at the cloud. The black vapor flowed into the bottle, and Ice threw the stopper over it, hoping he'd captured it all.

Instead, it leaked out the bottom, quickly re-forming inches from his face—then heading straight for him.

Think, think, think!

Ice abandoned the bottle and leapt away. He blinked hard, formed fists, focusing when every nerve in his head throbbed with the need for energy. He could not give out, could not give in. The Council needed him. Gailene needed to rest in peace. He needed Sabelle for his own.

Finally, he summoned a mirror. It quickly appeared in his hand, and he flipped it toward the cloud, praying the glass would deflect the mass back to Mathias. Instead, it passed around the little looking glass, re-formed, then went straight for his chest.

Now what? Ice wondered as he stepped back, back until he hit the force field. Nowhere else to go. He didn't dare look at Sabelle, at the fear he felt beating off her.

Suddenly, Mathias laughed, a screeching parody of joy. The sound dripped menace and scorn. "You can't outrun the spell. It *will* take you."

With his back against the force field, the black cloud began to surround Ice. He gritted his teeth, bracing himself to stay strong against whatever agony it brought. He would not show weakness or fear. If this was the end, if he never left this challenge ring alive, Ice wanted to die certain that Mathias knew exactly how he felt.

"Fuck off."

"So you've said before. Now . . ." Mathias smiled as the cloud smothered Ice, swallowed him, taking his vision, his ability to breathe—his hope. He choked, clutched his throat, needing air. There was none. Sabelle screamed, though it sounded far away. For a moment, he was glad she had never Bound to him. No need to mourn him once he'd gone.

The evil heat Mathias put off loomed closer suddenly, and the other wizard gibed, "Let's meet the *real* Isdernus Rykard."

What the bloody devil did that mean?

The cloud clung to him, hovering over his face. Ice continued to gasp for breath as dizziness spiked in his head. Panic for air set in. Surely at any moment he would pass out, die right in a heap at Mathias's feet, as the cloud paralyzed him from lifting a damn finger.

But a moment later, it passed through him. He drew in a desperate gasp of air and fell to his knees as the black mass drifted up the wall, clung harmlessly to the ceiling.

Mathias reared back. "Impossible!"

He reached a hand toward the cloud and hurled it at Ice again. Once more, it blanketed him, cutting off his air, his light, his hope. Then it left him, floating aimlessly in the enclosed force field. Why hadn't it clung to him as it had Bram? Why hadn't it damn near killed him?

"What does it mean?" he heard Sabelle ask.

Ice risked a glance at her. She looked pale, worried, as she turned to her brother, frantic for an answer.

"I don't know," Bram murmured. "It latched on to me viciously and didn't let go. Almost instantly, I felt . . . anger, arrogance. My worst thoughts all right in my head. Then I don't remember a bloody thing until the dark healer came to me."

"Is—is Mathias doing the spell incorrectly?"

Bram scoffed. "I think he's both familiar and ruthless with it."

"What the bloody—" Mathias fisted his hands, his blue eyes blasting rage. Fury hollowed his cheeks. Sweat slicked his chest and corded abs. "That is impossible!"

Ice stepped away from the wall, completely unharmed, untouched by the thunderous cloud. And amazed. He staggered, weakened and exhausted, but he was on his feet. He yearned to curl up against Sabelle and sleep for a year. But he'd lived through something he never expected to. Inside, he glowed with triumph.

"Apparently not," Ice taunted.

"No one," Mathias spat. "*No one* is incorruptible. Everyone has at least one flaw that makes them susceptible to the dark side. Take it!"

The furious wizard hurled the black cloud at Ice again. As before, moments of breathlessness, heavy chest, anger, and frustration. Then . . . surprising freedom.

Ice cocked his head and grinned. Finally, he understood. "I felt pure evil pass through me, looking to partner with its own kind. It found nothing useful, so it left."

"It must have latched on to you. Inside you. Somewhere. Surely, you have some—some flaw of character that could make you embrace the dark. Greed, lust, avarice, envy. Something."

The black cloud hovered in the corner . . . then started listing its way back to Mathias, as if drawn there. As if the mass sought evil, wanted a harbor in someone who hated or envied or felt too much pride or lust.

In Ice, the mass had found nothing it sought. It had scurried from the caring and love that flowed in his veins. From the light inside him.

And now Ice understood exactly how to fight Mathias.

With a snap of his wrist he conjured a sword. One thing Marrok had taught him well was to use a human blade. In a few short months, he'd perfected the art of slicing an enemy any way he wished, whether to defend, or in this case, to kill. Avenging Gailene was in his grasp, and for her Mathias must die now, by his hand.

At the sight of the heavy broadsword, Mathias scoffed. "A human's weapon for a wizard's fight You *are* mad. You'll get nowhere near me with that, you know."

It would be a challenge, but certainty fueled him, overriding exhaustion. He would succeed. For Gailene. For Sabelle. For the past and future.

Using the edge of the blade, he cut his own thigh. Sabelle gasped, and he did his best to put her concern from his mind. Bram stood behind her, offering comfort.

Now, he had to focus all his energy on delivering his blow to Mathias and ending two hundred years of agony.

The blood welled from the stinging wound on his thigh, and Ice wiped the flat of the blade across one side, then the other, coating the sword with the essence that beat from his heart. For a moment, he gripped the blade, bowed his head over it, and wrapped it in an enchantment that spread hope and joy. Love.

When Ice righted himself, Mathias's eyes widened, and he backed away, wary. His nostrils flared, and his face reddened.

"You will not touch me with that blade."

Ice didn't bother refuting him. He just took a step closer, wand outstretched with another paralysis hex ready.

The pungent stench of fear wafted across the challenge

ring, and Ice smiled, the gesture every bit as warm as his name. Mathias shook his head, stepped back through the cracking sheet of frozen water and slushy remnants of snow.

"*No!*" The evil wizard screamed, the raw sound reverberating through the force field. Then he thrust a hand forward, aimed toward a listing sheet of ice standing between them. Twisting his wrist, Mathias hurled the shards directly at Ice.

As he melted the frozen projectiles, Ice watched fury overtake Mathias. He laughed. Adrenaline charged Ice's system as he raised the sword. No doubt, Mathias would try to thwart him using some underhanded method, but he would not succeed.

Ice charged the other wizard, blood-wet sword at the ready. His nemesis retreated a step, then another. It seemed that Mathias feared the human weapon. Because he didn't know how to wield it? Possible. He'd never seen Mathias fight human. Perhaps he simply feared the unknown . . . and what Ice would do with it. The blood had to frighten him as well. Blood magic, though not practiced widely for centuries, was notoriously unpredictable and strong.

Mathias continued to back up—until he hit the force field. A few steps more, maybe two or three, and victory would belong to Ice.

"Cease!" Blackbourne called. "The break period has begun."

Bloody fucking hell. Everything inside Ice itched to lunge forward, finish off Mathias for good. Bury his ghosts. If he did, he would violate the rules of the challenge and forfeit all right to the Council seat . . . and any chance he had of spending his future with Sabelle.

With great force of will, Ice lowered the sword.

Mathias's gloating sneer nearly made him rethink his

position. Cheeky bastard would use the next fifteen minutes to his advantage, devise some new counterattack. Though Ice's limbs felt heavy, he'd rather keep fighting. A thinking Mathias was a dangerous one.

"You heard the esteemed gentleman," Mathias said, backing away. "Put the sword down. Unless you wish to forfeit."

And lose his chance for a proper revenge for Gailene, watch Sabelle slip through his fingers, because Mathias had goaded him into something stupid? No.

With a curse, he turned to find Bram standing nearby and handed the sword to the Doomsday Brethren's leader. "I don't trust him anywhere near this sword."

Bram grimaced at the blood-soaked weapon but grabbed it. "Nor do I."

But when Ice looked up, Mathias had fled, all but running inside the house.

Nodding, he made his way toward the house as well and the room prepared within for him to rest. Now that the imminent moment had passed, the adrenaline seeped from his system. Heavy limbs became a burden as he dragged one foot in front of the other to reach his appointed room. Mathias had a witch stashed upstairs, at the ready to provide a fresh dose of magical energy. While Ice . . .

He avoided Sabelle's concerned stare. The Council might not accept him if he and Sabelle looked too cozy. Despite recent discussions with Sabelle's brother, Ice knew it was unlikely he and Bram would ever be close again. He understood, however, why the elders might be wary.

But Ice was also keenly aware of a need to keep Mathias from looking again at Sabelle, plotting to use her as a weapon against him. He only prayed that ignoring her would at least confuse Mathias long enough for Ice to kill him and win the challenge.

He must keep Mathias off the Council at all costs. He must avenge Gailene today.

Inside the house, the artificial heat melted the December chill that had settled in his bones. Instead of relieving him, it smothered him like a blanket over his face.

Ice trudged upstairs, shutting the door behind him. He flopped across the bed, wishing like hell that he could hold Sabelle. Yes, the energy would be nice—blast and damn, it may ensure his victory—but he didn't like the thought of Mathias and his beloved within a hundred kilometers of each other, much less on the same grounds. Nor could he sacrifice the facade of Sabelle's indifference for his own comfort.

He'd simply have to dig deep, find the energy to carry on—without Sabelle's sweet touch.

No sooner did he complete the thought than someone tapped lightly on his door. It wasn't merely that no one else here would knock so delicately. Ice *felt* Sabelle on the other side of the portal, worrying.

"You shouldn't have come," he said through the door because he knew if he answered it, he would touch her, take her.

"Are you planning to leave me in the hall?"

"I won't risk calling Mathias's attention to you."

She sighed. "Dear, sweet man, he knows you've Called to me. My feelings, in his eyes, are irrelevant. Besides, do you really believe he would risk attacking me in a Council elder's home?"

Normally, no. None would dare such a feat. With Mathias, Ice feared anything was possible.

"Let me in," she murmured against the wood.

The sound ripped at his guts. "Sabelle . . ."

"The clock is ticking down. Let me help you."

His princess. Always wanting to help others, always selfless. Though he hated the fact she'd lain with Lucan, he understood she was not the sort of witch to sit idle and watch another's pain without lending a hand.

"I'm all right."

She hesitated. "Let me touch you."

Her voice cracked, squeaked in places. He heard her tears in those few short words. They wrenched his heart.

"I've gone mad with worry, watching you fight Mathias," she continued. "The black cloud frightened me nearly to death. Mathias looks so sure of himself, and I know memories of Gailene must be haunting you. Please let me in. Let me touch you."

Damn, the woman knew him far too well.

With a sigh, he rose and approached the door, gripped the knob. "Sabelle, if I let you in, you will not leave untouched."

"I hadn't planned to."

With a scowl, Ice ripped open the door. Sabelle stood there in simple clothing, her face a rich tapestry of emotion: concern, love, fear, joy. Everything he felt for her—had felt from the moment he set eyes upon her—rushed through him all over again. She scraped away all his defenses, the bluster and snarling he used to keep the rest of the world at bay. Only she saw the man beneath, the one still hurting from his sister's murder. The one who loved Sabelle more than his own life.

"Have a care! Mathias could see you—"

"He's busy shagging that brainless witch Rhea."

And he would return to the challenge ring shortly with much energy. Ice could all but hear Sabelle's unspoken words. Yes, he needed energy, but not if it risked Sabelle's safety.

"Yell at me," he demanded.

She scoffed, flipped long golden tresses over her delicate

shoulder, and breezed past him, into the bedroom, shutting the door behind her. "Little good that will do you, as you're well aware. You promised to touch me. I'm waiting."

Ice closed his eyes and all he could see in his memories were the times he'd possessed Sabelle. The first sweet moments of her trembling welcome in MacKinnett's guest house, deep in the midst of danger. Their shared joy upon his release from the hell of Mathias's dungeon. The poignant moments in his bed upon the eve of what was to have been her mating to Lucan. Each time, he wanted her more than the time before. And now, with exhaustion blunting his battle instincts, with fear blurring his strategy, with his anxiety for the future clouding his mind, he needed her more than ever.

Except he was sure Mathias would only hone in on her more if Ice revealed the depth of his devotion. For now, Mathias might be convinced Ice's Call to Sabelle had been motivated by ambition, not love. He'd prefer to keep it that way.

Ice drew in a shaky breath. "Please don't tempt me."

"But I love to." She sauntered closer, cupping his cheek in her palm. Even that light contact was electric, filling him with need and yearning. "I love you."

"Our feelings mean nothing until Mathias is vanquished and this challenge is won."

"And you will not win this challenge without energy, which must come from me."

Damn it, she was right.

"Besides, I disagree. Our feelings mean everything." Sabelle shook her head, golden strands catching the afternoon rays and shining as if they were pure sunlight themselves. Then she grabbed his hands. "As I become a part of you, you become a part of me."

Yes!

No!

Ice closed his eyes as her words washed over him. He loved them, loved her, soaked in her willing acceptance. Her voice embracing these sweet words gave his soul succor, his tomorrow hope. But he could not allow her to finish in this moment.

"I will be honest, good, and true. I heed your call. 'Tis you I seek—"

"Stop," he choked.

Sabelle continued the Binding as if she had not heard him, though he knew better. "From this moment on—"

"Not another word."

Tears and determination shimmered in her blue eyes. "There is no other for me—"

"Stop!" he growled, forcing himself to dig the word from the bottom of his soul. "Please, princess. No more."

He wanted Sabelle as his mate so badly. Being forced to put her off again was beyond excruciating.

The first of her tears fell. "You don't want me to finish the Binding?"

Ice grabbed Sabelle by the shoulders, willing her to understand that he hung on to his self-control by a thread. "I will always want you. Always. But there's your brother—"

"I've already told Bram that I don't care if he disclaims me. I want to be your mate."

He closed his eyes. What had he done to deserve this amazing, loyal woman?

"I am honored, more than you know. But I vowed to him that I would not take you as my mate unless I won this challenge."

Sabelle clenched her jaw, closed her eyes. "He doesn't deserve your steadfastness after the way he's behaved."

Silently Ice agreed, but that wasn't the point. "Politically, we cannot tip our hand and give the others on the Council any reason, real or imagined, to nullify this challenge. They've only allowed it because they believe me to be Bram's enemy, not a vote in his back pocket. Until I'm on the Council, we cannot upset that delicate balance."

"I don't think they can do anything to stop the challenge now."

"But do you know that for a fact?" He arched a brow at her. "I'm also concerned for your safety. I will not paint a larger target on your back for Mathias's sick pleasure and put you in more danger. He already knows I've Called to you, but if you Bind to me and become my mate, he'd only hunt you with more relish."

"We are stronger together."

His grip tightened on her shoulders. "I have enough fight for us both."

The lift of her chin, the stubborn set to her mouth was all the warning Ice got. "From this moment on, there is no other for me but—"

Ice could only think of one way to stop her: with a kiss. Pain at stopping her joining to him again jarred his heart, even as desire at the feel of her mouth beneath his thundered through his body. He cupped her head and clutched her tightly, pulling her flush against him, dying to merge with her, share the cacophony of feelings clashing inside.

Sabelle fought to tear her lips from his, to finish the Binding. His beautiful princess, so willing to fight for the cause and sacrifice for him. He couldn't allow that. Instead, he dove deeper into her mouth, leaving no part untouched. As always, she tasted of heaven and made him think of sin.

By degrees, she relaxed against him, lost herself in the kiss. Even being with her like this increased his energy. It filtered through him, wound down to his arms and legs, made his heart pump wildly. It would be enough. After all, he knew how to defeat Mathias—God willing, for good. All he needed was another opportunity and a minor distraction, and this power from Sabelle. All else was in place. No need to rush her out of her clothes and onto her back. He would not risk hurting her or treat her with so little respect.

Sabelle took the decision from his hands when she unfastened his trousers and pushed them down his hips.

Ice tore his mouth away. "There's no need—"

"I need!" she choked, and tears shimmered on the rim of her lashes. "I won't endure watching you face Mathias in a mortal challenge, knowing you lack proper energy when I could help you. It's all I can do to remain in my seat and wait helplessly for the challenge to end. This is something I must do, not because it's my duty, but my need. Please . . ."

How was he to refuse that, especially when he wanted her so desperately himself? "We have only a few minutes."

"We'll make it enough."

Amazing. Ice cradled her sweet face in his hand, drowning in her blue eyes. From the moment he'd first seen her, his life had careened out of control. For two centuries, he'd stood alone, without family, without friends. Solitary. Sabelle changed all that in an instant. And even if the possibility of their tomorrows ended today, he still would change nothing. "Thank you, princess."

Unable to resist her red mouth just beneath his, he dove back into her kiss, sinking deep, drowning even deeper in her, praying he never resurfaced. She enveloped him, arms around his shoulders, lips parted for his invasion. Sabelle clutched him as if these might be their last few moments together . . . because they were. She grasped that reality, and as much as he wanted to shield her from it, he loved her all the more because she understood.

With an impatient rip, he shoved the shirt from her shoulders. Her bra was in shambles moments later, her jeans mere shreds. Her sexy little lace knickers fell next to his rush of need. She gasped when he cupped her breasts, caressing her hard nipples with his thumbs. So soft, so perfect. No other woman compared to her. Sabelle was a rare beauty both outside and in.

A moment later, she grasped his erection, stroking him with a sure palm. He gasped into their kiss, his entire body bombarded by pleasure, not just because she touched him, but because it was Sabelle who held him as intimately as possible. Because she wanted him enough to arouse him more. Unnecessary, but a gift he wouldn't turn down.

"Isdernus . . ." she pleaded when he delved two fingers into her soft folds and found her wet and waiting.

"You know I hate that name," he choked out when she stroked him once more.

"You're far too warm in my arms and in my heart to call Ice."

Damn wonderful woman broke his heart all over again.

He kissed her once more, lowering her to the bed. She fell willingly into a sea of pillows and soft sheets, her thighs gently parted in waiting.

Breathing hard now, he grasped her hips. "I would rather take my time with you."

"We haven't more time. Take me now," she gasped as he caressed the hard bud of her clit with a pair of fingers.

Regrettably, she was right. And a part of him needed her now, needed the memories . . . in case this challenge did not end well. At least one of his last memories would be of Sabelle's sweet touch.

With that thought, he plunged deep inside her. She arched up to him, spreading her legs wider, then wrapping them around his hips.

"Please . . ." she pleaded, then her body tightened on him.

Ice was happy to comply.

He set a deep, steady rhythm, never wavering, never faltering, never stopping until she dug her fingers into his shoulders, cried out his name, and tightened around his cock. Ice clung to his self-control by a thread as he rode the storm of her orgasm.

As soon as her body sagged against the bed, he lifted his head from her neck and stared into her flushed face. Brushing the strands from her forehead, he was struck anew by her loveliness. She was exquisite each time he saw her, but with her eyes shining bright and naked with love, she was at her most beautiful.

Something welled up in him and threatened to swallow him. A feeling. More than need, way more than desire. Love, blinding in its intensity. Bloody hell, it threatened to choke him. It emptied his mind and lungs, even as it filled his heart and soul. He covered her mouth with his once more, delving inside. And with another deep stroke inside Sabelle, Ice exploded, calling her name.

She tightened her embrace on him, face buried against his shoulder. His skin there was wet, and it wasn't his sweat.

Ice lifted his head. Tears trailed down her pink cheeks, and he brushed them away with his thumbs. "If making love to you makes you cry, princess, I've done something wrong."

With a watery laugh, she held him tight, her blue gaze clinging to him. "*You* made a joke?"

"We haven't had much to laugh about together, have we?" He sighed. "Please don't cry."

"The thought of you stepping back into the challenge ring with that monster is intolerable. I know we said we cannot allow Mathias to win that seat, but at the cost of your life, I—"

"Five minutes!" Blackbourne's voice called up the stairs. "The challenge resumes in five minutes. Return to the challenge ring!"

At the summons, Sabelle grabbed his hand for dear life. Ice understood, truly. If their roles were reversed, he'd be terrified. But they must go on, even if he forfeited his life. He would not quit otherwise.

"We've agreed. This is something we must do." Ice disentangled himself from her silken body and rose from the bed before she used her aphrodisiac kisses to lure him back to her side.

Ice grabbed his clothes and yanked them on. Sabelle watched, wide-eyed, sitting up in the bed, the sheet scarcely covering the most delectable parts of her. He tried very hard not to be distracted, not to grab on to the woman he loved and refuse to let go.

Gritting his teeth and praying for strength, he kissed her forehead, then whirled away.

"Ice." Her voice trembled.

He wanted to reassure her that all would end well, but he couldn't lie.

"I need a word with your brother. Never forget I love you."

Before she could tempt him back, he sprinted down the stairs. Energy burst from every pore of his body, and he thanked Sabelle for her gift of the touch. Now, he simply had to put it to good use to stop Mathias from taking this Council seat—and continuing his reign of terror.

Today was Ice's day for revenge.

What Sabelle really wanted to do was tuck her knees under her chin and cry miserably. Succumbing to the urge would

accomplish nothing, however. And the challenge would begin
again soon. She needed to be dressed and sitting outside the
challenge ring supporting Ice . . . and praying.

Though Ice was a skilled warrior, and now well trained in
human combat tactics, thanks to Marrok, Ice was honest. He
would abide by the challenge's rules. Mathias would circum-
vent as many as he could possibly manage and still escape
detection. She felt helpless and frustrated—her least favorite
emotions—because she could do nothing more than tell him
to be careful and give him her support.

With a sigh, she rose, magically repaired the rips Ice had
made in her clothing, and dressed herself again. She didn't
take time for a soothing shower or to tidy the room. No time
or energy; it was all reserved for Ice.

Hurrying out of the room and down to the stairway, she
gripped the banister and began her descent—then felt a
presence behind her. Heart jumping in her throat, Sabelle
whirled.

Mathias.

He stood at the top of the stairs, clearly enjoying his
superior position several steps above. His smile looked pleasant on the surface, but she did not trust him for a moment.
He held his shirt in one hand, revealing the slick, rippling
muscles of his chest and abdomen. Even his hair was unusu-
ally disheveled.

A witch stood behind him, clinging to his arm, dressed
from head to toe in red. Lacy red that revealed more than
concealed her large breasts with hard nipples, the absence
of pubic hair.

Removing her hand from his arm, Mathias dropped a
quick kiss on her neck, burying his fingers in her tangled
hair. After he released her, the witch stepped away with obvious reluctance.

"Ms. Rion, have you been keeping Mr. Rykard company?"

Sabelle bristled. Whatever passed between her and Ice was not anyone's affair, particularly Mathias's. She turned away and resumed her trek down the stairs.

"I asked you a question," he snapped.

She refused to give him the satisfaction of an answer.

"You provided Mr. Rykard with energy, I presume. Tsk, Ms. Rion. Somehow, I don't believe your brother would approve of your association. Bram would think him rather beneath you. But from all appearances, I would guess it's you who's been beneath him."

Sabelle clenched her fists and bit her lip. And walked down the next step.

Mathias raced down until they stood shoulder to shoulder. "Have I offended you?" When she still did not reply, he entreated, "A thousand apologies, pet."

"I am *not* your pet," she growled, descending another step.

"Stop. Face me. Let me apologize."

Sabelle didn't dare. Lord knew what he truly sought. "You'll be late for the challenge."

"I have a few moments. Let me apologize."

Cold dread filled Sabelle's stomach. The wizard was up to something, likely something terrible. All along, she'd feared he would find some way to harm Ice. Now she saw that Ice was strong enough to fight this bastard, and Mathias was too clever to risk doing something underhanded to Ice that might cost him the challenge. Instead, because he had Called to her, Mathis knew he could instead prey on someone Ice would defend to the death.

Her.

Mathias had wisely waited to make his way to the challenge ring, likely lying in wait for her. If she hadn't needed a few moments to repair her clothes before donning them . . . if she hadn't needed a few moments to repair her emotions after Ice had refused to allow her to complete the Binding . . . if she had even believed that Mathias would risk harming her in Blackbourne's house . . .

"No?" he taunted, darting to the bottom of the stairs to face her. "Then come spend a bit of time with my . . . close friend, Rhea."

Rhea would only do his bidding, no doubt. Now that Mathias had her trapped between them, she had to defend herself and not allow him to use her safety against Ice.

Sabelle swallowed, cursing the fact no one was able to teleport in or around the house for the duration of the challenge. Now, she'd have to improvise a plan—quickly.

Swallowing hard, she summoned her courage. Each step toward Mathis spurred another tightening of the vise around her stomach, another rev for her heartbeat. Sabelle fisted her trembling hand behind her back, then opened it as she stood before the evil wizard. She had one chance, and she had to pray her abilities would not fail her now.

Cautiously, she reached out to Mathias. Her hand was just an inch from his and she eased closer . . .

Suddenly, she felt a jolt punch her in the chest. A spell clawed pain up and down her back, radiating down her legs, out her arms. Then her limbs froze. Her whole body followed, except for her lungs and heart. Mathias held her completely immobile. And he laughed.

"I know you're half-siren, dear. Did you really think I would let your touch sway me from my purpose? Very sorry, but no. I must kill Ice and you will help me. Now be a dear and spend some time with Rhea," Mathias drawled. "I insist."

CHAPTER EIGHTEEN

ICE SCANNED BLACKBOURNE'S WINTER-RAVAGED gardens. The spindle-branched trees devoid of leaves scarcely registered. Bram holding the sword and the empty challenge ring blazed across the front of his brain.

"Where is Mathias?" He approached the Doomsday Brethren's leader.

Bram looked him up and down, then growled, "You couldn't possibly muster that blinding energy on your own. Where the hell is my sister?"

Resisting the urge to hang his head or apologize, Ice met Bram's blue gaze dead-on. "I love Sabelle, and I've made my intentions very clear."

Bram gritted this teeth. "Was it necessary to flaunt her so publicly?"

"She insisted on coming to me and brushed aside my refusal. You know your sister can be quite determined."

Glaring at Ice for a long, uncomfortable moment, Bram finally cursed. "Don't touch Sabelle again."

"She is a grown witch," Ice argued. "She's no longer a five-year-old in need of your guidance. She loves you. But I know Sabelle, and you should as well. She is going to make her own choices, and anything you or I say will sway her little."

Staring at the winter-brown grass, Bram clenched his jaw so tightly, Ice wondered if it would break.

"Until you win this Council seat, this conversation is over. Then if she truly chooses you . . ." With a curse, Bram thrust the sword at him. "Take this. What the devil do you intend to do with it, anyway?"

"I think I've found the means to keep Mathias from this Council seat. It may even kill him."

That changed Bram's posture. "Truly?"

"The black cloud passing through me gave me an idea . . ."

"Yes. How *did* you fight that off?"

Ice shrugged, choosing his words carefully. "Somehow, it did not choose me."

"Because you aren't susceptible to the dark? That's what Mathias intimated."

Because he didn't live for ambition or greed, didn't covet anyone else's mate, didn't kill for sport . . . had nothing in his soul that could be used to tempt him to do evil. Bram, on the other hand, had always been ruthlessly ambitious, but since being smothered by the black cloud he hadn't hidden it well. At all. Now it ruled nearly his every thought and deed.

Rather than admit that and start an argument, Ice looked about Blackbourne's gardens. "Mathias has not returned from the break?"

"No," Bram confirmed. "And he's got less than two minutes or he forfeits the match."

Ice's blood ran cold. Mathias was still inside the house . . . as was Sabelle. Two minutes wasn't long, but when faced with an agent of death, it was an eternity. There was but one reason Mathias would not appear in the challenge ring: He had abducted Sabelle.

Tossing the sword at Bram again, Ice set off at a dead run for the house. Suddenly, Bram was by his side, the sword left leaning against the challenge ring's invisible walls.

"Go back to the challenge ring or you'll forfeit," Bram ordered.

"If it means letting Mathias hurting Sabelle, I don't bloody care!"

"She's *my* sister. I'll find her!"

"And the mate of *my* heart. If Emma were here, would you let Mathias anywhere near her?"

"Bastard."

Ice wasn't certain if Bram meant him or Mathias, and he didn't much care. He reached the back door first and threw it open. Just as he prepared to charge in, Mathias walked out.

"Going somewhere?" he asked. "The challenge will resume shortly, yes? Or are you admitting defeat?"

Narrowing his eyes at the ruthless wizard, Ice glared. "Why are you late?"

"One minute!" Blackbourne called.

"I'm not." Mathias smiled. "Just keeping Rhea occupied for as long as possible."

A vision of Mathias unleashing his malevolent passion on that witch nearly made Ice sick. He chomped at the bit to ask Mathias if he'd seen or harmed Sabelle, but didn't want to give the villain any ideas in the event Sabelle was merely resting or taking her time getting dressed. It seemed unlike her not to watch this upcoming phase of the match, but perhaps refusing to allow her to complete the vows hurt her more than he'd believed.

"A word with you, Rykard, before we begin again," Mathias asked with perfect politeness that made Ice want to grind his teeth.

"We have nothing to say."

Mathias grabbed his arm. "Actually, we do."

Bram glared at Mathias. "What the devil do you want?"

"To talk to Rykard alone, wizard to wizard."

Something was wrong here, Ice suspected. Very wrong. And it had to do with Sabelle. The certainty dug an icy claw into his gut. He swallowed fear, shrugged off Mathias's touch, then turned to Bram. A long look passed between them. Whatever their feuds, Sabelle was vital to them both. In that silent exchange, Bram agreed to search for her while Ice dealt with Mathias.

As Bram darted into the stately manor, Ice watched, dread raking poison-dipped talons into his gut.

He turned back to Mathias. "We're alone now. Say it and be done."

"Back to the challenge ring, if you please."

Ice understood the urge to murder all over again, but restrained it for Sabelle's sake as he crawled inside the ring. He grabbed the sword, comforted by its weight in his hands.

Mathias sent a sideways glance at the human weapon and dropped to a mumble suffused with evil glee. "I assume you have feelings for that lovely little siren you've Called to, and if you'd like to see her alive again, you'll forfeit the match as soon as Blackbourne resumes it."

Ice froze, then violence defrosted his system with the urge to kill. He raised the sword threateningly. "What the fuck did you do with her?"

"Nothing." He smiled. "Yet. Should you wish to keep it that way, you will bow out of this challenge. If not"—he shrugged—"let's say Gailene enjoyed my company far more than Ms. Rion will."

Visions of Gailene's body, twisted and broken, besieged him, and Ice forced the visions away. He could not think about the past if he wanted to have a future.

Clutching the sword, Ice's fingers crushed the handle. Veins bulged in his arms. His temper surged until he heard nothing more than pounding in his ears. He restrained the urge to kill Mathias—barely. He only did because he had to know what the bastard had done to Sabelle. "She's still here at Blackbourne's house, since no one can teleport out. And if you managed, you would be disqualified."

"Stop guessing like a fool and agree. You have less than thirty seconds to decide her fate. If you don't answer me before Blackbourne resumes the challenge, she dies before you can ever leave the ring to save her—and before Bram can rescue her."

Which meant Rhea was holding Sabelle prisoner in the house and probably had instructions to kill her upon Mathias's signal.

Oh dear God, had Bram been able to find Sabelle? How would he save her?

Ice wished to hell he could send Bram some mental message, but neither of them had been gifted with that magic. Instead, he surreptitiously reached for the phone at his waist to call Bram. Mathias's hissed warning stopped him cold.

"Don't be stupid. Do you forfeit? Decide now."

All Ice could do was pray Bram found Sabelle soon. Until then . . . he was trapped. Goddamned fucking trapped.

But nothing mattered more than Sabelle's safety.

He closed his eyes. Agreeing meant that he not only forfeited a Council seat, but also gave up both mating with Sabelle and avenging his beloved sister so she could finally rest peacefully after two long centuries. But Gailene would not have wanted Ice to risk another for her memory. She would have been pleased to see him in love.

Little good it did him. He'd foolishly left Sabelle upstairs, believing Mathias would use the opportunity to schmooze Blackbourne and further his political aspirations, not abduct a fellow Councilman's sister under their collective noses.

How naive he'd been.

He'd pay for his foolishness for the rest of his life. But Ice didn't deserve Sabelle if he couldn't win this battle, and he'd forfeit again ten times over if it meant saving her life.

Please, God, let her be safe. Even if she hated him for not protecting her. Even if Bram refused to allow him to ever speak to her again. Just knowing she was alive and well would be enough for him.

Ice didn't hesitate. "I'll forfeit."

"Very good," Mathias lauded softly. "Very good, indeed. After you've conceded the challenge to me, I will leave with Rhea and Ms. Rion. I need one other item from you before I return your beloved: the Doomsday Diary. At midnight, you will meet me at Hyde Park with the diary. I will exchange the book for Sabelle."

Those words hit Ice like a flight into a brick wall. This is what Mathias had sought all along, not a seat of power he had to share with six others, but the ultimate power to destroy or enslave magickind at will.

Bloody hell.

Had Mathias discovered the means to use the Doomsday Diary?

The evil wizard knew from imprisoning Caden's mate, Sydney, and stealing the book that only a female could write in the Doomsday Diary. Rhea, Mathias's whore, had held the book once and placed on it the bloody inconvenient tracking spell that had nearly gotten Ice and Sabelle killed after Mathias invaded Bram's house. But, if Rhea knew how to use it, why hadn't she? The wizard was many things, but not stupid. He must know that he needed a very powerful witch to manipulate the book and perform the awesome feats Mathias demanded.

What witch was more powerful than Merlin's granddaughter?

"You're both here," Blackbourne noted, his gaze bouncing between them as he stepped into the challenge ring. "Excellent."

Suddenly, Ice knew two things: one, Mathias would press Sabelle to use the diary to fulfill his twisted ambitions to rule and enslave magickind by force, and when she refused, he would kill her. Painfully. Two, he could never allow Mathias that chance. He prayed that Sabelle had used that clever mind of hers to break free or Bram had rescued her before Mathias could signal Rhea to begin Sabelle's doom.

"We are," Mathias confirmed. "Is it time?"

"The challenge has officially resumed!" Blackbourne confirmed.

"First, Rykard has something to say."

Gripping the sword tightly with one hand, willing his fury down until the right moment, Ice addressed Blackbourne. "Indeed, I do."

The older wizard frowned down his long, thin nose. "What is it, Rykard?"

"Excuse me, sir." Ice whirled to Mathias. "Fuck off."

With a battle cry, Ice lifted his wand with one hand. Mathias's eyes widened in disbelief. He swore and raised his own wand. One chance. One distraction. One opportunity to stop Mathias and his evil plan for Sabelle, maybe even kill the rotten bastard. He had to make it work.

Before Mathias could cast whatever nasty spell lay at the tip of his wand, Ice raised his other hand, which held the sword coated in his incorruptible blood.

Faster than the blink of an eye thanks to Marrok's grueling training, Ice skewered Mathias in the gut. He plunged deep, turned the blade, ripped it out. "That's for Gailene, you fucking madman. You brutally stripped her innocence and stole her life. So I'm going to slice you into little pieces, spit in the open holes, and let you rot until the maggots claim you." Ice then shoved the sword into Mathias again and, with a hard flick of his wrist, sliced open Mathias's abdomen. "And that's for threatening Sabelle. You'd best not lay a finger on her, or there won't be a death painful enough for you."

Mathias fell to his knees, and he clutched his stomach with both hands. All the goodness coating the sword was crashing Mathias's system. No doubt the bastard was trying to heal himself, but the effort was rapidly depleting his energy. Without it, healing any faster than a human would be impossible. Blood oozed from his wounds as quickly as it left his face. It dripped from his gaping mouth. Trembling, he raised his heat and glared at Ice with accusing eyes.

"You said you would," he choked. "Concede."

"I lied, just as you did. You abducted Sabelle and never had any intention of letting her go freely. You intended to use her to manipulate the Doomsday Diary, then kill her."

"Not so stupid, after all," Mathias hissed. "But it's too late."

"What's this you say?" Blackbourne interjected. "Mr. d'Arc has Ms. Rion?"

"Hostage somewhere in your house at this moment." And Ice was never so grateful that a wizard had locked down the property from teleportation or Sabelle would already be gone forever.

Ice dropped his sword and ran for the force field's door. He had to find Sabelle, now, in case Rhea had seen Mathias's injury through the window and harmed Sabelle in retaliation.

Blackbourne call out, "Wait! If you leave the challenge ring before I declare a winner or someone forfeits, Mr. d'Arc wins by default."

Damn! Bloody stupid rules. He didn't care. Sabelle was more important.

"No!" Tynan shouted just outside the ring. "Stay. Bram and I will find her."

"She could be in danger—"

"And all we've worked for will be lost if you step outside that ring now. I'll end this danger to Sabelle. You finish him." Tynan nodded at Mathias.

As much as he hated not to come to Sabelle's rescue, allowing Mathias to win the Council seat only gave him more power later to hurt her. His patience was at a the very end, but he gave Tynan a curt nod, then focused on the opportunity to ensure that Mathias never frightened or harmed anyone ever again. Time to dish out death.

Tynan addressed Blackbourne. "Lift the teleportation lock. I must reach Mathias's witch as soon as possible. I need the element of surprise."

If he hadn't already lost it.

Sighing, Blackbourne removed his wand from his coat, then gave it a dramatic wave. "It's been removed outside the house, except for the challenge ring."

Perfect, Ice thought.

Retrieving his sword, Ice crouched before Mathias and pressed the blade to the back of his neck. "How does all that pure-hearted blood that's seeped into your wounds feel? How do you like the enchantment of goodness?"

Mathias screamed in pure agony. Ice resisted the urge to wince. Instead, he noted that Mathias had grown paler. He coughed up blood. Ice had suspected earlier that his own blood, mixed with the enchantment, would serve as a sort of poison to Mathias's system that might kill him.

But for good measure, he would try to sever Mathias's head from his body. Ninety-nine percent of the time, that killed a wizard dead for good. And with the blade of the sword pressed against the evil wizard's neck, Ice's hand trembled.

"I'm going to make certain you never hurt anyone again."

"As you're so fond of saying, fuck off." Mathias crawled toward the challenge ring's door.

"Stop him!"

Blackbourne shrugged. "No one has conceded or won this challenge. I cannot interfere."

More bloody stupid rules. Did Councilmen have nothing to do all day but contrive them?

Shoving the thought to the back of his head, Ice leapt at Mathias. The other wizard clutched his stomach as he crawled out the nearly-invisible door. Ice latched on to his ankle before Mathias could break free of the challenge ring.

"No, you bloody bastard. This is a fight to the finish. To the death. Let's end it. Why don't you die?"

"You first," Mathias snarled as he tried to pull his leg free from Ice's grasp.

He wasn't about to let go.

Blackbourne tsked and clucked, observing with great concern. Ice ignored him and focused on Mathias, using every muscle in his body to reel the other wizard back into the challenge ring, one clawed inch across the floor after another.

With a roar, Mathias glared at Ice over his shoulder, then leapt up, pinning Ice to the floor. The maniacal wizard clasped his shoulders in a crushing grip and pressed his forehead into Ice's.

Fuck. Having Mathias panting in his face made Ice's stomach roil. Instantly, his energy began to drain, pouring out his body everywhere Mathias touched him. Ice grabbed the sword and, with Herculean effort, brought it crashing down on Mathias's back again. The other wizard bucked and snarled—but didn't let go.

Before Ice could yank the sword free and stab him again, Mathias bulldozed into his head, created a mental link, and filled it with images of Gailene. He'd shared links with others before and knew this was a true memory, one that only Mathias could have put in his head. Gailene naked, bloody, pleading for help. Begging for Ice to save her.

The sight was bad enough, but the words . . . crushing. Ice screamed as he saw Mathias crawl from between Gailene's thighs as she cried, tied down to a filthy bed, shaved, branded. A line of Anarki stood behind him, all hoping for a turn before the girl died. And too young to perform her own magic, too inexperienced with this sort of violence, she sobbed.

Ice heard her call for him over and over. The sounds ripped through his soul. Shreds of it flamed with guilt and fury and shame. When his own beloved sister had needed him, he had been unable to rescue her. Even now, he couldn't muster the strength to stab Mathias again.

The vision continued, and another wizard knelt to Gailene. Her sobs increased. She knew the death Mathias planned to deal her and begged for mercy. Mathias merely laughed and watched the carnage unfold.

"Are you ready to die, begging as your sister did?" Mathias taunted, wand raised.

This vision was the past. The painful, awful, twisted past, yes. But it was written. Done. And he could do nothing to change it. The future . . . That he could impact. He'd never bring Gailene back. But the future could be full of bright tomorrows if he could focus on it, on Sabelle, on escape and eliminating Mathias.

Ice sucked in a breath, dug deep inside him, then jerked his body away from the other wizard's, determined to break the physical link draining him and stop the haunting images poisoning his head. Muscles screaming, he lifted the sword and stabbed Mathias in the shoulder with the sword dipped in good blood and enchantments again, and the wizard howled.

"To kill you is a vow I made long ago," Ice rumbled. "Today, I will keep it."

Jerking the sword from Mathias's flesh once more, Ice roared, pain slicing its way through every muscle as he wobbled to his knees, still trying to push the disturbing, terrible visions of Gailene from his head. Weak. So damn weak. His vision swam and he saw double as his stomach pitched. He clutched the sword above Mathias, who staggered on hands and knees below him, bleeding profusely on the challenge ring's floor. The wizard's body heaved, bucked, and he vomited as the poison of good worked its way through his tainted blood.

There were two Mathiases blurring Ice's vision, and the smell of blood and vomit nearly made him lose his own lunch. But he held it back. One good swing with this sword through Mathias's neck, and he could put the past to rest, save Sabelle and magickind.

Vowing to finish Mathias for Gailene and Sabelle and all of magickind, Ice trembled almost beyond his control, the tattoo winding around his biceps pulsating, as he raised his sword. With a final battle cry, he lowered it.

CHAPTER NINETEEN

SABELLE CLASPED HER MAGICALLY-BOUND hands in front of her and stared out the window at the empty field bordering Blackbourne's lands. Nausea and cold dread vied for control of her stomach. By now, Ice knew that Mathias's witch, Rhea, was holding her captive. It was only a matter of time before the evil wizard used it against him, forcing him to do something unthinkable like surrender . . . or allow himself to be slain. Sabelle saw it all in Rhea's thoughts.

Neither could happen. She refused to allow it.

Nerves gripped her stomach in a cruel vise, and she twisted her fingers, thoughts racing. She must do something—and quick. But what? Sabelle cast a sidelong glance at Rhea. Dressed like a goth Victoria's Secret model, the other witch engendered both her fury and pity. She was helping Mathias with acts that would ultimately enslave and kill lots of witches and wizards . . . and she didn't seem to truly grasp that fact.

"Shouldn't be long now," Rhea bragged. "The most powerful, skilled wizard in all of magickind will be mine."

The witch was clueless. Mathias would never be exclusively *hers*. Though Rhea's breasts were in danger of spilling from her very brief top and her transparent knickers revealed a lush, womanly body, Mathias talked to the witch as if she were of no consequence. He merely used her. And when he was finished, he would discard her, perhaps in an unfortunately permanent fashion.

But Rhea's problems weren't Sabelle's. Right now, she had to get free. Escaping the other witch might be possible, but once Mathias returned, her own doom was likely sealed—surely after Ice's had been.

Think! She'd been foolish to believe that Mathias wouldn't be brazen enough to abduct her under Blackbourne's roof. Spilled milk now, and she couldn't afford to cry. She must devise a plan to escape.

With her hands bound and her wand tucked away, magic was impossible. She'd already tried reasoning with Rhea, but she was disgustingly loyal to the magical sadist she shagged. It really left her with no option but trickery.

And Sabelle had no problem using it.

"Indeed. I'm rather more concerned about the fact that Mathias bound my hands so tightly, I may lose them if you don't loosen his magic."

"You're trying to trick me," she accused, eyes narrowed suspiciously.

Hmm. So she wasn't completely daft.

"If you don't believe me, come test these bonds yourself."

The witch would have to touch her, since the bonds were invisible. Or she'd simply loosen them. Either way, Sabelle won.

"Mathias said I shouldn't touch you, so I won't. Besides, why do I care if you lose your hands?"

"Because Mathias needs me to write in the Doomsday Diary, yes? How am I to do that without hands?" Sabelle let that sink in for a pregnant moment, then added. "I wonder if Mathias will remain *your* wizard if he went to the trouble to abduct Merlin's granddaughter and you allowed her to become useless."

Rhea's eyes went wide. The thoughts crossing her mind

told Sabelle she'd hit her target. Likely, by the time she counted to five, the other witch would be loosening her binds. *One, two, three* . . .

"Nothing funny," Rhea warned, adopting a mean snarl as she grasped her wrists.

Gotcha. As soon as the woman's hands touched her, Sabelle sent out waves of compassion, laced with distaste for holding another captive. Rhea's eyes glazed over, and something soft passed across her face. Resisting the urge to tap her toe, Sabelle waited for her siren magic to do its trick . . . and hoped she could escape in time to save Ice from doing something stupidly noble that would cost them everything.

Ice's blade struck nothing.

He blinked. Blinked again, desperate to clear his vision. Ice wiped sweat and tears from his eyes as he prayed for strength and staggered to his feet.

Just in time to see Mathias crawl onto the brown grass outside the challenge ring. The wizard cast him a look of pure loathing . . . then disappeared.

"Where the bloody devil did he go?" Spencer asked, a concerned frown on his face.

"Teleported away."

Fury smacked Ice between the eyes. Sick defeat squeezed his chest, threatening to suffocate him. He'd tried. He'd disappointed himself, Sabelle, Gailene. Magickind. He dug the heels of his palms into his eyes, trying again to clear his vision, but he knew that once he tore his hands away, Mathias would still be gone.

Ice held in a curse and a cry. Instead, he stumbled to his feet. He must keep moving forward. Even if Sabelle never spoke to him again, even if she deemed him unworthy, he had to save her.

As he moved to leave the challenge ring, Blackbourne stopped him with a hand about his arm.

"You're alive."

Barely. And Blackbourne blinked as if astounded by the most recent events.

"Indeed. I must . . ." He stabbed his palms into his eyes again, trying not to see two of everything about him, and drew in steadying breaths. "Find Sabelle. That bastard you supported got away and threatened to kill her."

The rest of the Council frowned at him. "Your brother and O'Shea are in the house, so I presume they're looking into that. Before you join them, we have business to see to you. Since Mr. d'Arc teleported away during the challenge, I pronounce you the winner. Accordingly, you are now the next member of the Magical Council, with all the privileges and rights—"

Ice didn't have time for pomp and circumstance.

"Wait! Where are you going?" Blackbourne called to his retreating back.

Putting one foot in front of the other, Ice trudged toward the house. "I don't give a bloody fuck about anything right now except finding Sabelle."

Halfway across the yard, he could scarcely breathe.

"Ice?"

God, the voice of an angel, just like Sabelle's. Ice's vision had blurred more. It must have because, despite his head weighing a thousand pounds, he managed to look across the yard and see her dart through the back door, Tynan and Bram in tow, clutching a terrified Rhea.

Ice lurched over to Sabelle, and she met him more than halfway; he used the last of his strength to lift his hands and grab her shoulders.

She was here. Really here. Unharmed. "You're safe."

And though Mathias had escaped by unfair means, at this moment, Ice merely felt relief. The self-anger would come soon enough.

"You won!" Sabelle's voice trembled as she threw her arms around him.

Ice staggered back under the weight of her embrace. "Your safety . . . all that matters."

Sabelle looked at him, blue eyes shining love at him. "I overcame Rhea with my siren abilities after Mathias left us. It took a few minutes, but I coaxed her into letting me go. Bram and Tynan found us a few moments ago."

Clever as always. Ice clung to the fact she was unharmed for a breath, two, as he drank in the glory of her golden face. No sight would ever be so beloved. And she deserved more than he could ever give her.

Staggering to one knee, he bowed his head. "I failed. I'm sorry."

His vision blurred further, this time with tears. He'd been a fool to imagine he was good enough for her, and today had proven he was unworthy to be her mate.

"Failed?" She touched a hand to his shoulder and lifted his gaze to hers. "Ice, you won! You defeated Mathias. You're a Council member. You fought valiantly—"

"He escaped alive. I vowed . . . kill him. Did not succeed." Ice swayed, bracing himself on the ground with one hand to stay upright. He could not, would not, pass out. Even if he did not deserve Sabelle, he would walk out of here on two legs, like a man.

"No one expected you to kill him, just win. And you did." She knelt before him, and soon he was drowning in blue heaven and concern.

Ice closed his eyes. He didn't deserve her.

"Not enough." Ice sucked in a breath and focused so hard

that his head began to pound. But he must say this in a complete sentence, refused to embarrass himself more. "I am not worthy of you. I will love you always. Be happy. That will be enough for me."

Dizziness and nausea assailed him as he rose to his feet and stumbled past her.

"Isdernus Rykard!" Sabelle shouted at his back. "What sort of nonsense is that?"

The truth. She would see that someday.

She darted after him and grabbed his arm. Clearly, that someday wasn't today.

"Ice."

He couldn't look at her. Wouldn't. If he did, he'd bury his face in her neck, throw his arms around her, and stay there forever. He had to do what was right.

"Stop, Sabelle."

"Stop what?" she demanded.

He'd lost all hope of a future with this failure and didn't deserve to even set eyes upon her. But he heard the tears in her voice. Pain shredded his heart, and he closed his eyes. Strength, just a few minutes more. Then he could find privacy, rail at his failure, mourn her loss, and try to figure out how he'd live without her.

"Thinking of me. Find one who deserves you." Again, he strode past her, walking away from the challenge ring, the Council elders, and the woman he loved more than his own life.

"I have found a man who deserves me, Isdernus. One with the heart of a warrior and a selfless love I've never known. Please. As I become a part of you, you become a part of me."

"No," he moaned. Though each of her words were a balm to his soul, he forced himself to keep walking away.

And still, she kept saying the words he had so longed to hear. "I will be honest, good, and true. I heed your Call. 'Tis you I seek. From this moment on, there is no other for me but—"

"Sabelle, no."

"I say!" Blackbourne called to him. "Stop!"

Ice didn't answer. He merely put another foot in front of the last, the grounds swimming in his vision that had gone from double to triple. He came to the corner of the house, and managed a last glance over his shoulder. Blackbourne frowned under heavy brows. Bram and Tynan stood silently, as if uncertain or unwilling to interfere. And Sabelle looked at him as if he was breaking her heart. The fact he saw three of her only magnified his ache. That expression, so fraught with pain and confusion, cut him deep. She would move on, as she should. Must. But her sweet, tear-streaked face would haunt him forever.

"We're not finished here," Blackbourne shouted.

He drew in a deep breath. A few more steps, then he could sit, rest, until he could find the strength to teleport home. But as he planted his foot in the dormant grass, his knee gave out under him.

"Rykard! Where are you going?"

Apparently, Ice thought as gravity and unconsciousness took him, *I'm going down.*

The next morning, Sabelle paced Ice's caves, transcast mirror in hand. She had yet to see the stubborn warrior. After he collapsed at Blackbourne's, Bram and Tynan carted him inside the Council elder's house. Tynan stayed with Ice while her brother escorted her here. No matter how much she'd protested and railed, Bram insisted that she go.

After all, she wasn't Ice's mate, and Tynan was better

equipped to watch over Ice in case the Anarki struck on Mathias's behalf. Though Sabelle felt certain the crafty wizard was too injured and ill do anyone harm—at least for the moment.

"Did you find the mirror, Sabelle?" Caden called down the dark stone hallway.

Sighing, she followed the sound of the voice. In one of the larger rooms, she found Caden with an arm around his mate as she put the finishing touches on her lipstick. They looked so happy, so secure in their love for each other. In her head, she knew their road to happiness had not been an easy one. But her heart beat with pain and envy. She wanted that with Ice, had no question in her mind that she loved him—and that he loved her. This nonsense about deserving her? Perhaps that was true in Bram's mind, but she didn't care. She wasn't living her life to please her brother. She wanted to live to please the man she loved.

Too bad he was avoiding her. Honorable wizard, damn him.

"It's here." She held up the mirror for Caden to see, then turned to his mate. "Ready?"

"Indeed. Have you heard from the others?"

As much as it pained her, yes. "Bram called a few minutes ago. It's done. Officially."

Ice was now a Council member. Bram had no reason to stand between her and Ice, not that Sabelle would allow it. Yet the man still wouldn't speak to her.

"Then let's go."

Sabelle nodded. Whatever her ills, magickind must be made aware of all the changes and dangers going on around them. As disappointed and miserable as she felt, she was glad to have this opportunity to serve her people.

"Be sure to include this news, as well." Sabelle handed

Sydney a scrap of paper on which she'd jotted notes from Bram.

Sydney read them, eyes widening with each word. "Truly?"

"Indeed." Sabelle smiled faintly. Already Ice's involvement was making a difference, and she couldn't be more proud.

A few moments later, Sabelle put the mirror in place for Sydney, then cast the spell that allowed her to transcast to all of magickind. They waited a few moments, allowing the mirror in each magickind household to draw its owners to the magical surface.

"Good evening, magickind. I'm Sydney Blair-MacTavish with breaking news. Today, Isdernus Rykard, the first Deprived to join the Council in over five hundred years, was sworn into his position, replacing the late Thomas MacKinnett. Rykard defeated Mathias d'Arc in a Council-sanctioned challenge. He takes his place beside another new Council member, Tynan O'Shea, who replaces his late grandfather, Clifden.

"In related news, the new Council met today at the home of Carlisle Blackbourne. After a heated debate, they issued their first collective edict denouncing Mathias d'Arc's return and ongoing violence against the Privileged, women in particular. The edict, proposed by new Council member Rykard, passed by a narrow margin of four to three.

"Rykard delivered his first public statement after the vote: 'This makes Mathias public enemy number one. His actions, including the rape and murder of many women, among them my sister, and along with the assassination of my predecessor, MacKinnett, proves he's the most feared and loathed wizard in magickind. We *will* capture him and dispense justice.'

"I'll bring you more details as they become available.

Until then, safeguard your homes and families. D'Arc should be considered very dangerous. That's all the news for now. This is Sydney Blair-MacTavish. Good evening, magickind."

With a nod, Sabelle lowered the mirror. "Good job."

"The best, firecracker." Caden kissed her cheek, looking like he'd like to do a great deal more to his mate.

"My pleasure." Flushing, Sydney tucked a lock of red hair behind her ear. "I hope your Ice and the others catch him soon."

Her Ice? How Sabelle wished that was true. But no sense spilling her guts to Sydney—or anyone else. No one could shake sense into a hardheaded warrior like Ice. As soon as that wizard returned—

In the next breath, gentle *whooshes* sounded near the cavern's primary door. Bram appeared, then Tynan. Ice trudged behind them, watching the ground as he teleported in and made his way down the rocky hall.

As he passed her, he spared her a glance. Just one. It dripped regret and love, remorse and need. And exhaustion. Still, he would have nothing to do with her. Sabelle wanted to tear her hair out.

"Ice, wait." The plea tumbled out before she could stop it.

"Sabelle, we've nothing to say."

"*You* may feel that way. I, however, have plenty—"

"Not now, Sabelle," her brother cut in. "The Doomsday Brethren have grave matters to discuss. There are wider implications to the Council's newest vote."

She bit her lip hard to hold in her frustration—and barely succeeded. Magickind and the future, the Doomsday Brethren and the Council were all-important. But damn it all, so was her heart. Bram had taught her well over the years, however. Duty first.

As she followed her brother to the back of Ice's cavern and the massive dining table, the others emerged as well. Marrok kissed Olivia tenderly, then settled in a chair. Caden whispered something in Sydney's ear, then kissed her forehead. She smiled, then looped arms with Olivia. Together, they retreated to the back of the cavern. Sabelle stood her ground, refusing to leave, as Lucan, Tynan, Bram, Ice, Duke, and the twins all settled into a chair around the table.

Bram cast her a challenging stare. She met him head-on, arms crossed over her chest. "I'm not leaving before I hear about the Council initiations and the edict vote."

"There's little more to it than Sydney announced via transcast. Tynan and Ice are official, and Mathias is now wanted."

A partial truth at best, Sabelle was certain. "Did any of the Council members try to protest the initiation?"

"Blackbourne and Spencer are not pleased, but resigned," Tynan answered.

To Ice's presence. Everyone thought it, but no one said it. Why bother when the truth was obvious? The Council elders were elitist bastards.

"And Camden?" she asked.

"Suspiciously quiet," Bram added. "He may be resigned as well. Hard to tell. Either way, Ice will make a better Councilman than all of them combined."

Sabelle's eyes widened. Had her own brother said *that*? Was Ice more than a convenient vote to push Bram's agenda? Judging from the look on Ice's face, he was equally stunned and asking himself the same question.

Gnashing his teeth, Bram snarled, "Don't everyone bloody look at me as if I've grown a third head. Ice is strong and brave. I admit it. He brings the Council a perspective they lack. Along with Tynan, we'll accomplish the important things for magickind I've long sought. He . . ." Bram paused, grimaced. Whatever words he contemplated, they looked painful to admit. "He has a core of honor. Yesterday's challenge proved that."

Shocking! Bram's version of an apology, and he'd delivered it, not just to Ice, but with all the others listening. She was not only proud of Ice, but her brother as well. They'd spoken earlier, and Bram had confessed that, since the dark cloud, he found it hard to be diplomatic when his agenda was threatened, his ambition blocked. Tonight, he'd checked himself and clearly fought hard against his raw ambition, now barely hidden under his surface. In doing so, he'd both impressed her and provided instant acceptance for Ice. Bram didn't easily admit that he was wrong, and no doubt it was more difficult since Mathias's nasty spell. But Sabelle knew exactly the message her brother conveyed—and what it had cost him. He approved and accepted her choice of a mate. Though Sabelle didn't require it, and would have spoken the Binding to Ice regardless, having Bram's roundabout blessing was a relief. They may never be the best of friends again, but they could tolerate each other. It was more than she'd hoped for.

Now if she could just get Ice to understand that not only did he deserve her, she loved him . . . As soon as this bit of business ended, she would.

"And you suggested the edict?" Sabelle turned to Ice.

Blast it, she loved him so much that looking at him made her heart hurt. Especially when he merely looked away. Then he nodded.

"How did the vote go? Did the others agree to a directive?"

Bram grimaced. Tynan looked away. Ice gripped the arms of his chair. Ah, this was the something they wanted to avoid discussing.

Sabelle tapped her toe on the stone floor. "You know I'm not giving up until someone answers."

Under his breath, Bram cursed. "The vote was a four-three split as Sydney reported. Ice, Tynan, Sterling MacTavish and I supported the edict. The others opposed. No shock there. The original version of the edict contained a directive that allowed any of magickind to kill Mathias on sight."

Tynan turned to Caden and Lucan. "That's where your uncle parted ways with us. He doesn't want to condone what he believes amounts to murder among the masses. He prefers that we take care of Mathias."

"We?" Sabelle queried.

"The Doomsday Brethren," Bram supplied. "We alone have the directive to kill him. The rest of the Council has vowed to put up no other barriers between us and Mathias's death."

"That's not all bad, is it? Shouldn't that have been a part of our transcast?"

"What will Mathias do if he learns that he's free to kill at will among magickind, and those witches and wizards are allowed to take up their magic only in defense of themselves or their families, *after* it's clear Mathias means to kill them? By then, it's bloody too late. There will be more carnage. More murders."

"Stupid fools," she muttered.

"Exactly," Ice agreed, then looked down again.

Again, Sabelle wondered how Ice could see himself as unworthy and undeserving. He'd fought a battle with the most evil wizard of a millennium and survived. He'd earned a seat on the Council, despite the fact no Deprived had done so in centuries. He'd battled and nearly died, yet continued to come back stronger than before, full of the honor and valor she so loved about him. Yet he remained humbled, ashamed.

How could she embrace him and create a future with him if he couldn't stop focusing on his perceived failures of the past? Didn't he understand that he could have done nothing to save Gailene? That no one had expected him to actually kill Mathias in the challenge ring?

"The edict is behind us and nothing can change the directive we've been given, at least for now. Maybe after enough innocent deaths, the other Councilmen will concede, but until then, we have our orders: kill Mathias." Bram glanced down the table at all the Doomsday Brethren warriors. "That's a mission we can all embrace."

Amid nods and choruses of yeses, Bram sighed. "There's another matter we must address, our temporary residence. I'm planning to rebuild my own, bigger and better. Stronger. More secure. It will, however, take time. With Ice's blessing, I'd like to remain here until it's complete."

That snapped Ice's gaze up, straight to Sabelle. Again, the yearning and devotion on his face nearly toppled her, made her dizzy with want. Foolish, headstrong man.

"I—I . . ." Ice sighed as he looked away. "I prefer my privacy."

Sabelle knew better than to believe he didn't want her. What he didn't want was to weaken and give in to his need for her. She smiled. No way was she going to allow him to separate himself from her. No way would she let him prevent her from speaking the Binding one more time. The moment business was done, she was going to do whatever she must to make him see reason.

"As do I," Bram supplied. "But look at the others. Who among us has a location so well hidden, remote enough to be clandestine, with dungeons and proper safeguards?"

Ice had apparently completed the mental checklist. He turned to Duke. "What of your house? It's large and old, so likely equipped with dungeons. You've put safeguards around it, and we could add others—"

"And there are at least twenty humans underfoot at all times. Would you like to hide your magic from them twenty-four-seven? Or explain magic to them all?"

"You could give the human servants some time off."

"Months? Years? Besides, servants aren't the only consideration. Don't forget, my half brother and his fiancée are human."

Caden frowned. "They don't know what you are?"

Duke paused, cleared his throat. "No. And I'm afraid I must leave you soon, attend their wedding in two weeks' time, on New Year's Eve. At the manor. We'll have a house full of bloody guests for nearly a month."

"Well, Ice, looks like we'll have to trespass on your . . . hospitality a bit longer." Bram smiled, knowing he'd won his way.

"Damn it all!" Ice cursed.

Inside, Sabelle rejoiced. Not only did she like it here—the caverns provided a haunting natural beauty she would have never imagined possible— it kept her very close to Ice. As long as she was by his side, she would be able to work her way under his defenses and back into his arms.

"I think it's a good plan," Sabelle chimed in. "Mathias's witch, Rhea, is in the dungeon and since she isn't Mathias's mate, he should be unable to trace her. We've begun questioning her. Already she's admitted to placing the tracking spell on the Doomsday Diary. I . . . persuaded her to remove it. She's a valuable hostage, and relocating Rhea would be fraught with opportunities for her to escape or give Mathias the potential means to free her. I think it's best if we all remain here."

"Good. It's settled." Bram slapped the table. "Caden,

thank your mate for her prompt and excellent transcast. So glad I sent you to that silly human rag she worked for to lure her away."

Caden frowned. "You sent me there to shut her up."

Bram waved. "Whatever. It worked."

The wizards around the table laughed as they rose. Predictably, Caden went in search of Sydney, Marrok after Olivia, and Ronan sought out Kari, Raiden grumbling beside him about mating having turned his twin into a sap. Duke said his farewells and teleported away to tend preparations for the family wedding everyone knew he dreaded . . . which made Sabelle wonder why. She couldn't read Duke well; he was quite good at masking his thoughts. But enough of them revolved around a pink-cheeked blonde to raise Sabelle's brow. Finally, Bram and Lucan meandered side by side out of the room.

Her brother paused to give her a pat on the shoulder. In that single glance, she read his pained acceptance. Bram giving his blessing for a mating he'd long opposed was costing him effort, but he would no longer try to stop her. Ice had shown himself to be a worthy warrior, loyal to her and the cause. Now that Ice was a Councilman, Bram had no other logical objection. This wasn't perfect, but it was a start. She smiled in return.

With that, Bram turned back to his friend, murmuring that he'd had a call from Anka, who had information about Mathias's next move. She also wished to speak to her former mate. Intriguing, yes . . . but not Sabelle's first priority. Tynan looked as angry and introspective as always, a heartbeat away from an explosion of violence or grief. Sabelle knew one would break free of his control someday, and she wasn't at all certain which.

That left Ice staring at her with a mix of dread and resignation that made her wonder if he'd put too many obstacles between them to have any sort of future.

Once the others had left the room, Sabelle sauntered around the table. Ice watched her approach, torn between his need to grab her and pull her to him, and his honor, which screamed at him to leave her to a better future.

As she neared, Ice forced himself to take a step back.

"You cannot avoid me forever."

Her words shamed him. Bloody hell, he was mucking everything up. "Of course. It's cowardly, and I'm sorry. I want you to know that I won't blame you for Renouncing me."

"You daft, stubborn man." She stomped closer. "I'm trying to Bind myself to you."

Regret plowed through him. Releasing her was both the most honorable and most difficult thing to do. "Sabelle, no. I—"

"Just don't know when to shut up, do you? I don't want to Bind myself to you out of pity or spite against my brother or any other nonsense you might dream up. I want to be with you because I love you. And I know you love me."

Ice shuffled one foot against the stone floor. Love her? She was his whole world. For the sake of her future, he would give her up. "I don't deserve you."

"Because you failed to kill Mathias?" At his nod, she rolled her eyes. "That's rubbish. I told you, no one expected you to kill the ruthless bastard."

Except him. Ice clenched his fists at his sides. He had not only expected to kill Mathias, he'd demanded it of himself. The moment he'd realized exactly how to defeat Mathias in the challenge ring, he'd tasked himself with killing the nemesis who had ruined his life and shattered his hope of a future two centuries ago. Defeat was a bitter pill to swallow.

Something invisible crawled up his chest, closed up his throat. He didn't dare lift his gaze to Sabelle. He clamped his jaw shut, but his brows still slashed down, his face contorted. Tears threatened to unman him even more.

"*I* expected it," he roared, pounding his chest. "He deserved to die for what he did to Gailene, and I vowed to kill him myself. When I had the chance, I was too slow, too weak—"

"Too damn insistent on being a one-man army, if you ask me. He's evil in a way you can't grasp, thank God. But your refusal to embrace the future with me isn't about the fact Mathias is still alive."

"It is. I *failed* you and all of magickind. By God, witch, don't you understand that?"

Sabelle reached a tentative hand to Ice. He tried to steel himself against her sweet touch, but when she laid her palm on his shoulder, heat bombarded him. He jerked, winced . . . but couldn't make himself pull away.

"I understand that you think you failed Gailene. That you've spent two hundred years living for the express purpose of killing the villain responsible, thinking it would rest her memory. But Gailene would never have thought that you failed. You've become a great warrior, a Council member. You are a fine man I don't want to live without. She would be proud."

His face crumbled, and his throat seized up completely. Desperately, he pressed his lips together, determined to keep the sobs echoing in his head inside.

But it was no use. The sobs came, and with it, more fury. "I couldn't save her, I couldn't kill Mathias. How on earth could I save you if you ever needed me? Sabelle, I would never ask you to put yourself in my hands, in my protection—"

"Stop! Don't you dare think for me. I've had plenty of that from Bram, and I don't need it from you as well."

Her anger, her very words, silenced him. He hadn't meant to treat her like her brother, manipulate her into his way of thinking . . . but he'd done just that.

"There's no one I would rather be with. I've not asked you to save me, though I believe you could. I've asked you to *love* me. And if Gailene were here today, she would wish the same. She'd never want you to give up your life to pursue hatred and revenge. She'd only ask to remain in your heart."

The sweet, wise, pushy witch was right. Utterly. But did that change anything?

His shoulders shook as silent sobs wracked his body. "Gailene begged me to save her. As Mathias and the Anarki were slowly killing her, she begged me to rescue her, and I didn't."

"You had no notion what was happening to her, and even if you had, if you'd tried to save her alone, Mathias would only have killed you too." Sabelle wrapped her arms around him and held tight.

It was selfish, but he paused for a moment to bask in the warmth of her touch, of her love. How could he live without this for the rest of his centuries? He'd never wanted—needed—anyone more. But reality intruded, and he had to face it.

"At least I would have died with honor. As it is, I wonder if I remained alive so I could feel the weight of my failure for centuries more. Why did Fate take her and leave me?"

"You lived to fight another day. You lived because Gailene would have wanted it. You lived because you didn't fail her and because Mathias escaping didn't mean you failed her again; it meant you stayed alive, won the battle and the Council seat, and will live to fight the war ahead of us. *If* you're willing to let go of the past and embrace the future."

Letting go of the past. Ice closed his eyes. He'd sunk his

claws and every inch of regret into the past, giving little thought to the future, to any happiness. Until Sabelle. From the moment he'd seen her, she'd been a fever in his blood. She was his one reason to look forward.

He collapsed back into the chair. She knelt before him and grabbed his hands.

Ice clutched her delicate fingers like a lifeline, feeling her warmth and vitality. She was real. Now. He'd been clinging to ghosts for so damn long . . .

"You didn't fail, Ice. Your father did."

His head snapped up.

She squeezed his hands. "He didn't treasure the daughter who had been his to protect and love. He never knew her or the joy she could bring because he refused to see. Instead, he used her to purge you of all caring to make you the strongest warrior possible. He never understood that it was your heart that gives you greater strength than you would have otherwise known. Your love for Gailene pushed you today to battle a wizard who, by all rights, should have killed you. You devotion to her infused you with power and prowess. And you won because you cared.

"Gailene is with you, here." She touched his chest.

Ice gripped the arms of the chair and damn near crumbled under her fingers. His love for her swelled until he thought he might implode. His protective armor had been ripped off and he stood bleeding, raw . . . completely exposed for Sabelle to see.

She wasn't running away. Wasn't shamed.

"I'm there too," she whispered. "Just as you're in my heart. I need you. I need that caring core, that valor, that devotion. You've given it to me, and I won't live without it. You found strength in your love for Gailene. We can build a stronger bond together that supports us both. One that enables you to execute the Doomsday Brethren's new directive and still give you peace without giving up your future or your soul."

Total acceptance. It was there in her shining blue eyes. Sabelle didn't care if he was Deprived or allegedly insane, had a temper, was haunted by ghosts, or knew next to nothing about how to love. Somehow, she'd seen deep inside him . . . and still loved him with her whole heart.

Ice couldn't imagine loving her more than he did in that moment.

"If you could change the past, would you Call to me again?" Her lips trembled with suppressed tears as she asked the question.

She was afraid. His courageous, amazing witch was frightened, not of the fact Mathias got away, but of rejection. The realization tore down the last of Ice's resistance. He could stand to walk away if only he hurt, but to purposely wound Sabelle? Unacceptable.

"Without hesitation."

"You're certain?" She sniffled.

Ice knew he could assure her again or simply prove what was in his heart. An easy choice. He never wanted Sabelle to have doubts that he loved her. And he knew Gailene would not only approve of his happiness, but applaud it. Another day, soon, he would resume his quest to kill Mathias, not out of hatred, but love. To ensure no brother ever had to lose his sister in such a savage fashion or suffer such untold grief again.

Ice cradled Sabelle's face in his hands and smiled into her teary eyes. "Become a part of me, as I become a part of you. And ever after, I promise myself to thee. Each day we share, I shall be honest, good, and true. If this you seek, heed my call. From this moment on, there is no other for me but you."

He finished the vow with a soft kiss, one tinged with love and forever.

Sabelle eased away. "You won't interrupt me this time, I hope."

"I'd cut out my own tongue first."

She smiled as she stared right up into his eyes, and Ice swore he could see his forever.

"As I become a part of you, you become a part of me. I will be honest, good, and true. I heed your Call. 'Tis you I seek." She brushed her lips across his, pouring all her devotion into the kiss. "From this moment on, there is no other for me but you."